CHRIS ALMEIDA & CECILIA AUBREY

ALTERNATE
Connection

A COUNTERMEASURE SERIES NOVEL

ABOUT THIS BOOK

CIA Operative Nathan Nelson has built his life on secrets, especially those that have shaped the man he is—secret feelings for a woman he has viewed as off-limits for a decade, events that have taught him to keep his shield up. Now those secrets have come barreling down on him at the worst time.

Foreign Service Specialist Rachael Moore's personal crusade puts her in the crosshairs of very dangerous people. She has risked her life to free herself from the past, and in doing so, has exposed her battered heart and deeply concealed dreams to the man who once told her he would never touch her.

Unknowingly, their connection may not only bridge the chasm between them, but may also shed light on a puzzling mystery. Their perilous journey becomes a race for their lives, leading them into a conspiracy rooted deeper than their tangled emotions.

Will their present collaboration shatter the tenuous links of their woven past, or forge a future bond they never expected?

Check out the other books in the Countermeasure Series

Visit your retailer today for the complete list of books in the series.

Praise for
CHRIS ALMEIDA AND CECILIA AUBREY

"A riveting, clever spy story full of intrigue, modern-day espionage and a scorching hot romance."
—*Misty Evans, award-winning author of romantic suspense*

"If you like nonstop action and sexy heroes and heroines, don't miss the Countermeasure Series."
—*Desiree Holt, best-selling author of erotic romance*

"Almeida and Aubrey had me from the first paragraph and I couldn't put it down. Electrifying thriller!"
—*Becky Condit, Mrs. Condit and Friends Read Books*

"It is beautifully written with the perfect mixture of action and suspense and in the midst of all that there is a beautiful emotional love story entwined."
—*Rhayne Risque, Guilty Pleasures Book Reviews*

"I highly recommend Countermeasure for any fan of a fast-paced erotic romance. I know I'm looking forward to checking out the duo's next collaboration!"
—*Silla Beaumont, Just Erotic Romance Reviews*

TRADEMARK ACKNOWLEDGEMENTS

The authors acknowledge the trademarked status and trademark owners of the following wordmarks mentioned in this work of fiction:

Star Wars: LucasArts

Guinness: Diageo Ireland Private Unlimited Company

Marvel Superhero character names & likenesses: Marvel

ACKNOWLEDGEMENTS

Alternate Connection's journey was a long and arduous one. Much to our readers' chagrin, we took our time. Like good whiskey, the story needed time to mature; the characters needed time to grow inside us so we could do them justice. A greater amount of time was dedicated to research, to ensuring we dotted our i's and crossed our t's. With that said, we would like to thank all of our friends and readers who have stuck around, waiting patiently (and impatiently) for this installment in the Countermeasure Series.

To our Beta Readers, who brought big smiles to our faces with their excitement over each chapter we passed into their caring hands for their thorough review and critique. We hope that our reader riot chapters kept you on your toes.

To the whole of our Street Team and Discussion Group, for putting up with our merciless teasing. Thank you for being such good sports and joining in our fun.

We would like to also extend our gratitude to all of those we consulted and who corroborated the facts in our fiction, answered our endless questions, provided us with invaluable information, and kept us on the straight and narrow. In particular, thanks to Deanna Fisher for having been our bridge to the military world and to the many military men and women who offered their expertise to make our fictional operations as close to reality as possible. We thank each and every one of you from the bottom of our hearts.

Last but not least, to the few, the many, the proud who took up the mantle of our daily chores and personal responsibilities to allow us time to write. Without you, this novel would still be a WIP.

We have thoroughly enjoyed writing this installment in the Countermeasure journey and hope you will enjoy revisiting old friends and meeting new ones. It has been an honor to bring Nathan and Rachael's journey to life, and it's with humility that we place it into your hands.

Sláinte,
Chris & Cecilia

TABLE OF COTNENTS

"Do you really think it is weakness that yields to temptation? I tell you that there are terrible temptations which it requires strength, strength and courage to yield to."

–Oscar Wilde

Prologue

The Code

London, England – Ten years earlier

THE GLASS DOORS TO THE Arrivals waiting area of one of the busiest terminals in the world parted with a whisper-soft whirl. Nathan Nelson's confident strides—in contrast to the emotions swirling in his chest—took him straight into the throng of people holding flowers and name signs. Taking advantage of his towering height, he skimmed their faces, focused on finding Phillip's among them.

He squinted against the sunlight bouncing off the terminal's polished floors, welcoming him back to London. Blue skies were a rare commodity in England even in warmer months, and he hoped the pleasant weather would hold. The last thing he needed was a forecast to match his gloomy mood for the length of his brief visit. His gut churned with anxious expectation for what promised to be the longest two weeks of his life.

"Rachael and I want you here. You should receive your ticket soon. I'll be at the airport to collect you." Phillip's tone during the brief

overseas call had been decisive, leaving no room for excuses.

"It seems I'm being summoned."

Phillip had laughed. *"Whatever it takes to get your ass here. Rachael has already reserved one of the guest rooms at my parents' house for you. She knows it means a lot to me to have you here."*

Against any shred of common sense, Nathan was there. Not spotting Phillip, he weaved through the milling bystanders at a brisk pace, hauling his duffel in one hand and his tuxedo's garment bag in the other.

"There you—"

Startled, he pivoted abruptly toward the feminine voice and crashed into the woman at full force. In swift response, he dropped his bags and wrapped his arm around her waist, catching her before she toppled to the floor.

"I'm so sorry. I wasn't looking," he muttered hastily as her hair fanned him, her scent colliding with his senses like a freight train at full throttle.

"It's okay." Laughter laced her voice. He released his hold and supported her by the elbow while she steadied herself and smoothed her clothes. *Way to go, Nathan.*

Her rich, dark hair hid her features, but Nathan didn't need to see her face to recognize her. Heart thundering in his chest, he frowned at the spike of awareness that flared and licked its way under his skin—the response to her velvet-smooth voice, a sensation he was familiar with and feared all at once. One of the reasons he'd been glad to leave England when he did. His frown deepened and he let go of her arm, putting space between them.

He heard what sounded like a chuckle as she swept her hair away from her face. "I caught you by surprise." Indeed she had. The woman looked up into his eyes and smiled. "Hello, Nathan. Always so polite."

Nathan stared at Phillip's fiancée, half stupefied. Despite understanding what he'd be walking into, he'd been unprepared for the impact looking into her twinkling brown eyes again would bring. The murmur of voices in the terminal faded. A lump formed in his throat and his palms grew sweaty. He'd been a fool to think that distance would have dimmed the attraction or muted his need. Suddenly, he found himself stumbling over both his words and his feet. The same way he had the night he'd met her, before he knew who she was. His hormones still kicked into overdrive at the mere sight of her. His eyes roamed over her features, soaking her in. She looked different. More...alive. Or maybe the old saying that the heart grew fonder with distance was true—and if so, he was undeniably screwed.

After a moment of silence, he realized he'd been gaping at her like a bumbling idiot. He cleared his throat. "Rachael," her name burned its path out of his mouth. "What...what are you doing here? I thought Phillip was picking me up."

"He was, but he got pulled into another endless meeting and sent me to collect you." Her eyes studied him with a curious intensity, almost as if trying to read him. An easy smile played at the corners of her full lips, completely unaware of the intense discomfort twisting his stomach.

Nathan retrieved his duffel. "Ah. I see. You didn't have to drop what you were doing to come and get me. I could have taken a cab."

"Don't be silly." She grabbed his garment bag. "Come on. I'm parked this way."

Without another word, Rachael brushed past him and headed out the exit without checking to see if he was following. With a couple of strides, he caught up and matched his steps to her much shorter one. He'd always felt like a giant beside Rachael. She wasn't petite, just the perfect size to make him feel he could protect her from any harm if he could only wrap her in his arms. He'd loved that about her since the first time they'd met. He continued to do so even after he'd realized how far out of his reach she was. How many times had he molded her body against his? How many times had he heard her sighs as he brushed the curve of her waist with the worshiping touch of his fingertips? All figments of his wild imagination. Dreams he had learned to subdue, to snuff over time—and that had evaded extinction with a simple look at her.

Enveloped in awkward silence, they walked to her car. He glanced at Rachael out of the corner of his eye, trying to gage her reaction to seeing him again, but nothing in her expression told him she was unsettled in his company. She didn't seem to feel the same way he did—brittle, disjointed.

"Here we are." She stopped beside a sporty red Peugeot and popped the trunk with her remote. Her eyes traveled the length of him. "Might be a tight fit."

He eyed the tiny car. "No kidding." After dropping his bags in and closing the trunk, he squeezed his six-four frame into the passenger seat, struggling to keep from bumping against any part of her in the confined space.

Conversation wasn't his forte where Rachael was involved, but he tried his best, blurting out the first thing that came to mind once she maneuvered onto the highway.

"All ready for the big day?"

"Hope so. At least you're finally here." She flashed him one of her radiant smiles that always left him breathless. It dimmed slightly and a hint of undefined emotion clouded her eyes. Rachael returned her attention to the road. "Next week's rehearsal is the last step."

The crazy idea that she might have cold feet crossed his mind and the fist in his gut tightened. Hope and disgust at his own thoughts warred inside him. What the hell was he thinking? He shouldn't have come. Phillip wouldn't have considered asking him to be his best man if he had even so much as suspected how Nathan felt. He should have declined. He should have used his course load as an excuse to bow out of it, but he couldn't bring himself to do it. He owed Phillip his presence on such a significant date. Hell, he owed Phillip his life, his sanity.

Nathan sucked in a deep breath and cursed under his breath when her perfume—a flowery mix that reminded him of exotic landscapes, wild and free—teased his senses once again. An unwelcome surge of desire rushed through him. He closed his eyes and clamped his teeth together in an attempt to stem the tide.

"How was the flight? Any problems getting through security?" she asked, her voice bringing him back to reality. "Some people are frustrated with the lengthy procedure now."

He shook his head and fought the dryness in his mouth. "The flight was uneventful. As for the security, it is what it is. A necessity in the world we live in now. But I have to admit, having an embassy stamp has its perks. It helped cut down some scrutiny and sped things along."

"Hope you got some rest during the flight. Phillip wants to take us out tonight to celebrate your arrival with a pint."

Nathan's heart twisted in his chest. He didn't want to be a spoil-sport, but he knew each day would pose a bigger challenge for him if he had to spend every waking hour around her. The best thing he could do for himself was to avoid it. "He shouldn't bother. He'll probably be tired."

"He said helping you break the law amuses him and that he wouldn't miss the opportunity. Something about it being the only time you'll ever do it."

The neutral conversation gradually relaxed Nathan's frayed nerves and he settled into the plush seat. "Well, I'd only be breaking the law if I was on US soil."

"Technicalities," she scoffed. "You're not twenty-one yet, so not legal."

Her teasing was contagious. He managed to smile back. "You're one to talk. It's not like you're that much older. What? Six months? Besides, the drinking age here is eighteen. That makes me not only legal, but a late bloomer."

"Late bloomer, hmm?" she teased.

Nathan's cheeks warmed at the innuendo. He rubbed the back of his neck. Why the hell did he have to behave like a twelve-year old with a crush around her? To hell with his hormones and his unwanted attraction to his best friend's fiancée. That was a boundary he would never cross. He searched her face again and only found humor etched across it. "Well...," he racked his brain but couldn't find a witty comeback. He opted for the facts. "I was taught to follow rules. That's just who I am."

"I know. I'm glad. It suits you."

Unsure how to take her last comment, he swung his head to look out the passenger window for the remainder of the drive, clenching his jaw to quell the hunger inside him. A hunger he'd never satisfy, because as much as he craved everything about Rachael, he was solidly bound to uphold the code. Honor and ethics. The two things his father had taught him well, and which he had in spades.

It was that deeply imbued honor he hoped would hold him together before he unraveled. Neither Phillip nor Rachael could ever know of his inner battle; that burden was entirely his to bear until time and distance erased it all. If this was a taste of how the next two weeks were going to play out, he was in for one hell of a ride.

Chapter One

Neighborhood Watch

Ten years later

THE SHRILL RING ALMOST KNOCKED Naveed Abboud from between the soft thighs of the woman sharing the bed with him. Although his hard cock begged to stay buried deep in the warmth of her flesh, he couldn't ignore the call. It was one he'd been expecting. He disentangled himself from the woman, brushing aside her halfhearted grab for him.

"Don't answer…." Her words matched the plea in her eyes.

Sweat beaded on his temples as he rose to his feet and put distance between them. No one could know he had female company. No one could know about *her*. Fornication was forbidden. It went against the teachings of the Holy Book. An offense that carried a heavy price. He locked eyes with hers in a hard stare and, bringing his finger against his lips, picked up the cell. The widening of her eyes and tilt of her head communicated that she understood his silent demand. Satisfied, he brought the phone to his ear and answered the call.

"Go ahead," the clipped words flowed off his tongue in Arabic. No greeting was needed. He knew who it was and the nature of the call.

"Took you long enough," the caller huffed.

The woman's bliss-induced hooded eyes tracked his every movement as he paced the room. He caught her gaze and his stomach tightened; it carried the promise to finish what they had started. A promise he was looking forward to seeing fulfilled.

The male caller's voice cut through his thoughts. "The guests are confirmed and will be arriving on time for the party." Having been briefed on the perils of digital communication screening, the two men used short, nondescript dialogue. They were links in a long and unforgiving chain, one created with the sole purpose of keeping their mission off the radar.

"I'll let the hosts know," he responded in a low, controlled voice.

"What about your neighborhood watch? Anything new?" The question was the same each and every time. A routine he'd become familiar with over the last couple of years.

"No. Same boring shit. How's DC?"

"If I wasn't so rooted here, I'd ask for a transfer. This place is a sewer." If Naveed didn't know Arabic wasn't the caller's first language, the man's flawless pronunciation would have fooled him.

"We all have a purpose. Yours is to continue your watch there. If anything changes regarding the visit, he'll want to know as soon as it happens. They can't afford any surprises."

"I don't need you to remind me. I understand my duties." The man's sullen tone told him he didn't appreciate being chastised. *"Ma'a salama."*

"Allah yasalmak." He disconnected the call, once again free to continue where he'd left off minutes before.

It had taken him awhile to succumb to the temptations of the

West, but once he had, he'd done so without blinking an eye. At times, his craving for a taste, a bite of that forbidden fruit caused him to forget the true purpose of his life in the US.

He returned his gaze to the naked woman lounging on the rumpled sheets. Her heavy-lidded eyes brightened as he approached her. A seductive smile played on her lips as he parted her legs and covered her soft, welcoming body with his. A warning light flickered in the corner of his mind, but it was quickly snuffed by the touch of her lush mouth against his, the sweet clench of her heat around his cock. In that moment, all that mattered was the woman melding her body to his. A groan of need rumbled up the back of his throat as he laid claim to her teasing lips. There would be time to play courier pigeon later.

Chapter Two

The Party

‡————————‡

ACHAEL MOORE HURRIED THROUGH THE security check, flashing her credentials as she passed the guards at the staff entrance of the US Embassy in Tel Aviv. On her heels was Mark Stratton, one of the Diplomatic Security Service special agents assigned to her boss's team.

Located on one of Tel Aviv's busier streets, the boxy concrete building didn't have the historical appeal of the consulate in Jerusalem, but it had one spectacular redeeming quality: the ocean view from the fourth floor—where Rachael often escaped to think things through—was magnificent.

For the past few days, the embassy had been teeming with US citizens and their families, a direct result of the latest travel warning issued by the State Department urging them to leave the region. In the last phases before the closure, a skeleton crew of employees, also anxious to leave, were the only ones left handling the stragglers flocking to the building.

Rachael whisked past the line of men and women clutching

passports, birth certificates, and Department of Defense identification cards, waiting to have their documents screened for departure. She veered right and jogged down the corridor toward her boss's office.

Gerald Blair, the US Special Envoy to the Middle East to whom a few months earlier she'd been assigned to assist, had received an order of departure over night, instructing him and his team to leave the country on a scheduled diplomatic flight out of Ben Gurion International Airport.

Overseeing the peace talks between the Palestinian and Israeli states had put him in the spotlight and, after making suggestions that had ruffled feathers on both sides of the table, he'd become a target. As his personal assistant and attaché to the mission, she had been placed in the same line of fire. Their time in Israel and the West Bank was over until the talks could be resumed.

Rachael rushed inside his office while her shadow stood guard outside. Wasting no time, she began stuffing files into a courier bag. Working in the politically unstable region of the world had landed her in hairier situations before. The evacuation should be a piece of cake—and also the perfect cover for what she needed to do. She rummaged through the file cabinet, flipping through folders, pulling out only those containing confidential and classified information they couldn't leave behind.

Stratton walked in while she packed. "Are you done here, Ms. Moore? The convoy will be leaving shortly."

She froze, heart beating out of control, as he approached her. The man wore a well-cut black suit that screamed Secret Service and was damn good at his job. But it wasn't the muscles rippling underneath that suit as he walked or his chiselled good looks that jolted her. It was the way he carried himself. His stance always reminded her of…. She gave herself a mental shake. *Focus.* She dismissed the familiar presence from her thoughts and continued with her task.

"Almost. I just need a few more minutes."

"Is that it?" He nodded at the bag on the desk by the file cabinet.

"There's not much left." She looked up and shrugged. "Most of the documents are saved in digital format on a remote server. My main concern right now is securing the last of the physical files Mr. Blair wants to take with us." She glanced down at the ones in her hands. Her tone was firm and gave away none of her personal tribulations. She set them aside and pulled open the top drawer of the last cabinet. "Just give me ten, will you?"

"Roger." Turning her gaze to him, she recognized the sudden faraway look in his eyes. Someone was talking in his ear. Stratton paused and raised his wrist to his mouth. "Yes sir."

"If that's Mr. Blair, tell him I'm almost done."

He nodded as he reported over the communication device, "ETA ten minutes." His steely eyes indicated the deadline was firm before he turned on his heel and strode from the office.

Rachael blew out a sigh of relief. She didn't need him looking over her shoulder. But she also knew he hadn't gone far. The security agent would be stationed outside the door, waiting to escort her to the convoy. She had to be quick.

She began flipping through the tabs until she found the folders she needed. Thumbing through pages, she located the one she wanted. It was the first of several documents that, to the unsuspecting eye, appeared to be just ordinary reports—but to her they were gold. Documents she had seen but not been able to copy before. Dots she hoped to be able to connect. As she pulled the cell phone from her pocket, she darted a glance over her shoulder before turning back to the desk and taking a snapshot of the page. She shuffled through the pages until she'd captured images of them all.

"Time to go, Ms. Moore," Stratton's voice boomed from the

hallway. Rachael's already knotted stomach tightened even more.

Her pulse jumped and she flicked a nervous glance over her shoulder again. "Coming."

She stowed the last of the files and shoved the drawer closed. Plucking the micro SD card from her phone, she took a deep breath to calm her nerves. Eyes pinned on the doorway; she opened the locket at her throat and tucked the card behind the precious photo she kept inside. The documents on the card were critical to the goal she was committed to achieving. She tucked the locket back under her blouse, crammed the last of Blair's folders in the bag, and zipped it closed. Shouldering the hefty load, she hurried from the office and, as expected, the DSS agent fell in step behind her.

He herded her across the building, wading through employees milling around like scattering ants in a colony.

Two unmarked standard sedans composed the convoy leaving the city. They headed in the direction of the parked cars waiting on the last of the passengers. As she approached the vehicles, agents were escorting Jason Wolfe, a representative from the European Union, and Goh Min-Sook, the UN Secretary-General, to the lead vehicle. Both men had also been participating in the peace talks and were guests at the embassy. Stratton led Rachael to the second vehicle and, in a gentleman-like fashion, helped her into the back seat.

Once the DSS agents took their positions in the vehicles, they sped off. In fender-to-fender formation—a clue to anyone that they transported valuable cargo—the convoy snaked through the streets of Tel Aviv, heading in the direction of the airport.

Rachael, wedged in the back seat between Blair and DSS agent Hank Thompson, settled into a more comfortable position. Stratton rode shotgun and, from time to time, she overheard him conferring with the driver or talking through the radio with Alex Norwood, one of the agents in the lead vehicle.

It wasn't long before the landscape transitioned from towering skyscrapers, congested streets, and crowded sidewalks to green pastures and fertile lands. Rachael focused her attention inward and lost herself in the images and instructions playing in her head. The stress and exhaustion of the last few days beat at her, but she was determined to stay awake. She snapped her head back each time it drooped, even though instinctively she knew it was a losing battle. After almost finding a soft pillow in the form of Thompson's solid shoulder, she leaned her head back against the seat. Soon her eyelids became too heavy, and she succumbed to exhaustion.

"WHAT THE HELL is going on up there? Tell them to hurry up. We're supposed to be at the airport in ten!" Blair's voice boomed over the loud exchange between the agents and the screeching sound blaring from the radio going amok, snatching Rachael from her uneasy nap.

Her eyes widened when she realized the cars were inert in the middle of the highway. She darted her gaze to the slim watch hugging her wrist. They'd been on the road for less than twenty minutes.

A crease marred Blair's brow as he checked the back of the car. "Damn it, Stratton. We're boxed in," he rasped as he turned back to the stone-faced agent.

"Let me find out what's going on," Norwood's steady voice sounded through the speaker.

"Copy," Stratton replied.

Rachael sat tall in her seat and shot a look at her boss. His expression was taut. "What's happening? Why are we stopped?"

Caution clouded his features. "It looks like a checkpoint. No way to get through it. We might need to notify the flight crew and instruct them to wait on us if we need to head back to the embassy."

A buzz of energy flooded her. Something was wrong, and in a big way. "There isn't supposed to be a checkpoint in this area. Especially not on a main highway. Do you think this has anything to do with the evacuation?"

Concern flared bright in his eyes. They'd witnessed the gruesome images of what the religious dissent could unleash on its residents. That he'd been thinking the same hadn't left her warm and fuzzy, but the idea that her past—the need-to-know part she had omitted when she took the job—might have finally caught up with her worried her.

"No." The pause in Blair's voice wasn't reassuring.

It was winter in the Middle East. Day and night temperatures varied wildly from sweltering hot to frigid cold. The idling vehicle's air conditioning, even set to high, couldn't fight off the heat building inside. Sweat beaded on her temples and trailed between her breasts. They watched an armed man wearing fatigues approach the lead vehicle's front passenger window. Silence descended over them, fear a choking smog in the car. Over the radio, they heard the exchange between the man and Norwood. The armed guard spoke in a harsh, rapid dialect, the tension in his voice palpable to her. Her pulse jumped and blood thrummed in her veins.

"Something feels wrong," Stratton mumbled to himself. The tension in his voice tightened another band around Rachael's heart. He lowered the window and surveyed the area, his hand seeking his sidearm, his posture rigid and predatory. Out of the corner of her eye, she caught movement. An armed man approached and circled their vehicle. His eyes scanned those inside as if looking for some-thing, someone. She saw Thompson push back his jacket and wrap his fingers around the grip of his piece in an almost synchronized movement with Stratton's.

Rachael's eyes travelled to the interaction taking place around the lead vehicle, her thoughts willing the guard to walk away and let them by, but the dialogue continued to flow through the radio. The lead car's driver translated the man's demand.

"He wants to see our passports."

"Why? This is a diplomatic convoy," Norwood argued. *"Everything is in order."*

The same armed man who had screened them approached the lead vehicle. Rachael caught his furtive shift toward the driver's door and the nod to the man standing by Norwood's side. Her fingers dug into Blair's arm.

"Why is he—?"

A pop sounded, cutting her off, and a red splatter burst like confetti on the passenger side. Norwood's shattered skull flopped against the edge of the open window, blood trailing rivulets down the side of the door.

"Fuck! Ambush!" Stratton yelled. The team's response was swift. The security detail called out their positions in a chaotic cacophony over the radio while covering their protégés. "Get down, get down!" Stratton shouted.

Rachael gasped in shock when Thompson gripped the back of her neck and shoved her head down against her knees. "Stay down," he grumbled near her ear.

The loud roar of rapid fire, the clang of metal, and screams filled the air. When bullets sprayed the cars, simultaneous cries split the air. Rachael squeezed her eyes shut tight and put all her trust in the agents' ability to keep them alive.

"Shit!" she heard Stratton curse from the front seat as he and the other agents returned fire. "There's no time to call for air support. Get us the fuck out of here! Now!" Stratton ordered the driver, who slammed the car in reverse, ramming the car behind them, trying to force a way out. The impact flung them about in the back seat like crash test dummies, but did nothing to get them out of the line of fire still raging. They were pinned, deadlocked between the assailants and other civilians' cars who, in their haste to escape the attack, had abandoned them and run on foot.

Rachael's heart jumped when Thompson's hold on her loosened and his weight suddenly slumped on top of her. Wet warmth slithered down her side. Pinned and unable to turn her head, she reached over and strained to get him off her. Icy dread coursed through her veins when the heavy weight wouldn't budge. Struggling against the constraint, she inched a glance upwards. A hole gaped in the side of his head, his once friendly brown eyes lifeless and staring into nothingness. The blood seeping from his wound stained his expensive suit and pooled between them on the plush leather seat.

She swallowed the scream that clawed at her throat. "Oh my God, Hank." Sorrow for him, for his young family she had seen in pictures not so long ago, shredded her. She pushed at him until his body crumbled against the door, freeing her to sit up once again.

"Keep your head down, damn it!" Stratton yelled.

Her heart lurched in her chest as she hunched forward, bracing her knees in the tight space between the console and the back seat. Blair did the same behind the driver's seat, his eyes crowded with horror and locked on the dead agent while the crossfire between the agents and the armed attackers transformed the highway into a death zone.

An explosion of glass rained down on them as the back window shattered into a million pieces and the acrid smell of gunpowder permeated the air in the car. The sounds of agony and screams of pain mixed with commanding orders as the agents shouted their positions and status. Their voices, riddled with urgency, mingled in the air with the harsh yells from their attackers. The assailants spoke Arabic, a language she understood well, but under all the chaos and the popping of guns it became almost impossible to discern a cohesive sentence from the words they screamed at each other.

The buzz and whooshing noise was painful to her ears, but not as painful as the concussion of the explosion set off somewhere behind the sedan, nor the heat that washed over them following the blast.

"Rachael? Rachael? Talk to me. Are you okay?" The ringing in her ears muffled Blair's voice.

"Yes." She shook all over, heart accelerated to a mile a minute, her whole body falling prey to the adrenaline rush. "Is there any way out?" Her gravelly voice sounded foreign even to her.

Pops rang in the distance, followed by a grunt and a scream.

"I'm hit. I'm hit!" they heard the terrified voice of the driver in the lead car scream before the radio became eerily silent.

"Carter! Report!" Stratton tried to reach the other agent trapped in the car in front of them.

When there was no reply, Rachael followed Stratton's careful check over the dashboard. Before they could take in the full scene, their front windshield shattered and warm drops sprayed her face. They both ducked again.

"Stratton, get us out of here!" Blair commanded when their driver slumped to the side.

Each time Stratton tried to open his door, a rain of bullets peppered the area around them. One by one, the agents and drivers in their convoy were being picked off by enemy fire. She knew their chances of leaving Israel alive were declining with each shot, each second gone by.

"Who are these people?" Her voice barely registered above the conflict outside the car.

Blair's arms flew up to cover his head as another round of shots arrowed through the passenger windows, peppering them with more glass. "Who knows?! Hamas, Fatah, Mossad—it could be anybody!"

Just when her ears felt as if they would burst, silence descended over them. It was soon broken by a voice yelling instructions from a short distance. The banging of her heart against her ribs replaced the ringing in her ears. Suddenly, the door flew open and a man, little more than a teenager, stared down at them, a deep frown above his eyes. He jabbed Stratton's face with the butt of his AK-47 and, with a grunt, Stratton dropped his gun to the floorboard as blood gushed from his nose.

"Get out," he barked in Arabic. "Move!" he repeated in heavily accented English.

The back door popped open and another man grabbed Blair's arm, dragging him from the car. Blair tumbled to the ground and Rachael's stomach tightened as the guard jerked him to his feet and shoved a black hood over his head before pushing him toward the front of the car. Her pulse raced faster as a third guard gestured her out of the back toward him. Swallowing hard, Rachael slid across the seat and stood on wobbly legs. Fear coated her tongue when a similar hood covered her head, enveloping her sight in darkness. She bit back a startled cry when a heavy hand jerked her arms behind her back and restrained her.

The same hand gripped her elbow and hustled her to where she guessed the others were gathered. She hadn't gotten a chance to see who else had survived from the other vehicle. Wolfe and Min-Sook had been the peacemakers when negotiations had gone sour and were there under the umbrella of the United Nations. She prayed they had survived, especially given the importance of their roles during the peace talks.

"Go, go." The man shoved her forward. She could hear the shuffle of feet and the thunderous roar of an engine approaching them. Tires squealed to a stop, and the pungent smell of burnt rubber teased her nose. She bit back a gasp when calloused hands unceremoniously hauled her up and pushed her onto what she could only assume was the flatbed of a truck. Rough hands shoved her further back and she cried out as her ankle rolled and pain shot through her kneecap like an electric current.

"Ms. Moore? Rachael? Are you hurt?" Stratton's gruff voice called out and then cut off in an "oomph." Sounds of scuffle filled the air and another man screamed in Arabic for silence. The back end of the truck dipped three more times under the weight of people climbing in. Relief flooded her when she heard the voices of Blair, Wolfe, and Min-Sook.

A swoosh sounded above them, and she no longer felt the sun beating against her nor could see any vestiges of sunlight filtering through the cloth covering her head. A flap? A cover so that no one would see them? Those questions and many more revolved in her head as she catalogued any available information to use later.

Within minutes, the truck raced away leaving the bullet-riddled sedans—silent witnesses to their abduction—behind. The whole incident seemed to have lasted a lifetime, but she knew it had been mere minutes since Norwood had taken the shot to the head.

Blinded by the hood, Rachael concentrated on sounds—the revving of the engine, the clanking of what sounded like a chain hitting metal, the rumble of the tires against the asphalt—and direction, mapping their way to wherever they were heading like crumbs on a path in her mind.

Moments later, the truck veered left and the ride became bumpier. Dust tickled her nose. She tried to brace herself as the truck barreled down what had to be a dirt road. Her heart thumped in her chest at the sudden realization that none of the civilians who had witnessed the attack knew who they were, where they were being taken or by whom. She sucked back the sob that threatened to burst from her lips. She couldn't die. Not when she was so close.

"Hang on, sweetheart."

Renewed hope burned inside her as Phillip's words echoed in her head.

"I will," she whispered back.

Chapter Three

Like Father, Like Son

"I'LL BE A BLAST, CASSIE. I can't wait." Jessica Connellan's contagious excitement could be felt even over the phone. "Thank god, that second round of antibiotics finally kicked in before you hacked up a lung."

Cassandra kicked her feet up to rest on her desk and grinned. "No kidding. Knock on wood it doesn't come back again. I'm glad we'll get to spend your first New Year's in Ireland together. It makes things feel like home again. Especially now that we can't make it to your place for dinner tonight."

"Stephan's already fretting. But I kept the list intimate. Just family and a few friends."

"Pity Bob won't be able to make it, but it'll be great. Your last big hoorah before you begin to waddle like a duck." Cassandra's grin spread wider. *Wait for it…*

"What the hell, Cassandra Cristina. That was a low blow," Jessica grumbled. "I refuse to waddle."

Cassandra burst out laughing. "Honestly Jess, I don't think you can stop it from happening."

Jessica snorted. "Thanks for reminding me." Sarcasm dripped from her words. "Before I forget, did you two reach a decision?"

"No. I'm scared to think how Bob will react to it."

"Yeah…it won't be pretty. I'm glad I'm not the one who has to break it to your dad. Let me know how it goes and if I can begin to plan the welcome party," Jessica joked. "Damn. Look at the time. I gotta go. Stephan's holed up in the office."

"Does the man ever stop working? It's a holiday, for crying out loud."

"I know, right? He wants to get as much as he can done before the baby arrives. Oh, I almost forgot. I finished the report you wanted and will email it shortly. Interesting stuff, but not much there."

The humor bled from Cassandra's voice. "Not what I wanted to hear, but thanks. I'll take a look. Let you know if we need to dig some more."

"Give me a few minutes and then check your inbox. Later, chica."

Cassandra hung up. A heavy weight of disappointment pressed against her chest. She turned her chair toward the big windows in the office. Water beaded and trailed in little rivulets down the glass panes. Funny she hadn't noticed that the rain had started again. That was one thing she was still coming to terms with—the never-ending rain. She loved it, but it wasn't the same as a nice California downpour, which hit you, lasted a couple of days, and was then beaten back by the sun. Instead, Dublin's rain lasted for weeks on end. What she never got tired of was its scent—the rich, old-world earthy aroma that found its way inside no matter how tightly you closed the windows.

Turning back around, she glanced at Trevor, who had his eyes locked on his screen and, more likely than not, hadn't heard a single word of her conversation with Jessica. Cassandra pushed from her chair and walked over to his side of their work area. Resting her hands on his shoulders, she checked his monitor.

"Anything new?"

"No." His gaze never veered from its target. "This damn case is pissing me off. Just when George and I think we have something solid, the digital trail hits a brick wall."

Frustration knit her brows. She had nothing to give him either. Her own analysis of the case before they'd left for Russia hadn't yielded anything new. The target was a slippery bastard, a target the CIA had pressed them to locate before another tragedy pummeled US soil.

"I'm sure if we keep at it something will pop."

The usual playfulness was vacant from Trevor's eyes as he flicked his gaze to her. "Not how I expected to be spending Christmas Day."

She shook her head in agreement. Although she and Trevor had an atypical job with no allowance for extended vacations or scheduled breaks, it *was* Christmas. She was looking forward to making the most of the holidays with him without interruption, even if it meant working on difficult cases together.

"We knew the NSA would have priority when we started this. It can't be helped. Especially due to the ties to national security." She gave his shoulders a reassuring squeeze before moving away. "Jessie sent me some dossiers I had requested. It seems we'll both be busy tonight."

As she took her seat, her cell phone vibrated on the desk with an incoming text message. A quick swipe on the screen revealed the sender's name. *Nathan.* She bit her lower lip, contemplating whether to read it. *Whatever Nate wants, I'm sure it can wait.* She turned off her cell, tossed it on the desk, and checked her inbox. The report hadn't come through yet.

Glancing once again at her husband, she noticed that the lines of concentration had deepened along his brows and under his eyes. Her stomach churned with disquiet as he kept his attention glued to the screen. She'd hoped Jessica would find something, some nugget of information that would miraculously set them on the right track, set them free to pursue what really mattered to them in the long run. She needed to breathe, clear her head.

"I'm going for a cup. Want one?"

He grunted a half reply and she left him to his work while she refilled their cups and tried to organize her thoughts, unfortunately without much success.

Back in the office, she set Trevor's cup on his desk and, nursing hers in her hands, walked to the window for a glance outside. Mother Nature pummeled the eerily quiet street with large watery globes. Under the dark skies, the picture-perfect Dublin had the somber hue of winter.

As she stared out the window, her focus blurred and turned inward. It fluttered around the unread text message she had just received from Nathan. Guilt's unforgiving fingers pinched her for ignoring it. Since their return from St. Petersburg, their friendship had been tenuous at best, and that saddened her. Their joint mistake had created an awkward and high hurdle to overcome, but she missed the brotherly figure that had been a part of her life for so many years. Although it was Christmas, she was fairly certain he wasn't calling to extend his well wishes. Still, she should have read it.

The familiar beep of incoming email cut through her musings, almost as if signaling Cassandra to get her ass moving. She dropped the curtain back into place and moved to her desk. Setting her cup aside, she opened the file Jessica had sent her and scanned the first page.

The dossier on Jamad Assir—one of the many minor names associated with the case driving Trevor and George mad—contained details on his routine, but nothing that could be deemed a strong link to the man they were searching for. Assir frequented the local mosque, but that in itself wasn't out of the ordinary. His work life was quite uneventful as well. At the bottom of the document, Jessica had listed his past known associates, individuals with whom he'd been in contact through the time he'd been under surveillance. Trevor's mutterings periodically broke the silence and a smile tipped the corners of her mouth. She really loved the man.

The document-screening came to a halt when one of the names listed in the file caught her attention: Abboud, Naveed. Cassandra's smile faded and her body stilled. The profile didn't have a lot on him, only physical description and parentage. Naveed Abboud, son of Ahmed Abboud. A niggling of recollection stroked her mind.

She opened a new browser window and searched for that name to spark her memory. Skimming through the results, disappointment lined the back of her throat. Nothing of value jumped at her. On a hunch, she filtered the results to videos and scrolled down until one caught her eye. An old news clip—specifically, an interview that appeared to have been cut from an old British television newscast. The caption at the bottom of the screen displayed the name Timothy Worthington directly above his title, Oversight Commissioner of the Police Service. Putting on her headphones, she watched the clip.

"Eyewitness accounts claim two men were seen walking away from the building moments before the explosion occurred. Through CCTV footage secured from the area at the time of the blast, we can confirm that we were able to identify one of the men as Ahmed Abboud, a known munitions expert. He was taken into custody earlier today and is now being held for questioning. The unidentified man is still at large."

"Commissioner! Commissioner!" voices shouted in tandem.

He raised his hands, palms out. *"Ladies and gentlemen, that is all I can release at this time."* Worthington then turned his back to the cameras and, without a backward glance, left the room.

Cassandra's eyes were riveted on the frozen image where the clip had ended. Hope surged through her veins. The name had indeed triggered a memory. An old case. One that had become a case study for new recruits.

The man held for questioning was a suspect in one of the most daring terrorist attacks in London. The fact that someone had been able to infiltrate a restricted area within MI5's headquarters and execute Abboud had been a monumental embarrassment. MI5 had been left with egg on their face and a hole in their organization. It had never been established how the execution had taken place, and questions revolved around whether or not it had been an MI5-sanctioned kill.

Cassandra drummed her fingers on the keys and tumbled the facts she could recall from Trevor's case around in her head. Unable to find any glaring connection, she bookmarked the video for later scrutiny. She added Abboud and Worthington's names to the file and shot off an email to Jessica asking her to check into them further. It was weak, but there was a chance it could be related to the case in some way.

She suddenly became aware of how dark the room had grown. It was getting late; hunger clouded her mind, making it difficult to concentrate. Rolling her shoulders, Cassandra dropped the headphones and pushed from her desk. She could bet Trevor was so engrossed in whatever he was working on he'd ignored the hunger signs. She shook her head. *What a pair we make.*

"I heard that," Trevor's voice rumbled, breaking the silence cocooning the room.

"What? You can hear my thoughts now?"

"No. But I heard your stomach growling at me." His voice brimmed with humor.

"Sorry for the ruckus. How about you? Craving anything special?" Cassandra stood and he pushed his own chair back as she closed the distance between them.

"Was that a trick question? It sure opened a door to the gutter section of my mind." He flashed a wicked grin.

She enjoyed the repartee as much as he did. "I would love to have some delicious meat—hey!" Her yelp echoed throughout the large room as a tug on her hand sent her tumbling onto Trevor's lap.

He chuckled and kissed her hard on the lips. "Keep that up and you will." He wrapped his arms around her and captured her mouth again in a soul-branding kiss.

Cassandra pushed away from his chest, gasping for air. "Down, boy-o," she laughed. "God, I can't believe I'm saying this, but hold that thought. I'm starved, and when that happens, as you well know, grumpy becomes my middle name. I need food. So? What'll it be? Fend, in, or out?"

Heat flared in Trevor's eyes. "Back to the gutter, are we?"

She punched his arm. "Jeez. I didn't plan a festive meal since we should've been at Stephan and Jessica's. It's fend for ourselves with leftovers. Order in. Or go out to a restaurant."

"Not sure about the last two. This is Ireland, not San Francisco. Everything closes on Christmas day, even pubs. Remember?"

She hung her head in defeat. "I still can't get over that," she huffed. "Looks like we're fending for ourselves, then."

Trevor tucked her under his arm and dropped his head against the high back leather chair as if pondering world hunger. "Leftover Chinese it is. Do you think you can wear last year's Christmas present at the dinner table?"

Heat flooded Cassandra's cheeks at his reference to the first

Christmas gift she had given him: herself. "Wouldn't I be a little underdressed?"

Trevor's eyes sparkled with humor. "Chopsticks, me, and you dressed in a little six-inch-wide gold ribbon. Definitely understated, but delectable as hell."

Cassandra flicked his chin. "It will all depend on how quickly you feed me."

"Okay then. A challenge. I like it," he laughed, tugging her toward the kitchen.

"NOT AS GOOD as you can find in San Francisco, but pretty damn tasty, even the second time around." Cassandra uncurled herself from the couch and began gathering the empty cartons from the coffee table.

"I don't know about that. In San Francisco, you probably have 'Merican' Chinese, not the real thing." Trevor's teasing tone as he took their glasses and chopsticks to the kitchen hadn't escaped her.

"Whatever. You'll change your tune the next time we're there. Chinatown's food is off the hook." Cassandra scrambled, juggling the cartons, but one slipped her grasp and spilled its contents on the floor. "Damn—"

Trevor's laughter echoed in the open-concept room. "Nice juggling act," he peeped from the sink. "I think you need practice." He tossed her a rag and relieved her of the rest of the cartons.

Cassandra narrowed her eyes. "You laugh."

Trevor flashed a lopsided grin and the corner of her mouth twitched. She sank to her haunches and wiped the rice that had scattered across the floor into a pile. As she reached for the grains that had scattered near the Christmas tree, a shimmer of green caught her eye. It seemed a gift had been missed, one that she didn't remember seeing or placing under the tree.

"Trevor?" Curiosity flooded her. "Where did this come from? I don't remember seeing it. It certainly wasn't here yesterday."

"Bugger. I totally forgot about that." He wiped his hands and walked back toward her, sporting a deep frown. "Stephan stopped by earlier and dropped it off while you were in the shower."

While Cassandra finished the cleanup, Trevor retrieved the box covered in cheery Christmas paper and set it on the coffee table. "Any idea what it could be?"

Trevor studied the gift. "No. Stephan's only comment was that I'd be glad to have it." He was curious about its contents, but a part of him shied from ripping the paper off. His stomach churned just at remembering the tone in Stephan's voice and the uncertain gleam in his eyes.

Cassandra's voice broke softly through his introspection. "Do you want to open it by yourself? I can go upstairs." Her eyes almost burned holes as she studied him. That was the one downside to having a wife who could read just about anything from facial expressions. He glanced at her and knew by the firm set of her mouth that she was holding back from voicing her opinion. He also knew that waiting for him to make up his mind was just about killing her.

"No. I want you with me. Always." Aware of her watching his every move, he ripped off the paper. As he lifted the lid, he froze in place. A lump constricted his throat as he stared at the box's contents.

Cassandra moved to his side and glimpsed over the rim. Reaching inside, she pulled out one of a dozen neatly wrapped packages and carefully tore the wrapping material.

"Frames?" She turned it over in her hands to reveal the image of his parents.

Air was sucked from his lungs as if he'd received a sucker punch to the gut. In the undated photograph, his parents held each other close against the backdrop of the beautiful old house in Sligo, their wide grins beaming at him from the photograph. He could swear he saw a twinkle in his ma's eye.

"I think Stephan went digging when I asked him for help with our anniversary gift." His eyes traced the familiar features in the picture.

"Is this your home?" she asked, handing him the picture and reaching for another.

He dropped to the edge of the couch, unconsciously rubbing his thumb across the glass. "Yes."

Cassandra continued to remove the pictures one by one from the box, stacking them on the coffee table and chuckling as each new frame of his life was turned face up and unveiled to their eyes.

"Oh, this one's cute. You had that mischievous gleam in your eyes even as a little kid."

An involuntary smile pulled at the corner of his mouth. "These were all taken in Sligo." Trevor's heart raced a mile a minute and his legs turned to rubber in repetition of the night he'd sat in front of their Sligo house a few months earlier, unable to face the images residing within its walls. Being confronted with a kaleidoscope of the past left him stunned.

With each frame Cassandra set aside, the band around his heart loosened a tad more. *Damn the old man.* Stephan had picked the right moment, even if he hadn't known it himself—Christmas with the woman who had come to mean so much to him—to force him to confront memories of the time before she had stormed into his life, attitude and determination glinting fiercely in her beautiful brown eyes.

Trevor's gaze followed Cassandra as she began to walk around the room, strategically placing the pictures on shelves.

"They can sit here until we hang them on the wall next to the two you gave me for our anniversary."

Just like doctors exposed people with phobias to the triggers of their fears in order to eventually desensitize them, he figured she intended to expose him to the snippets of his family life. She could be onto something. Seeing the image of his parents arranged on the mantel next to her parents' wedding picture had somewhat eased the discomfort in his chest.

Cassandra returned to his side and surveyed her décor work. He engulfed her hand with his and caressed it, brushing his thumb across her wedding band. "Thank you for putting them up."

She leaned down and kissed his lips. "Another terrific present. You'll need to call Stephan and thank him." She gestured at the frame in his hand and he passed it to her. "You know? You truly favor your dad. To tell the truth, when I first saw him in the pictures I thought it was you and some old flame."

He cocked his head to study the picture before he shrugged. "Nah. I have my mother's smile."

"I can see it, but trust me when I say you are the spitting image of your father. From looking at this picture, I can expect you to age like a good bottle of wine. I am looking forward to experiencing the mature version in a few decades." Humor flickered in her eyes and warmed him up inside.

"And I expect you to keep savoring that wine for a *very* long time. They say it's good for your heart." He could barely keep a straight face.

She chuckled as she set the picture on the table and climbed back onto his lap. "It's been a great Christmas." She cupped the sides of his face and kissed him. "Thank you."

Trevor brushed his knuckles against her soft cheek. "I still think you should've worn the ribbon."

"If you're a good boy, maybe later…." Cassandra ran a finger down his chest to his waistband in a slow tease. The generalized warmth grew into a more localized fire.

"Fuck later!" He pushed her off his lap and her raspy laughter wrapped itself like a silky ribbon around his heart as he tugged her to the stairs.

Chapter Four

Be Careful What You Ask For

THE PHONE'S CHIRP ALERTED HIM of an incoming message. Not the first one Nathan had heard hit his cell that night, but none a reply to the message he'd sent Cassandra earlier that day. He didn't need to look at the device to know what the message read or who had sent it.

The clock on the sterile white wall told him he'd have to move his ass if he wanted to make it to the restaurant on time. Nathan had considered heading there earlier, but being Christmas Eve, he hadn't had the stomach to watch families enjoying the holiday evening while he waited. He'd killed that time at work instead.

He'd gotten caught up with report-writing but had lost track of time in the process. Nathan cursed under his breath and clamped his jaw tight, mulling on the meeting ahead. No way to avoid it. He might as well get it over with.

With a deep intake of air, Nathan grabbed his coat and scarf from the hanger on his way out. He punched the elevator button, running through different scenarios in his head on how to get out of the meeting with Luke: an accident, an after-hours briefing, even an emergency call to duty in the pits of hell would be better than having to face him. *It's so fucked up.* He doubted anyone else in the world would have that same kind of reaction.

The pounding of his long, purposeful strides on the polished marble floor echoed in the empty lobby of the CIA headquarters as he crossed to the exit. It was dark by the time he stepped into the brisk December night. His stomach rolled, palms sweaty, and a cold wisp chilled him to the bone. Or maybe it was his dread of the upcoming event that caused the chill. He couldn't tell the difference at that point.

Aware that their warmth would shelter his body from the cold but would never melt the ice in his chest, Nathan shrugged on his wool coat and looped the scarf around his neck as he trekked the short distance to his car.

He slumped in his seat and gripped the steering wheel while his gaze roamed the dark sky. *Damn it. There is no way out of it.* He keyed the engine and sped out of the CIA's parking lot, fishtailing as he punched the gas, propelling him toward a conversation he was far from comfortable having.

He drove the short distance to Ray's The Steaks in a state of numbness that morphed into his usual shield the closer he got. The cool exterior he'd always presented to the world hardened and was securely in place by the time he walked into his favorite restaurant twenty minutes later. The mouthwatering aroma of delicious food invaded his nostrils the instant he crossed the threshold, the clinking of glasses and hushed conversation a soft white noise in the background as he scanned the restaurant for the familiar face.

He spotted Luke seated at a table in the back. *Great.* The place was not as busy as usual, which would provide them with some privacy. A good start to a reunion he knew would turn sour, as it usually did. Nathan would say something, Luke would shoot it down. It was how the damn story pretty much played out when it came to them.

Nathan was making his way through the maze of tables set with crisp black tablecloths, gleaming cutlery and wine glasses when Luke caught sight of him. His eyes flashed with something Nathan couldn't identify, but which strangely resembled longing. He stood as Nathan drew closer. Luke's larger frame—honed through long and intense military training—encased in a navy suit instead of the usual fatigues, blended with the environment. His military crop of blond hair, green eyes the exact shade as Nathan's, height, and prominent cheekbones so similar to his own made it impossible for anybody who saw them together not to recognize the connection.

"Hey, little brother." Luke extended his hand as he reached the table. A smile spread across his lips but didn't quite brighten his eyes. Aside from their appearance, they had nothing in common.

Luke was their father's favorite. The good son. The one who'd followed in their father's footsteps. The one who'd made all the right career choices and spawned the perfect family. Luke had married his high school sweetheart straight out of the military academy, and they had two boys whom Luke was actively grooming to be in the army, just as their father had expected of his own sons.

Nathan shook his hand and took the seat across from him. He didn't bother taking off his coat or wasting time with pleasantries. "So, why are we here?"

"I think you can guess."

The meaning embedded in Luke's words pricked under his skin and his anger singed the corners of his control as it ripped loose.

"Why in the world would you come all this way to talk about Jay? You know how I feel about it." His words were as crisp and cold as ice water.

"It's been too long, Nate. Dad wants you home this time." Luke hesitated, then rephrased, "Mom wants you home."

Nathan's heart sank in his chest. He avoided Luke's eyes, focusing his attention on his own hands clasped on the table. As much as he had his reasons for evading home and as much as he resented his family, he still loved them.

He raised his eyes to meet Luke's, now devoid of any warmth they might have held. "Tell her—" A bitter taste coated his tongue. He pushed from the table, ready to leave the brief family reunion behind. "Tell her I send my love."

Before he could stand, Luke's iron grip on his forearm halted him. "I didn't come all this way to leave empty handed, Nate."

Nathan snared his gaze. "I guess you'll just have to tell him you failed."

"He won't be happy."

"Honestly, I don't give a shit," Nathan smirked. "Anyway, what you really mean is he will be disappointed with *you*. Which means you'll finally get a taste of what Jay and I experienced our entire lives."

"Don't drag Jay in this. This is between you and me."

Rage churned in Nathan's gut as he leaned over the table, his temper flaring hot. "You and Dad both dragged him in, fucked him up, and spit him out like a discarded rag when he needed you most." His voice grew dangerously low as he snarled his contempt. "I hope you're satisfied with the results.

Luke's face blanched. *Good.* Nathan hoped his words had cut deep. He wanted the wound to fester, like the one festering inside of him with each year that went by. He wished he could leave it all behind, that he could move on and forget where he'd come from and who he was. For a while, he had done just that. Thrown himself into the hardcore world of espionage, but even that hadn't turned out so well. It seemed he had a propensity to disappoint or lose those he became attached to, one way or another.

Luke's eyes hardened. "That was uncalled for. You know damn well I loved him as much as you did."

Nathan's sarcastic chuckle bubbled up before he could hold it down. "Are you fucking kidding me? You *tortured* us our entire lives. You *laughed* when we got in trouble. You even tricked us into our demises more often than not." Nathan watched as another flash of undefined emotion crossed Luke's eyes. "Was that only so you could stay on the old man's good side, or did you get off on watching him punish us?"

"We were kids, for Christ's sake. Kids do stupid things." Luke continued to restrain him, anchoring him down, well aware that Nathan would split the moment he let go.

"I'd actually believe that if you'd had the guts to stand up to him when we were all grown men, but you didn't. You were our older brother. Kin. Blood. You should've stood up for us." Nathan almost spat the words at him. Luke's face grew paler. "We done here?" Nathan stared pointedly at Luke's white knuckles twisted in his jacket sleeve.

Luke's gaze dropped to his hand, as if he had no clue it had been there all that time. He bunched his fingers one last time then almost hesitantly released his grip. "I guess we are."

Nathan rose to his feet and gazed down at Luke. Tension pulsed between them. In spite of their convoluted history, blood was a strong link. He wished it wasn't. The only hope his nephews had of not ending messed up like him or his brothers lay with Jeanie, Luke's wife. Unlike them, Jeanie didn't come from a military family and would balance out the strict upbringing they'd had. She would keep Luke on the right path.

"Tell Jeanie I said hello." Nathan turned and strode to the door without a backward glance.

He snapped a look at his watch. The whole ordeal had taken less than fifteen minutes. *Almost a new record.* He was always amazed at how simple conversations could go down the shitter in the blink of an eye when it involved members of his family. They all carried a heavy burden where Jay was concerned. Each saw the events that had taken place from different perspectives and seemed unable to reach a common ground for forgiveness.

Nathan carried his own share of guilt and shame, but his were of a different nature from the rest of the family. He and Jay had been close. His guilt stemmed from the fact that he hadn't recognized the signs that something was horribly wrong. He'd been so caught up in his own world back then, he'd forgotten to look around him and realize that Jay was also going through his own personal hell. It was too late to fix that mistake.

He climbed in the car and beat those painful thoughts back into the Pandora's Box in his head, but couldn't get rid of the heaviness in his heart. He wiped the sweat beading on his temples as sharp-edged emotions churned in his stomach.

"Fuck. Fuck. Fuck!" He slammed the heel of his palm against the steering wheel and turned the engine. It was gearing up to be a painfully long week, filled with memories and heartache. He could never get used to that, regardless of how many years swept by.

The restaurant wasn't far from his apartment and, as he drove back home, images of Luke's eyes and the odd glimmer he'd caught in their depths a couple of times during their dysfunctional conversation crawled into his memory. Could it have been remorse? He doubted it, but miracles did happen. Maybe deep inside his older brother, there was a small—a minuscule—amount of goodness.

Each and every day, Nathan was reminded of his origins when he looked at himself in the mirror—reminded that he shared the same genes with the man who called himself his father, but who had acted as their commanding officer all their lives. He'd rather have forgotten that fact, but the past was something he couldn't erase. Especially after the last few months spent digging for answers inside himself. Clues to his emotional Sahara.

He didn't have to delve too deep to find them. He was lucky he hadn't turned out worse. Not him. It just made him work harder. His father had not given them much affection, instead forging them with steel, and that steel had differentiated him from the others when he had taken the leap into the CIA.

It had been that steel and determination to prove his father wrong that had made him a prime candidate for the distinctions he'd received. Nathan had grown confident of his skills, of his capabilities, and of his strength. But their differences still created a chasm between them most times. Times like those. Christmas. New Year's. It was always when it hit him the hardest.

Nathan parked in his assigned spot at the complex and climbed the stairs to his apartment, the weight of the meeting still heavy on his mind. He closed the door behind him and dumped his tie and jacket on the back of a chair on his way to the bedroom, numbness making him more like an automaton. Not bothering with the light, he kicked his shoes off by the door and set his standard-issue SIG and cell on the nightstand. Down to his briefs, he tossed his clothes in the hamper and fell like a log on the bed.

The chill of the room skipped across his bare skin, leaving a peppering of goosebumps in its wake, but he didn't slip under the covers. He needed that forced cooling down. With his gaze locked on the white popcorn ceiling illuminated by the faint glow of the streetlight outside his window, he worked hard to push away the bitterness and hurt that burned inside him. He didn't quite understand why his father had sent his lapdog after him in the first place.

Why now?

Whatever the reason, it wouldn't have changed his determination never to set foot back home again. *Home.* He wasn't a religious man, but in that moment, he found himself praying to be sent miles from where he was. Worlds away. He turned to his side, chaos still swirling in his chest. He breathed in deep and expelled the breath in a slow release, forcing himself to take advantage of the blessed oblivion sleep could give him. But before he could escape, the shrill ring of his cell phone startled him.

Shit. He dreaded answering it. He was in no mood to talk to Luke again, but he reached for the device anyway.

When his eyes registered the number on the display, he swung his feet to the floor and sat on the edge of the mattress, answering the call before it rang again.

"Nelson."

"Zero eight hundred hours. My office." David Franklin's voice was stern, no sign of his usual humor. It didn't surprise Nathan. The CIA Director hadn't been too happy with him since the Russian incident.

"Zero eight hundred. Will be there, sir."

The second the call ended, his gut told him something big was up. Short-notice briefings usually meant action. Action meant he wouldn't have to dwell over Christmas. Adrenaline shot through his system. It was almost as if the heavens had answered his prayers.

STANDING IN FRONT of the closed door, Nathan stared at the shiny nameplate. Mixed feelings surged through him. The director was someone Nathan looked up to. He'd been the one who had seen potential in him, had handpicked Nathan out of his class long before he'd reached his current position. Despite their close relationship, he'd avoided Franklin as much as possible over the past few months. Out of sight, out of mind had been his MO. He'd figured if he stayed off Franklin's radar, things would smooth over and the faster he could get back to what he liked best. Did best. He squared his shoulders and knocked.

"Come in."

He pushed open the door and Franklin turned as he entered the office.

"Nelson, have a seat."

"Sir," Nathan acknowledged and took the seat in front of the desk across from where his superior stood.

Franklin sat at his desk and studied him with a sharp, assessing gaze. "How do you like your assignment?"

"If you call pushing paper around, typing fancy emails, and surfing the net an assignment," he shrugged.

A small smile twitched Franklin's lips, but it faded almost immediately. "You know damn well we couldn't send you back into the field right away after you were almost compromised in Russia." Nathan held his hard gaze with a matching one of his own. Franklin heaved a hefty sigh and tapped his fingers on a standard manila folder on his desk. "I've called you in because of this." He pushed it in Nathan's direction.

Nathan snatched it up as it hit the rounded edge of the desk. He pulled out the neatly stapled stack with the Top Secret stamp on the cover and began leafing through the pages. His eyes snapped to Franklin's.

"This happened yesterday?"

The director tipped his chin toward the file. "Four agents killed. Six hostages taken."

Nathan flipped through the few sheets. "Is this all?"

Franklin slipped another folder across the desk and rested his chin on steepled fingers as he examined him. Nathan's skin began to crawl under the scrutiny.

"Take a look and tell me what you think."

Nathan's pulse jumped with the adrenaline spike. He lowered his eyes to the file and scrutinized the paperwork. The more he read, the more his frown deepened. The report contained information that, if corroborated, would cause heads to roll.

"This is one hell of a clusterfuck, sir."

"That's why I'm putting you on it. Don't make me regret it."

Finally. Back in action. "I won't. Do you have the dossiers on the hostages? I want to familiarize myself with them before I leave."

"No. They're in transit."

"When can I expect to have them in hands?"

"Zero five hundred. Lieutenant Commander Daniel Hanson will meet you at the base and brief you in the air."

Nathan's stomach sank. Though he'd been given a reprieve, he was still in the doghouse after all. "You're saddling me with a partner? You've got to be fucking kidding me. You know me. I work better alone. Cancel the lieutenant. Have him courier me the details. I can study the dossiers on the way out. I've got this. My field experience—"

"We both know you can handle your share of the mission," Franklin cut him off. "But due to the nature of the operation, the Eighth Special Warfare Logistics Group has been called in."

Nathan had heard of the 8th but had never had the opportunity to work with them. It was known that hushed rumors circulated among civilian online forums as to whether they even existed. Those with high enough clearance knew who they were and what branches of the forces they came from. They also knew that if a mission was big and ugly, they were the go-to crew.

Franklin's next words removed any shadow of doubt over their existence. "Hanson's team is the best there is when it comes to these types of extractions. Their skills and competencies are off the charts. We really have no choice. Some serious shit is hitting the fan. Hell, Washington is breathing down our necks on this one. Besides, his contacts alone are worth their weight in gold." Franklin's stern expression didn't allow for argument. "The same way your contacts played a part in why you were chosen for this mission."

Nathan's narrowed eyes focused on Franklin's austere expression. "What do you mean by *my* contacts?"

"You're going to pay a visit to an acquaintance of yours. Someone whose expertise is essential to the case. The details of your assignment must remain classified Top Secret, even to Hanson. As far as they know, you are there to oversee the discovery and extraction of the hostages. The less they all know, the better."

Understanding slammed into Nathan's skull like a club. The situation was more critical than he'd originally thought. That was his chance to make up for the mess he'd gotten himself into, a way to forget what time of the year that was, a way to make amends. The old saying was true—be careful what you ask for.

Chapter Five

Good Morning

T REVOR SPRANG UP IN BED, HEART pounding in his ears. The foreboding dream had left its calling card—the sheen of perspiration glazing his skin, the unsettled squeeze in his heart. Unlike the other episodes, there were no vivid images playing in his head like a movie reel. The only things left behind this time were the physical reactions to the images that had held him captive in his sleep: jumping pulse, racing heart, rage bursting in his chest—and a scream still lodged in his throat.

He sat on the edge of the bed and scrubbed his hands over his face. *Shite!* Looking over his shoulder, his eyes found Cassandra sound asleep. She lay sprawled on her side of the bed, covers twisted and bunched around her waist, hair tousled across her face and pillow.

When his dreams returned, they did so with a vengeance, tearing at his nerves and leaving her restless in her sleep as well. He couldn't tell if it was because he tossed and turned under their onslaught, or because she, on some level, sensed the nervous energy in him as they happened. Either way, those dreams—nightmares, premonitions, whatever one wanted to call them—were disrupting both their lives.

He'd learned to handle the dreams that teased and poked at him with subliminal clues he wasn't able to decrypt. He'd learned to use them to fuel his drive but couldn't predict what they would do to her, to their still-developing relationship. And that scared him more than the possibility that he'd never uncover the answers he sought. Concern tightened around his chest like a vice as he gazed upon his sleeping wife.

Releasing a shaky breath, Trevor pushed from the bed and padded to the bathroom. The cold tiles stung the soles of his feet as he crossed the room to the stall in hopes that a hot shower would help ease him back into sleep, or at least help him gather his chaotic thoughts.

Time stole away as mist covered the glass walls surrounding him. Eyes closed, he faced the spray and let the water rinse the lather from his hair and, with it, the remnants of the dream.

A smile broke across his face when gentle hands caressed his stomach and Cassandra's low, raspy voice murmured against his ear, "Just what the doctor ordered." She pressed her bed-warm body against his and nudged him from under the jets, stealing his hot water.

"Hey. Shower hog." He turned in her arms and pulled her against his chest, his arms tightly wrapped around her soft shoulders. He tucked his face in the curve of her neck and let both her presence and the heat of the water ease the tension from his shoulders. Her fingers strummed along his lower back, each tender stroke, each caress in direct correlation with his growing erection.

Trevor's stomach bottomed out when she dropped a hand between them, wrapped her fingers around his now-rigid cock and pumped him in gentle strokes. A groan rumbled in his chest as he shoved his fingers in her hair and pushed her back against the tile, canting her head and capturing her mouth. His tongue delved into moist silk, seeking and teasing. He pressed his skin against hers—hard planes against soft and giving valleys—and the full-on contact coerced all the chaotic emotions from his mind, leaving only one thing there: her love.

The content purr that vibrated low in her throat was like a velvety glove stroking his whole body. God, he wanted her. Would always want her.

She circled her arms around his neck while smoothing her foot along his calf. "Couldn't sleep?"

Trevor dragged his palm down her thigh and curved his fingers behind her knee. "Not really." Shifting his stance, he raised her leg and draped it around his hip, melding them against each other. He flashed a crooked grin. "Maybe you can rock me back to sleep." His straining cock pulsed and brushed at the entrance to her heat, almost as if begging for relief. Her chuckle morphed into little gasps of pleasure with each touch.

He fisted his cock, rubbing it back and forth against her slick folds before driving deep into her flesh with one smooth push. His heart thrummed in his heaving chest as her body welcomed his, enveloping him in warmth. Cassandra's back arched from the wall as he pulled almost all the way out and thrust back in to the hilt. Her shaky moan mingled with his in the steamy stall. He wrapped his hand in her hair and pulled her head back, tilting her chin, bearing her neck to his seeking mouth while keeping a lazy cadence with his hips.

He nipped her jawline, scraped his teeth along the tendon of her neck and sucked on the soft silky skin at the base of her throat before trailing feather-light kisses back along the column of her neck. He followed its line to the shell of her ear and teased the sensitive spot that drove her wild.

"You, *a bhean,*—" he continued to thrust through his words while she quivered around him, gripping him tight, his voice hoarse to his own ears, "—are so hot, so tight around me."

She turned her head, baring more of her neck to him. "Trevor...." His name was barely a whisper on her lips.

"Tell me, Cassie girl." He wrapped her other leg around him, leveraging her weight against the tiled wall. Palming each round cheek, he lifted her higher for each withdrawal and pulled her tight against him for each plunge. Cassandra's hands hooked around his neck, her fingers combed through and grasped his hair as she rocked her hips, meeting his every pump.

"You. Just you." Her gasp flowed into a moan of pleasure and she dug her heels into his lower back, pulling him closer.

A tingling ran from his chest to his stomach as she held his gaze. He was undone by the desire darkening her irises as her body grew tight around him.

"Trevor," she whispered when he thrust up, deeper, harder into her pulsing flesh. "Yes!" she cried out, biting down on his shoulder as her release rippled around his aching cock and her body clamped down so hard around him he could no longer hold it together.

Her shaky cry and taut body drove him over the edge. "Fuck!" All the pressure and heat that had built deep in his balls crested in hot surges until he thrust one last time. His arms tightened around his wife and he buried his face in the curve of her shoulder, his breath choppy as they held onto each other while riding out the tiny electrical shocks assaulting them.

Moments later, Cassandra's legs slid languidly from his hips. She leaned heavily against him and he continued to hold her to him until their breaths lengthened out and she could stand on her own.

She looked up at him, pushing the hair from her face. "Wow,

that's what I call a good morning greeting." She stood on tiptoes and smiled against his lips, "And to think all I wanted was to share your shower before you used up all the hot water."

Trevor chuckled and grinned mischievously as he looked down and handed her the soap. "The morning is definitely looking up, now." Cassandra cast a droll look at his groin and raised an eyebrow. "Hey, don't judge me, woman. I've just been ravished!"

Cassandra's other brow lifted in feigned surprise. "Hold on. Who ravished who?"

Trevor burst out laughing. God, it felt good to laugh. She had the ability to brighten his day with a single look, erase his worries with a single word and fan his resolve with her own. He raised his hands in surrender and backed out of the shower. "You, love, ravished *me*."

"I did, didn't I?" Cassandra grinned as she began to lather her body. "You owe me coffee as a show of gratitude."

His grin broadened. "Yes, ma'am." He toweled himself dry and left the room with a gentle prod. "I'm going back to bed for some shuteye. You can join me anytime and greet me again later."

Her laughter followed him to the bed and a smile played along his lips as dreamless sleep finally overtook him.

Chapter Six

Same Old Grind

THE TIPS OF POLISHED BLACK shoes came into Nathan's field of vision as he riffled for the hundredth time through the paperwork he'd received from Franklin. He raised his eyes from the pages to find the captain of the small jet stationed on the tarmac frowning at him.

"We need to board shortly, sir. Our flight plan has departure at zero five thirty."

Nathan's gaze dropped to his watch. *Shit. The asshole is late.* He gave the man a curt nod. "We'll give him a few more minutes; if he doesn't show we'll have to reschedule."

As much as he would love to leave without Hanson, he couldn't. Hanson had details of the operation in his possession. He wondered if Franklin hadn't done it on purpose so Nathan wouldn't leave him behind. His boss knew him well enough that he'd considered that a strong possibility.

From where he sat in the small waiting area, Nathan's eyes followed the pilot's retreat to the plane and then roamed the hangar.

The massive metal structure housed only one aircraft undergoing maintenance. Members of the crew worked in and around it, their ongoing conversations a buzz in the background. Bulky stainless steel chests lined the white walls, neatly arranged for easy access, making it clear that it was a military installation.

He flicked his eyes to his watch again. "Damn it."

He had no clue what Hanson looked like. All he had to go by was the little information Franklin had handed him before kicking Nathan out to gather his gear and prepare for the flight.

Franklin's comment still echoed in his mind. *"You'll need the operator's experience, skills, and contacts on this assignment. His team has been deployed on many missions in the region. Some on his team are familiar with the language and he knows the territory like the back of his hand."*

Aside from that, the only solid piece of information he'd received had been the man's name. A name that had turned up very little— and most of what had turned up was classified beyond his grade access. That in itself was a red flag; there was not much beyond his reach. He didn't need that aggravation, but he'd put up with it to get back in the field.

Helping Cassandra and Bauer in the summer had grounded him with the worst desk job in the service. After months of menial work—data analysis and reports—he was about to go nuts. He was chafing to take on challenging assignments again. In addition to getting him back on track with the boss, that mission promised to deliver the blood-pumping action he craved, even though he didn't quite care for the cloak of secrecy.

Nathan could hardly wait to get his hands on the mission files. He didn't know what annoyed him more: the fact that Hanson had firsthand access to them, or that he'd been saddled with a stranger as a quasi-partner. To top it off, his nerves were already frayed from his meeting with Luke. He'd managed to keep his tangled emotions under wraps during the meeting with Franklin, but there was no way to deny he was on edge. He felt like a pressure cooker about to explode into a million pieces.

Burning resentment ate at his gut and crept into his throat, almost choking him as memories skidded across his mind. He shook off the unpleasant thoughts as he stuffed the paperwork into his briefcase and pushed to his feet. Straightening his tie and buttoning his coat, he leaned against the entrance to the hangar, where he could see down the length of the tarmac.

He tipped his head back and filled his lungs with the brisk air. The bright lights of the hangar reflected off the plane's fuselage, making it appear painted against the slate gray backdrop of the early winter morning.

Nathan checked his watch again and shook his head. "Just great. Just fucking great," he muttered under his breath while crossing his arms in frustration. "Bastard better not miss this goddamned flight."

"Hel-lo, sweetheart." The deep, raspy voice coming from the opposite side entrance drew Nathan's attention. He frowned. A scruffy-faced man sauntered in his direction, his eyes locked on a female crew's ass. His cocky gait and the oversized military-grade canvas duffel bag strapped to his shoulder gave Nathan a clue as to who that man could be. *No fucking way.*

He stopped a few feet from Nathan and spoke to the target of his greeting—a petite blonde in a green military flight suit. He caged her in an intimate yet casual way, one hand latched around the strap of the bag and the other braced against the wall by her head. He leaned his face down to whisper in the pretty woman's ear. She giggled at whatever he said and smiled. He must have sensed Nathan's scrutiny because he cast a glance his way and winked.

Nathan sized him up. Roughly six-feet, lean build, wearing beige multi-pocket cargo pants and a Hawaiian shirt. His scraggly dark brown hair was in disarray and, of all things, he sported an unkempt beard. A leather flight jacket and heavy boots rounded out his appearance.

The man had Black Ops written all over him. Most people expected to see cleancut, uniformed, stiff types when they thought of special ops, but Nathan knew better. The unconventional clothing and longish hair, the overly confident stance, the build. He was the perfect nobody. A man who could blend in like a ghost, given the need, and execute the cleanest surgical strikes. Hanson was a sanctioned killing machine. And it seemed it would be up to Nathan to handle his overactive libido during the operation. *Great.* And he thought things couldn't get any worse.

Nathan clenched his teeth when the woman slipped a card into the operator's front pocket and walked away with an enhanced rocking of her hips. The man's eyes followed her until she disappeared from view. With a shake of his head and a wide smile spreading his lips, he swaggered toward Nathan.

When he reached him, he extended his hand. "How's it going, buddy? Lieutenant Daniel Hanson."

Nathan took his hand. "I know who you are."

Hanson's eyes pinned his and sharpened. "Glad to know we've passed the awkward phase then." An amused smile quirked his lips as he looked him up and down. "Nice look, G-Man." It seemed Hanson also knew who he was.

"That would be Special Agent Nelson to you. You're late." Nathan turned on his heel and stepped toward the sleek jet, fully expecting Hanson to follow him. "I hope you understand this kind of delay is unacceptab—" He turned to see Hanson still standing where he left him, arms crossed. "What are you waiting for? The clock is ticking."

Humor and icy calm flashed in Hanson's eyes "We need to clarify a few things first."

Nathan expelled a deep breath. "You gotta be kidding me, right? We can go over the case on the plane."

"I didn't say case." The smirk never left Hanson's lips.

"What then? Can't we play this little game later?"

"Nope. No can do. I'm not working with someone I or my team can't trust. Especially with our lives on the line. Besides, I have a date with—" he retrieved the card from his pocket and read the name on it "—Donna Parker in two weeks. I don't plan on missing it. It took me longer than I expected to break her into agreeing to go out with me. I need to stay alive for that to happen, which brings us back to why we need to clarify things."

The whirl of jet engines powering up filled the air. "For Christ's sake, move your ass. We need to take off on schedule."

Hanson adjusted his stance and the bag on his back. Nathan wondered what the hell he concealed in the damn thing. The ease with which he carried the obviously heavy load hinted at a hidden strength and deceptive power only forged through arduous training.

"First, you may be CIA, but you don't rule my roost. My men, my orders. We both follow protocol and communicate with each other."

Nathan couldn't share his real thoughts on that requirement of his. He needed to play the part to achieve his goal. He also couldn't deny Hanson had a point on the open communication. Trust was an intrinsic part of teams like his, as opposed to Nathan's solitary work, but it was a two-way street and he could gain needed knowledge from it.

"Understood. Is there anything else you're compelled to add?"

Hanson's eyes hardened, the humor faded. "Second, we need our focus on the job. If you have any personal issues, leave them on the tarmac before you get on that plane." He set his bag on the ground and kept his steely gaze on Nathan's every move.

Nathan's stomach bottomed out. He frowned and cocked his head, trying to read more from Hanson's expression, but the man didn't give anything away.

"What the hell is that supposed to mean?"

"Exactly what I said. I'm a man of few words, but you can expect them to be straight to the point. Nothing good comes from lies and deceit. We deal with enough deception as it is in our trippy line of business."

Nathan narrowed his gaze, trying to read any underlying meaning from Hanson's expression, but there was nothing there.

"Fine. If this concludes the lesson, we need to get our asses on that plane." Nathan started toward the plane without giving Hanson a chance to add to his list.

Hanson matched his stride. "Oh, one last thing. Chill, dude. Once we have coordinates, this'll be a walk in the park," he quipped as he gave Nathan a good-natured slap on the back.

Nathan had other ideas as to how the mission was turning out, but he kept his opinion to himself. If they could make the long flight without coming to blows, he would consider the rest viable. Until then, it was a tossup.

They boarded the comfortable jet and took their seats. Within minutes, the plane began taxiing and gaining momentum for takeoff. While Nathan's small luggage had been stored in the cargo, Hanson had held tight to the duffel that sat in the aisle at his feet. Nathan's curiosity about the man reached new heights when Hanson unzipped the bag and he caught a glimpse of polished black metal. Hanson reached inside and retrieved a thick bundle of folders, which he tossed on the little table in front of Nathan's seat.

"There you go. Have at it."

Nathan removed the rubber band holding them together. "Is this everything?"

"Yep. Other than a last-minute fax. The reason I was delayed. Well…if you don't include Anna, but that's another story."

"You mean Donna." He glanced in Hanson's direction before turning his attention to the folders.

"What? Right…Donna. And no. I meant Anna." A wide grin lit up his face. "I was instructed to stop by Headquarters to pick those up"—he nodded at the folders in Nathan's hands—"and I did. A call came through saying there was something we needed to take with us. Sat around waiting, but the damn fax still hadn't arrived by the time I hightailed it out of there. Be thankful I didn't stay, or you'd still be waiting for me."

Nathan raised an eyebrow. "What about the fax?"

"Meh." Hanson shrugged. "Would you have preferred I missed the flight? If it's important, they'll send it to our destination."

Nathan shook his head and pulled out the first folder containing the personal file of Gerald Blair, US Envoy to the Middle East. The report was thorough and contained a detailed account of both his professional and personal life.

He raised his eyes to Hanson. "Do you want to split them?"

"Nope. I'm done. They are all yours."

"When—?"

"While I waited for the fax that never came. I'm a fast reader." Hanson's lips quirked in a cocky grin as he leaned his seat back and closed his eyes. His disheveled appearance and the hickeys decorating his neck were a clear indication he needed some shuteye. "Let me know when you're done so we can discuss the case."

Nathan sank into his own seat, his mind teeming with questions. Sizing up the pile of files in front of him, he didn't think he would have answers to those questions any time soon. Particularly because his search extended to pieces of a puzzle unknown to Hanson and included scrutinizing the lives of everybody targeted in the attack.

With that in mind, he returned his attention to Blair's file and began studying the first of those they were supposed to know inside and out before they set off for ground zero.

They had a very unusual situation in their hands. While religious extremists were quick to claim responsibility for kidnappings, hoping to drive the world's attention to whatever cause they claimed to support, those who'd abducted the six remaining members of the diplomatic convoy two days earlier hadn't made any demands through the media. They'd simply dropped off the radar as if they'd never been. There had to be a reason, a purpose for that divergence from the norm, and that reason could be tied to Nathan's prime directive. The answer could be in any of their pasts or presents and, if he was to be successful, he had to find it.

As he read through the pages, he looked for inconsistencies, hidden information, or activities that could have made Blair or any in the convoy a target. Anything that could have put them all in the crosshairs of whoever had taken them.

He beat his way through Gerald Blair's file. Blair had been in extensive contact with Palestinians and Israelis—unavoidable contact since it was an integral part of his job to mediate peace in the region—and that in itself could have placed a target on his back, but nothing in his file stood out.

Nathan set Blair's file aside and moved on to the next in the bundle. As he flipped it open, his whole body stiffened in his seat. A buzzing noise flooded his ears and his sight dimmed. His field of vision narrowed to the picture on the page and the name listed. Moore, Rachael. Status: Widow.

Rae.

His blood iced in his veins. For a moment, he felt detached from reality, expecting someone to pop up in the seat in front of him, pointing a camera and screaming, "*Gotcha!*" He fixed his eyes on the file again. Phillip Moore's wife. Was that why Hanson had made that comment about setting personal involvements aside?

Nathan stared at her familiar image for a moment before diving in. Some of the information was known to him. Some was brand new. He read the report on Phillip's wife with a heavy heart and the thumping in his chest rose to such a loud racket he thought it would wake Hanson from his beauty sleep.

Nathan's internship in London had been a core requirement of his BA in International Studies and Political Science at the Virginia Military Institute. Acing the National Security Policy course had given him an edge, and he'd been accepted for a work program at the US Embassy in London.

His role had involved direct liaising with British Intelligence. What had promised to be an inconsequential work-study experience took a sharp turn when, halfway through his stay, terrorists had attacked the World Trade Center.

He'd met Phillip in one of the first international coalition against terrorism meetings he'd attended, and Phillip had been his main contact and source in the British Intelligence from then on. Despite their age gap, they'd found many things in common.

He could never have foreseen that their friendship would be the source of so much comfort and anguish. Nathan, only nineteen then, had never experienced from his father or older brother the sort of friendship or mentorship Phillip had offered. They had often met after hours at Phillip's favorite hangout in London, their time spent in lengthy and heated discussions about politics and foreign policies. That common ground had served as fertile landscape for a friendship that had quickly extended beyond the work environment.

He'd thirsted for that sort of positive interaction and looked forward to invitations to join Phillip after work, but when Phillip had introduced him to his fiancée things had gone south. After that, he'd dreaded invitations to join them. He'd feared they would hear his heart racing every time she drew near, or that they would catch him secretly admiring the color of her hair, the delicate shape of her hands, the perfection of her skin.

He had battled those feelings often, but never regretted one single visit because those memories were all he would have left. After all, he knew he would be going home in the spring and leaving them both behind.

As his friendship with Phillip grew into a tight brotherhood of sorts, he'd welcomed Phillip's attention as a replacement for his own dysfunctional relationship with his older brother. Their strengthened friendship competed in his heart with the feelings he kept simmering in there for Rachael.

Nathan would never have expected to see the day he'd say no to Phillip, but it had come. Phillip had reached out once, long after Nathan had joined the CIA. What he'd asked him to do would have gone against every rule in the book. Every rule he'd learned from growing up in a military family. Every rule instilled by Phillip himself. And the most critical point, it would compromise several ongoing investigations. He had no choice but to stick to the rules, even if it left their friendship shaken.

Months later, he'd received an email from Rachael informing him of Phillip's passing. His death, and the circumstances surrounding it, had packed a phenomenal punch and left him questioning whether his help would have made a difference, would have kept him alive.

Guilt had ravaged him to the point of forgetting even the most basic training like gun maintenance, or self-preservation for that matter. It all had come to a head during a surveillance operation in which his distress had placed Cassandra and the rest of their team, including himself, in danger. She had followed her principles and reported him to their superiors. He'd gotten a good yelling at from Franklin and been told to snap out of whatever he had going on.

Cassandra's honesty and diligence had drawn him to her even more than when she'd stumbled into him in the maze of cubicles. His heart had sped up as the live images merged with the memory of the bump into Rachael at the airport. The cascade of dark hair hiding her face from view, her build, her skin color. But she reminded him of Rachael in more ways than the physical one. Like Rachael, she was tough, feisty, driven. For the first time since he'd met Rachael, he'd dared to imagine what it would be like to have a relationship without it eating him from the inside out. The way just thinking about Rachael had. The way it still did.

Guilt punched him in the gut once again and he held his breath, squeezing his eyes shut to keep self-flagellation at bay. He'd gone through that cycle many times before. He wasn't about to slide down that road again. If saving Rachael was how he could redeem himself, even if it meant he had to face her one more time, he was going to take it. He had to put all his feelings—those he thought he'd buried long ago and yet which stubbornly resurrected at the simple thought of her name—aside and work the case.

The more he read Rachael's dossier, the more his frown deepened. Why was she working at the embassy in Israel? How had she come to be assigned as a personal assistant to Blair? Those questions and many others piled up in the back of his mind as Nathan read the files on each of the convoy's members. Aside from what color underwear each of them preferred to wear, he'd learned everything to be culled from their dossiers—their past and current activities, routines, dealings, and associations.

What he didn't find was a definitive link to any extremist organization, nor to what triggered the kidnapping. It was now up to their next stop on the itinerary to provide clues as to where they were and how he and the 8th were going to rescue them. And they would.

Rachael Moore's involvement had turned that professional mission into a personal act of penance. He would make sure Phillip's wife made it out alive, even if he had to trade his own life in the process.

Chapter Seven

A N IDLE MIND IS THE DEVIL'S PLAYGROUND. NATHAN understood the saying all too well. With nothing to do once he'd gone through the files, the rest of the flight had left him with time on his hands. Too much time to reflect on the clusterfuck his life had turned into. By the time the jet touched ground again, he'd gone through every single scenario of how the next few hours would play out. He hated even more that Hanson had commandeered the wheel of the sedan waiting for them at the airport, taking away his chance to do something other than stare out the window and let his mind play games with him.

He stretched and shifted in the passenger seat, rolling his shoulders in an attempt to loosen his tense muscles, but it didn't do much to improve his mood. When he'd prayed to be anywhere else in the world, he hadn't taken into account that fate was a fickle bitch.

Nathan wiped his palms on his thighs and turned to look out the window. The streets were peppered with tourists and locals alike still recovering from holiday hangovers. Cars zigzagged, people rushed down the streets bundled up and going on about their lives. Different city. Different country. Same old grind.

As much as he wanted to avoid the subject, his thoughts shifted inexorably in one single direction. What would his reception be like? Nathan's throat constricted and stomach clenched. "Christ!" he muttered, scrubbing his hands over his face.

"Hey, bud. Say something?"

Out of the corner of his eye, he caught Daniel's scrutinizing glance. Blood rushed and pounded in Nathan's head. He pinched the bridge of his nose and tried without success to ignore his unwanted companion. "No."

"Are you sure?" Daniel's eyes pierced the distance between them. "You look like you've just been run through the wringer."

"You don't know how right that statement is," Nathan muttered. Hanson's prolonged glare as if expecting Nathan to sit down for a much-needed therapy session pushed him to snap, "Just stay out of my business, Hanson."

Hanson raised his hands in the air in mock surrender. "Whoa. Chillax." He grabbed the wheel again and returned his gaze to the road ahead.

Nathan sighed heavily and dropped his head back against the seat. He had no clue how it all was going to go down, but his gut told him it wouldn't be a walk in the park.

THE RAIN-WASHED SIDEWALKS glimmered and reflected Christmas lights still twinkling with holiday spirit when they reached their destination. Stepping from the vehicle into the mild winter evening, Nathan lifted his collar against the crisp wind and waited for Hanson to join him on the sidewalk.

He studied the building in front of him with clinical eyes. The clean, well-kept exterior didn't give away the importance of the location to US Intelligence or how much one particular person living in that house meant to him. For a fraction of an instant, he considered turning away. But that visit was business, work. It was not personal. The image of Phillip's widow flickered in his mind's eye and he corrected himself: not *too* personal.

Somehow, standing there, staring at the ambiguous façade, made it harder to ignore its existence or the impacts of its residents on his life. He shook his head to clear those thoughts. He needed to focus on the task at hand if he was to get through the days ahead with his sanity intact. He sucked in a deep breath, hoping to quell the raging inferno burning in his stomach.

"Ready, buddy?"

Nathan turned his eyes to Hanson. He hoped the frown crowning them would give Hanson a clue to refrain his happy-go-lucky self, but he seemed oblivious to Nathan's inner turmoil.

"I'm always ready."

"Whatever you say, pal," Hanson shrugged, his stance changing into a more salute-like one.

Something must have gotten through after all. Nathan exhaled another deep breath and approached the door, followed closely by Hanson, who sported a shit-eating grin. The words *easy boy, easy boy* looped in his head. Squaring his shoulders, he pressed the doorbell. As the first notes of the chime reached him, his frown deepened.

CASSANDRA LOVINGLY TRACED the words on the cup she nursed in her hands. She couldn't resist one last caffeine shot after dinner, even though she knew she'd pay dearly for it later that night. Each time she took a sip she smiled at Trevor's gift idea.

He'd been antsy and could hardly wait for her to open the box on Christmas morning. Tears had sprung to her eyes upon seeing his gift. Not only was the cup large enough to hold a massive dose of caffeine, but he'd had it personalized with something close to their hearts. Inscribed on one side were the words "You're part of me," and on the other, "I'm part of you."

It had become her favorite treasure, surpassing even Trevor's humorous take on her love affair with the elixir of life—a humongous cup decorated with the words "SIZE MATTERS."

Chuckling at her husband's antics, she took another sip, but this time her smile faded to a frown as her eyes caught the words scrolling on the ticker at the bottom of the television screen across the room. She approached the coffee table and, grabbing the remote, turned up the volume.

"A diplomatic convoy was ambushed on Christmas Eve outside Tel-Aviv. Six members of a team mediating the peace talks in the Middle East were taken under heavy fire exchange."

"Trevor?!"

"Up here." His voice floated down from the office.

"Did you see the news? The ambush?"

"Yeah, I—" The Imperial March reverberated through the house, drowning out Trevor's words.

Cassandra frowned and set the remote back on the coffee table, along with her cup. It was too late for couriers and Jessica hadn't mentioned she'd be coming by—but knowing Jessica, she'd possibly popped in to show her something new she'd gotten for the baby. Excited at another chance to gush over little outfits and booties, Cassandra jogged down the stairs and jerked the front door open. The smile on her face died and she stopped dead in her tracks as if a hand had slammed against her chest.

NATHAN COCKED HIS head and leaned closer to the door, trying to identify the familiar chime playing inside. Hanson held a similar puzzled frown. As they both leaned closer, the door jerked open and the unmistakable notes of The Imperial March flowed over them, loud and clear.

"Nate!" Cassandra's tone rang with surprise, her face startled as she stumbled back a step.

He raised an eyebrow. "You've gotta be kidding me. He has *that* as a chime?"

Hanson's hearty laugh resounded beside him. Cassandra's expression morphed into a cautious stare as she leaned against the red doorframe and pulled the door toward her, closing the once-welcoming gap. Her blank gaze locked with Nathan's.

"What are you doing here?"

Nathan observed Cassandra from a brand new perspective, one acquired since their last encounter in Russia. Barefoot and dressed in a pair of jeans and a teal t-shirt, hair gathered high in a ponytail, Cassandra looked...happy.

"National Security business."

Her assessing gaze touched on Hanson. "Who's your friend?"

"Hanson. Lieutenant Commander Daniel Hanson. Pleasure to meet you, ma'am."

In disbelief, Nathan watched Hanson's smile grow into a white glow of teeth only found in toothpaste commercials. His disbelief increased when Cassandra smiled back at him. Where was the always-suspicious Cassandra he knew? It seemed her caution was only directed at him. A painful pang stroked his chest.

Cassandra's eyes flicked to the car parked at the curb, hopped to the briefcase in his hand, and locked with his eyes again. "So why are a CIA agent and a Special Ops operator on our doorstep at this hour of the night?"

Hanson frowned, but Nathan wasn't surprised by her accurate assessment of him. Cassandra was exceptionally good at what she did. "An urgent matter. We flew out as soon as they dropped the directives in our lap. I thought Bauer would have gotten the heads-up by now. Didn't he tell you?"

At that moment, a loud bang resonated from upstairs. "You've gotta be fucking kidding me! Fuck!" Bauer's indignation was evident even from the distance.

Nathan smirked. "Foul-mouthed much?"

Cassandra rolled her eyes and opened the door. "Come in. Let me figure out what's going on," she called over her shoulder as she headed up the stairs.

Carrying his briefcase, Nathan followed her. When he reached the first floor, his eyes absorbed every inch of the place. Behind him, Hanson whistled. The spacious, airy, open-concept room had another set of stairs leading to the upper floors and was divided in two distinct areas. One side housed a modern kitchen—from which the tantalizing aroma of freshly brewed coffee wafted—and a family-style dining area, the other a sleek sitting area with plush leather seating and a ginormous flat screen TV tuned in to the night's newscast.

The floors were covered wall-to-wall in warm-toned hardwood, and colorful fabrics peppered the place in stark contrast to the retro Star Wars movie posters on the walls. A clear statement that people with opposing tastes lived there. Two people who had melded their lives in a puzzling yet oddly homey and eclectic combination.

"Trevor's upstairs in the office." She nodded to the second set of stairs and continued that way with the two men tagging along behind her. "He was doing some penetration testing earlier. He may have hit a firewall somewhere," she chuckled as she led them up.

Nathan trailed her to one of the two doors opening to the hall and, as he walked into the room, his eyes widened.

"Whoa," Hanson peeped beside him.

Their office reminded Nathan of a mini version of the command deck in one of those sci-fi movies. Low lighting, big screen monitors on the desks and flat screen TVs on the walls, hum of electricity, and blinking lights everywhere.

Nathan saw the gleam of appreciation, almost admiration, in Hanson's eyes. He had to exercise a boatload of restraint to keep himself from rolling his. *Great. Another Bauer groupie.*

Two desks sat predominantly in the middle of the room, facing each other like a captain's station. One was littered with disks, gadgets, cables and other computer components. He assumed the other, much tidier one, was Cassandra's.

"Fuck me!" The curse boomed from the corner of the room where Bauer stood next to a fax machine housed in the wall-to-wall cabinet.

Bauer expelled an exasperated sigh. Fully engrossed by the contents of the several sheets of papers crumpled in his hand, he absently raked his fingers through his already-mussed hair and rubbed the back of his neck. As Cassandra closed the distance, he became aware of their presence and snapped his gaze in their direction. His expression slid from irritation to surprise to anger in the blink of an eye.

Bauer's stormy stare narrowed on Nathan. "How did you get here so fast? Lit the gas up your ass to rocket yourself across the ocean?"

Hanson half snickered behind him and Nathan had to exercise all his restraint not to elbow him.

"I take it you just heard?" Nathan reined in his dislike for the man. *If only I didn't need his help.*

"Damn right! Whoever dragged me into this…this partnership

can ki—"

"Trev," Cassandra admonished as she met him halfway and slipped the papers from his fingers, quickly skimming them while Bauer's scowl continued to hammer at him.

Nathan couldn't quite blame him. He'd done and said a lot of things in the past to garner Bauer's dislike. Some quite out of line, even by his own standards. But the man's cockiness—even if he had the skills and reason to back it—raked his nerves and rubbed him the wrong way.

Knowing he needed Bauer's expertise on that mission was a bitter pill to swallow. Yet, with what he had at stake, Nathan was willing to set animosity aside for the sake of the people involved. He was counting on Bauer to do the same once he looked over the intelligence they had and understood the gravity of the situation.

Nathan avoided Cassandra's questioning gaze. "Believe me when I say that I didn't ask for this assignment. After the desk duty I got as a result of the little snafu in Russia, I just couldn't refuse." Nathan glimpsed at the source of another snicker. Hanson leaned in the doorway, arms casually crossed over his chest. His relaxed stance gave away the fact that he seemed to be enjoying every second of the exchange. His head bobbed from him to Bauer as he followed the conversation, the corner of his mouth twitched, restraining a smile. Nathan did his best to ignore the needling. Regardless of the discord among them, they all had work to do and they had to do it together. "I'd have taken anything to get back in the field. Even this."

Cassandra raised her eyes from the paperwork to meet Nathan's and he saw the note of reproach in them as she spoke. "We all came out alive, and that's all that matters." Her gaze slid to Bauer. Surprise hit him as he observed a troubled expression slip through her defenses when it paused on him before returning to the sheets in her hand.

"I don't regret asking for your help, even if you two continue to hold grudges," Nathan said.

"Un-freaking-believable!" Trevor muttered and lifted his chin in Hanson's direction. "Who might you be, mate?"

Hanson's smile grew wider and he approached Bauer, hand extended in friendly greeting. "Lieutenant Daniel Hanson, Eighth Special Warfare Logistics Group. Extraction specialist at your service. Love the doorbell, by the way."

Nathan had witnessed the heated look in Bauer's eyes as he followed Cassandra, he'd experienced the cold stare when Bauer looked at him, but never had he seen a friendlier smile than the one that lit up Bauer's face as he approached and shook Hanson's hand.

"I thought about getting the original theme song, but The Imperial March is much more ominous. You never know who might show up at your door—" the look he shot Nathan dripped sarcasm, "—as was well proven today."

Cassandra cleared her throat and Bauer retreated. "We'll need to be briefed. The fax states you have the case files?"

Nathan set his briefcase on top of the keyboard and other techy debris on Bauer's desk and removed the stack of folders from it. He handed them to Bauer and waited until he'd scrutinized the first page to begin his briefing on the mission at hand.

"Two days ago, at approximately twelve hundred hours local time, a convoy heading to Ben Gurion International Airport was overrun and its occupants taken. We believe it to be the work of a lesser-known terrorist organization. The assets in the convoy were high-ranking members of the security council assigned to oversee the peace talks on the Strip."

Bauer narrowed his eyes. "Is this the case on the news?

Nathan nodded. "They're all over it."

"Is the number of hostages on the news correct?" Cassandra kept her eyes on the pages as she fired off her question.

"Six taken. Four killed on the spot."

"Any demands via audio, video, internet, not disclosed to the media?" Cassandra flipped through the documents.

"Zip." Nathan watched his own puzzlement cloud Bauer's expression.

"Why have we been pulled into this? I'm a digital communications analyst. Not Black Ops. This sounds more like a case of military extraction than digital infiltration, and you already have your man for that," Trevor tipped his head at Hanson, who in turn nodded in acknowledgement.

"You're right. We do have the right team for the extraction. What we don't have is a location."

Bauer's frown deepened. "Cryptocity can handle that. Why did they request Operation Countermeasure be involved?"

"It seems your little pet project has caught the head honchos' attention. They think your out-of-the-box tactics are the best thing since sliced bread and can get us the information we need faster than conventional channels. Your reputation has skyrocketed since your brush with the Russians." Nathan couldn't stop sarcasm from bleeding into his words. "It gave you rock-star status among the operatives." He snickered, "Nobody can figure out how a geeky desk jockey handled that and lived to tell the tale."

Bauer's eyes flashed with anger at the disguised insult. "Watch your mouth, *amadáin*." Cassandra's hand reached out and gripped Bauer's elbow when his hand balled into a fist.

Hanson stepped between them. "This has been fun kids, but you're wasting our time." He directed his commanding tone at Bauer. "We need whatever information you can dig up so we can get our asses on the next flight out. Lives are on the line. The clock is ticking."

While Hanson talked, Bauer's eyes never left Nathan's, temper smoldering in their depths, but he held it in check. Nathan acknowledged his silent warning with a nod before Bauer turned his full attention to Hanson.

"Once we've locked in a position, then what?"

"Hanson's team and I go in for the exfil," Nathan interjected.

"You?" Bauer scoffed. "I thought you said you were grounded."

"Let's just call this job a redemption." The statement was true in ways none of the others in the room could fathom.

Bauer leaned back against his desk and crossed his arms over his chest. "Let me get this straight." He raised his eyebrows, his expression serious even though his tone rang with suppressed humor. "You need *me* to help *you* wipe your slate clean with the Agency." A broad grin spread across his face. "Hot damn. You need *my* help. Freaking ironic, isn't it?" he chuckled.

Nathan itched to punch the smart-ass grin off the Irishman's face, but he couldn't let his personal conflict with the man jeopardize their mission. Hanson moved into his field of vision, his frown drawing his attention. Nathan could almost see the warning in the man's eyes. The same one he'd given Nathan during their earlier conversation back on the tarmac.

"Yuk it up all you want, Bauer. But we're on a deadline."

"Right." Bauer swallowed his humor and nonchalantly switched to operation mode. He circled the desk and shoved the briefcase off his keyboard, then tiled the sheets of papers over the clutter. "What do you know about the details of the convoy? Was that advertised anywhere?"

"No. The convoy itinerary was not in the public domain."

"Could it have been a coincidence? Wrong place, wrong time? They grab westerners all the time."

"No." Hanson added, "It was an emergency evacuation. There

was chatter over the last couple of weeks pointing to another uprising. Things are getting tense in the region. Several embassies are being closed as we speak. Only Blair and top brass in the Foreign Service knew of their evacuation time and route."

"Have you screened the hostages?"

Nathan pulled the second stack of folders from his briefcase and handed them to Bauer. "Personal dossiers. There's nothing in any of them that struck me as out of the ordinary." *Nothing I want you to know.* His personal interest would remain undisclosed to all but himself.

Bauer passed the folders to Cassandra and she opened the first. He rubbed his hands over his face then braced them on the desk, staring down on the scattered paperwork. Nathan observed as Bauer's eyes tracked from one document to the other, as if willing a miraculous link to appear.

"There's no personal connection among the hostages or victims, either," Hanson spoke up. "Only two of the DSS agents were part of Mr. Blair and Mrs. Moore's detail from the moment they entered the region. One of them is dead. All others rotated in over the course of the talks."

"You got all that from the files in less than what? Thirty minutes?" Nathan scoffed.

"No. After I read the files, I made some phone calls before I reached the hangar. The beauty of having friends in high places." Hanson's smile never reached his eyes.

What the fuck does that mean? Again, Hanson's comments left Nathan wondering about his role in the mission.

"That's useful." Bauer interrupted. "We can focus on searching for other connections outside of the current players. Do you have any ties to any of the hostages or victims?"

Bauer's unexpected question threw Nathan for a loop. His stomach bottomed out before he noticed Bauer was looking at Hanson and not at him.

Hanson shook his head. "I met one of the DSS guys years ago on a job. Other than that, no personal contact with any of them."

Nathan knew he should disclose the connection to Rachael, but he couldn't. He lashed out instead. "Why do you need to know?"

Bauer cocked his head and studied him for a moment. "Because anything, and I mean anything, matters. If anybody has details not available in the dossiers, it might help us locate a digital footprint we didn't consider before and, in turn, a motive. Find the motive, find the culprit," he commented as if he were pointing out the obvious to a child.

Nathan's conscience beat at him. As much as he saw the need to lay all the cards on the table, he couldn't take another blow. He couldn't take their judgment—and they *would* judge him. Especially Bauer. So he gave them a half-truth. "Rachael Moore. I knew her husband."

All eyes converged on him.

"Elaborate." Hanson crossed his arms over his chest.

Nathan could almost feel the waves of suspicion emanating from him. "Not much to tell. Her husband was SBS. We met when I was in London for a college internship. Became friends. As I said, not much else to say."

"Interesting." Hanson's tone was cold, assessing.

"Have you two been in touch lately? Via phone? Email?" Bauer pressed.

Nathan's eyes tracked Cassandra. She was doing what she did best: weighing every microexpression of his. He had to use all his training to hide his reaction to the images that popped into his mind at Bauer's prompt. Memories of a day in San Francisco. A day he'd made more than one mistake, a day that haunted him in many more ways than she could ever imagine or know. His stomach twisted in a knot.

"No. Not for a while."

"That's not much to go on." Bauer exhaled a sharp breath. "We need to find someone who might have had direct contact with any of them immediately before the kidnapping. I'll hit their emails and social media accounts. Anything helps. Any digital trail at this point is better than none. If we can get a solid hit on a cell phone signal, even better."

"I'll make some more calls." Hanson spoke with cool authority.

"I'll check in with the director," Nathan interjected.

"Brilliant. I'll get a hold of George and we can strategize together on how to trace them."

"Let's get down to business then," Cassandra chimed in as she moved to the desks and began clearing them. Bauer stepped in to help, and soon the four of them had a mini command center.

"They are an efficient team," Hanson commented as he watched the almost-synchronized collaboration.

Nathan didn't need anybody pointing out the obvious. Bauer and Cassandra worked like a well-oiled machine. He'd seen that machine in action in Russia, and it had prompted him to ask himself difficult questions. He was still working on the answers.

The Bauers' smooth collaboration should be a good starting point. They all needed to become a cohesive team if they were to make that rescue happen. With all the resources available in the room, it didn't take long before they rolled into full-on operation mode. He pulled a chair closer to the desks and surveyed the action.

Hanson had made himself comfortable. He'd stripped down to his undershirt before kicking back in the chair, propping his feet on the desk and crossing them at the ankles. Vibrant tattoos encircled his chest and weaved down his left arm all the way to his elbow. The deep rumble of his voice droned in the background as he spoke on the phone.

Nathan's gaze travelled to Cassandra. She chewed on the end of a pen while immersed in profile analysis, eyes flying from documents to screen and back. Nathan had seen that focus before. She was like a bloodhound when looking for answers.

Across from him, Bauer had his unblinking gaze locked on his screen while his fingers flew over the keyboard. If there was one thing Nathan could admire about him, it was his tenacity even through the hardest of heartaches. Based on the little Cassandra had shared with him in Russia, Bauer had had his share of loss. That was the only thing they had in common.

A hippie Black Ops, an ex-CIA operative with serious trust issues, a geek with the luck of the Irish, and a man with a secret mission of his own. Nathan tried to get his head around the absurdity of it all.

Whoever had devised the twisted plan that had pulled that ragtag team together must have been high. Nathan scrubbed his hand over his face, expelled a long breath, and tackled his share of the quest. They had no time to waste. He *had* to find Rae. Alive.

Chapter Eight

Good News, Bad News

*T*REVOR RECLINED IN HIS CHAIR, arms crossed above his head and eyes locked on the live chat application, willing it to come to life. He'd sent all the data he'd gathered to George in hopes he would pick up a trail through ECHELON filters. As usual, the downtime made him antsy. The sooner they could solve the new case, the sooner they could return to searching for their elusive target. And also the sooner Nelson would be gone from their home.

Almost as if in sync with his thoughts, the sound of snapping joints caught his attention. He raised his eyes from the screen and observed Nelson stretching in his chair, working out the kinks.

Across from him, Hanson held the phone to his ear, his voice a low rumble. He'd been tapping his many connections and maintaining an open line of communication with his men in preparation for the surgical operation of extracting the hostages from captivity.

From the bits and pieces Trevor had caught of his conversations and a quick check of his own, he understood why Hanson's team had been pulled into the fray. Although they hadn't had time to talk, Trevor gathered the man was brilliant at what he did. His calm precision while discussing details and his relaxed attitude toward an operation of that magnitude spoke volumes. Only someone confident in his own and his team's skills would see what lay ahead as routine.

Trevor's attention migrated back to Nelson. He studied him just as he had done in Russia, fishing for anything he could draw from his behavior. The CIA operative flaunted the same confidence as back then, yet there was a new bite—or maybe it was bitterness—he hadn't seen before, and it didn't seem to be related to Cassandra. Trevor had caught Nelson gazing at her earlier, but his expression lacked the yearning he'd seen reflected there in the past.

He watched him from the corner of his eye, trying to pinpoint what in the Hulk's demeanor tickled his inquisitive OCD. Since their brush in Russia, Nelson's edges had been sharpened to Ginsu knife quality. From the time he and Hanson had shown up on their doorstep, Nelson had felt like a ticking time bomb in a calm-before-the-storm kind of way. He worried that ignoring the length of the man's fuse could cause that bomb to blow up in their faces faster than they'd like.

Trevor's curiosity had been piqued when Nelson had mentioned his association with Phillip Moore. His cool, impersonal tone had made Trevor's bullshit meter go berserk—one of the benefits of having a former CIA analyst for a wife. He'd absorbed enough from her about body language, voice tone, and facial expressions to know that Nelson was not telling them everything. He didn't know what it was, but it was definitely something worth digging for.

The information on Phillip was limited to the few lines in Rachael Moore's dossier. He'd served as a Middle East Envoy after leaving the SBS and before being murdered in Israel a few years back.

Rachael's profile wasn't that extensive either. Employment records with the US government started when she'd moved to the US after her husband's death. Nothing in it explained Nelson's unease when Moore came up in conversation. On paper, she looked almost too clean. Trevor made a mental note to search for more on her life prior to that.

A beep on his screen pulled him out of his thoughts.

Are you there? George's message flashed on the monitor.

Trevor's fingers flicked across the keys. *Here. Find something?*

Maybe. Got my hands on the satellite imagery and footage from the area where the kidnapping took place. Pretty gruesome, even from a bird's eye view.

Trevor grimaced. *I can imagine. Anything useful?*

The kidnappers intercepted the convoy just outside of Tel Aviv. They loaded the hostages onto a truck and headed south. That's when it gets interesting.

Were you able to track it?

Nope. The satellite window dropped. The timestamp on the last image is only a minute into their escape. Timed to precision, or a very lucky coincidence. Can't tell which. They jump in the truck, window goes down, end of story. No imagery trail to follow.

Fuck. Trevor inflicted his frustration on the keys.

Totally. BUT…

When the rest of the sentence didn't pop up right away, Trevor's impatience reached new levels. *Stop teasing. BUT what?*

I screened all digital communication from that particular area and time of the kidnapping. Mostly calls by looky-loos shitting their pants with all those bullets flying over their heads. There was one call that stood out, though. The caller was calm. Cold. Indifferent to the attack.

And?

I was able to pull a couple of digital signatures.

Trevor shook his head and smiled. He could almost see the smirk on George's face. *That's brilliant! Have you triangulated their current location?*

Not yet. The signals are dead. Haven't been used since, but I'm on it. I'll let you know when they go live.

Keep me updated.

Hold on. There's more. This is where it gets freaky. The digital signature of the recipient of the call is a match to one of the signatures we isolated in Waldo's case.

A sinking feeling swarmed in Trevor's stomach. George had nicknamed the man they'd been tracking for months "Waldo" because of their inability to find his whereabouts. It was as if he had been hiding in plain sight, blending into the environment, morphing like a virus every time they got close.

What the hell are we dealing with here, George?

Not sure yet, bud. But I'm positive it's something bigger than the CIA or SOCOM ever imagined. I'll send you a copy of the transcripts once I get my hands on them.

Stay in touch. I'll break the news to the Hulk and Hanson.

LMAO! What? Not best buds yet?

Shut up, George. Just keep me posted on any new developments on your end.

Don't I always? TTYL

As Trevor logged off the chat, details from the two cases swirled incoherently in his head. Who were the players orchestrating the kidnapping? That question was now joined by more pressing ones. How in hell could the two cases be connected? What was the common thread between them? They would need every single possible resource they could get their hands on to find those answers.

The sinking feeling widened into a chasm. He and George had followed every single lead directly into a virtual wall. They still had no idea who the man was, but one thing was clear. Whoever Waldo was, he wasn't a newbie—and neither were his immediate circle, the ones protecting him. Digital communication could reveal a lot, but could also hide plenty if you knew how.

Trevor lifted his eyes from the screen. "I have good news and bad news." Everyone dropped what they were doing and focused their attention on him.

"Bad first," Hanson commanded from his chair, setting aside the report he'd been studying. "Always end on a good note."

"What are you? Pollyanna?" Nelson grunted at Hanson. When his eyes locked on Trevor's face, a mix of expectation and something Trevor could only identify as hope flashed in Nelson's eyes.

Hanson's lips curved into a wide snarky smile. "Shoot, Bauer."

"Right. Bad news. We still don't have a lock on their location. Good news. We have a digital signature from cell phones we can trace when—if—they ever use the damn things again. Pray they do, sooner rather than later."

His frustration must have been evident because Nelson looked at him, expectation bleeding through. "There's more. Am I right?"

"Sorta. George and I have been working a case for the CIA. Earlier this year, we were tasked with locating and identifying a person of interest. All we had to go on were old records and a few known associates. We've made almost no progress because he seems to favor pigeons instead of email and phone calls." Hanson chuckled at his sarcastic remark. "A little while back, George was able to isolate a digital signature belonging to one of his associates. We don't know if they're still in contact as we haven't been able to trace anything to him since."

"And what the hell does that have to do with our case?" Nelson challenged.

"A device used by the recipient of a call made from the area of the kidnapping matches the signature we have on file for that case. George is submitting a request for a full transcript of the call as we speak. Soon we'll be able to analyze the content of the conversation and see what clues we can extract from it. At least, that's the plan."

"This is big." Hanson leaned forward in his chair.

"Yep," Trevor nodded.

"So we'll be sitting here waiting for the intel we need?" Nelson's question bled controlled coldness.

"Correct."

"That's not acceptable." Nelson's eyes roamed the room before fixing back on Trevor.

Trevor narrowed his eyes when he noticed beads of sweat on Nelson's temples even though the temperature in the office was always much lower than the rest of the house.

"It's out of our control at this point," Trevor said.

"We need to locate them. Each minute counts. We're losing precious time," Nelson bit out through gritted teeth.

Trevor leaned back in his chair and held his stare. "Let me put it in perspective. If they use the phones or if we can find another signal we can follow, it might happen faster. Otherwise, we're hosed."

"Fuck!"

"Easy, Banner. Easy." Trevor couldn't hold back his smart-mouth retort.

"Fuck you, Bauer."

"Boys, boys!" Cassandra raised her hands. "How about we take a break. It's late. You'll play nicer after some shuteye."

Trevor held Nelson's gaze silently for a moment. The air in the room thickened, rife with the tension of months of unresolved differences between them. He dismissed the blatant invitation for a good old-fashioned fist fight. That could come later, when there were no lives at stake.

"Agreed. We might as well recharge for the next round."

As they stood, Nelson glanced at his watch. "Do you have a place we can bunk? It would save us time if we didn't have to commute between a hotel and here. Especially if we get a hit."

"It'll be a couple of hours yet before George gets the transcripts," Trevor replied. "There are several hotels within walking distance. You should be able to huff-it back in no time."

Hanson chimed in, "We have reservations nearby. Regroup in a few hours?"

"Nonsense," Cassandra interrupted. "We have plenty of space. Besides, it's more efficient this way. No need to travel back and forth."

Nelson's eyes met Trevor's, their animosity closely matched.

"Brilliant," Trevor grumbled under his breath.

"Hanson, Nate. Follow me." She turned and headed upstairs to the third floor.

"Yes, ma'am," Hanson grinned.

Trevor watched Nelson's lips curve into a smirk as he followed Hanson out the door.

"Fucker."

Cassandra ushered them into a guest room taking half of the top floor. "Here you are." She pointed to a door on her right. "That's the bathroom. Towels are in the cabinet under the sink."

Nathan scanned the room. It was almost like stepping into a sophisticated suite in a high-end hotel. A dark brown leather-upholstered full size bed occupied the left side of the room. Light-toned wood nightstands with moss green shaded glass tops flanked the bed.

A simple wooden desk and office chair sat in front of a bank of windows overlooking the park across the road. A comfortable looking overstuffed chair in the same shade of green as the nightstands sat in the corner facing the door. The room was practical and tidy. He could see Cassandra's hand all over it. He returned his eyes to the bed and frowned.

"Sorry, it's only a full." Cassandra must have seen his expression. "I'll leave blankets on the couch downstairs in case you don't want to bunk together. You can flip for it," she called over her shoulder as she headed out the door.

Hanson stretched out on the bed, crossing his arms behind his head and legs at the ankles. "Been a while since I slept in a bed this comfortable."

"You can have it," Nathan snapped. "I'll take the couch." He grabbed a pillow and made his way downstairs. A warm glow shone from under the Bauers' bedroom door as he walked by.

Bauer's low brogue reached him through the closed door. "Hey, just saying. Remember when we had Jessie over and she complained the house was not made with visitors in mind? Not sure they will appreciate the night's symphony."

"Trevor!" Cassandra's soft laughter washed over him in a gentle wave.

Nathan took off down the stairs, shaking his head as memories of another night, a different door, and their hushed voices assaulted his ears.

"Freakin' rabbits," he muttered, tossing the pillow on the couch.

Chapter Nine

The Messenger

KHALIL ABBOUD LEFT THE hostages under the competent hand of his second-in-command after the midafternoon *Salaah*. He drove a little over an hour to the *Rasūl's* compound for a report on the progress of the operation.

Khalil had stepped into his father's shoes as frontman in the cause a decade after his father had been killed during one of their operations. He'd been raised from the age of ten by family members under the distant yet watchful eye of the *Rasūl,* almost as if he'd been groomed to take a bigger role within the organization, while his little brother had been sent abroad, groomed for a more menial job. Since then, Khalil had grown to admire the man they called "The Messenger," for good reason. He was a brilliant strategist and a skilled survivor. He'd escaped—not always unscathed—countless assassination attempts and had grown stronger in his determination to take the jihadist cause everywhere. Each and every one of his escapes had added to his arsenal of techniques, helping him conceal himself in the world like a wisp of magic—something Khalil hoped to master by observing and learning from his mentor.

The rain, abnormally frequent that winter, made for a miserable drive through the northern edge of the Negev Desert. The unseasonably cold temperatures didn't faze Khalil. His many years in gray England as part of his schooling had given him an advantage when facing the year's challenging weather. Although the rain was a nuisance, it was also a needed gift from Allah. Water brought life to the land; each drop would be needed to face the many months of dry spells.

With the help of his Israeli papers, Khalil crossed the checkpoint into the West Bank without too much hassle, and took the highway heading north toward Hebron. The landscape gradually changed from golden desert sands into metropolitan gray as he approached his destination. His plan was to return to their camp long before nightfall, in possession of further instructions regarding the six people they held captive and in time to observe *Maghrib*, the after-sunset prayer.

Arriving at the familiar property located in a residential area of Hebron, the sentinels, warned of his arrival and familiar with his vehicle, let him through the gates without delay. The twelve-foot-high walls not only kept the main pink-and-beige brick-stucco residence and outer buildings from neighbors' prying eyes, but also kept any meeting within its circle a secret to the outside world. From the street, the place looked like a typical upscale residence. As the *Rasūl* had once put it, the best hiding place was in plain sight.

He parked in the courtyard and made his way to a second metal gate decorated in intricate arabesque design, the entrance to the two-story building. Again, he was allowed passage without ceremony and escorted to a sitting room he'd been to many times before. The tiles covering the floors in a rich red-and-gold geometric pattern never ceased to amaze him. He stood by the couch and let his eyes roam the place as he waited.

The interior of the house, though well-furnished and immaculate, lacked telephones or internet connection. The *Rasūl* credited his survival and that of his organization to the direct avoidance of any type of traceable communication within the walls of the compound. In his youth, Khalil had carried messages between the *Rasūl* and other members. During the many years it had taken to climb the ladder to become a trusted member of the organization's inner circle, he'd become accustomed to reporting updates in person and never questioned any of the *Rasūl*'s decisions.

He didn't have to wait too long before the *Rasūl* joined him. The man held an aura of power about him, one that impressed all in his presence—including Khalil—with awe. The *Rasūl* removed his headscarf as he always did when they met, and Khalil felt blessed by that gesture, one he interpreted as a sign of trust. The *Rasūl* observed him through deep, dark eyes like bottomless pools as he closed the distance between them. Extending his hands, he clasped Khalil's and said *salaam*, as was etiquette.

"Peace be upon you." The *Rasūl*'s grip was as firm as his drive.

"And peace be upon you also and the mercy of Allah," Khalil replied in proper form before sitting, as indicated by a wave of the *Rasūl*'s hand.

The man in front of him had changed in appearance many times since Khalil had come to serve him. The *Rasūl* was like a chameleon adapting to the environment. Like any observant Muslim, he dressed modestly. To those who didn't know who he was, he appeared to be just a regular Arab businessman in a city where strife and tension permeated the very air they breathed. To those who knew him, the humble clothes did not disguise his importance to the cause they all had embraced. Khalil felt blessed and fulfilled in his presence. He understood the path the *Rasūl* was forging was one of greatness, and that the operation they were executing was one more step to achieving their goal.

"How was it?"

"As well as we expected. We have six of them."

"Six?" The *Rasūl* frowned.

"We had to cull the drivers and a couple of agents."

The *Rasūl* nodded, mouthed an "Ah," and continued his briefing. "That was not part of the plan; however, it might work to our advantage. The guests. Are they enjoying their visit?"

"Aside from whining, begging, and demanding their release?"

A quiet laugh rippled from the *Rasūl's* lips, but the humor never reached his eyes. "Have you spoken with them?"

"No. Just as you had instructed, we let them simmer."

"Good. When you do, observe them carefully. Interrogate them all. We can't allow any of them to return with suspicions of what is at stake. Dispose only of those who show any inkling before their release."

"What will you need for the broadcast?"

"Only their fear. That should be enough for now." The *Rasūl* paused, and a gleam Khalil had never seen before flared in the depths of his eyes. "America makes such a big deal about us and yet is blinded to the disease within. We will watch it consume them from the inside out."

The *Rasūl's* assuring words renewed Khalil's confidence in the plan. "What Allah wishes."

"Wait for word from me. I'll send a courier with instructions when the time comes. Until then, keep them alive and well. They are worthless to us dead."

Contentment radiated like a bright star within Khalil. All he had to do was follow the plan and wait for the pieces to fall into place. With that, he rose to his feet. "May Allah look over you."

And all of us. For the time of great victory had arrived, and with it the fruits of their pious labor.

The *Rasūl*, Salman al-Boshnak, watched with gravity as Khalil exited. Khalil's father had been a good warrior for their cause, but, like others before him, he'd gotten too close. As much as he'd trusted the man, he'd known too much about the past and his true identity. He'd become a liability to the cause simply by existing. Khalil, like his father, knew too much—but handling that new threat would have to wait until this stage of the plan was complete. He wondered if his hesitation to deal with Khalil lay in his attachment to the young man. After all, he'd doted on him as if the boy had been his own. His mistake. He'd have to fix it soon enough. For now, his focus lay on the men under Khalil's orders. Some of his recruits were young and careless. He needed them all to follow his orders to precision. And when the time was right, they would all earn their reward—if not in this lifetime, in the next.

His people had fought for so long it had become second nature. From the Middle Ages to modern times, Arabs had revolted against many empires, but for one single reason. Their right to land and identity. They had been either stripped of their birthplace or segregated on it. Their voices muted, their hands tied, their rights raped.

They had lived in the vastness of the area from the Mediterranean Sea to far beyond the Jordan River for over a thousand years, only to have it ripped piece after piece from under their feet by foreigners, non-believers. His hands balled into tight fists.

The British had given away their land without a second thought as if those inhabiting it were nothing but grains of desert sand. Since then, Arabs had been squeezed, pummeled, crushed into the minuscule areas they inhabited today, prisoners in a modern-day concentration camp, forgotten by the world.

He took a deep, angry breath as images of the past haunted him and the echoes of his mother's wails deafened him to his surroundings. The coppery tang of blood and the stench of singed flesh attacked his senses from the deep recesses of his mind. When one lived the gruesome reality of checkpoints, destruction of homes, and expulsions without notice, one developed a harder view of what's fair or not.

The efforts to return his people to what they once had would not be rewarded in one single swoop. Jihadists that had performed enormous attacks on military operations abroad or sought mass destruction in the past garnered no empathy from the rest of the world. Although they had achieved their immediate goal of punishing those responsible for many massacres in the past using the old eye-for-an-eye method, the results were diluted by the backlash.

He had a better way of achieving their goal. A smarter way. One that would give his people the future they deserved. One that needed time and patience—and he was a patient man. Many would say a cold and calculating one, but he hadn't bested most Intelligence agencies for years by chance. Their time would arrive in the shape of betrayal, and he would enjoy the developments like a director enjoyed opening night.

Chapter Ten

Strategy Game

ON THE DAY OF THEIR CAPTURE, Rachael had been dragged from the truck, bound and hooded, into the cell she currently occupied. Soon after, gentle hands had ministered to her swollen ankle and, later that first night, one of the men had returned with food. He'd removed her hood and shoved a *hijab* in her hands, barking instructions and gesturing for her to wrap it around her head and cover her hair. She had quickly complied with his demands and accepted the meal.

Food was a positive sign. It meant that whoever had planned their kidnapping wanted them alive. The balaclava the man wore was another good sign: if their captors were taking precautions to keep their identities hidden, it also indicated they wanted to keep them alive, maybe trade them for money. If that was the case, they were more valuable alive than dead. Or so she hoped. Her stomach knotted and dread ripped through her.

It had been three long days since they'd been taken. Rachael still hadn't a clue as to why, but she knew there was some purpose.

Extremists and mercenaries always had a reasonable excuse for their acts cemented in their psyche, even if the rest of the world thought them insane.

Bone-chilling cold clung to the air and the rain pelting the outer walls of her cell reflected her mood. It was as if the skies wept, for they understood the uncertainty eating at her. Rachael tucked the blanket closer around her legs and the *hijab* tighter around her head, more for warmth than modesty. She'd always thought of it as a nuisance, but that day she was grateful for its added comfort.

Her eyes roamed the poor excuse for a room. The mudstone walls appeared as rough as they felt on her skin when she leaned against them, and, despite the discomfort, she thanked the heavens for the poor state of the building—particularly the considerable gaps around the doorframe, perfect to allow sound through.

Dim lighting penetrated the room through a single opening, not much wider than the size of her open hand, on the wall opposite the door. The little she could see outside gave her no clue other than to tell her they had to be somewhere isolated, she guessed a compound in the middle of the desert; otherwise she was certain she would have heard the world in motion beyond those walls.

Even during daylight hours, there was no rush of cars, honks of horns, or buzz of humanity assaulting her ears. Instead, she'd only heard the murmur of voices or shuffle of steps outside the door and overheard snatches of trivial conversation among the wardens as they walked by. Rachael had been able to piece together that the other members of their group still lived, but she wasn't sure if they had all been spared from harm.

The exhaustion of captivity—physical but also emotional—hammered at Rachael. She rubbed the back of her neck and rolled her head in a tight circle, attempting to loosen cramped muscles, but the kink ran deeper. Unable to relieve the discomfort, she focused on her goal, the only thing keeping her sanity intact.

Unconsciously, she rubbed her thumb over the gold band encircling her ring finger as her thoughts careened in her head. Over the last few years, she had pushed all memories of her life with Phillip to the background to keep it from tainting or weakening her hunt for information on what had truly happened to her husband. However, during the solitary nights in the compound, those memories broke loose, flooding her mind and leaving her restless and edgy.

Rachael shifted into a more comfortable position and hissed as pain shot from her ankle up to her knee like an electric current across a live wire. Riding it out, an isolated point in time pushed forward, overwhelming her senses.

Rachael stood next to her father in the reception line at the Israeli Embassy in London; she greeted diplomats and political figures alike as they arrived for the night's functions. She was only seventeen. Her mother's flight from New York had been delayed and she was forced to play hostess in her place at one of the embassy's gala balls. Out of the corner of her eye, she saw a tall man in dress uniform walk in and scan the room. Dark blue jacket immaculately pressed, medals shining on his chest, he held his navy-blue-and-white cap under his arm in a casual but intense stance.

The weight of his gaze made her stammer as she greeted the guests. She brushed her sweaty palms across her thighs and ignored him as best she could. An older gentleman, also wearing a Navy dress uniform, joined him and they fell into place at the end of the line.

She could barely wait to be done with the greetings. She already had cramps from her overextended smile and feared she'd gouge out her eyes from sheer boredom before her mother relieved her.

"Rachael?" Her father's voice demanded her attention.

Pasting the plastic smile back on her face, she turned on her heel. She stopped dead in her tracks when her eyes collided with the soldier's dark brown ones. He stood beside a shorter and older version of himself. The many years attending diplomatic events saved her from embarrassing herself.

"Yes, Father?"

"Rachael, this is Captain William Moore," her father introduced the older man. "He is our liaison within the British Special Forces. Captain, my daughter."

She nodded and shook his hand, sporting the required wide smile. Her father then turned to the younger man.

"This is Lieutenant Phillip Moore, Captain Moore's son."

Rachael stuck out her hand and the lieutenant's much larger one engulfed it.

"Pleasure to meet you, Mr. Moore."

"It's Lieutenant Moore, Rachael," her father corrected, and she blushed at her lack of tact.

She knew the etiquette surrounding formal events, but somehow the look in Phillip Moore's eyes made her forget her place.

A smile crinkled the side of his mouth and humor twinkled in his eyes. "The pleasure is all mine."

"Rachael, why don't you show the lieutenant around while I talk to the captain?" Her father's question sounded more like an order. "We have something pressing to discuss. Lieutenant, if you'll excuse us. Rachael will keep you company."

Momentarily stunned, Rachael watched their fathers retreat.

"—your evening?"

She turned her attention back to the lieutenant when she realized he'd been talking to her.

"I'm sorry. You were saying, Lieutenant?"

He cracked a smile. "I asked if you were enjoying your evening. Please call me Phillip. Unlike our fathers, I have no need for formality."

Relief flooded her and her first real smile of the evening curved her lips. "If you consider wearing a long dress and pantyhose, sweating like a pig under tons of makeup, and dying to get out of here enjoyment, then yes." Her heart beat loud in her ears as Phillip threw his head back and laughed. Mortified, she stammered an apology. "Please tell me that didn't just happen?"

Humor shone from his eyes. "Indeed, it did."

Searching to regain some dignity, she pushed forward. "Tell me what I can do to redeem myself. That was unconscionable of me.

"There's nothing wrong with being truthful. Rather refreshing for a change." He flashed a wide grin.

Rachael's eyes snapped open and her throat tightened at the vivid images of that day, which now lived solely in her memory. Her fingers reached for the locket tucked under her blouse—a gift from Phillip on their first anniversary. A faint smile brushed her lips. He would have gotten a kick out of the use she'd recently made of it. She missed him. Missed his acceptance, humor, and friendship.

Leaning against the rough, uneven surface of the wall, she watched the last of the day's dim light fade away behind the cracks, taking her hopes with it.

Darkness fell swiftly, and she wished she could escape the four walls surrounding her just as easily as the light had. She listened intently and, as expected, the musical murmur of the *Maghrib* reached for her. The chant of voices should have soothed her, but they only served to inflame her anxiety.

Once prayers were over, a man yelled orders—spoken in a dialect she understood—to get one of the prisoners. Her body tensed as dread bubbled through her veins. She shut her eyes and listened. The order was followed by a loud racket of slamming doors and the shuffle of feet.

"Where are you taking me?"

Rachael's stomach dropped when she recognized Jason Wolfe's panicked voice in the distance, followed by another flurry of discussion in Arabic between two men. Wolfe, although hardcore when it came to human rights politics, had the gentlest of souls. Her heart thrummed loud in her chest as she limped across the floor and pressed her ear against the door. The commotion faded and an eerie quiet descended. Rachael held her breath, waiting, listening for more, for any tidbit of information she could collect that would give her an understanding of what was happening outside. Nothing. She released a frustrated sigh and returned to the pallet and the warmth of the blanket.

Her segregation was both a curse and a blessing. Familiar with the local culture, she understood why she hadn't been locked up with the others, but it didn't make the wait any easier. She would have preferred to have been placed in the company of the other women in the camp. The ones who had tended to her ankle each day. That way she could try to play on their sympathy. Maybe claw her way out somehow and disappear into the darkness to find them all help. She hugged her shoulder and rested her chin on her chest as she pondered on ways she could get them out of that mess.

She reached out to her husband's memory, seeking strength. Phillip had been one of the strongest men she had known. He also had a way about him that seeped into others, made them think their actions through and find the right way. Weird how some people made others feel comfortable and compelled to share pieces of themselves. Maybe because they truly listened. Phillip had been one of them.

After their first meeting, she had found herself crossing paths with him often due to their fathers' work collaboration, and in those chance encounters she got to see that side of him in action. Phillip had given her the courage to pursue her dreams, encouraged her to follow her heart, even if it meant leaving the nest and ruffled feathers behind. In following her heart, their paths had taken different directions, but they'd kept in touch through email. She had looked forward to each one of them as a boat in a storm seeks a lighthouse beacon. And Phillip had been that and more.

When they had met again a year later in London during another visit to her parents, it was as if they had never parted company. The laughter, encouragement, and connection had all still been there. But that time there was more between them. His maturity had brought out the best in her, grounded her. Pushed her to be all she could be. He had opened a world of possibilities to her, something her own father had never done. She had moved to London to be with him that year.

In the partial darkness of the makeshift cell, she clung to the knowledge that Phillip had molded her into who she'd become and he deserved a show of the strength he'd brought to the surface. She'd survived worse in the past—had survived losing him—and would endure the new ordeal ahead. Just one more obstacle on the route to her goal.

★ ★ ★ ★ ★

THE CLANK AGAINST the door and creak of hinges tossed Rachael out of a fitful doze. A light flared in the room; instantly alert, she squinted and covered her eyes against its brilliance in the open doorway. A chill flared up her spine and her palms grew sweaty as a man walked in, his predatory gait indicative of his role among them. *My turn.* She knew they would eventually make their way to her, but she was still unprepared for the reality of it.

Her thoughts raced a mile a minute as she tried to read the man, but his face was hidden by a black mask, leaving only his dark penetrating eyes and thin grim lips uncovered.

He moved closer and studied her, almost as if peeling layers to reach her core. She felt like a live bug under a microscope, and just as vulnerable as she sat on the squalid pallet with no license to walk away from it. As the dissecting stare continued, she became agitated under his assessment but resisted the urge to squirm.

His dark eyes stopped their roaming when they reached her hair. "Cover your head."

His English held a faint British accent. It was the same voice she'd heard when she'd been pulled from the truck the day they'd arrived there. Something in his tone sent another surge of adrenaline coursing through her veins. Her fingers trembled as she adjusted the *hijab* back into place.

"Not all men under my command are as in control of their urges as I am...Ms. Moore." His pause was more unnerving than his words.

A warning whispered in her head. She clasped her hands in her lap to hide their shaking and watched him warily. Her throat went dry. "How do you know my name?"

"Your colleagues enjoyed some of my persuasion." Satisfaction colored his voice.

His words set alarm bells ringing in her head. She reached for the locket and the secret it guarded as she gathered her scattered thoughts. "Why are we here?"

"I'm the one asking questions. Not you."

His eyes narrowed, but instead of shrinking under the cold stare, she forced herself to straighten her shoulders and sit taller.

She tightened her grip on the locket until the edges dug into her palm. A raging heat flushed through her body, eating away at her earlier fear. She looked him straight in the eyes. "We offer nothing of value to you."

"You are wrong. You are extremely valuable. You and your friends are—how do you say? A bargaining chip?"

"For what? You know our government will never negotiate." She rubbed the locket between her fingers as she tried to douse the anger bleeding in her tone.

"That is yet to be seen." He frowned and cocked his head. His eyes narrowed to slits as they focused on her hand.

A sudden chill hung on the edge of his words. She'd pressed her luck. Rachael had seen the warning burn in the eyes of many in that land. She understood the challenges women of that country withstood. In some sects, women weren't allowed to vote, drive cars, or leave home without a male escort. They didn't lead. They followed. She could be stepping on unsteady ground by being inquisitive, and it could lead to painful consequences.

Her heart dropped and her breath caught in her throat when the man moved in long strides to the opposite corner of the room. He grabbed a chair and dragged it to the pallet, making a grating noise as he approached her. When he set it in front of her, she lifted her chin in defiance and braced herself. She took a deep breath and forced herself to relax, but his calculating stare only heightened her unease. Without warning, his hand shot out and wrapped around hers and the locket.

"No! Please!" she cried out, keeping a tight hold. His eyes were devoid of emotion as he pried it from her fingers and lifted the chain over her head.

Her captor took his seat and leaned back in a slow, deliberate motion. He crossed his legs and his eyes bounced from the locket to her face then back to the silver charm. He rubbed the etched design on its front with his thumb. A shiver ran through her when he opened the pendant and eyed its contents. His gaze slithered to her left hand then pinned her own and, in that moment, she thought he had discovered her secret. Rachael's eyes fluttered closed, her throat clogged, and her gut clenched with fear under the weight of his eyes.

"Are you married?"

Rachael almost wilted as relief loosened fear's grip on her. She licked her lips nervously. "I was."

"The man in the picture?"

"My late husband. The necklace was a gift from him." She wanted to scream and shout, demand the locket's return, but she held it all in check. She had to play it cool or he would suspect he held more than a sentimental token in his hands.

He returned his eyes to the picture. "An officer?"

The photo was an old one of Phillip in his dress uniform. "No. That's an old photo. Discharged." She hated the taste of the lie that rolled off her tongue. Rachael reached out her hand. "I'd like it back. It's all I have left of him."

Panic sucked the breath from her lungs as she watched it disappear into his pocket. *No!*

"Let us try this again, shall we, *Mrs.* Moore?"

The smooth flow of the English words dripping from his tongue irritated her less than the knowledge that he had been educated in Phillip's country. She noticed it in the way he enunciated some of the words. Little nuances in his speech.

Frustration and anger once again swallowed her fear. She needed that locket back. Sentimental value aside, she needed to review the card's data. Finish what she started.

"Try again? What do you want that you don't already have?" she rasped.

He motioned a hand and a young man appeared at the door carrying a chipped ceramic cup. Her inquisitor handed it to her. "Drink." He waited for her to do so before he continued. "You are the assistant to Gerald Blair. As his assistant, you must have overheard discussions."

She swallowed and stared at the toes of his stained combat boots. Her heart bounced against her ribs and she banked the anger that pounded in her head.

"I'm just an administrative assistant, not privy to confidential discussions. I don't have clearance."

Khalil leaned forward in his chair and studied the woman in front of him. She had been unexpected. He had observed her wrap the *hijab* and noticed she knew their ways. And although she had shown the proper respect, when their eyes locked he had seen myriad emotions tumbling in their chestnut depths. Fear and uncertainty the two obvious ones, but also something he didn't expect to see. Anger. Fire. Life. Her eyes had flashed red-hot temper, but she had snuffed it when she noticed his scrutiny.

He had seen the nervous shake in her hands and the perspiration at her temples. There was something incongruous about the woman. He eased back and observed her eyes fly now and again to the pocket where he'd stashed the necklace. He had something valuable to her and he'd use it.

His second-in-command and two others stepped into the room, interrupting his musings. They stopped at a lift of his hand.

"We will continue this discussion later, Mrs. Moore. But first you will assist me." He stood and turned to his men, speaking in Arabic. "Is everything prepared?"

"Yes, Kahlil."

A name. Khalil. The one who dealt the cards.

He nodded at the two men in the back. "Take her. I will follow in a moment."

They jerked her to her feet and pain rippled across her face. "Take care with her. We need her in one piece."

"Where are you taking me?" She held his gaze as the men dragged her from the room.

Once they were alone, his second-in-command shook his hand

and exchanged the three traditional cheek-to-cheek kisses with him in greeting. *"As-salamu alaykum.* Everything is set according to your instructions."

"We must keep our guard up." Kahlil kept his emotions in check. He didn't want to show too much confidence. It led to carelessness among the ranks. "First we must send the *Rasūl's* message to the infidels. And then we wait for our next orders.

"The longer they are in our possession, the more danger we bring upon us."

Kahlil ignored the concealed warning in the man's words, eyes locked on the spot where Rachael Moore had sat before being half-dragged, half-carried by his men out of the room.

"Do you doubt me? The *Rasūl?"*

"No, *Sahib.* I meant no disrespect."

Kahlil nodded his head in dismissal and led the way to the inter-rogation room. His hand slipped into his pocket and wrapped around the woman's trinket. They would use her first. The Americans had a weakness where women were concerned. She would be the instrument to push their plans forward.

He smirked when he reached the room. All had been orchestrat-ed as directed. The woman sat tied to a simple wooden chair facing a video camera. The flag of a sovereign Palestine had been stretched across the mural hanging on the wall behind her. The perfect backdrop. He ignored the woman's piercing eyes and approached the desk in the far corner.

One of his trusted soldiers turned to him. "We are ready, *Sahib.* " He moved to the side, and Kahlil stepped closer to watch her read the words printed on a sign. Satisfaction and joy filled him. The message was perfect. The initial move in their strategy game. It delivered the threat without giving away their true intent. That would come much later.

Chapter Eleven

"*N*ATHAN...." THE GLIMMER OF TEARS marred Rachael's beautiful face. His heart lurched in his chest when she extended her arms to him. He knew he shouldn't, but he took her hands in his and pulled her toward him. The skin under his touch was as smooth as he remembered. He tugged her closer and wrapped his arms around her, unsure if he could ever let go. He tucked his face in the dark curtain of her hair and inhaled the sweet scent of lilacs. He couldn't let go, as much as he knew he couldn't hold on.

"Oh God, Rae...I'm so sorry."

"Nelson."

Nathan frowned. Rachael had never called him by his last name. He pushed from her embrace and his eyes collided with Phillip's intense gaze. Nathan's throat closed and he took a step back.

"Phillip...I—"

His dear friend's expression was serene, not angry or accusing as he'd expected. *"It's okay, mate. Just get her out of there."*

"Nelson!"

The images blurred and faded as the roar ripped him from his dream. Eyes wide open, he tried to focus on its source.

"Finally. Time to wake up, Sleeping Beauty." He turned on the couch and found Hanson at the top of the stairs.

Reality sank in as he identified his surroundings. *The Bauers' house.* He rose to his elbows. "What's going on?"

"New developments. There's coffee in the pot, get upstairs pronto."

Nathan had tossed and turned through most of the night, and what little sleep he'd gotten had been plagued by unsettling dreams. He shook their last threads from his head and filled a cup before dragging his ass upstairs. Despite his prompt response, he was the last to arrive. He walked into their makeshift command center just as news of a recent broadcast identified as the abductors' hit his cell phone.

Hanson eyed him from the middle of the room, sporting the same disheveled appearance as the day before. Despite the typical military stance, the guy looked like he'd stumbled out of a pub after a night of heavy partying. Bauer stood next to him, clean cut, looking bright-eyed and bushy-tailed. They looked so different, but seemed to be on the same wavelength where he was concerned, both throwing darts at him with their eyes. Nathan could almost feel their sharp tips piercing his flesh.

Further in the room, Cassandra leaned against the desk facing the window, a pensive look blanketing her face, her eyes adrift in nothingness. Unusual for her—she always seemed to be turning people inside out rather than lost inside herself.

"Now that we're all here…." Bauer threw a condescending look at him and it took everything Nathan had not to shove his fist down his throat. "This is the video broadcasted by an online Arab news outlet approximately two hours ago. It was picked up by a stateside news channel and now it's gone viral." He aimed the remote he held in his hand at the TV mounted on the wall and with a click, the segment came to life on the large flat screen.

"My name is Rachael Moore. I'm an American citizen. I beg that the United States government do all that they can to release me and the others taken during the attack on our convoy. The mujahideen's demands are simple."

Rae.

Nathan's limbs felt heavy, each breath tightening his chest to near implosion as he focused on her and how uncomfortable she appeared to be with her wrists tied to the chair's armrests. A black *hijab* covered her dark hair. Her white blouse and black slacks had dirt stains and were wrinkled from her ordeal. Seeing her again, especially under those circumstances, was like a punch to the gut, but Nathan kept it to himself—or at least he hoped he did. No one in the room seemed to notice how much the video affected him; their eyes were glued to the images on the screen. He studied her, searching for reassurance that she hadn't sustained any injuries while also trying to focus on what she was telling them. The camera zoomed in on her face.

"…Please act quickly and release the Palestinian people from oppression. Return the land that is rightfully theirs. Evict those who have wrongfully ripped them from their homes and we shall live to rejoin our families. They have given us only a week from the time of this broadcast. Our lives are in your hands."

The news anchor's face replaced Rachael's.

"The President gave the following statement a few hours after the broadcast hit the airwaves."

The image switched to the press conference held at the White House.

"The United States condemns the kidnappings and will join efforts with the other nations affected to return the hostages safe and sound to their families. With that said, I must reiterate, the United States government does not and will not negotiate with terrorists."

Bauer paused the video and a solemn silence cloaked the room. An echo of Rachael's words bounced around in Nathan's head. *Our lives are in your hands.*

"So, where does that leave us?" Hanson's biting tone cut through the quiet.

Bauer turned on his heel and strode to his desk. Pulling the keyboard closer, he focused on something on his monitor, fingers flying over the keys. "We're tracking the point of origin of the video in the grid as we speak and should be able to give accurate coordinates in a little while. Once that happens, George will acquire satellite imagery of the location."

"How long will it take you to have the details on access routes?" Nathan interrupted.

"Once we have eyes on it, not too long. We can't provide you with an in-depth risk analysis without audio or video surveillance. That would require days, months, of continuous data collection. It took the NSA years to collect the data that corroborated Bin Laden's position to one-hundred-percent certainty." The clacking of Bauer's fingers on the keyboard punctuated his every word.

"Yes. I know," Nathan snapped. He was well aware that some CIA operations could take eons to come to fruition. Usually, no steps were taken until Washington could verify the intelligence collected as solid. But that case was different, unusual. They already had the necessary clearance for invasive surveillance due to the Top Secret nature of his mission. "We are not dealing with apprehension of enemy targets here. We are dealing with US citizens' lives on the line. I'm sure they would be grateful for any percentage of certainty we can get at this point. Just make sure that whatever you manage to get *is* reliable."

"All my team needs is the X on the map. We'll hit it as soon as the authorization comes down the line. Shouldn't be a problem, considering the latest developments," Hanson nodded at the screen.

"This is a CIA operation. Leave the authorizations to me." Hanson raised one eyebrow at Nathan's interruption. "Just focus on achieving a positive outcome. The director is expecting no casualties among hostages." The words tumbled out of his mouth before he could think them through. His concern for Rachael's recovery made him tactless, clumsy.

Hanson's narrowed eyes pierced his. "That's always our goal. A successful mission is always first priority for any USSOCOM team."

Nathan nodded. "Of course. I didn't mean it that way."

Cassandra stared at him as if he'd grown a second head. She knew him as a smooth operator, the rule-follower, the one who ironed each operation's wrinkles. His background in political science made him a diplomat when it came to all aspects of his job. Sadly, that didn't translate well into his personal life.

"As I was saying," Bauer diverted their attention back to the case, "George and I will work on finding and intercepting any other communication to and from the source once we locate it. And we are still listening for the cell phones identified in the attack. Maybe now that we have more targets, we'll get lucky." His eyes sparkled with anticipation for what Nathan could see was like a game to him.

Nathan had never seen the Irishman in action before and, as he observed the geek in his habitat, he came to the realization that he might have grossly underestimated the man's know-how. He truly hoped he had because the hostages' lives, most importantly Rachael's life, depended on his and Miller's skills being as big as their cocky attitudes.

Nathan's gaze drifted to Cassandra. She'd moved to her desk, her trademark determination again stamped firmly on her face. Hope bloomed in Nathan's chest. Cassandra was tenacious when on a case. She had a keen eye for detail and for tracking anything amiss. Having her onboard could only be beneficial to their cause. He left Bauer and Hanson geeking out over the technologies and the process they would use to lock in the location and walked toward her. When he sat on the corner of her desk and she didn't divert her eyes to him, he knew without doubt he was on her shit list.

With all the commotion of Bauer's arrival at the safe house in Russia, they'd never finished their conversation. Eventually, they'd have to sit down and lay all their cards on the table if they were ever to keep their friendship alive. He wanted that, needed that. Needed contact with anybody who was willing to see some good in him, and Cassandra had been the only one to do that in the past. From her expression, he would have to prepare for some serious sucking up, something he wasn't used to doing.

"What do you want, Nate?" Her tone was cold. It pained him that he deserved it.

He could answer in myriad ways, but he opted to remain on target, focus on the job. "Your take on it?" He kept his voice low. "You've always had a sixth sense for this kind of thing."

She turned her eyes to him then. Her gaze was as cold as her tone had been. "It's failed me on more than one occasion."

Flashes of the day she was shot crossed his mind, but he brushed it aside. She was okay now. She was happy with the Irishman.

"Your intuition is better than all science analytics combined. You know it. I know it."

Cassandra scoffed. "That's the smooth talker I know." The humorous glimmer in her eyes left him with an odd sense of satisfaction. It told him she wasn't past the point of forgiveness.

"Only speaking the truth." He gave her time to think on his request, but deep inside he wasn't so sure she would.

Cassandra shook her head and released a heavy sigh. "Fine. I don't have anything substantial at this point. I've barely cracked open the case. Once Trevor and George have more details on the location and the people connected to it, we might be able to tie in to existing active cases. If that happens, I'll be able to delve into the dossiers of the ones involved. Unlike Trev and George, I work with real people. Not machines."

"I know that. But how about your gut? What's it telling you?"

"That we need to tread carefully."

"Yeah, but you are a planner; you always tread carefully. Well, that is unless—" Nathan stuck his thumb over his shoulder in Bauer's direction "—he's concerned."

Cassandra threw him a narrowed look. "Are you really going there again?"

Nathan inhaled deeply and let out a long breath. "Sorry. Force of habit." He didn't even know why he'd said that. He had no claim over her. Never had. He'd done a lot of soul searching since the events in Vyborg. His life since childhood had been a collection of clichés. The strict military father, the sibling rivalry, the rebellion. Even with all the conflict—or maybe because of it—his life was quasi-normal. But then it switched from cliché to a collection of train wrecks. Jay, Phillip and subsequently Rachael, Cassandra, and even Petrovna, each an added car to the pileup. He could honestly say that most of those wrecks had been out of his control, all except for one. The one he'd brought upon himself. That had been Cassandra. Although he understood himself—his reasons and motivations—a lot better than before, it didn't make the weight of past mistakes any easier to shoulder. She stared at him, waiting for more, something other than a flimsy excuse. "All I can say is that it won't happen again."

She searched his eyes for a while, almost as if trying to decide whether or not he was being truthful. She might have found her answer there because when she spoke, the ice in her attitude had melted a bit.

"Does that mean you're finally going to play nice?"

He almost choked on the laughter that bubbled up in his throat. "With him, you mean? You gotta be kidding, right?"

"As a matter of fact, no. Come on, Nate. He's a great guy."

How could any man refuse to do as she asked when she turned her powers of coercion on? He almost pitied Bauer. *Almost* being the key word.

He raised the shields higher and retorted, "Have you asked him to do the same?" The rosy hue that flooded her cheeks and sheepish look on her face told him she'd gotten the same response from her husband. "That's what I thought. I can work with him. It pains me to say it, but I need his skills on this. But friends? That's a stretch, Cass."

"Well, the least you can do is to give him a break."

"I am. That's why we're here. I know he's good at what he does. I hadn't realized how good until now."

"Stubborn men. One day…." she grumbled dismissively, rolling her eyes before focusing her attention back on her screen.

A deep-throated chuckle broke Trevor's concentration. He sought its source and found Nelson leaning on Cassandra's desk, the two in animated conversation, as if the last six months she had avoided him like the plague had not happened.

"Anything?"

Hanson's question forced him away from his thoughts, but his gaze remained locked on the two across the room. "No. George is checking for new intercepts. I'm following a different trail."

"So, they worked together at the CIA." Trevor raised his eyes to Hanson and found him observing the targets of his own attention. It wasn't a question. It was a simple statement, similar to those people made when bringing up the weather or a sports match to strike a conversation.

"Yes. They were working a case together when she was shot. She left the Agency shortly after."

"I read that in their dossiers. Didn't realize they had developed a friendship from such a short-term assignment." He shrugged. "But I guess it's like the service. Once you serve with another man, go into battle together, he's your brother for life."

"They knew each other before they were assigned to that case. They met on Cassie's first day on the job." Trevor had never thought of it that way. Although he understood that Cassandra had an older friendship with Nelson—one he didn't like but accepted would always exist—he'd never stopped to think that their connection had been forged by having to rely on each other. By joint experiences. Like Mulder and Scully, they had drifted closer because of it. The difference in their case was that Cassandra didn't love Nelson. "But I guess you are right on the friendship for life."

"And you hate that she still has contact with Nelson." Again, Hanson didn't word it as a question.

"I don't think it's a state secret that I don't like the man," he smirked. "And for the record, it's a mutual thing."

"I got that. You two aren't very subtle about it."

"Let's just say we both have our reasons." Private details were best left unsaid.

"Yet you're not pounding him for chatting up your wife."

Memories of the less-than-pleasant exchanges he'd had with Nelson filled his mind, closely followed by the infinite times he'd heard the words "I love you" from Cassandra over the length of their marriage. The knowledge he held her heart made it easier to resist the urge to wring Nelson's neck, but didn't fully erase his gripe.

He shrugged off the burning in his stomach. "No need. She'd do that herself if he crossed the line."

Hanson smiled. "Why doesn't that surprise me?"

Trevor returned the smile. "She's stunning. You should see her handling that Glock of hers."

"Not sure I want to find myself under the muzzle of her pistol." Hanson's mouth quirked with mirth.

Trevor smiled and shook his head. "I can assure you, you don't."

The familiar ring of the video chat application sounded from Trevor's speakers, bringing their attention back to the case.

Nathan followed Cassandra toward Bauer's desk, hoping for the news they'd been waiting to hear.

Miller's face filled the screen when Bauer accepted the call. "You are on speaker. Tell us what you've got."

"Not sure what to make of it, Trev. Hope you can help solve this riddle. I have the coordinates. The source of the upload points to a residence south of Jaba', in the West Bank. And we got eyes on it."

Nathan's heart pounded in his chest. *Finally. A strong lead.* "Were you able to get anything else?" he cut in before Bauer could respond. "Any movement in and out? Any other communication?"

"No. That's why I said riddle. I checked the footage from the area. Backpedaled twenty-four hours from the upload time and checked for movement. From the activity, I couldn't see anything that spelled 'hostages on board' for sure. You'd expect at least increased security when there are six adults being held against their will. Based on the footage, there isn't much activity there. Nothing out of the ordinary during the last day, anyway. I'm not sure what to make of it."

Cassandra turned to Nathan. "We should sit tight and wait for confirmation of more activity." Her voice carried the usual analytical tone she adopted when in work mode. "If we go in without reassurance, we might jeopardize the mission and put the hostages' lives at risk."

"Usually I would agree with you, Cass," Nathan replied. "That's CIA standard protocol, but this case requires thinking outside the box. We can't just sit and wait. We only have one week. Not months or years. Even if the hostages aren't at that location, there might be critical intelligence in that house, something that could lead us to them."

Cassandra's brow drew into a frown as Nathan spoke. He could almost see the questions rolling in her mind. Although there was a lot about him she wasn't fully aware of, she knew his professionalism.

"Nate—"

"I agree with Nelson," Hanson interrupted. His eyes had lost all sense of humor as he stood behind Bauer's chair, arms crossed over his chest. "We can set up a reconnaissance incursion. My team can be in and out of there in the blink of an eye."

Cassandra, always the voice of reason, cut in. "What about detection? If the hostages aren't there, the insurgents will know we are onto them the moment you raid the place."

"Stealth is just one of our greatest strengths," Hanson rebutted calmly. "We'll be able to make a more educated decision when we have boots on the ground and eyes on the target. If we find no sign of the hostages, anybody else on the premises can become a valuable asset."

Hanson's input solidified his own desire for action. Cassandra's hesitation made Nathan uneasy, but she'd always preferred the comfort of certainty to the torment of doubt. He'd been like that himself not long ago, but at that moment the need to take action preceded caution.

Armed with all the details and cell phone in hand, he broke from the group.

Cassandra returned to her desk while Nathan made calls and Trevor discussed the pros and cons of physical incursion with Hanson. *Let the boys be boys*, she thought as she raised her mug from the desk for a sip. She grimaced when its contents touched her lips. Cold. Just like the shoulder she'd received from both Nathan and Hanson.

A new email from Jessica popped in the inbox queue and she opened it right away, hoping it was something new and relevant to the case.

Good morning! Happy birthday, chica. Let me know when you're available for some girl time. I didn't want to ruin any plans Trevor has for you by calling or stopping by. I'm sure they involve a lot of Irish charm. I'm positive it's already started with a loud bang. Picture me rolling my eyes. See you soon. XO

Jessica's enthusiasm made her smile. She made a mental note to invite her over as soon as the guys were gone. As disappointed as she was that neither Trevor nor Nathan remembered the date, she couldn't blame them. The case took precedence. The meaning of the day was insignificant compared to the danger the hostages faced.

She set the cup down and let her eyes drift back to Trevor and the others, then to the image of the press conference frozen on the screen. Her thoughts scrolled out of control in her head like an old-style ticker tape, leaving in its wake a pounding headache, one that matched the faint ache of the scar tissue etched in her hip.

In her mind's eye, she replayed the video segment over and over again. Something felt off, but for the life of her she couldn't put her finger on it. The message Rachael Moore had delivered was simplistic at best. Gave nothing of the true intent or identity of the kidnappers. Why just the old rhetoric? They had the world's attention, but there had been no demands for immediate military withdrawal, nor any prisoner exchange demands either.

When it came down to it, the video hardly helped them in un-covering the ones behind the attack. Moore's scripted speech mentioned only the *mujahideen*. The word originally used to describe any Muslim struggling in the path of Allah now encompassed several radical groups.

Cassandra pictured Moore tied to the chair. She was another conundrum. While her speech had been shaky in its delivery, her eyes and set of her jaw screamed defiance. Between her dossier and the video, Cassandra was beginning to like the woman who seemed to have had some sort of connection to Nathan in the past.

She sat back in her chair and rested her chin on steepled fingers, turning her focus to Nathan when he rejoined the group. He hadn't noticed her scrutiny while he'd watched the video, but she'd seen the concern carved into the grim set of his mouth and in the flare of his nostrils. Moore was more than an acquaintance. She was sure of that. It worried her that Nathan's personal feelings toward Rachael Moore might interfere with his judgment. She, like everyone else, under-stood time was precious, but that didn't merit jumping into something half-assed. People were bound to get hurt, no matter how stealthy they were.

"Think outside the box, my ass," she grumbled, reopening the folder and diving again into what she did best. If she dug deeper into Mrs. Moore she was bound to find something others had missed.

"Did you say something, Cass?" Nathan glanced at her.

She met his eyes and shrugged. "Not really."

Nathan's phone buzzed on the desk and he grabbed it. "Nelson. Yes, sir." Nathan's gaze traveled to the other men, who stopped talking and approached him. A shiver crawled up Cassandra's spine when Nathan's eyes fixed on Trevor. He listened for a moment and, as the caller continued to talk, his eyes sought hers. His expression was clouded with discontent, and instinct told her something was amiss. "When? Yes, sir." Once he hung up, Nathan became silent, his eyes locked on hers as if searching for the right words.

"Just spit it out, Nate."

He took a deep breath and avoided her gaze, turning to Hanson instead. "The CIA has moved the operation to Jordan, effective now. We are to report to the air base, where your team is already on standby." He then turned to Trevor. "You are coming with us. They want you filling the role of communications specialist. We'll need someone with the right skills on site. Seems being famous has its downside."

Cassandra's gut twisted into knots as she crossed the room and stood next to Trevor, clutching his hand in hers. "When are we leaving?" They were heading into the fire again, this time hotter and more volatile than the last one.

Nathan's expression confirmed her worst fears. "Sorry, Cass. You're not coming."

Her mouth dried and her heart thumped in her chest as she sought Trevor's eyes.

"What do you mean she's not coming?" His gaze bounced from Nathan to her and back again. "She's a valuable asset. Part of the team."

"I know, Bauer. But they only want essential personnel. It's bad enough that we'll be taking you to handle this. They don't want more civilians than strictly necessary on site."

Hanson's eyes collided with hers and the dread in her veins amplified with the iron she found in them.

Trevor drove his hands through his hair. "You can't be serious. Cassandra can handle herself, and her skills will come in handy if we cap—"

Nathan spoke through gritted teeth. "Israel is not Russia, Bauer.

If something goes south, we are talking guided missiles, IEDs, insurgent fire. Do you really want her there?"

"Hello? Standing right here. Stop talking like I'm not in the room—"

Hanson moved closer to Trevor and held his gaze. "Think about it, Bauer. What would happen if something goes wrong and she's taken? It's for the best. One less worry for us."

Cassandra slid her eyes to Trevor. He couldn't hide the struggle from her, nor the play of emotions taking place in his head. Refusal rolled into doubt and finally into acceptance before her eyes. Her heart thudded against her ribcage when he took her hand and brushed his thumb along the back of it in a soothing motion.

"Cassie, they're right. You can still continue the investigation and help us from here."

She could feel the weight of all eyes on her. Her heart pounded in her ears, drowning out his words and the concern etched in his tone. Once again she was being left to work in the shadows. Once again the decision had been taken out of her hands.

She jerked her hand from Trevor's and stepped back. "My skills would be of more use in Jordan. Where you excel in decoding signals and machine language, I excel in decoding human emotions. I'll be needed *there*. Not here." She pinned first Hanson then Nathan with her gaze. "You know I'm right. You just don't have the balls to—" she snapped her mouth shut before she said too much, and with one last disappointed glance at Trevor, she strode from the room.

Trevor's stomach tightened as he watched his angry wife disappear toward their bedroom. Raw and primitive emotions warred within him. Part of him rejected the idea of being apart from Cassandra once again. Some couples thrived with distance, with "me" time. He and Cassandra thrived on sustained contact, the strengthening of their lives together with each locking of eyes first thing in the morning, each achievement reached together, each smile and moan they exchanged. Being away from her was his Kryptonite. But for once, he saw sense in what Nelson said. He wouldn't be able to focus on the task if he was worried about her safety. Knowing she was in the comfort of their home and among friends made things easier to bear.

She'd always been the voice of reason; once she cooled off she'd see they were right—but until then, there would be hell to pay.

"And that boys, is why I avoid attachments." A cautious look crossed Hanson's face as he continued to stare out the office door. "Ah, hell. Should I be worried about her Glock?"

Trevor frowned. "I'm thinking we should all watch our asses."

Nathan's nod of agreement did nothing to take the edge off his concern. "Hate to be you, Bauer. We don't have time to sit and wait for makeups. Plane is scheduled to take off as soon as flight plan and refueling is complete."

Trevor shot one last look at the empty doorway and followed Cassandra's path. He might as well jump into the fire.

"Shite. Let's get this over with."

Chapter Twelve

Men Like Trevor

TREVOR STOOD NEXT TO THE closed door of the suite he shared with Cassandra, and for the first time, instead of the passion and hunger he'd always felt in connection to the room, hot apprehension coursed through him. It was clear that Cassandra was disappointed. The thought tore his insides. He couldn't blame her, but a part of him was relieved that the choice had been taken out of his hands. In fact, out of all their hands. Neither Nelson nor Hanson could have overridden the authority of those making the decisions.

Cassandra's skills could still be of use to aid their case. He hoped she would understand they weren't kicking her out, only keeping their asset—his most precious one—safe. He counted on her practical side to help her come to terms with the rationale behind their decision, but he also knew she'd be reeling until that happened. He took a deep breath and braced himself before walking in. He swept the softly lit room with a glance and found her standing by the window, all solemn stance and rigid shoulders.

"Did you convince them that I should be going with you?" He couldn't read her expression, partially obscured in the reflection on the glass, but the quiver in her voice told him she was struggling to keep it together.

He squeezed his eyes shut as a painful pang engulfed him. He was split between the need to shelter her and the need to fulfill her wants and wishes.

"You know it's not that easy. The order came from much higher up the chain. You're still part of the team. Just not on the ground."

"So this is it?"

"I'm afraid so."

She released a sharp breath but still didn't turn to face him. "It's like living a groundhog day. You stuck somewhere under gunfire while I have to watch from the distance as you put your neck on the line." Her tone was flat, and that scared him more than tears or anger.

Trevor padded toward her. She shivered under his touch when he turned her to him and lowered her eyes to his chest, avoiding the eye contact he sought. He took a deep breath and rubbed her arms soothingly.

"It's not the same, Cassie. We'll be in touch. It'll be as if I'm sitting across from you in the office. God! How many days have we spent more time looking at screens than at each other?"

Cassandra pulled away from him and wrapped her arms around her midriff to ward off the chill stabbing her in the gut. The voice in her head echoed the reasoning in his words, but her heart wouldn't listen.

"You don't have any experience in these types of situations. It's a hot zone out there, Trevor. Men like you are taken hostage, killed."

Trevor's eyes narrowed. "What do you mean 'men like me'?"

Cassandra's fears for his safety blurred her judgment and turned off filters. "Geeks. Analysts. Businessmen. Reporters. You name it." Hurt clouded his eyes but it didn't stop Cassandra from adding salt to the open wound. "Unlike the others, you don't have *any* combat training. I know you can handle yourself in a bind, but this is different, Trev. This isn't Paris or Russia. This is the Middle East, for crying out loud. An erupting volcano of destruction."

His eyes cooled, his tone flattened. "And I'll be at a command post at an Air Force base far from field action."

"Really?" Cassandra rolled her eyes, a part of her unable to stop from inflicting the same amount of pain she'd received, unable to see the line she'd crossed. "You'll be in the field, a really hot one, just by being there. Are you aware of what goes on in and around those bases?"

Trevor's scowl deepened and he shoved his fists into the pockets of his jeans before taking a deep breath. "The base in Jordan is not in hot territory. We should be relatively safe. Having me there will give them the advantage of real-time intel if they come across encrypted material in any hardware they recover. They would waste precious time transporting the equipment to someone capable of cracking it or moving the personnel to Jordan after the fact. With me on the ground, there's no delay."

"I'm sure they have cryptanalysts in the military. Why don't they take one of their own? Someone more capable of defending himself?" Although a shard of reason had crept in, the words slipped out of her mouth faster than common sense could stop them.

Trevor stared at her in silence for a moment, his narrowed eyes holding a world of hurt in their depths. When he spoke, his voice carried a mix of impatience and anger.

"Because they're not me. They have skilled personnel, grant you, but I'm better. You know that. Besides, it's to our benefit. Their case ties to our own. George and I have been trailing the guy for months now. Handing the intel we collected to another team at this point would be a complete waste of time. They wouldn't know where to go with it and, if you can remember—" he glared at her with burning, reproaching eyes "—lives are at stake." He turned on his heel and headed to the closet. "I need to get my stuff. You heard Nelson." He cast one last openly hostile look at her and her stomach bottomed out. "If there's time, I might be able to make a run to the store for bubble wrap. You know...men like me need that to keep from getting hurt."

"Trevor...." She watched as he set his duffel on the bed and began rummaging through the closet.

Emotional helter-skelter welled up inside her. Regret, disappointment, hurt, and anger came to blows in her head. As much as the logical side of her knew that everything he'd said made sense, she couldn't come to terms with how easily they'd excluded her, how easily Trevor was walking out the door, leaving her behind. Again. Her heart thumped in her chest and she grew lightheaded. That simple thought realigned her reasoning. It dawned on her that the issue lay within. Old fears she had thought buried in the past fizzed and multiplied like a Gremlin watered by their summary ruling. Their refusal to include her in the boys-only club they seemed to have created didn't bother her. She'd grown confident of her worth, nurtured by Trevor's reassurance of his love for the real her. With him, she'd overcome the old her. What she clearly hadn't overcome just yet was her fear of loss, in particular of losing him. Not now. Maybe not ever. The old what-ifs from the past, the ones that had almost kept them apart when they'd first met, wiggled their ugly corpses out of the dark recesses of her mind.

Cassandra covered her mouth with trembling fingers. She'd tried so hard to bury those old fears. She thought she had, but every risk he took, every dangerous situation they went through—some not far behind them and still fresh in her mind—brought them back from what she realized was barely a shallow grave. She had unleashed those ghastly fears on him in the worst possible way. Her heartbeat raced out of control and she pressed one hand to her stomach, trying to soothe the knots that had formed there. *What have I done?*

More than ever, she couldn't let him go. Not angry or hurt. She not only needed to put the past to rest, but also to fix the damage she had just inflicted. She wracked her brain for a compromise.

If they wouldn't allow her to be there in an official capacity, she would hole up in a hotel in Amman. Close enough to douse her jitters. Close enough to find a way to make it up to him. A smile crept up her lips when she thought he might not resist staying with her instead of at the military quarters on the base. They'd be able to look into each other's eyes and talk it through in person instead of a faceless chat via VOIP connection.

Reason whispered in her ear that it would do more harm than good to push the matter further at that heated moment, but she ignored it. She stepped into the closet and pulled down her own bag. Unlike Nathan and Hanson, she was certain Trevor would welcome her being there. Setting it on the bed, she moved to the dresser to gather what she'd need.

"What the hell is this?" Trevor's voice was harsh.

She turned to find him glaring at her bag, underwear and socks forgotten in his hands.

"My bag."

"For?" He zeroed his focus on her. His eyes, narrowed to slits, were unyielding. Adrenaline shot through her body.

"I'm taking the first flight to Amman. My visa is still good, I think." She continued to select sensible items for the Jordanian climate. "If not, I can still pull a few tricks out of my hat to get a visa quickly. I'll let you know when I'm there."

A tide of red crept up Trevor's neck before he shook his head.

"No. You are *not*," Trevor replied calmly. Dropping his clothes in his luggage, he picked up her bag and returned it to the closet.

"The hell I'm not." Cassandra stormed to the closet and grabbed the bag. The moment she stepped out, Trevor tore it from her hands and tossed it in again. "Damn it, Trevor." Her voice shook with the uncertainty that sliced through her. "Cut it out."

She turned to retrieve it a third time and gasped when Trevor gripped her elbow, spinning her around to face him. Cassandra's heart rose to her throat. She'd never seen Trevor's eyes flash with anger directed at her as they did in that moment. All marriages had ups and downs, and she'd known the day would come when they wouldn't see eye to eye, but facing the mounting rage in his expression still brought an unexpected wave of trepidation to the surface.

"You're not going, and that's final. Damn it, Cassandra. We just discussed this. You said it yourself. It's too dangerous."

Cassandra scoffed and pulled her arm from his grip. "You're joking, right? Hello? Who whipped *you* into shape? Helped with your marksmanship? Besides, if you acquire footage of informants tied to the hostages or even of Mr. No Face, I can analyze it on the spot. I'm not staying here. Where you go, I go. Partners, right?"

For an instant, a faint light twinkled in the depths of his shadowed eyes and she thought he'd agree with her, but then she noticed the tightening of his jaw, the muscle ticking in its stubborn set.

"Don't fight me on this one, Cassandra Cristina. There is no way in hell you are going on your own." He took a loud deep breath and his eyes softened slightly. "I can't see you hurt again."

Cassandra's control snapped. "Hurt? Me?" She pounded his chest, pushing him back. "The one who sat in comfort and watched *you* take risks last time. Me?" She slammed her palms on his chest again. "The one who had to sit on my hands while *you* were being hunted by a psycho and almost died?"

Trevor reached for her wrists, but she pushed him away, evading his grasp. She turned her back to him. Tears of frustration burned the back of her eyes and she pressed the heels of her palms against them to keep them in. *I will not. I will not.* She willed them not to fall. She hated that show of weakness. How many times had her father told her to suck it up, that tears were a coward's way out? She sucked in and blew out a deep breath. "Fuck!"

His fingers brushed her shoulder and he turned her to him again. "Cassie—"

"I never had a chance. Did I?" Cassandra held his gaze. His eyes said it all. She bit back the anger that squeezed her heart and pushed past him, blindly seeking to put as much distance between them as she could.

"Cassandra!" Trevor's footfall on her heels gave her a burst of speed as she skirted the end of the bed.

Struggling for control, she growled in frustration when Trevor's hand slammed against the door, thwarting her efforts to escape. She turned and found him a breath away, towering over her. She looked up into his eyes, her heart lurched, and she gasped, "Let me out." She pushed against the solid wall of his chest, but he wouldn't budge.

She couldn't breathe, think, or even hold onto her anger with him that close. She needed air, space. She dashed under his arm, but Trevor caught her around her waist, effortlessly carrying and tossing her on the bed, pinning her under his weight.

"Get off me!" She kicked her legs, twisting from side to side. Straddling her hips, he clasped her arms above her head, his hold firm but not hurtful, and locked eyes with her. The determination that shone from them gave her pause. She stilled and eyed him warily.

He held her gaze, his eyes solemn. *"A ghrá,"* he sighed heavily, dropping his chin to his chest. Silence blanketed them, broken only by their heavy breathing and the loud pounding of her own heart in her ears. When she flexed her hands in his grasp, he lifted his head. "If you managed to get to Amman—" he snapped his jaw shut and clenched it, breathing in deeply through his nose as if to center himself before continuing, "—knowing you were there would tear me apart."

Cassandra's heart ached in a way it never had since she'd met Trevor. In the past, she'd had her desires, wants, needs, dictated or ignored. When she'd met him, all that had changed. With Trevor...with Trevor, everything was different. For the first time, she'd felt empowered. Felt she had a purpose. Felt she was loved for who she was. She tightened her fists, digging her fingernails into her palms, but that pain didn't compare to what she saw in his face.

"I can't—" Trevor choked out, "—I can't lose you. I've lost enough." Torment darkened his eyes to black pools. "If you come to Amman, you'll be even more vulnerable than ever before. Western women are often targets for violence in that part of the world. Do you remember the news about the tourists who were attacked with acid not long ago?" Silenced by the raw emotions she saw on his face, she managed a brief nod. "How do you think I'd be able to focus on helping with the case if my head—" he paused, "—and my heart weren't in it because I'd be worried sick that my wife, the woman that makes me who I am, who is and will always be a part of me, was out there without an official cover or protection?" He squeezed his eyes as if even the thought of what could happen to her was physically painful to him.

His words shed new light on the argument, and slowly, understanding filled the void in her mind. The gunshot wound she'd taken in France, the split from her in Russia, big scares he'd endured since their paths had crossed. She recognized that the love and fear entwined in his heart were the same shrouding hers. They both had lost love in the past. They both feared losing it again, because they understood well the pain it would bring in its wake. Although the veil of denial had been lifted from her eyes and she could clearly see his logic—and loved him more for it—she needed him to understand she shared that same worry.

The man was as reckless as a bull in a china shop when the excitement of a challenge took hold of him. He was the yin to her yang, the free spirit to her conservative edge. It was that same recklessness that made him who he was, that completed her. But it also scared her silly. He seemed to take pleasure in making acquaintance and tangoing with danger. She feared the kidnapping had become more than a job, more like a personal crusade the second George mentioned a connection to the case they'd been chasing for so long. Locating the hostages and finding his target's identity had become a priority to him, and that was a recipe for disaster where Trevor was concerned. Cassandra had seen it in the glint of his eyes. She would never in a million years change the enthusiastic way he embraced his causes, but her heart cracked at the thought of what kind of sacrifice it might require from them in the end.

His grasp loosened and he shifted to give her more room. When he spoke again, his voice wavered. "If I let you up, can you promise me you won't storm out?"

She nodded and he let her go. She hesitated before scooting off the bed and moving back to the window, putting some distance between them so she could think clearly. The soft glow of lights from the posts peppering the paths inside St. Stephen's Green sucked her in. Time was against her. Trevor would soon be gone and Cassandra wasn't sure that she knew how to mend the tattered bridge between them. She'd never been good at patching relationships. Nathan and her father were both proof of that.

Snow flurries billowed on the other side of the glass. They were due for a good dusting, something unusual for Dublin, even in the winter. She could remember the first snow they'd gotten in Ireland. She'd dragged Trevor to the park and he'd indulged her, making snow angels with her until she'd turned into a human popsicle. He'd also warmed her up in the privacy of their room.

She let go a heavy sigh and her breath created a wide disc on the glass pane. She watched the circle of condensation recede and increase with each breath she took. Focusing on something so menial and ordinary helped quiet her mind.

She heard Trevor's soft steps as he closed the distance between them and stood behind her, close enough that the heat emanating from his body enveloped her. Her stomach bottomed out when her eyes collided with his in the reflection on the window. Nervous anticipation raked its claws down her back as she held his gaze.

"Cassie…." The more Trevor searched for the right words, the more he realized there were none he could use to express all he felt.

"Yes?"

Trevor watched her jaw tighten. Such a stubborn lass.

"This is a military operation. We have our orders. Nothing I could have said would have changed that, *a ghrá*." His chest constricted with guilt at the relief he felt that she would be home safe. He breathed a sigh of relief when she didn't repel his touch as he rested his hands on her arms.

Cassandra turned to face him. "I understand—"

"I understand—" Trevor paused, surprised and more uncertain than ever as their unfinished sentences hung between them. "You understand?"

"That I have to stay. But that doesn't mean I have to like it."

His parents' disappearance had choked his faith to an ounce of its life. Strangely, when she frowned and turned back to face the window, for the second time in his life he found himself praying for guidance to make it right, to make everything all right again.

"I get it, Cassie. I understand your reasons for wanting to be there and for not wanting *me* there. I *get* it. I get *you*. I know you well enough to see through the tough façade you put up. But you can't blame me for doing my job. At this stage of the game, it's not like I can refuse to help them. But you can't blame me for being relieved that you aren't going to that hellhole either." He paused, searching for the right words and settling on the simple truth. "The mere thought that you could get hurt again or that I could lose you forever is enough to drive me mad. I wouldn't focus on what they need me to do. My focus would be on you. Always you."

Cassandra felt Trevor's eyes boring into her. She returned her gaze to the street and absorbed his words. The sky had turned a dark slate gray matching the darkness in her chest. The intermittent swirl of snowflakes, Tasmanian devils dancing on the sidewalks, did nothing to improve her mood.

"I know." She dropped her eyes and stared at her clenched hands, unable to meet his gaze in the reflective surface. "It'll kill me to sit here wondering if you're okay. Waiting for some word. Any word. Not knowing what's going on out there firsthand." Anguish gripped her heart as she raised her eyes back to his. "Let me be clear. I want to be there with you. Working with you. And if something ever happened to you, I'd want to feel I did all I could to help you; otherwise I'll feel lost. The same way you do about your paren—" Cassandra caught herself. It was too late.

"Oh, fuck." He wrapped his arms around her and pulled her back against his chest.

Cassandra covered his arms with hers and leaned her head back against his shoulder. The ache that set off inside her heart took root and spread through her. She closed her eyes and in the quiet that enshrouded them she heard the rumble of voices and the thumping of feet on the wooden floor above as the men gathered their gear. She blocked it all out. All but Trevor. His arms around her, his warmth pressed against her back.

"Shite, Cassie." Trevor dropped his forehead to the curve of her neck. "I would never willingly make you go through that. *Never.*"

"I know." She nuzzled his temple and inhaled deeply, filling her lungs with his scent, a mix of tea and musk. He'd never doubted her ability to handle herself, even when he feared the outcome. Now it was her turn to pay back his trust with her own.

Cassandra brushed a kiss on his cheek before she span in his arms to face him. She cupped his chin and locked eyes with him. His longish five o'clock shadow abraded her palms. Tears stung the backs of her eyes. The burn of his whiskers on her skin one more thing she'd miss.

"Do you promise me you'll stay away from any walls?" His eyebrows raised a fraction and she saw relief bloom in his eyes. "You and walls don't get along."

The beginning of a smile tipped the corners of his mouth. "Cross my heart." Tugging her closer, he kissed her temple. "I promise. No walls." His lips brushed her cheek. "Scout's honor." He tightened his arms around her as his mouth crushed hers, his tongue sliding across the seal of her lips, demanding access.

Cassandra moaned, overwhelmed by his touch. Being at odds with Trevor was so alien to her; a few minutes of discord felt like an eternity. Reveling in the reconnection and his touch, she allowed him in. His tongue pushed past her lips, plundering her mouth, powerful and demanding. He explored its recesses, then pulled back to trace her lips with whisper-soft kisses as his hands cupped her ass and hauled her tighter against him.

She wrapped her arms around his waist and neck, holding him

snug against her. Acceptance and understanding morphed into basal need. Tears pricked her eyes. She wanted more, had to have more before he was gone for God knew how long.

"Cassie girl," he murmured against her mouth and deepened the kiss, sending electric shocks from her chest to her pulsing clit with each thrust of his tongue. Her nipples ached and tightened into puckered buds, begging for his attention.

Trevor's growing erection swelled between them and desire lit her up from the inside out. She lowered her hand from his waist to the button of his jeans, undid it, and slipped her hand inside, wrapping her fingers around his girth. It thrilled her when his shaft grew even harder in her hand. It never ceased to amaze her how quickly he responded to her touch.

"Hold on," Trevor groaned and pushed away from her, holding her gaze as he pulled her shirt off over her head. He traced the edges of her lacy bra with the tips of his fingers, his nostrils flaring with each heavy inhale and exhale as he did so. His hands slid behind her, unhooked it, then pushed the straps off her shoulders and down her arms. She caught the reflection of her desire burning in his eyes as he dropped his gaze to her breasts. Their little taut tips hardened, anticipating his touch.

His hooded eyes skated across her tummy to the waistband of her jeans. She held her breath and bit her lip when the pads of his fingertips brushed up her hands and followed the path of his gaze to the button. With nimble fingers and her eager help, he had it undone and her pants and undies stripped in no time, leaving her bared to him.

His ragged breath was a match to her own shallow gasps. "So stubborn. So beautiful," he whispered reverently. "So mine."

She was putty in his hands. Cassandra's gaze tracked his every move as he shed his own shirt. The ambient light in the room played over his corded shoulders and arms. She watched how his muscles bunched and flexed as he stripped off his pants. He was breathtaking. Trevor stepped closer and a surge of goosebumps flicked across her when, taking her hand in his, he guided her to their bed. She was more aware of him than ever before. Maybe because she sought to soak in everything there was of him while she had those few stolen moments.

He tugged her onto the bed and knelt on the covers, prompting her to do the same. They sat there, facing each other, eyes speaking for their hearts. She closed hers when he extended his hand and brushed her hair from her cheek with the back of his fingers, fingers that knew how to play her like a fine violin. They continued their exploration, skimming down the valley between her breasts and trailing further across her stomach.

She sucked in a breath when the light touch of his fingertips brushed across the sensitive skin inside her thigh, then stopped its trajectory, detouring playfully across her hip. The ache between her thighs intensified, leaving her squirming with need. She opened her eyes to find him sporting a wide wicked grin.

"Tease," she grumbled jokingly.

Cassandra smiled into his eyes and drew his hand to her breast, pressing his palm against her turgid nipple. Heat suffused his cheeks and grew taut with want. She hissed when he tweaked it and trailed his tongue along her exposed neck.

Trevor traced her curves once again, his fingers making slow and deliberate circles on her supple skin. He enjoyed the sight of the goosebumps that bloomed under his touch. He circled her breast once, twice, before leaning down and covering it with his mouth. He sucked and teased her nipple with his tongue and teeth, dragging gasps of pleasure from her. He repeated the same with the other breast, then blew over the moist skin and watched both dark rosy tips pebble instantly.

"You're mean," she groaned.

"You haven't seen anything yet," he chuckled as he pushed her back against the bed. Instinct might have told her what he had in mind because she eased her thighs apart in invitation. "Antsy?"

"Ver—" She choked on the word when he slipped his finger inside her.

He couldn't peel his eyes away from her face. She was a beautiful woman, but she became absolutely stunning when pleasure overtook her expression. Eyes closed, lips parted, back arched. He loved painting that expression on her face over and over again.

He withdrew his finger and she tightened around it, as if trying to keep him from doing so. She moaned when he thrust it in again, but that time he rubbed her clit in lazy circles with the pad of his thumb, each gentle stroke in sync with the plunge of his finger. He leaned over her and explored the fullness of her lips with his tongue, nipping at the corner of her mouth as she panted into his with each push and pull of his hand, each flutter of his thumb on her swollen nub.

His cock twitched, begging to be surrounded by her heat. With each ripple of her hips, he throbbed to take her fully. Yet there was so much more he wanted to give her before he had to go. He had no right to take her until he'd at least given her far more than he'd received. He trailed kisses from her mouth to the hollow of her neck and farther down, leaving a moist path along the length of her body as he settled between her parted thighs.

She couldn't possibly know how much her taste pleased him, excited him. It didn't matter how many times they made love; her touch, her taste, inebriated him. Each new throaty moan drove him crazy, and that time was no different. He loved basking in the knowledge that he satisfied her every desire. The same way he could expertly decrypt code, he could also read her need from the sway of her hips, from every hitch in her breath. He knew what she wanted, and he was more than happy to give her all of it.

Cassandra raised her head from the bed to look down at him with the sexiest heavy-lidded eyes. He held her gaze as he lowered his mouth to her sex.

"Tell me when you are close," he whispered before he laved her wet folds with his tongue in one long stroke.

He closed his eyes and savored her taste as it exploded on his tongue, the sweet scent of her arousal thrilling him and boosting his own. She cried out and arched her back as he flicked her clit with his tongue before sucking on it. She gasped and shuddered under his mouth's plunder. Her fingers combed through his hair and grasped at it, holding him in place as if afraid he'd pull away. There was no need. He'd remain exactly where he was forever if he could.

"So sweet." He continued his onslaught, alternating nips, sucks, and flicks of his tongue in tandem with the rhythmic thrust of her hips against his mouth.

"So close. Please…don't stop." Desire laced her broken whisper.

"Never." He massaged her slick folds with his fingers and plunged them deep before grazing his teeth across her clit, hurling her over the edge.

"Yes," she hissed, tensing under his hands as she fell apart, rippling and quaking around him. He continued to taunt her with spaced licks and flicks of his tongue on her over-sensitized flesh, making her squirm over and over. A rush of warmth radiated in his chest when she pushed at him. "Enough. You're killing me."

He rolled onto his back and laughed quietly. Her taste lingered on his tongue and a satisfied smile spread his lips. His cock jumped to attention as if telling him it still hadn't had a turn but, as she lay boneless on the bed, he'd happily ignore the demands of his body for longer in favor of doing what he'd just done all over again.

Cassandra lay panting, chest heaving. The pounding of her heart in her ears echoed the power of her mind-blowing orgasm. A satiated languidness clung to her limbs as she turned her head and met his eyes. The satisfied smirk curving his lips made her laugh out loud.

"Proud of yourself, aren't you?"

"Bloody right." He flashed a boyish grin and her heart stalled in her chest. That crooked smile coupled with the thick brogue would spike any sexy-meter.

She chuckled and, crawling over him, braced her hands on the bed, caging him. Unable to resist the unmasked pride displayed in his eyes, she hungrily covered his mouth with hers, tasting her own essence, her saltiness on his lips.

"Two can play that game, Mr. Brennan."

Trevor clamped his hands on her hips and tried to push her off him. "Ready for round two, *a bhean?*"

"I don't think s—"

They both jumped when a thunderous bang sounded at their door.

"Bauer, enough playing house. Move your ass. We leave in thirty." Nathan's voice died away as he moved down the stairs.

Cassandra's mouth dried and her heart revved, more determined than ever to brand Trevor the way he'd just branded her. She pushed against his broad shoulders and sat back on her knees, straddling his hips. "Cassi—"

"Shush." She pressed her finger against his lips. She wasn't ready to say goodbye just yet. Holding eye contact, she leaned forward and kissed his dark brow. She brushed her lips across his cheek and whispered in his ear. "We have unfinished business, husband." A groan rumbled deep in his chest in reply.

She shifted further down his thighs, trailing her lips and tongue across his jaw, down the line of his neck until she reached his tight, hard nipple. His fingers clenched in response, digging into her hips as she scraped her teeth across its hardened tip. She nipped and swirled her tongue around the delicate skin just as he had done to hers. His hips surged and his cock jerked against her stomach.

"Jaysus. It won't take much at the rate you're going."

She raised her eyes and they collided with his hooded ones. "My turn to make you suffer."

His eyes narrowed when she shifted again and began a slow descent to her target, tasting her way down his tight stomach, nipping at the soft skin of his hip, and trailing wet kisses along the inside of his thigh.

He hissed when her hot breath grazed his erection and groaned when she left his straining cock begging for her touch. She inched lower and a shard of desire speared through her as her gaze skimmed over his body. God. She wanted to lick every inch of him, retain every inch in her memories.

Lured by his musky scent, she pushed his knees further apart, settled between them, and, leaning over, traced her tongue along the seam of his sac. The warmth of his tender flesh was intoxicating, and she loved the rough texture of its skin against her tongue as she licked and fondled each ball.

Trevor's fingers dove into her hair and entwined with the strands. Cassandra smiled when he all but growled, "Shite. You'll be the death of me, lass."

She hummed low in her throat and wrapped her fingers around his cock. Its hardness electrified her and sent a wave of passion coursing through her veins. God, he was beautiful. His lean athletic body and muscular thighs gave a whole new meaning to hot hardware. She edged higher and ran her tongue along the bundle of sensitive nerves ringing the underside of his shaft's crown.

"Fuck!" Trevor rasped as she swirled her tongue over his silken skin and teased little pearls of liquid to the surface of the slit before licking them. "Not like this, Cassie."

Before Trevor could stop her, she wrapped her lips around his pulsing flesh and sucked him in a long, drawn-out pull. When she reached the hilt, she reversed the motion, pulling slowly back, caressing the base and length of his shaft with her tongue.

Her throat flexed instinctively around him and he growled out, "No."

Reaching for her, he rolled them on the bed, inverting their positions. Their groans mingled as he drove into her in one smooth motion, consuming her with his need, their need. She shifted her hips and met his thrusts, rocking against him skillfully, searching to match his rhythm. Her heart thumped loud in her ears, almost drowning out the sensual sounds of their lovemaking—the cadenced slap of their sweat-covered skins, the gasped half-moans, the smack of wet lips. They were all powerfully arousing on their own; combined, overwhelmingly so.

Cinching his hand behind her neck, he crushed her mouth with his, kissing and nibbling her lips, swallowing her pants and moans. He released her mouth and stared long and deep into her eyes, communicating an unspoken promise as he thrust deeper, harder, branding her his once again.

She cupped his face and pressed her lips to his. "I love y—" Her breath hitched, and for one heart-stopping moment she felt her whole body engulfed by a rippling heat. It drew her into a whirl of sensations that threw her over the edge again. "Trevor!"

Trevor couldn't hold his release any longer. It flowed through him in an unstoppable wave, drawing everything from him as he poured inside her. Spent, he sagged atop her, burying his face in dark chestnut waves of fanned hair on the bed. The speed of his inhales and exhales matched the beat of his racing heart. He shifted to the side, ready to roll onto his back, but Cassandra wrapped her arms around his chest, stopping him.

"Wait. Not yet," she whispered in his ear.

"I don't want to squish you." Her soft laugh dispersed his worries and he settled into her embrace.

He caressed her exposed skin, brushing lightly along the curve of her breast and waist. As their breaths evened out, his thoughts spun out of control. Closing his eyes, he drew deep breaths to relieve the anxiety churning in his stomach. He'd have to leave shortly. While Nelson would be chomping at the bit to take off, Trevor dreaded the thought of stepping outside of that room, afraid that by leaving after hurriedly patching the hairline cracks in their marriage's foundation, those cracks would splinter into wider gaps. He had to trust his gut, trust that the love they'd found and shared was strong enough to withstand the frustration of being apart once again.

Heavy footsteps crossed the hall toward the stairs, and he knew he couldn't delay their departure any longer. A cold knot formed in his throat as he rolled to his side and pressed his lips to Cassandra's temple. She turned her face to him; she had that distinctive glow about her that made him hate to taint the moment with goodbyes.

"It's time." Her voice didn't waver, her eyes didn't cloud with tears, and that brought him some peace. It was almost as if she knew that if she cried, he would fall apart.

"Yes."

"I'll help you pack." Kissing his chin, she rolled to the edge of the bed and fished her clothes from the floor.

He followed her example and slipped back into his jeans and t-shirt while she did the same. Silently, she helped him pack his clothes while he packed his gadgets, Jack II, the laptop that had replaced his old one destroyed in France, cables, and chargers for everything he carried and then some.

He was checking his mental list for anything he might have forgotten when she set his duffel on the bed beside him.

"A couple of pairs of jeans and a few of your favorite T's. Sweaters, socks, and underwear. Toiletries and a brand new box of teabags. I wasn't sure they would have them there. Put the cup in there too. Just in case. You're on your own for milk and sugar."

He pulled her into his arms and hugged her tight to his chest, placing a kiss on the top of her head.

"Bauer! Hurry the hell up!" Nelson barked. Trevor broke the embrace to grab his bags.

Cassandra followed him downstairs where Nelson and Hanson waited, packed and ready to go. Both men grabbed their own bags and headed down to the foyer, giving her no opportunity for a long farewell, barely time for a brief goodbye.

Hanson walked out first, closely followed by Nelson. Trevor stood by the open door with Cassandra. His grip tightened around the straps of his bags. Desolation burned in his chest.

They watched in heavy silence as Hanson stowed his duffel in the trunk, took the wheel, and turned the engine. Nelson also stuffed his bags in the trunk, leaving it open for him as a hurry-the-hell-up sign before he claimed shotgun. Both men stared at them impatiently from the car.

She wrapped her arms around his chest and tucked her face in the crook of his neck. "Go." The word was in absolute opposition to the tightness with which she held onto him.

She lifted her face to him and he covered her lips—still swollen from his plundering, he noticed—with his hungry mouth. He tightened his grasp on the handles of his bags when the kiss sent the pit of his stomach in a wild swirl. He was certain that if he let go of them and took her in his arms, he'd never leave.

"Oh, come on already!" Nelson's loud grumble startled them.

"Shut up, Nelson," Hanson retorted.

Trevor ignored the two and sought Cassandra's eyes. "I'll make contact as soon as we touch down."

She cupped the sides of his face and looked deep into his eyes. "I love you." She attempted a smile he knew was only for his sake.

"I know." Somehow, it felt right to mimic his favorite scene between Han and Leia right before Han was frozen in carbonite. Trevor felt frozen inside, too.

She brushed her fingertips along his jawline. "Go."

He moved toward the car in a daze, each step felt like he was being hung, drawn, and quartered. He dumped the bags in the trunk and closed it before slipping into the back seat. As Hanson pulled away from the curb, Trevor couldn't stop himself from looking back one last time. When they turned the corner, he dropped his head back against the headrest, eyes shut, trying to ignore the maelstrom of emotions blasting him.

Cassandra watched the sedan's taillights disappear from sight through tear-blurred eyes. Raw ache unfurled in her chest. Numb, she crossed the threshold into the house, closing the door behind her. The sound of the turning bolt echoed in the empty living space.

She reached the first floor with lethargic steps. No music blared from the entertainment unit. No cursing drifted down the stairs from the office. No heavy tread of feet sounded across wooden floorboards. The house, which had been filled with holiday cheer and life only a few days earlier, was an empty shell. The strangeness of it hit her all at once.

The phone shrilled nearby, making her jump. Thinking it to be Trevor, she ran to it. "Hello?"

"Hi, this is Shannon from the Brazen Head." Her heart sunk as the girl continued in an animated tone, "You guys never showed up so I called to see if you wanted me to hold the reservation."

Cassandra frowned. "Reservation?"

The girl paused. "Oh man…was that some sort of surprise? Trevor said he'd drag you out of the house even if he had to carry you on his back. He didn't say you didn't know."

He'd remembered. A warm glow cracked the layer of ice that had chilled her earlier and she smiled at the idea of her stubborn husband dragging her to the pub. "No. It's okay. Trev had to leave on a sudden business trip. He might have forgotten to cancel. Sorry about that."

"It's all right." The girl offered to change the date, but Cassandra declined before hanging up.

Lost in an emotional mayhem, Cassandra made her way to the second floor, where she stood just inside their bedroom door. Their sanctuary. Her heartbeat fluttered erratically as her gaze swept the room. The sight of the rumpled bedcovers knocked the breath from her lungs. The memory of their last moments together—a birthday gift he'd unwittingly given her—sent an intoxicating tingle feathering along her skin, mirroring the path his hands had taken. His scent, fresh and spicy, lingered in the room, torturing her senses. With each bombardment of images—his hitched breath when she reached for him, his warm flesh under her tongue, the deep rumble of his whisper against her ear—the ache intensified.

Their argument played in her head and shame flogged her already-torn conscience. She'd never meant to hurt him. She hadn't been able to think beyond the danger he was flying into. Cassandra rigidly held her tears in check and sucked in a deep breath to center herself. She was in limbo until the guys' boots hit the ground in Jordan. Cassandra shivered and rubbed her arms to ward off the wintry chill wafting from within. Her eyes drifted to the window. The flurries of earlier were sticking. The ground would soon be buried under a layer of snow.

Another shiver snaked up her spine and she blindly reached for a discarded piece of clothing on the chair. As she slipped it over her head, the rich, earthy scent of Trevor's aftershave overwhelmed her. A lump rose to her throat and she swallowed hard. His favorite Aran cable-knit sweater. Bunching the front of the oversized garment in her hands, she buried her nose in it and breathed him in. She squeezed her eyes tight. God, he'd only been gone five minutes and it already felt like a lifetime. The sweater's warmth comforted her, but it would never be the same as having Trevor's arms around her.

Shaking her head, she turned on her heel and crossed the hall to the office to escape more vivid images flooding her mind. The muted TV screen displayed the news; the low hum of computers surreal compared to the bustling activity taking place in that room mere hours earlier.

Cassandra took a deep breath, raised her chin, and boldly walked in. As she approached their desks, she avoided looking at Trevor's and began putting the place back to rights—moving chairs, straightening files, rolling maps. She cleared her desk and finally walked around to his. Her eyes roamed across the surface and the eclectic chaos that reigned supreme. Cables, external drives, and other small equipment mingled with more trivial items like elastic bands, coins, and batteries—lots of batteries. She brushed her fingers over his wireless keyboard. He was always complaining that it ate them like candy. The messy desk was just as he liked it, how he'd left it. It was him. It was all that she had of him in that moment.

His absence washed over her again, shattering the last shreds of her control. She collapsed in his chair and curled into a ball, pulling his sweater tight around her as hot tears, the ones she had held in through the day, slowly found their way down her cheeks.

Chapter Thirteen

Damsel in Distress

𝒯HE EVENING SOUNDS DISRUPTED RACHAEL'S already limited rest. The shuffle of feet outside her door had become habitual at that time of the day, helping her keep track of the routine within the compound. Not today. Each and every sound near her door squeezed the pit of her stomach tighter. Rachael rose to her feet, draped the thin scratchy blanket around her shoulders, and sat in the farthest corner of the room.

She could still feel the heat from the rudimentary lamp shining in her face, the stiffness of the chair she'd been tied to. That had been the first time she'd ever experienced a sense of claustrophobia. Rachael's chest tightened and a lump formed in her throat at reliving the vulnerability she'd experienced under the watch of the men while she recited the words to the camera, the helplessness at understanding their meaning. She wiped the cold sweat beading on her face with numb fingers as her thoughts veered into a dark, bottomless pit. Darker images inhabited it. Images of news stories of the many journalists and civilians who had been in her shoes before they met horrible ends in the desert by the executioner's hand.

She hung her head and cut those thoughts off. She'd been certain that they were going to walk out uninjured. Now she wasn't so sure. Her heart thrummed in her chest and she gripped the blanket tighter. Ignoring her aching body's scream for more rest, she wrapped her arms and the blanket around her knees and focused on the sounds beyond the door.

She knew that at some point, one of the two women who brought her meals and tended her ankle would arrive, bringing her the day's meager allowance.

The younger woman seemed to be about Rachael's age, but she couldn't be certain. The harsh living conditions in the region ate away at its people, aging them faster than their lived years. The older woman reminded Rachael of her own grandmother. She had a friendlier but shy quality to her touch. Her eyes were clouded by cataracts, most likely brought on by age and poor nutrition, a common malady among the Palestinian population to whom basic healthcare was a luxury.

War took years from people in more than the physical sense. It ravaged their health, but also their spirits. Through her father's work as an Israeli Diplomat, she had come to experience the good as well as the bad in the world. They had lived in many peaceful countries, but also in war zones, just like the one in their own backyard.

Her own ideologies had driven her to try to make a difference, but instead she had seen firsthand the effects of territorial conflict, extremism, and ignorance, also the results of unbridled war. There, she had found a bigger web of lies than she could ever have imagined. One that sickened her, but one she had to rely on in her search for those who'd betrayed Phillip's confidence, not only to honor his memory but to free herself from the past.

Rachael sat up and stretched, turning and testing her injured ankle. The homemade cataplasm the women applied to her ankle when they'd brought her food was dark and smelly, but whatever they'd ground together in it worked wonders. Under their care, the sharp pain had subsided to a dull ache and the swelling had gone down to a small lump. She no longer felt the sting of the injury when she put weight on it.

Like clockwork, she heard the jingling of keys outside and the clanking of metal before the door opened revealing the guard and the older woman carrying the tray in her hands. The woman bumped into the imposing guard as he cleared the doorway and she scrambled to save the meal from hitting the floor, but some splashed on the guard's pants and boots.

Fear, stark and vivid, glittered in her eyes as she stared at his pants in horror. "Forgive m—"

"Idiot!" the guard snarled in Arabic. He backhanded the older woman, sending her and the tray's contents flying.

"Leave her alone!" Rachael yelled in her defense.

A cold knot formed in her stomach as Rachael lurched across the floor on her sore ankle and fell to her knees next to the woman. She hissed when Rachael lifted her chin to check her face. Reaching for the edge of her shirt to dab the blood trickling from the woman's mouth, Rachael's breath caught in her throat and pain flared across her scalp when a violent jerk snapped her head back, undoing the *hijab*. She cried out, reaching back to her nape and scratching at the guard's fist twisted into her uncovered hair. Tears flooded her eyes when he pulled her to her feet.

"Meddling American whore." He yanked on her hair, bending her head back until she was arched like a bow and fear left her with a sensation of small insects crawling under her skin. His gaze snared hers and Rachael saw scathing hatred in his eyes.

"Do your worst, coward." She spat the words carelessly, her own anger making her reckless. She knew he didn't understand them, but her tone clearly communicated the anger that burned inside her.

His fingers captured her jaw in a painful grip.

"Don't!" the woman cried out, rising to her feet and pulling at the guard's fingers. He growled low in his chest and shoved her out of the way with a sweep of his arm. His eyes, brimming with icy contempt, never left Rachael's face as he tightened his grip, fingers digging into her tender flesh.

"What is going on here?" The guard's attention snapped to the door.

Rachael almost cried out in relief.

"Nothing." The guard released his grasp and shoved her away from him.

She collapsed to the floor, breathing in shallow, quick gasps. From the man's tone and reaction, she gathered the new arrival wasn't just one of the lowly pawns in that game. The tension between the two men hung like a heavy mist in the air and drew her eyes to them. Her savior stood just inside the door; the guard faced him, his stance spelling defiance.

The man's glance flickered over her. "Khalil ordered she was to remain unharmed."

Rachael stored that little piece of information.

"She's nothing but an infidel whore."

The guard's superior didn't correct him, but his eyes narrowed as if wondering what to do about his contravention. "Go. Leave her alone."

"What does it matter?" he spat. "She will be gone soon." The guard scoffed and exited the room, leaving his words etched in her mind.

Rachael's rescuer picked up the *hijab* from the ground and tossed it at her, then turned to the old woman. "Clean this up and get her food," he ordered in his native language.

The woman nodded, cleared the bulk of the mess as best she could, and, with a grateful parting glance at Rachael, scurried from the room, leaving the two alone in the cell.

"You need to cooperate with us," the man said in heavily accented English. "Your time here is limited. You don't want it to be worse than it needs to be, do you?"

She shook her head and clamped her teeth shut to hold back the rash words that rose in her throat.

"Good." He turned away and, with a last glance back, left the confined space.

When the click of the lock jangled in the room, she let out a deep, shaky breath. Her entire body trembled and her stomach quivered in reaction to the faceoff. She rubbed her arms briskly to ward off the chill, but nothing could warm the ice in her veins or wash the bitter taste from her mouth.

Rachael moved back to the pallet. As she leaned back against the wall, a powerful wave of hope filled her. She hadn't expected the woman to come to her defense, but in doing so, she'd revealed to Rachael she could be open to helping her. Rachael had to find a way to get through to the woman. She'd had it with playing the damsel in distress. She needed to find her own way out of that nightmare.

Chapter Fourteen

Dance with the Devil

HE HINGES CREAKED WHEN KHALIL opened the door. He paused and let his eyes roam over the man sitting at the table. The incandescence of the bulb flaring above his head darkened his features but exposed wrinkles and dirt from days of confinement. He wore the same well-cut suit—minus the jacket—he'd had on the day they had been pulled from their luxury vehicles. The man also carried the same stiffness of entitlement so typical of Americans. The man's hands turned to fists when their eyes met and it was clear to Khalil he was used to commanding and directing, to holding people's lives under his control. Khalil almost scoffed at the thought. So much for control. They all lost that eventually under duress. Even him.

Khalil approached the table and sat across from the prisoner, who glared at him with obvious hatred.

"Why kill them? There was no need." The man's voice bled indignation. "Why?"

Khalil smirked. "Why not?" The man peered at him for a moment and frowned as if he couldn't comprehend the question. His eyes shifted to the guards posted by the door, almost as if expecting them to object to Khalil's actions. Other than a few words, none of his men spoke fluent English, making their conversation somewhat private. "If Americans can shoot first and ask questions later, why can't we do the same?"

"You are insane," the man bit out.

"Am I?" Khalil casually leaned back in his chair and pulled the pocketknife from his belt. With deliberate, slow movements, he opened the blade. The man's eyes locked on the shiny surface and his stance changed to cautious. His reaction was exactly what Khalil wanted. He wanted to show who was in charge and who asked the questions there. He twirled the blade in his hand. "Are you done with the pitiful whining?"

The man's eyes continued to follow Khalil's fluid motion with the knife. "What do you want from me?"

"Information. What do you and your cellmates talk about when we are not around?" Khalil tilted his head, observing the man's reactions. "Do they have any theories about why you are all here?"

The man rolled his eyes and huffed, "No. Of course not."

"What do you and the others talk about then?"

"They're afraid. It's only human. Nobody expected to face the carnage you and your men inflicted," the man spat out contemptuously.

Khalil raised an eyebrow and leaned forward. "You are truly pathetic. Great gains require great sacrifice, great effort." He'd had enough of that fool. He flipped the blade in his hand and stabbed the knife into the table so it stood as a warning. The echo of the impact bounced off the unadorned white walls.

The prisoner narrowed his eyes, unfazed. Khalil almost admired his bravery, but the man didn't deserve it. He shouldn't hold either admiration or appreciation, only hatred for the American.

Khalil still couldn't see how that worthless piece of human garbage would lead them to their objective, but he trusted the *Rasūl* to know the outcome. *Sometimes you must dance with the devil to get what you want.* He sneered at the infidel, but the man held his ground.

"I want to know what they know. If they know. Everything."

"Why would I hide anything?" The man crossed his arms and leaned back against his chair.

"I don't trust you." Khalil remarked matter-of-factly. "Traitors will always be traitors. It doesn't matter that you are helping our cause now. You are still doing it for your own advantage."

"I'm not stupid. I don't trust you either. I know if it wasn't for the *Rasūl's* wishes, we would all have been slaughtered on that highway. You'd claim it was an accident, which I'm certain you've already done to cover up the mess you left there." The man held Khalil's glare with the same disdain and contempt. "Try not to screw up any more. You should have kept them all alive. They're not leverage if they're all in body bags."

"You don't tell me what to do. As you said yourself, accidents can happen." Khalil shrugged and waved his statement off with a flick of his fingers.

"I wonder what the *Rasūl* would think about you fucking up the execution of the plan he went to such extent to put together." The American spoke in fluent Arabic this time, smirking as he rested his arm on the back of his chair.

Khalil's blood chilled. Although he played a crucial part in the plan, Khalil also knew that if he messed up, he would be holding his own death certificate in his hands. The *Rasūl*, he would stop at nothing to achieve his goal.

His expression must have given away his thoughts because the man chuckled. "Glad to see you've come to your senses." He shook his head and exhaled a heavy breath. "I'll keep my eyes and ears open. If any becomes a liability, I'll let you know." He stood and rounded the table toward Khalil. "I can't return unharmed, since you've bloodied the rest of them. You better enjoy it. This is the one and only time you or your men will ever lay a hand on me."

Khalil smiled. He'd take more than simple satisfaction out of bloodying the unbeliever. He stood and grabbed the front of his expensive dress shirt.

"My pleasure." His voice was cold, his knuckles precise as they connected with the man's face.

Chapter Fifteen

Scary Bunch

*N*ATHAN HADN'T BEEN ABLE TO sleep during the first leg of the flight to Jordan. On landing in Germany, the last operators from Hanson's team—those who had been delayed by another engagement and had missed the first transport to the Middle East—joined them for the remainder of the trip. After a short layover, the second leg of their flight began without a hitch.

The manifest included the flight crew, himself, Hanson, Bauer, and the three late arrivals, Cesar "Heinz" Mendes, John "Ranger" Norton, and Neil "Mac" Wallace. Once they boarded the C-130 and secured their luggage, Nathan took a seat beside Mendes and Norton on one side of the plane, while Wallace, Hanson, and Bauer sat across from them.

Nathan crossed his arms over his chest and stretched out his legs once they were safely in the air. The weight of the past four days began to take a toll on him. His stomach rolled uncomfortably and he couldn't determine if it was because of hunger—he hadn't had anything to eat since they'd left the Bauers'—or because the case was slowly eroding his steely attitude.

Nathan's eyes roamed the cavernous fuselage. Nothing read comfort. Light green painted metal mingled with metallic braces and cables in the bare belly of the beast. The center rails had been removed, leaving a much wider gap between the red canvas foldable seats lining both walls and giving them much more room than the usual cramped military troop transport.

Backpacks and duffel bags, their only belongings, hung from hooks above their heads while they sought comfortable spots for the almost five-hour flight. Aside from the human cargo, the C-130 also carried the weekly load of mail to be dropped off in Amman before their short trek to the air base north of the capital. The bulky mail pallet wrapped in heavy-duty cellophane sat in the center far back, closest to the tail ramp.

Nathan leaned his head against the seat's mesh back and considered what they had in store in the days ahead. They'd have a short time to get acclimated while the last details of the assault were put in place. He expected they'd hit the target on day two. The Crew's men already on the ground had been briefed on the target location, and Miller should have already sent additional surveillance footage to their base of operations while they were airborne.

As much as it was essential that they detached themselves from the case to maintain objectivity, Nathan couldn't stop his mind from splitting between Rachael's and Cassandra's faces, both fear-stricken and solemn.

The knot in the pit of his stomach tightened. Bauer, who sat directly across from him, hadn't fared much better since they'd left his house. He'd spent the flight to Ramstein in silence. Nathan's guilt grated on him.

A couple of hours into the flight, there was still no change in

Bauer's disposition. Nathan raised his voice above the hum of the engine and prodded him.

"Are you in the game?"

Bauer looked at him with a distant expression, as if he hadn't heard the question, but within seconds Nathan saw the usual sarcasm flare in his eyes. Bauer raised his eyebrow and scoffed.

"Of course I am." He then closed his eyes and let his head fall back.

"You don't look like it."

Bauer straightened in his seat, irritation flooding his eyes when he fixed his gaze on Nathan again. "What the fuck do you want me to say, Nelson?" His belligerent tone matched his humorless smirk. "That I'm bloody happy to be away from my wife again? Just for the record, I'm not."

Heat suffused Nathan's cheeks at the comment. "It's not my fault you and Miller have a reputation that garnered attention from the upper clout. Besides, you'd be on this flight regardless of who was running the show. Don't worry," he drawled with distinct mockery, "we'll make sure you get back to your wife in one piece." He lowered his voice and muttered to himself. "Lord knows you two can't be apart. Freakin' rabbits."

He cast Nathan a dark look through narrowed eyes. "Seriously? Are you that dense? Is that what you think? That we're together only because we enjoy a decent round of sex?" Bauer's question, delivered with a hint of admonition, stunned Nathan into silence.

He wanted to shout "Fuck, yes," but in reality, it wouldn't be the truth. He'd seen the emotions playing on both of their faces in Russia and again during his short stay in their home. Nathan recognized there was more to their relationship than simple lust. Bauer shook his head and glared at him with stern, reproving eyes. That legendary Irish temper Nathan had heard so much about had just kicked up a notch. He watched as Bauer's hands curled into tight fists. Nathan tensed, ready for his onslaught, but just as quickly as his temper had flared, Bauer's expression morphed into pity and his stance relaxed.

"There are three types of physical satisfaction." Bauer lifted his hand and counted on his fingers, explaining in the same tone he would have used with a child, "Sex, fuck, and love. You can have sex with just about anyone; you can have an exceptionally good fuck with someone you enjoy being with and even better if it's someone you love; but you only make love with that one person who makes you whole."

As simplistic as his definition was, it explained why he'd felt more hollow after every sexual encounter and relationship he'd had. Nathan met Bauer's gaze and his inner dialogue brought up memories that made him uncomfortably aware of his mistakes. Cassandra. That single night had weighed even heavier on his conscience because of the events that preceded it and, to some extent, caused it to happen.

Bauer paused, as if waiting for what he'd said to sink in, then drove it home once more. "I love Cassandra. I miss being with her because she makes me a better man."

His words seeped insidiously into Nathan's mind and hurled him back in time. To a time when he'd felt at the wheel of his own life, captain of his destiny. But instead, it had abruptly veered out of control toward a cliff. Life had given him few options then. Jump off or turn around and endure the rough terrain. If there was one thing his upbringing had taught him, it was that failure was a part of life, pain was fleeting, and quitting was permanent. He wasn't a quitter. The same way he'd plowed through in the past, he'd do it again. He'd been raised to be a fighter, and he would use all he'd learned and all the assets he'd acquired over the years to bring the case to a close.

Trevor took notice of the unsettled emotions in Nelson's eyes. For a split second he expected Nelson to apologize, but snapped back to his stiff stance when Hanson, who had been so quiet in the seat beside him Trevor could've sworn he'd been asleep, spoke up.

"She's better off back home, Bauer," he reasoned in a strangely comforting tone. "She doesn't need to be in that place. The carnage we see in those places...." He didn't need to complete the sentence to communicate its entire meaning.

Trevor's mind had made peace with the decision to leave her in the safety of their home the moment the directive had been delivered. Yet his heart didn't see things the same way.

"I know." He exhaled a deep breath. "Doesn't make it any easier, though."

"She's safe," Nathan blurted out, and Trevor flicked his gaze back to him, frowning at the flash of emotion he found in his eyes. "Believe me. You don't want to feel what it's like seeing her in hostile hands."

Trevor cocked his head. Even though discord still ebbed like a heavy cloak over them, they'd been able to hold a somewhat civil conversation without jumping down each other's throats. Maybe Cassandra had a valid point when she'd suggested he try to see Nelson's good side. Up until that moment, he hadn't even considered Nelson had one. He'd noticed something was out of whack when Nelson had arrived at his doorstep, but to him the man always felt like an unpinned grenade on the best of days. He'd written it off as his normal Hulkish attitude.

The more he thought about it though, things just didn't jive. But before he could ask questions, Nelson diverted his gaze as if he'd revealed more than he'd like. The moment to do some digging stole away. Unable to sleep in the uncomfortable military transport,

Trevor sought a distraction.

"How is it? I mean, living on the edge twenty-four seven," he asked Hanson, who didn't seem to miss much of anything. Trevor didn't know if the man didn't sleep because he was tuned into the exchange or because he just couldn't.

Trevor had done a bit of research and unearthed some crazy information about the 8th Special Warfare Logistics Group, including a list of high-profile operations in which they'd been involved. It was mind boggling. The 8th's striking uniqueness came from being the only USSOCOM group that recruited from all branches of the military—Airforce, Army, and Navy—to form a cohesive team of top operators. Those who passed the grueling selection were proficient in any environment—in the air, water, and on earth—any climate. Their all-encompassing ability also gave them the nickname the AWE Crew, which they preferred to the unit's formal designation.

"It's wild, man." A faint smile curved Hanson's lips. He paused, as if searching for words to describe it. "Before I joined the Navy, I didn't think I could be good at anything. Enlisting was my escape. But I excelled through every challenge in BUD/S and then SQT. That's when I realized I'd found my calling."

He had a good idea of what BUD/S—the gruelling basic training program all aspiring Navy SEALs had to complete successfully before they could move on to further qualification training to become a SEAL—entailed. He'd watched a documentary, fittingly entitled *Hell Week*, on the subject. The things those guys went through to earn their tridents made him cringe. The men who completed the program were a few of a kind. Steel-coated determination, brains, and brawn combined into one powerful weapon; yet they were still human, susceptible to injury and death like any other.

"Are you ever afraid you'll die without saying a proper goodbye to those you love?"

A shadow crossed Hanson's eyes. "I have no one to say goodbye to. It works for me," he shrugged, but Trevor heard the buried sorrow in that nonchalant statement. It took a special kind of man to not be shaken when asked to name their pallbearers as part of their sign-up for the job.

Disconcerted by the sudden silence growing between then, Trevor diverted the conversation to safe ground. "How confident are you that the team can deploy this in such a short time?"

"The Crew only recruits the cream of the crop. We are as prepared as a team can be." Hanson's confidence in his team was unwavering and fanned Trevor's own. "Plus, we've done this sort of thing several times. Right up our alley. It's muscle memory now."

"I can only imagine." Trevor observed a twitch in Hanson's jaw. His calm demeanor couldn't quite conceal his restlessness. "I'm sure you're glad we are heading to Jordan. It's obvious you'd rather be in the action than watching things from the distance."

"The day will come when I'll be overseeing from the sidelines." Hanson's mouth twisted in a grim smile. "Until then, I'm with my men all the way. Might as well enjoy the fun while I can. Watching the action instead of being a part of it is the downside of moving up the ranks, I guess."

"Or a sign you're getting old." Trevor couldn't contain the humorous jab.

Hanson guffawed. "I'm not that much older than you." His smile grew wider. "Just well worn."

"Too much action?"

"Oh, yeah. Women. They wear the hell of out me."

Trevor stared at him a moment then burst out laughing, shaking his head. "Right."

"I'm no expert on relationships," Hanson chuckled, but the humor never reached his eyes. "Not really fit for the long-term thing like you."

"I didn't think I was either. That was until Cassie came along. Now I can't see myself growing old without her."

"On that note, sorry she was pissed, man." Genuine apology shone in Hanson's gaze. "It's just how things go. If she still had that official job with the Agency, we could probably have fudged an excuse to bring her, but to be honest, I wouldn't want her there anyway."

"Point taken."

"I'm sure that after what? A year of marriage? You've become an expert in finding ways to appease her," Hanson snickered. "You'll need it, considering you ditched her right after the holidays." He grinned widely, his meaning clear by the raised eyebrows and wicked gleam in his eyes. "Women have this thing about special dates. Just make sure you're extra thoughtful when you get back. Flowers, wine. You're golden."

A niggling dread overtook Trevor and he fished his phone out of his pocket in a rush. With the commotion of the day and their hasty departure, he hadn't checked his messages since he'd lost signal shortly after boarding the jet to Germany. When he unlocked his screen, the missed calls alert popup glared at him. One from Stephan, the other from the Brazen Head.

"Fuck me," the curse escaped through gritted teeth.

Hanson frowned at him. "What's up?"

"As if I didn't feel already bad enough." Trevor raked his hair with his fingers while a fist squeezed his heart tighter than before.

His reaction got Nelson's attention. "What's going on? Got anything from Miller?"

"Shite. No." Trevor scrubbed a hand across his jaw. "Cassie's birthday. It was yesterday." He sighed heavily, numbly staring at his cell's screen where the dinner reminder mocked him in big letters.

"Oh, shit. You are hosed, buddy." Hanson's words did nothing to soothe his churning stomach.

Trevor almost laughed when he saw the embarrassed look on Nelson's face. "At least I'm not alone."

A flush crept across Nelson's cheeks. "Yes, but it's not the same. I'm not married to her. You are."

Nathan was right. He was in trouble. Big trouble. Trevor hunched back against the canvas mesh seat and took a deep breath, seeking comfort in silence, but found none. His wool jacket wasn't enough to warm him. The dinner date was only part of the surprise. He'd been waiting forever to see the sparkle in her eyes and hear the excitement in her voice when she saw the tickets to London. He'd never live that whale of a fail down. He was sure of it.

THE SUN HUNG high in the sky when they stepped out of the C-130 onto the tarmac at King Hussein Air Base. Trevor squinted against the brightness reflecting off the sandy landscape and spotted the two Humvees on the tarmac waiting to transport the newly arrived to their forward base of operations, the buildings housing the Jordanian Air Academy and the American air base. Two uniformed soldiers greeted the Crew men with tight handshakes and slaps on the backs as they cleared the ramp. It was clear they were all part of the same brotherhood.

"Trevor Bauer, Agent Nathan Nelson," Hanson introduced the two once the greetings subsided, "I'd like you to meet Michael Wright. The Reaper. He's the meanest tactical knife fighter I've ever served with. He named his favorite blade 'Scythe'—hence the nickname." They exchanged curt nods and Hanson turned to the other man. "This here is Cameron Acer. We call him Ace, not just because of his last name. The man can hit the target over two thousand yards away. He's also my second-in-command." Hanson slapped Acer's shoulder comradely.

Trevor shook hands with the special operator. He was surprised to see his clean-shaven jaw and crisp clothes instead of the apparently popular man-cave style sported by a number of them. It screamed career military.

Acer flashed an easy smile. "You must be the geek I've heard so much about." He turned to Nelson and nodded. "Special Agent. Now that we've got introductions out of the way, let's roll."

Although winters in the Middle East didn't compare with the extreme low temperatures in parts of Europe and North America, they weren't balmy either—unless you were in a vehicle, protected from the elements, and in direct sunlight. It could get stifling, as they discovered when they all jumped in the Humvees for the quick trip to the main building housing their temporary base of operations.

As soon as they had stowed their belongings into the assigned quarters, they were immediately directed to the room that had been converted for use as operations control. After a brief introduction and a few handshakes, Hanson led the way to the room.

Trevor studied the men in front of him. Scary bunch. If they were in a bar and wearing leather, they could easily pass for a biker gang. Only a few were sort of clean shaven, with the vast majority having opted to grow beards and sporting wild tattoos like Hanson's. Although they all wore the standard-issue camo pants and t-shirts and their appearances varied greatly—from Acer's blond Californian surfer to Mendes's mellow Hispanic lover to Ranger's lethal build wrapped in proud dark skin—they all held an air of unwavering confidence.

Hanson stood in front of the rows of chairs occupied by the Crew's men and cleared his throat to get their attention.

"Listen up! For those who missed the intro earlier, this is Agent Nathan Nelson, CIA. He'll be overseeing Operation Argus Strike." Hanson nodded at Nelson and then at Trevor. "This is Trevor Bauer. He's the NSA specialist who'll be supporting the mission from a communications standpoint. I know most of you have already received some information, but since some were not present when the green light came through, we'll go over everything again and again until we have the raid's best-case scenario and contingencies down."

"While we're still collecting and processing intelligence, we have identified a place of interest. The intel points at three occupants. We have not yet been able to confirm or deny if there are weapons in the house. Hope for the best, but expect the worst, as always. Although we are almost one hundred percent sure the hostages are not at the target location, we have reason to believe we'll find critical information that can lead us to them."

Norton, one of the soldiers who had met them at Ramstein, raised his hand. "What's the probability that we might not find anything of use?"

Trevor took the question when Hanson looked pointedly at him. "About fifty-fifty."

An air of incredulity covered Norton's face and was mirrored on the others'. "Are you serious? We're going in with such odds?"

Nelson shifted forward, becoming the focus of their attention. "This is merely an intelligence-retrieval operation. We want computer equipment, documents, scraps of paper, any photos you may find. The goal is to seize the equipment used to upload the kidnappers' broadcast and record any information we can uncover from the residents.

Wright raised his hand. "How many teams?"

Hanson shuffled the papers then directed his gaze at him. "Two standard six-man teams. Infil via air. We have two stealth Black Hawks scheduled to arrive from Afghanistan this evening to support the operation. For the purposes of this mission, we'll call them Eagle One and Eagle Two. Bravo Team, in charge of the recon mission, will be on Eagle One. Eagle Two carrying Delta Team will be on standby a few clicks away in case Bravo Team runs into hostile fire." Hanson threw a mocking look at one of the team members. "But let's try not to repeat that snafu in Afghanistan."

The whole group laughed at what was clearly an inside joke. Hanson proceeded with the briefing, answering technical questions about the raid and contingencies. "The only thing we need to be aware of right now is that there will be a command net communication blackout once we're in. It'll be short. A few minutes and we're back in business. During that window, all video and audio communication with Command will be severed. Troop net will be up as usual."

Hanson answered a few questions that popped up and, once he finished his briefing, dismissed the men. "Go get some shuteye." Trevor had learned that the majority of the team's missions were nocturnal and the operators often traded day for night in preparation for the activities. "We should have more intel in a few hours."

As the bulk of the men dispersed toward their quarters, Trevor approached the small group gathered around Hanson. Acer, whose pensive expression and deep frown hadn't eased since the beginning of the briefing, asked, "What if the materials we bring back don't reveal their location?"

"Bauer and Miller are still working on collecting more intelligence, but whatever we find will be another link in the chain. As it stands, this location is the only solid connection we have to the hostages. It's not a hundred percent, but it's the closest we've got and the clock is ticking," Nelson countered. His frown grew as if he wasn't entirely comfortable with the idea himself.

"We're following breadcrumbs we found along the way in the investigation. If we're lucky, we might hit the jackpot with what you bring back," Trevor added.

Acer's doubt was evident. He was the planner, the strategist in the group. He, like Cassandra, wanted all the information to be nice and tidy before they made a move. Trevor, on the other hand, wasn't too squeamish about taking high risks.

"With all this breadcrumb talk, it's like we have Hansel and Gretel to show us the way. What if we don't hit the jackpot?"

Trevor cocked his head, contemplating Acer's words. A lightbulb lit up with an idea, a crazy one, and he evaluated its merit. After a moment, he realized they were all looking at him, expecting an answer.

"Huh, we'll have to play it by ear." The answer didn't seem to draw reassurance from any of them, but it was all he had—at least until he could pass his idea by George.

George had always been the one who saw his crazy moves for the brilliance they carried. He'd be levelheaded enough to assess its worth without bias, even if he worried that it could get them into more trouble.

"Can you show me your communications room? I need to set up shop."

Not knowing the plan swirling in Trevor's mind, Hanson nodded. "Ace will show you."

The adrenaline of the hunt was a drug in Trevor's veins, kicking excitement through him. His pulse coursed faster and he smiled to himself. "Brilliant. Let's get the party started."

ONCE TREVOR WAS able to make himself a little home away from home, it had only taken an email to have George up and running in no time. He'd been camped out in his office at Cryptocity scouring intercepts since he'd found the link to Waldo.

He shot his idea to George and, while he waited for his assessment, Trevor continuously watched the activity around him. The Middle East was a perennial hot cauldron, and from time to time it erupted with the force of a dormant volcano. As it was, the men and women based in Jordan were prepared for another insurgent uprising in the surrounding region. US Intelligence had just made public new threats they'd had under watch for a while.

His foot tapped under the desk almost by its own volition as he waited for George's return. Trevor glanced over his shoulder to make sure nobody was close enough to read their text conversation on screen, and prodded George.

Are you alive?

A beep alerted him to an incoming message. *I'm here. And you are as impatient as usual.*

Trevor ignored the blatant scorn. *What's your take on it?*

I think it might work. One thing is certain. This case stinks. Trevor could almost picture the frown puckering George's forehead.

Tell me about it.

So, what do we have?

They had always brainstormed a case that way, be it in person or by text, to help spark ideas. Trevor began listing what they knew.

1 – Waldo's buddy is connected to the kidnapping somehow. Which can mean Waldo is back. Waldo has been off the radar for a while. Why surface now??

2 – Details of the route were classified as Secret. We found no chatter to indicate anything different.

3 – The video upload has an identifiable source.

All put together can mean only two scenarios:

A: Whoever took them is an amateur, maybe trying to strike out on his own, branch out, and got lucky with his first catch.

B: Waldo is the mastermind behind it and we have a mole on our hands.

If A= =true it might mean Waldo's buddy has made the first mistake since we got on his case. We can only hope he'll make many more.

If B= =true then we're SOL because that means well organized and deadly.

Knowing of the connection with Waldo and the fact that he's been successful in hiding his identity for years, I'm hedging our chances of finding a link from digital communications directly to him between zero and none. We need better tricks to foil this one. Which brings us to my idea.

Shit. George's only retort left Trevor with a sinkhole for stomach. After a few moments of silence, George replied, *With what we have right now, I'd say we go for it. It might be the only way to track them.*

Relief swept over him. It was nice having George's corroboration. *Don't think we have any other option.*

Are you sure you don't want to bring the others in?

And have them try to clear it with Washington all over again? Trevor frowned and considered the time they would lose on a new round of authorizations. From an operations point of view, there would be no critical changes that would compromise their team's safety. All of the contingencies had been explored. *That would mean sitting on it for days again.* The clearance they already had covered that; therefore, there was no point in delaying the raid, especially when they didn't have a lot of time to squander on politics. *I want out of here as much as the others, George. I'm pretty damn sure the hostages would agree with me. Plus, how do we know if we can trust all of them? We don't know how deep this runs.*

You are nuts. But your gut never failed you or us before and your ideas, although unconventional, get the job done. I'm in.

Can you start visual surveillance ASAP?

Yep. Everything was already set to go for the op. Only need to widen the window. We should be good to go by tomorrow night.

Don't "should" me, George.

Have I ever let you down? By the way, you owe me big time.

I know. Keep me posted on the other signals too.

Will do.

Trevor stared blindly at the screen once the connection ended.

"Are those signals tied to the phones you're tracking?" Nelson's voice boomed immediately behind him, jerking him from his introspection and sending a surge of adrenaline through his veins.

Trevor closed the chat window before he spun in his chair to face him. Nelson towered over him, arms crossed over his chest, sporting a deep frown. It had been Nelson's default expression since the first time they'd crossed paths. The guy didn't seem to know how to relax and have a good laugh.

"Yes. He'll keep me posted if something comes up."

"I saw that."

Trevor paused; the confrontational tone in Nelson's voice rubbed him the wrong way. His temper warmed up.

"Spying on me, Nelson?"

"Do I need to?"

"Not if you want results. And I do believe you want them." Nelson stiffened even more than his usual stick-in-the-ass posture—if that was even possible. Trevor knew he'd pushed the right button.

"We both know we all need results, and fast. The deadline is looming over us." Nelson's frown grew deeper as he stared him in the eye.

"Even if we all put one hundred and ten percent into this mission, there may be casualties. We all know that. They know that. The nature of the beast."

Trevor watched Nelson's expression closely. He noticed the sudden tick under his eye and the blanching of his skin, making him increasingly curious to what had the power to shake Nelson that way. One more reason to dig deeper, start further back in time. He might have to add a few high profile government servers to his list of hacked systems.

"Let's aim at bringing them all home alive," Nelson snapped, but his voice was devoid of its usual confidence.

"If you got your head out of your ass and told me the truth, things would be much easier."

Nathan's heart sunk. His CIA file should have been sealed. Only those with the highest clearance had access to it. And as for the personal side of his life, that was a closed book, one sealed in his chest and mind a long time ago. But Bauer was handy with a computer. What if he had dug into it? Nathan's mind scrambled through his history, looking for any possible exposed parts that Bauer could have inadvertently accessed during the course of his data mining.

Anger bubbled up inside him and spiraled out of control at the thought that Bauer had snooped into his personal life. He lunged. Grabbing Bauer by the front of his t-shirt, he dragged him from the chair and pinned him by the throat against the wall.

"Do your job." He leaned in closer. "And keep your nose out of my business."

The personnel in the room froze in place like deer in the headlights, observing the action, unsure how to handle the two non-military guys about to get into a fist fight.

Bauer clutched his wrist and pushed back. His eyes fired with rage, and Nathan could almost see the wheels turning in his head.

"Maybe you should practice what you preach, Nelson." For a moment, Nathan couldn't determine if Bauer was referring to the case or something of a more personal nature.

He pushed Nathan off him at the same time Hanson's voice rang behind them.

"What the fuck is going on here?" Hanson sounded baffled and pissed off at the same time.

Nathan almost laughed as he released his grip on Bauer's shirt.

"Nothing." He kept direct eye contact with Bauer and lowered his voice. "Do your part and we'll all be happy. How about that?" Nathan raised an eyebrow when Bauer's hands balled into fists.

"Fine with me. But if you're concealing anything from us," Bauer's tone challenged him once again, "any vital piece of information that could have facilitated the operation, I'll have your ass on a platter."

Hanson moved closer, almost as if expecting to have to extricate the two. Nathan was tempted to have a go at some good old-fashioned use of pent-up energy, but they couldn't waste any more time. Besides, Bauer's warning was inconsequential. Nothing regarding Nathan's connection to Rachael was relevant to the case. The fact that she was more than just another US citizen to him didn't affect the mission in any way. He was there to do his job and he'd do it well, regardless of whom they were rescuing from enemy hands. At least, that's what his head told him. His heart sang a different song. A much different one.

Nathan took a step back and straightened his suit. "You won't, Bauer. Let's focus on the job."

Bauer smoothed his shirt and walked back to take his seat. He turned his attention to the screen and began typing, ignoring both Nathan and Hanson.

Hanson's frown deepened and his eyes bounced between the two, but he didn't say a word. Good. Nathan didn't need a new inquest. His hackles were raised high enough.

"Anything on the phone sigs, you tell us," Hanson directed at Bauer.

"Copy. Looking forward to my first real-live operation. With the live radio and night vision goggles' footage, this will feel like playing one of my favorite games." Bauer's almost morbid excitement was evident in his tone.

"You two should get some shuteye. We all should. We'll need to be in top shape to pull this off." Hanson didn't need to add that the days ahead didn't promise to bring much sleep.

Chapter Sixteen

Two Men

ACHAEL SAT CROSS-LEGGED ON THE thin sleeping pallet, eyes lost on the whirls of dust hitching a ride on the rays of afternoon sunlight. She was thankful for the small opening in the wall, typical of older buildings in the region. It could be worse. She could have been imprisoned underground without even specks of dust to entertain her. She would have gone crazy by now. Three days had slipped by since her grand video performance. Three days she'd been living with the knowledge that their lives could be ticking down with the clock.

She had spent that time bouncing between shock and denial, divided between hopelessness and the drive to do something to save herself and the others, no matter the cost. She just couldn't accept that time was running out, and with it, her window of opportunity to close Phillip's case. Try as hard as she could, she still couldn't shake the roll in her stomach and the tightness in her chest when his name and the reason she was there surfaced in her mind.

Phillip.

The floodgates opened again, drowning her in a memory reel of her life's choices.

Phillip's image broke free and flashes of their time together came in bright bursts. Blue skies, the sweet fragrance of marigolds in the park, Phillip down on his knee. The day he'd proposed to her, she'd thought life couldn't get any better. Phillip, seven years her senior, was larger than life, mature, worldly, and caring. The perfect partner. He'd swept her off her feet with his confident support of her choices, something she'd never received from her parents. Particularly not from her father. She didn't hesitate to say yes. They had been sharing a flat in London for a year. Marriage had been the logical progression of the comfortable relationship they had. There was no doubt in her mind that they should be married.

Shortly after they'd announced their engagement, Phillip had introduced her to Nathan. Phillip had invited Nathan for dinner at a favorite restaurant of theirs, hoping to ask him to be his best man. The news surprised Rachael, since Phillip hadn't known Nathan for that long, but she assumed that if Phillip regarded him so highly, spoke of him so fondly, Nathan must be worth that honor. She was sitting at the restaurant bar waiting while Phillip checked on their table when she'd seen him for the first time. The memory steam-rolled through her mind.

"Is this seat taken?"

The smooth masculine voice edged with control snapped her from her musings. She turned to respond and froze on the spot. Her heart raced and heat rose to her temples. Rachael stared at the man, her tongue tied in knots. She could barely voice her reply.

"No. It isn't."

He had to be at least six-two and didn't look much older than her. His black suit jacket and black slacks were pristine and creased to military perfection. Her fingers itched to run over his buzz cut and feel it tickling her palms. The thought scared and surprised her. She tightened her hand around her glass to keep from acting on that crazy impulse, unsure of the emotions bombarding her from all sides.

He sat at the bar and signaled the bartender. "The usual."

The heat radiating from his body sent a scattering of goosebumps across her skin. Distracted by the effect and without thinking, she blurted, "Oh, you're a regular?"

He reached for the ale the bartender set in front of him. His steady gaze traveled over her face then dropped to her lips before returning to search her eyes. The corners of his mouth tipped in an easy smile.

"A temporary regular. A friend introduced me to the place."

"I see." Butterflies fluttered in her chest as she listened to his low chuckle. Her own smile faded under the intense gleam of interest in his green gaze.

After what seemed like a lifetime, he broke eye contact and took a large gulp from the glass.

Rachael dropped her gaze to her own drink, stunned at her visceral reaction to a total stranger.

Out of the corner of her eye, she saw him turn to face her. "Are you here alo—?"

"Nathan. There you are, mate." Phillip pulled Nathan into a hug and thumped his back.

Rachael's stomach turned. The stranger she'd been conversing with was the man Phillip considered a friend. No, more like a brother.

"Have you introduced yourself to Rachael?"

"No. Where is she? His eyes searched over Phillip's shoulder.

"You're sitting right next to her. Rachael, this is the friend I was telling you about, Nathan Nelson."

Nathan's eyes widened and she could have sworn disappointment had skated through them before all the fire that had burned in them *disappeared behind a cold wall of pleasantries.*

"Nice to finally meet you. Phillip has told me so much about you."
He reached for her hand and placed a soft kiss on her cheek in greeting.

That night had marked the beginning of many she had spent in his company, uncomfortably aware of his presence. Nathan had never evoked the same warm and comfortable feeling she felt for Phillip. Nathan prompted a raw response, one she had initially tried to avoid. Unfortunately, unaware of her conflicting emotions, Phillip took his self-appointed older brother role to Nathan very seriously. He made a point of including him in outings or inviting him over for tea or drinks. Gradually, she began to give in to the emotional trepidation she got when Nathan was around. Deep inside, she was looking for an explanation for the difference, for why she didn't feel the same way about the man she was about to marry.

While Phillip had always felt safe, Nathan felt unbridled under all that control of his. Like standing at the edge of an abyss, unable to take that last step. With Phillip, she'd been content to sit for hours talking, laughing, sharing a quiet evening. When she had looked at Nathan, she had visions of seeking lips, bodies crashing in heated embrace, moans mingling in the midnight breeze. The more she knew about him, the more she saw of him, the more he puzzled her. Nathan's honor, strength, and vulnerability became apparent when she saw his reaction to his brother's passing. His pain made her own heart ache and compelled her to soothe him.

An innocent hug flipped it all upside down. From that day on, she noticed he avoided her at all cost, making her well aware that she might have worn her confused feelings on her sleeve. She'd panicked. What was she thinking? She was engaged to a wonderful man who would give his life for her, who had supported her, and yet, she was taken with his friend? Shame and guilt had racked her, shocking her into setting her head straight once and for all.

When Nathan's internship had ended and he'd returned home, she'd welcomed the time away from him, time to overcome the doubts—but they'd continued to plague her even in his absence. Her gut told her she was making a mistake, told her that it wasn't fair to Phillip. She was swimming against a current of emotions, drowning in doubt. The strongest current had pulled her toward a life of certainty with Phillip and away from the embers she'd glimpsed in Nathan's eyes a few times in the past.

Breaking off the engagement was not an option. She'd made a commitment to Phillip when she'd said yes, and she intended to honor every letter of that yes. Besides, with the involvement of their parents in the big day, everything had already been taken care of. Dress, invitations, catering…. She would marry Phillip. The feelings she'd had for him had not changed. She still admired him for the honorable man he was, even if there was no fire ravaging her insides when she thought of him. Rachael could only hope that the question of who she would have been with had she met Nathan first stopped pestering her along the way.

That question had been answered when she ended up having to meet Nathan at the airport when he returned for the ceremony. While she'd waited for Nathan's flight to arrive, she'd stood in the crowded airport, reassuring herself it had all been just a silly crush she'd long smothered. But when he'd strode into the waiting area, the instant attraction she'd experienced before and that had died down while he'd been away flared to life once again. She could swear she saw the same heat flare in his eyes when he'd stumbled into her and wrapped her in his strong arms to break her fall. But if they had been there, he'd buried them well once they had stood face to face.

Something had changed him during the few months he'd been gone. The cold walls of indifference he'd built after their introduction appeared taller, thicker. The wide berth he'd given her had finally proved that she'd been right in proceeding with the wedding. He'd helped solidify her decision.

Walking down the aisle toward the two men that had impacted her emotions so differently had been one of the hardest things she'd done in her life. While she may not have felt the earth move under Phillip's touch, she did care for him deeply. She'd poured all she had into their marriage, but it hadn't been enough.

As the memory faded, Rachael released a shaky breath. She had never voiced it, but somehow Phillip had recognized that their marriage had grown into a deep caring between friends, lacking the unbridled passion shared by lovers. He'd never held her emotions against her.

A lump swelled in her throat. She knew that she'd disappointed him, even though he'd never questioned her. She wished with all her heart that he'd been the one, that his kisses made her forget who she was, made her want to lose herself in him, but the spark had died. If she were to be honest with herself, she had to admit that it had never really been there. Not like she was sure it would have been with the one man who had hovered on the fringes of her thoughts all those years.

Pulling her knees closer to her chest, Rachael rested her forehead on them. After Phillip's murder, she couldn't go back to her work. Her head hadn't been in the game, and she'd been concerned she'd become a liability. The idea of staying in the flat they had shared had been too painful, so she'd holed up with her parents in California to regroup.

Little did she know that California had its own little surprise in store for her, in the form of the man that had fluttered in and out of her thoughts over the years. Nathan. She'd been surprised to get his call asking if he could stop by. He had dropped off the face of the earth after she and Phillip had married. She hadn't had any contact, except to receive a clipped note of condolence the day of Phillip's memorial.

When they'd faced each other, the part of her that had still harbored feelings for him had wanted to hug him, soothe away the sorrow she'd seen shadowing his eyes. A bitter taste coated her tongue and her heartbeat revved as anger radiated across her chest at the memory of the last time they had crossed paths. *"I hate you...I never want to see you again."*

Those words still burned on her lips. Words she'd used to cut Nathan as deeply as he'd cut her. It hadn't been the reunion she'd expected.

She dropped her eyes to the gold band gracing her left hand. Rachael's heart lurched as it always did when Nathan burrowed into her consciousness. The dreaded question popped out again. How different would her life have been if she'd met Nathan first? Would that spark have grown into a wildfire over the years? She would never know.

As he'd explained the reason for his visit, the warrior part of her had wanted to make him bleed. Even a year later, the shock of his confession and the knowledge he could have changed the course of both hers and Phillip's paths shredded her.

One positive thing had resulted from his visit. It had reignited a fire in her gut. It had driven her to finally rummage through Phillip's personal effects and, in the process, had led her to the case Phillip had been working on at the time of his death. In the end, it had set her on a course of redemption, one that could release her from the cage of guilt in which she'd lived since his death and allow her to pay back Phillip for everything he had given her. When she'd said "I do," she'd meant it. And she was going to honor Phillip in death.

Rachael had locked all her feelings for Nathan deep in a far corner of her heart never to be reopened and focused all her attention on the last case Phillip had handled. An investigation on terror cells in England and their particularly startling links to the '95 London bombings. Tapping his loyal friends, she'd gotten her hands on the report on Phillip's murder. Her stomach had rolled while she'd gone through the medical reports on the wounds and the findings on the possible murder weapon. Phillip was a very precise and organized man. He'd left several notebooks locked in their safe, which she found to be thought processes on the cases he'd investigated. She had spent long hours reviewing his notes and reconstructing the sequence of events that had led to his death. She'd tracked each lead he'd documented, each person of interest he'd flagged, until she'd understood where the trail he was following ended. A leak in the US Embassy in Israel.

Rachael had wasted no time picking up where he'd left off. Making use of her father's influence and pulling a few favors from his contacts, she'd secured the position as Blair's assistant and, while in Israel, had collected several pieces of evidence that could help her pinpoint the origin of the leak.

She rubbed her palms over her face and pushed to her feet, stretching the kink in her shoulders. Rachael paced the confined space, chafing at her current state of inactivity. Up until the time of the evacuation, she'd been making progress on the case. The files on the SD card hidden in the locket included documents that were key to pinpointing the leak and solving not only his case but his murder. The locket weighed heavily on her mind. If the hidden card was found, it meant swift punishment. Icy tentacles spread through her body and she wrapped her arms around her middle, seeking warmth.

"I'm so sorry, Phillip." Her whisper filled the room.

She needed his reassurance that it would all work out. She wasn't so sure she would complete her mission. While victims of kidnappings for ransom were more valuable alive, the victims of ideological kidnappings were more valuable when dead. It seemed as if she'd barely breathed since the day of the videotaping. With no tangible demands, the video had simply been a taunt aimed at the American government. A small part of her still hoped it was a bluff; the other dreaded they'd been elected as vessels to send their government a message. The world knew that the United States did not negotiate with terrorists.

Her mind twisted to other hostage situations she remembered seeing on the news in the past. Very few had happy endings. Rachael rubbed her breastbone, trying to ease the burning sensation spreading from her chest to her throat, and grimaced at the sour taste filling her mouth. In most cases, within a short period of time a second video surfaced, that time showing the outcome of non-compliance. Who's to say that the same wouldn't happen to her?

Her stomach rolled. Rachael squeezed her eyes shut and took a deep, cleansing breath. That wasn't going to happen if she could help it. She had too much at stake. Had come too close to fulfilling her self-imposed mission to find Phillip's murderer. She had less than four days to get her hands on the memory card and figure a way out of that mess.

She opened her eyes as she listened to the soft murmurs of conversation between the women passing in the hall. Their voices administered a dose of adrenaline to her veins and the sour taste in her mouth began to fade as a plan finally took shape in her head.

Chapter Seventeen

Man Down

"*WO MINUTES.*" THE ELECTRONIC TONE of the pilot's voice crackled through the speakers, hyping up the tension among the ground crew.

Radar beeps and traffic-control chatter buzzed in the room as Trevor watched the monitors expectantly. Part of him wished he was in on the action, yet he knew that an operation of that caliber should be left to the pros.

"*Men like you get hurt.*" Cassandra's words, although true, still stung like hell.

He blocked the thought and locked his eyes on the screens. One by one, the live feed from the cameras mounted on each of the men's helmets lit them up with hazy green infrared images. Through the feeds, those in the control room would have direct access to the ground crew's activities and live through each of their moves. In the monotone glare, he could discern the focus on the mission etched on the men's faces. What he couldn't determine was whether they were all aware of the special instructions he'd given Hanson before their takeoff.

"Are you fucking nuts? I'm not putting my men at risk for a hunch."

Hanson's narrowed eyes and crossed arms hadn't stopped Trevor from pushing his case forward.

"If you want this mission to be successful, you'll need to trust me."

"You're asking for a lot, Bauer. I'm not even sure how the hell this mission got the approval on the little actionable intel we got. I'm not losing any of my men over this."

"I'm not asking you to put your crew at risk. We're on the same side here. We want the same thing. In and out."

Hanson's hard stare had locked on Trevor for a long time before he'd taken a deep breath and nodded in agreement.

"I hope this works out." The warning in his eyes had been clear.

Watching the somber faces of the men about to raid the target, Trevor hoped he'd read Hanson right the first time around. Loyal, dedicated, proud of his service—but also a rule breaker like himself. Hanson would do whatever had to be done to accomplish his mission.

"Thirty seconds," the pilot's voice broke through the static.

"Has Miller sent you anything new?" Nelson stood beside him, watching the action unfold as the mission support personnel bustled around them.

"Nope. I'd have told you if he'd found anything relevant."

Nelson crossed his arms over his chest and turned his eyes to the screens, ignoring him once again.

"Eagle One landed. On target. Bravo Team is set."

Trevor held his breath, his attention riveted on the screens like all the others in the control room monitoring the raid as it unfolded. The live satellite feed locked on the helicopter as it touched down on the selected Landing Zone, a treeless patch of dirt two hundred and fifty yards west of the target. The two-toned images captured the men as they jumped off the Black Hawk's deck and fell into formation. They double-timed across the LZ's muddy field toward a dirt path leading to the house. With each of their strides, Trevor's heart accelerated a beat.

DANIEL SIGNALED THE team to roll. Everything from the second they hit the ground was pure muscle memory. A simple hand signal and they closed in on formation for the short uphill hike to the building.

They split into groups of two as they reached the target. Daniel and Reaper, Bravo One, set off for the front door. Ace and Heinz, Bravo Two, headed for the back of the building followed closely by Bravo Three, Ranger and Mac.

Each team member carried two radios for the mission; each radio had its own earbud. One allowed the teams to communicate among themselves on the ground; the other allowed them to maintain communication with the command center at the Forward Operating Base. For that mission, Daniel expected most of the traffic to be restricted to the team.

"I'm going explosive," Daniel reported, already setting the breaching charge across the main door's knob and lock. They took cover to the side, and with a loud crack, the lock fragmented. The distinct scent of spent charge surrounded him when he approached the door to verify the breach. "Main entry breached," he notified the team.

Another crack sounded from the back of the house. Seconds later, Acer reported, *"Back entry breached."*

"Roger."

Word exchange was restricted to the bare minimum to keep track of the team's location and their status as they scoured the rooms on the main floor of the two-story building. Pausing before the last door, Daniel squeezed Wright's shoulder, signaling him to open it, and cautiously moved forward into the room taking the left, his partner the right.

They checked every nook and cranny for a sign of the residents. Once they found no sign of life, he notified the team, "Clear."

"What do we have here?" Wright mumbled from an alcove in the room.

"Jackpot." A computer desk was tucked in the corner, flanked by two file cabinets. Engaging the safety on his MP7 submachine gun, Daniel let the weapon hang by its strap at his side and pulled open one of the drawers. "Fuck me." He stared at its contents and calculated the amount of work they'd just inherited.

"What'd you find?" Wright came up behind him and looked over his shoulder.

"Heavy lifting. That's what. Bravo Two, status."

"Back of the house is clear. Bravo Two and Three heading up to the next deck," Acer's hushed voice sounded in his ear.

"Secure the upper deck, then bring your duffels. We have to pack a lot more than just a few hard drives."

"Roger that."

Wright cursed when he opened another drawer. "I think heavy lifting was an understatement."

Daniel retrieved the folded duffel from his pack and tossed it to Wright. "Start loading. I'll take the comput—" A loud commotion upstairs followed by wailing and screams cut him off.

"What's going on up there?" Daniel called into the comm.

"Found two tangos. A male and a female," Norton, Bravo Three leader, reported.

"How about the third?"

"Not with these two."

"Zip-tie them and bring them down so we can keep an eye on them. Heinz, speaks Arabic. He can get intel from the two when they get down here."

"Roger that," Norton replied.

"I'm sending Heinz down to help out." Acer's voice came loud and clear over the troop net.

"Are you done with clearing the rooms?"

"Only one left."

"Don't send him. Just follow procedure. Clear the room and get back ASAP. We need all hands with this shit."

"Copy."

Within a few minutes, Norton and Wallace arrived with the residents, now immobilized, and more canvas bags.

"Bravo team, be advised communication blackout will begin in T-minus thirty seconds."

"Roger," Daniel replied as the men filed into the room.

While Wallace kept watch and tried to interrogate the couple in broken Arabic, the other three men proceeded to load files, hard drives, cameras, and other items that could provide them with intelligence. They knew the impact even the smallest scrap of paper could have on any operation.

As they stuffed anything and everything into the satchels, Mendez walked in and whistled.

"Holy shit. You weren't kidding. Hell of a lot more to transport than we were told. Is this going to tip us over the bird's weight capacity?"

Daniel inspected the load. "Nope. We should be good."

With the extra pair of hands, they started shoving every device they found into the bags. Any files, documents of any sort, were collected for later translation and assessment. Minutes passed before Daniel turned his attention to the door and frowned.

"Where the fuck is Ace?"

Mendez paused mid-action. "He told me to get my ass down here to help. Said the clock's a-ticking. Said he could do the last room himself. He should be down with the last hostile by now."

"Bravo Two, do you copy?" Daniel called in. Precious seconds slipped by without a response. Clearing a room didn't take long unless.... A flare of unease tapped Daniel's gut. Acer was the anal-retentive nut on the team. If he was taking longer on deck two, it was for a pretty damn good reason.

He released the safety on his machine gun and shouldered it. "Reaper, come with me. Heinz, get what you can from those two. Ranger and Mac, finish down here. We're heading up to see what's keeping him. Shout when everything is bagged."

"Copy," Norton acknowledged for the rest of them.

Halfway up the stairs, Daniel's senses pricked into overdrive. Wright, second in marksmanship skills only to Acer, followed on his footsteps and they padded almost as one up the stairs. He removed the troop net's noise-canceling earbud and listened, trying to pinpoint the origin of the sound he thought he'd heard.

"I'm not going to hurt you." The quiet words, soft whispers in the night, reached him when he hit the top of the stairs. The hair on the back of his neck stood on end and a ripple of adrenaline surged into his veins. "It'll be okay." There was an ominous ring to the tone of Acer's voice.

Daniel cursed under his breath, pushed the MP7 to his back and drew his Sig Sauer P226. He cocked it silently as he padded toward the open door and Acer's hushed murmurs, Wright covering his six.

The low-wattage glow in the room allowed him to see his buddy standing immediately inside the partly open door. Acer's MP7 hung by its strap over his chest, handgun still holstered.

"See?" Acer waved his hands in a friendly gesture while a tentative smile played on his lips. "Nothing. Won't hurt you. How about we put that down, now? Slow and easy." He gestured to the ground in a slow movement.

His buddy's stance spoke volumes. He was staring down the barrel of a gun. *Fuck.* A knot of tension rode low in his gut as he inched forward, searching for a good line of sight to neutralize the hostile, but the angle of the door blocked his view. He signaled to Reaper he was doing a wall flood. Finger on the trigger, he burst through the door, gun drawn at chest mass height, and straight into a nightmare.

"Hold fire!" Acer shouted at the same time the loud crack of unsuppressed gunfire exploded in the room.

The scene played almost in slow motion before Daniel's eyes. The AK-47 assault rifle's kick, throwing the small child back against the wall. The clink of the spent cartridge hitting the floor. Acer's grunt as his body absorbed the impact of the high-velocity shot before landing on his back. To their luck, the boy lost his grip on the rifle when the impact knocked him out cold, otherwise they would have been under a spray of bullets and riddled with holes.

As he rushed to Acer's side, in his peripheral vision he saw Wright punt the rifle away from the child. *Fuck, fuck, fuck.* The word looped in his head and a heavy feeling settled in his stomach as he kneeled beside his friend.

Acer swallowed hard and groaned, clutching his vest with his left hand. Heavy footsteps clambered up the stairs as Daniel searched for the point of impact, praying the bullet had ended its deadly trajectory on the vest plate. Dread ate his hope and spat it out when he found the hole at the top of Acer's sleeve and blood soaking his fatigues. He also found Acer's troop net radio dial turned to off. A cold tendril of fear rode on the coattails of the familiar coppery tang when he remembered they were cut off from the FOB.

"Fuck. Ace, talk to me, man."

Acer's face contorted in a makeshift grin. "Fuck. That's the last time I play chicken with a bullet," he hissed between clenched teeth. "How bad?"

Daniel exhaled a deep breath and checked the wound. It bled like a sieve. "Bullet won." He assessed for broken bones while Wright removed the strap off Acer's gun to use as tourniquet and passed it to him. The location of the wound, close to the shoulder, was tricky. "Can you move your hand?"

"Let's just say jerking off is out of the question right now."

"Bravo Team, communications are restored," the base operator's voice crackled over the command net radio.

Ignoring Acer's sarcasm and Wright's nervous chortle, Daniel took a deep breath and made the call no troop leader ever wanted to make.

"Man down. I repeat, man down. Requesting immediate exfil."

Mendez ran into the room as the broadcast hit the waves and stopped dead in his tracks when he faced the bloody scene. "Holy shit."

The reply crackled across the radio, *"Copy, Bravo One. Stand by for ETA."*

"Double? The kid?" Acer rasped.

"Not hurt. Knocked out."

Wright tightened the strap, prompting a colorful expletive from Acer.

Daniel glanced at Mendez. "Are we done on deck one? The bird is inbound. We need to get Ace back to the LZ."

Mendez picked up the rifle from the floor and nodded at the child. "What about the boy and the adults?"

"Make sure he's okay. Disable the AK and release the adults once we are all out of here."

Mendez nodded. With Wright's help, Daniel hauled Acer over

his shoulder. SOCOM teams took the "light is right" motto to heart for a reason. If Acer had been hauling the full standard kit, it would have been almost impossible to drag him out of there. Acer's weak grunt didn't bode well. He was losing too much blood and slipping in and out of consciousness.

Daniel reached the bottom of the stairs just as the others walked out of the room with the stuffed bags. The acrid smell of explosives still permeating the air blended with the scent of Acer's blood soaking his fatigues.

"What the hell happened up there?" Norton yelled over the panicked wails of the two residents still being held in the room.

"I'll tell what I know when we're out of here. Let's roll. Heinz, bring up the rear and release the residents."

Heinz frowned at the order. "We're not taking them with us for interrogation?"

Daniel held Heinz's stare and spoke for all to hear. "We won't—I repeat—*won't* be taking any of them in for questioning. No detainees."

Heinz nodded. "Roger."

Daniel forced himself to clear his head as a flood of adrenaline urged his body to move, to carry Ace to safety. His men didn't question the order. Just saddled the heavy bags and led the way to the door.

"Bravo Team, be advised, Eagle One's ETA is five minutes."

"Roger that. On our way to LZ."

The farther from the house, the closer to the exfil, Daniel chanted in his head. Acer's dead weight wore him down with each step, but they all had been conditioned to never give up.

"You're a heavy son of a bitch, Ace," he mumbled almost to himself, and was rewarded with a low chuckle. Relief flooded him. If Acer still had a sense of humor, they were in good shape, he tried to reassure himself.

When they reached the designated Landing Zone, there was no sign of the helicopter.

Daniel dropped to one knee. "Alpha Team, where the fuck is that bird?"

"Inbound, Bravo Team. ETA one minute." The faint distinctive whomp-whomp-whomp of Eagle One's blades slapping the air in the distance confirmed the command's status update. The sound intensified as the black aircraft rolled in.

Heinz reached them just as the stealthy Black Hawk set down, hurling dust all around them. The men dumped the bags inside and pitched in to help Daniel drag Acer onto the deck between the seats.

With Wallace's help, Daniel cut Acer's fatigues and checked the damage with his mag light as the bird gained altitude with all of them aboard. *Shit.* The jagged edges of the gaping wound spelled trouble, but he kept it to himself. He didn't want to alarm Acer.

"Sorry, man. This is gonna hurt."

Acer groaned and cursed when Wallace tightened the strap to staunch the bleeding. He bucked, fighting the needed intervention, but soon the pain knocked him out cold. Satisfied that his friend had found temporary relief, he let Wallace, who had been recruited from the Para-Rescue team into the 8th, handle the emergency care.

"Can you—"

"I'll do the best I can." Wallace's somber tone wasn't making things any easier.

The helicoper's vibration had always soothed him during exfils. This time, the noise and incessant shaking grated on his raw nerves.

"Can this bird fly any faster?"

"We are going as fast as we can with the extra load," the pilot replied. "ETA is fifteen minutes."

"Copy."

For the first time in his long career, no tactical breathing technique seemed to help him regain control of his mind. He'd been in worse combat situations before, he'd seen friends die, but none had been as close to him as Ace.

"Fuck!" He punched the bird's frame. Pain reverberated through his knuckles and arm, but didn't dissolve the fist in his stomach. He leaned his head back against the seat and the scene in the room played out in front of his eyes. The rancid taste of failure filled his mouth.

The somber faces of the other team members didn't give their feelings or thoughts away. They were trained to subdue them. Suppressing emotions kept them alive and sane, but Daniel knew they all had the same bitter taste filling their mouths, the same fist in their stomachs at seeing a brother hurt.

"He'll be fine," Daniel whispered to himself. Acer's stillness mocked him, making his words sound more like begging than reassurance as they zipped through the dark skies toward Jordan air space. One man down, but mission accomplished.

Chapter Eighteen

Long Shot

ASSANDRA FORCED HER EYES OPEN to the blurry outline of the mouse and the pile of files next to her nose. By the crick in her neck, it became painfully obvious that the copious amounts of coffee she'd downed during the night hadn't been enough to keep her awake.

"Shite." Trevor's favorite curse tumbled from her dry lips as she peeled the side of her face from the keyboard. *Talk about a crash and burn.* She stretched back against the chilled leather chair, wincing as her cramped muscles screamed in protest and scrubbing her face in lieu of a cold splash before reaching for her cell phone. She squinted against the brightness of the phone's screen. The world clock application displayed the current time in Amman, Dublin, and Baltimore, making her well aware it was a brand new day and they still had nothing to go by on the case. A quick glance showed her there were no messages. She'd been on enough field assignments that she hadn't expected Trevor to establish contact until things had stabilized.

A wicked thought burrowed its way into her mind. What if she gave him a taste of his own medicine? A little demonstration of how much she missed him, the same way he had when she was in Langley not long ago. She would have loved to see his eyes widening with surprise. A cocky smile and half-mast eyes would follow. Cassandra was so tempted. She knew her husband would thoroughly enjoy that kind of spontaneity. But in his case, he would be surrounded by military personnel on a base in the middle of the desert without the sliver of privacy she'd had in the cab that steamy night. Her stomach sank again.

Even though she knew he, Nathan, and Hanson had most likely jumped from the frying pan into the fire as soon as they'd hooked up with the rest of the team, disappointment still sat in her stomach like a lead weight.

Cassandra shivered against the cold morning air and pulled Trevor's sweater tighter. *No news is good news.* His lingering scent wafted around her head and she breathed it in with a heavy heart.

"That better be the case, Bauer," she mumbled.

Her thoughts rolled back over the activities since Trevor, Nathan, and Hanson had left. After she'd indulged in a good cry, one she wasn't proud of, she'd picked up where she'd left off on Trevor and George's active case, resurrecting her notes on Ahmed Abboud and the old video newscast she'd saved the day before Nathan and Daniel had descended on them in a swirl of chaos.

Hours, days, had dragged by since Cassandra had last been in contact with another human being. Jessica had called the evening of her birthday. During the brief call, they had gotten into the why Stephan hadn't been able to reach Trevor to let him know Tatiana, Dmitriy Vlasov's wife, had been in an accident. Aware of the importance of the mission and Cassandra's need to see it complete, Jessica had reassured her of Tatiana's progress and that she'd let her know if things changed.

With Jessica covering for her at the hospital, Cassandra had spent the last two days scouring for what she could find on the bombing. She directed her gaze to the open document on her computer screen. Apparently, her cheek's affair with the keyboard was a gift that kept giving. She had to delete two pages of Ks from the bottom of her notes on the MI5 case. Despite her in-depth research, it appeared as if the second bomber had vanished into thin air. Abboud had claimed responsibility for the bombing before he was executed, but a tingling in her gut told her that his murder had the same, if not bigger, importance in the story as that of MI5's failure to determine the identities of the other bomber and Abboud's killer.

Although she'd hit a dead end, Cassandra couldn't let it go. She'd work that suspicion to death if it had the potential to lead her to the answers Operation Countermeasure needed to close the damn case. But for now, she had to put it aside before she went crazy.

She closed Abboud's file only to reveal another one open behind it. Rachael Moore's dossier. Cassandra lifted her eyes to the large flat screens decorating the office wall where the news clip of Moore's plea—the one Cassandra had watched over and over looking for microscopic clues in her expression—displayed Moore's taut expression.

A Mills College graduate. Her father, the former Israeli Ambassador to the United Kingdom; her mother, an American foreign relations specialist. Rachael had married Phillip Moore, a British Navy officer, immediately after graduation. They'd alternated between England, Israel, and off the radar for the length of their marriage. It wasn't until after her husband's death that she'd resurfaced in California, where her parents had resided since her father's retirement. They owned a large property not far from where Cassandra used to live.

Cassandra had only scratched the surface where Moore was concerned. The hunch that there was a lot more to the woman burned at her, but it was the relation to Nathan that intrigued her the most. In all the years that Cassandra had known Nathan, he'd never once mentioned Phillip or Rachael. She could still recall the glimmer in his eyes and tightness in his voice when he'd mentioned knowing them. It was time to delve deeper into the Moore's lives, into Nathan's life before she'd met him, and find out what he'd omitted. Find out whether Rachael Moore was a victim or a threat. Find out why Nathan had to work so hard at keeping his emotions from showing to all.

A wide yawn held her jaw hostage and her stomach erupted in a loud rumble. The itch to get back to work pressed on her shoulders, but first Cassandra needed food and coffee—lots of coffee. She pushed herself from the chair and headed down to the kitchen. Later, when the sun was up and the rest of Ireland had started their day, she'd check in with Jessica regarding the status of her earlier request for additional information on Abboud.

★ ★ ★ ★ ★

CASSANDRA'S CELL PHONE rang a few times before she diverted her eyes from the screen and picked it up. From the number on the display, she knew just who it was.

"Morning, sleepyhead."

"Don't judge. Anybody walking around with a bowling ball for a stomach is entitled to extra sleep." Jessica barely stopped to breathe between sentences. "Before you ask, Tatiana is doing fine. No follow-ups are expected and the baby is hanging tight. I'm actually looking forward to having someone close to share the whole newbie mom experience, since you won't listen to me and take the leap." Her voice brimmed with humor. "I can't wait to watch you waddle and joke about it the same way you tease me. And to think, you call yourself my best friend."

"When that time comes, you'll be so busy with three or more of your own that you won't have time to bug me." Cassandra tried her best to school her tone, but Jessica knew her too well.

A long pause silenced the call. "I'm sure it'll happen sooner than you think."

"To be honest, I'm not sure I'm ready. It's a big step. Besides, I have no clue how to be a mother. I'll probably end up drilling the poor thing like Bob drilled me.

"Stop. You're going to be a fantastic mother. And Trevor will balance your drilling tendencies with his spontaneity. Don't forget, you'll get lots and lots of practice when you babysit. Hint, hint."

Jessica's words rang true to what she already knew. Cassandra took a deep cleansing breath. "No time to dwell on what-ifs. Trevor and I have a lot to do before we can be free to contemplate that sort of change in our lives. So, do you have anything for me?"

Jessica must have sensed her discomfort because she shifted gears without arguing. "That's exactly why I called. It should be in your inbox. I hope what I found is enough. I can keep digging, but it's not like he seems to be hiding much."

"Damn. I must have missed it. Let me take a look and I'll let you know. I might have you dig into a few more things for me if you're up to it."

Jessica had been working from home at their request. No point in making her drive to their house when she could achieve the same results in the comfort of her home, especially as she got closer to having the baby.

"That's what I'm here for, Auntie," Jessica chuckled, and disconnected the call.

Cassandra didn't waste any time diving into the new material Jessica had sent over. A good portion of it was old news. A copy of birth records confirmed that Naveed was indeed Ahmed Abboud's son. It was the second birth record Jessica had located that made excitement bloom in her chest.

She opened the last file, pausing to read Jessica's comments on the last page: *I thought you would find this connection interesting. I'm still looking for a current address.*

Adrenaline thickened Cassandra's blood and her pulse kicked up a notch. She re-read the highlighted section. Naveed Abboud had an older brother. Shortly after their father's death, Naveed, who was barely a toddler at the time, had been sent to live with a family member in the US while his brother, Khalil, had been raised by family in the West Bank. Naveed had been living in the States ever since.

Too anxious to wait for Jessica, she decided to tap her best bet— George—for the information she needed. She opened an email and requested his help in securing an address and anything else he could dig up on Naveed Abboud. With any luck, he'd see the email as soon as he hit the office in a few hours. A smile curved the corner of Cassandra's mouth for the first time in two days as she added the latest information from Jessica and hit send. It wasn't Waldo, but it was another dotted connection within her file. A long shot at best. And she loved long shots. After all, it was one that had led her to Trevor.

Chapter Nineteen

Wait and See

*T*HE PERSONNEL AT MISSION CONTROL monitored the movements inside the house through the live feed, somber expressions all around as they witnessed the action miles away. They all lived through the surgical breach of the building, through the team's clearing of the rooms, everything going according to plan up to the communications blackout.

"Communications restored in T-minus thirty seconds," the radio operator announced.

As the satellite signal returned to fully operational, they all held their breaths in communal disbelief. Dread descended upon the room as the screens filled with the live images once again and the speakers broadcasted the anguish in the men's voices.

Before the blackout, Trevor had been confident about his plan, sure of the outcome. Now, while watching helplessly as the men struggled to keep one of theirs alive, doubts crowded his mind. The room exploded into action, pieces of conversation among the team members filling the gaps of what had happened.

"Man down. I repeat, man down. Requesting immediate exfil." Hanson's tone didn't reveal much about Acer's condition. It wasn't necessary. The helmet cameras fed them the graphic depiction of the reality outside the wire.

"Copy, Bravo One. Stand by for ETA," the radio operator replied to Hanson's call. The team on base bustled to have the men extracted and ready the MEDEVAC. Trevor stood in silence beside Nelson while the arrangements were made and sighed in relief when mission control radioed in again, "Bravo Team, be advised, Eagle One's ETA is five minutes."

"Roger that. On our way to LZ." More shaky images, now back to two-toned infrared, showed the troop's organized egress to the meeting point from every man's angle. Those with eyes glued to the monitors were silent witnesses of the team's unparalleled training. Swift and efficient, they double-timed downhill across the dirt path and reached the landing zone before the Black Hawk arrived.

Seconds dragged into minutes before the images showed them all safely onboard the helicopter and inbound to the base. One by one, the screens went dark as the men turned off their cameras, almost as if seeking privacy to deal with the outcome of that mission.

"What happens when they get here?" Trevor asked Nelson, his mind reeling for the entire team.

"MEDEVAC will take Acer to Ramstein."

"And?"

"He'll be taken stateside as soon as possible." *If he survives or not.* The unsaid words hung in the silence.

They stood to the side while the room stirred with activity around them. For once, they were drawn together by a common bond. Trevor's limbs felt heavy, numb. Shock and desolation tumbled inside him, and he barely knew Acer. He couldn't fathom the range of emotions his brothers-in-arms were going through during that flight. His thoughts veered to the mission and ignited a spark of hope—hope that he was right about the residents, otherwise Acer's sacrifice would have been for nothing.

"ETA three minutes. Is the ground crew on standby?" When the pilot's voice announced the helicopter's approach, Trevor followed the other staff outside.

The illuminated tarmac crawled with emergency and support personnel. The MEDEVAC Black Hawk's engine hummed to life in preparation for the injured soldier, readying for takeoff. The sound of another set of blades slicing the air reached them long before they saw the inbound vessel, its black fuselage disguised against the dark curtain of night.

Moments later, gusts of sand peppered the air around those welcoming the teams to base. Controlled chaos erupted as the emergency team took charge, moving Acer into the medical evacuation version of the same helicopter that had transported him back to base. Trevor observed the faces of the two crewmen working on stabilizing the wounded soldier, their focus and determination etched in every creased forehead even as the flight crew completed their pre-checks for departure. Without a second wasted, doors closed and the bird lifted off and left the base under the somber watch of Acer's team members.

The AWE Crew members stood on the tarmac until the sound of the blades slapping the air could no longer be heard, their strong stance turning into something else Trevor couldn't quite identify. Mourning and hope mixed into a sobering concoction.

Slowly, they dispersed toward the base quarters, some huddled in groups, others seeking solitude, each dealing with the unexpected developments in their own way.

Trevor stayed behind, standing beside Hanson, whose eyes were locked on the distance as if tracing the helicopter's path in the dark sky. After a period of silence, Hanson's head dropped and he took a deep breath before raising his eyes to meet Trevor's.

"Tell me it fucking worked."

Nelson's stance stiffened and Trevor squeezed his eyes shut. *This should be fun.*

"Tell him *what* worked? What have you kept from me, Bauer?"

Trevor chose to ignore his question and answered Hanson's instead. "No way to know just yet. We should find out soon."

"What the fuck have you two done without my express authorization?" Nelson's eyes threw shards at both of them. His hands balled into fists; Trevor knew what came next if the guy flew into a rage. He'd given him the Hulk nickname for a reason.

"We're out of options, so we tried something a little...unorthodox." Trevor barely had time to finish before Nelson was crowding him.

"You Irish shithead!" Rage made the veins in Nelson's temples pop. He grabbed Trevor by the collar of his graphic t-shirt, ready to decorate Trevor's face with his fist. "Did you consider the fact any deviation of the plan could jeopardize the entire operation or cause a tragedy like the one we just witnessed?"

"Cut it out, Nelson!" Hanson shoved between the two, releasing Nelson's hold. "His plan didn't get Ace shot. Not following procedure did. My fault." While guilt weighed prominently on Hanson's words, his hard stare told little of his state of mind.

"We have the whole operation recorded, Hanson. I doubt anybody would find you at fault." Nelson turned to Trevor. "What did you do? I need to know so I can minimize the fallout from your stupidity."

"Down, boy. We're playing the waiting game now." Nelson's frown deepened and Trevor took a long breath before explaining. "I've been tracking this same group for the CIA for months. They have become exceptional at hiding."

Nelson's eyes narrowed. "What do you mean tracking them for months? Did you intercept any intel about the kidnapping before it happened?"

"No. Nothing like that." Trevor looked around and made sure they were out of earshot before lowering his voice. "This stays here. Absolutely nobody else can know. I shouldn't even be telling you anything. Classified Top Secret, got it?" After receiving nods from both men, Trevor continued, "Operation Countermeasure has been handling a particularly puzzling case for a while. It has ties to terrorist activity in and out of the US." Both men's eyes narrowed on him like sniper sights on an enemy. "After the news that Osama had been tracked using digital signatures splattered the news, terrorists adjusted the way they communicate. They don't use digital communication often, and when they do, they are smart about covering their tracks. Let's just say it has made our work that much more challenging. We've been hitting brick walls at every turn for a long time. That was, until the kidnapping happened. We identified one signature among those picked up at the coordinates of the abduction as one previously linked to our case. Aside from that small link and a gut feeling, we didn't have much to go on, but as you said yourself, we use unconventional methods. We went with it."

"And how does that tie in with tonight's operation?" Nelson's expression was taut, his jaw clenched. The man was still a powder keg about to blow.

"We have eyes on the ground. George has the area under high-def surveillance twenty-four seven."

"I still don't see a connection."

"The operation's goal was not to recover physical assets or intelligence; it was to stir the hornets' nest. We know there is a link between that house and the kidnappers. We also know there is a connection between the kidnappings and our high-profile target. That being the case, there is no way in hell they'll use digital communication. It would make it too easy for us to trace them. But a run-in with a US military op intent on securing computers and documents would force their hand. They would have to report it to whoever is in charge." A light of understanding began to shine in the men's eyes.

"That's why you told me not to take anybody into custody." Hanson's mouth curved into a half smile. "Son of a bitch."

"You're watching for movement right now?" Nelson's tone had cooled down, but he wasn't as enthusiastic as Hanson. Not that Trevor expected Nelson to be enthusiastic. Ever.

Trevor smiled, confident in his strategy. "We have an entire crew on duty watching every move they make. Eventually, they will feel safe to report the raid, and when that happens, we'll be right there with them."

Nathan's heart thumped in his chest. For a change, Bauer's words gave him hope. "What if this theory of yours doesn't fly?"

The Irishman shrugged. "We'll try something else. But for now, this is the best shot we have."

Nathan listed their options in his head. Nothing else made as much sense as Bauer's trick. "So when can we expect to see results?"

"We are not dealing with dumbasses. It's clear they've been instructed not to use cell phones or traceable devices if it can be avoided. Give them time to make sure the coast is clear, and I'm positive we'll see movement."

Time. Something they didn't have. Nathan didn't know if he could wait any longer. His body was wound tight from the effort to keep his composure. The need to keep his mission under wraps, as well as his much deeper link to one of the hostages, weighed heavily on him.

"Understood. I have a few calls to make. Keep me updated." He locked eyes with Bauer. "I mean it: no more fucking secrets."

"Aye, aye, captain." The Irishman's tone riled him, but he needed Bauer functional more than he needed a punching bag on which to unleash his frustrations.

Nathan's mind teemed with information as he headed outside in search of a private place to make a call. Pulling the secure satellite phone from his pocket, he dialed his superior.

"Any news?" His boss's tone gave nothing away, but the fact that he was awake and picked up on the first ring did.

"We haven't located the hostages, but we may be close." He damn well hoped Bauer was right. "Some new intel came to light. Look into all active NSA cases. Something about a terrorist organization with ties to the country. There may be a link to our guy there somewhere."

"I'll get someone on it right away."

"I'll need clearance to join the crew when we zero in on the target." Nathan knew he was stretching the limits of his position within the CIA.

A longer pause silenced the call before his boss spoke again. "I'll make it happen. And Nelson? Proceed with caution. There's too much at stake."

"Yes, sir." The line went silent, indicating the end of the call. Nathan couldn't help but think of his very personal stake in the mission. Something way more crushing and closer than finding a traitor among those whom his country had trusted.

He pocketed the phone and stared into the distance where the sun was about to break free. The strange serenity of the moment, not long after they had witnessed the evacuation of one of their own, triggered memories he'd rather have kept locked down. They rushed at him, reminding him of his past, exposing the lies he'd lived with for years.

From the day he'd returned to the US after his last visit to the Moores, he'd managed to craftily stow away his feelings and move on. He could see clearly now that it had been out of self-preservation that he'd sought Cassandra's attention. The idea wormed its way into his mind until he'd convinced himself that she was the key to his happiness, and he'd worked hard to convince her of the same. Unwittingly, Cassandra had become a proxy for the one he couldn't have. Why couldn't that have been clear to him then? He'd have avoided a world of hurt for all of them.

Nathan turned his face to the pitch-dark sky. His eyes roamed the emptiness while his mind filled with images of the fateful day that had triggered his headfirst dive into his present agony. He squeezed his eyes shut, unable to ignore the lurch in his chest. Having sex with Cassandra had been by far the second worst decision he'd made that day, and maybe his entire life. The first had been caving to the need to see Rachael during that trip to California. One would have said masochism was the propelling force, but he just needed to see her, even if he knew she was still out of bounds. He'd known she had moved to the Bay Area to be closer to her parents after Phillip's death. He had no way of knowing that paying a visit to Rachael and sharing with her the details of his last contact with Phillip a few weeks before he'd been killed in action could turn out that wrong.

"How could you have ignored his request? He was your friend." Rachael's accusing gaze had torn through Nathan, slicing deeper than the wounds he'd already inflicted upon himself.

"He was the one who taught me about honor, and that to be ethical in my work was the only way to make those I loved proud." Nathan's eyes had stung with unshed tears. *"I loved him too, Rae."*

"Right. You loved him so much you caused his death by omission."

Deep inside, he knew she was just lashing out because she was still mourning the loss of her husband, but it hadn't taken away the impact of the blow. *"Or maybe you just wanted him to die so you could reap his spoils."* Her eyes had shot cold shards at him.

Nathan's heart had sunk to his knees then, and it repeated the dive in recollection. The old guilt that he'd carried with him for so many years had flared and engulfed him like a bonfire out of control. He could have ignored what she'd had said all he wanted. As much as he'd never wished Phillip any harm, he had coveted the one thing Phillip treasured the most—Rachael. What had compounded matters was that she'd seemed to have always known it.

"I would never—never—*have caused him harm. No matter how much I've wanted you, I could never…. You're Phillip's wife. You'll always be."*

Her eyes had widened and then hardened more under a heavy frown. She paused as if processing his words.

"He's gone and I hate you." If pain had an audible synonym, it would have been Rachael's tone when she'd finally spoken.

"I know. And for that I'm truly sorry."

"I don't ever want to see you again." Her words had killed a part of him he didn't expect to revive. They had also made him weak.

He'd left her that night and had driven around the streets of San Francisco in a daze. Numb to everything around him except the fact that he'd not only lost his best friend but also severed the only link he might have had with the woman he'd loved for most of his life. Shame slinked its way into his mind when he remembered how the night had ended. How he'd aptly masked his pain and followed through with meeting Cassandra for dinner. How he'd tried to forget the hatred in Rachael's eyes in Cassandra's arms. What a fool he'd been. One day he would have to face the consequences of his idiocy, but not just yet.

He took a deep breath to clear his head and reset his directives. Find the hostages, rescue them, identify the traitor. Those were the only three things that mattered. Rachael's eyes, full of rage and hurt flashed before his. Nothing would come between him and getting her out of there alive. He couldn't afford to fail, even if saving her meant losing her once again.

Chapter Twenty

Secret

*H*USHED VOICES, SHUFFLING FEET, and the echo of long strides penetrated Rachael's awareness. The reality of her captivity slammed her once again as her eyes slowly adapted to the penumbra in the small cell.

Rolling to her back, she draped her forearm across her eyes and listened. Rachael kept track of the activity in the house through the routine around prayer times. The compound roused for *Fajr*, the first prayer of the day. She breathed freely, knowing the guards would be too busy to drag any of them out.

Pulling the blanket tighter around her, she lay still, her senses on high alert. She couldn't remember the last time she'd actually slept for more than a couple of hours. Ever since her video appearance and the loss of her necklace, Rachael's mind had been strapped to a rollercoaster in an endless loop. She racked her brain to piece together a profile of their captors, hoping to identify which terrorist group was calling the shots.

The precision with which the kidnappers had popped off the

security detail, the setup for the video recording, even the fact that they appeared to have had the compound prepared and stocked to hold them painted a picture of a well-organized group.

Other than the first time she'd been taken out of the cell for the ridiculous plea, she'd been left alone. The men hadn't been so lucky. She'd heard them being escorted, sometimes dragged, often to the small room she'd been taken for her tête-à-tête with Khalil. She assumed all had gone through the same grilling she had.

Rachael frowned as her brain worked harder to make connections. From her knowledge of the demand, she assumed an ideological drive behind the kidnapping. Those types of terrorists weren't in it for money. They were radicals. They acted for shock value. A cold tendril of fear slithered down her spine. She couldn't die. Not before she'd solved Phillip's case.

Rachael forced a deep breath into her lungs and let the distant hypnotic melody of the morning call take hold, cleansing her mind of all darkness, infusing it with hope. Perseverance was the only thing that could get them out of that bind.

The hum of prayers died away and a cloak of silence descended before the compound stirred to life again. She turned her head toward the door and a flicker of apprehension swept through her, twisting her stomach into knots. Activity outside her door was both welcomed and dreaded. Her fluency in Arabic was still unknown to her captors. Assuming she didn't speak the language, they were careless, discussing and gossiping while near her door. It had been through those conversations that she'd gathered critical information on them, like the name of their leader.

Every day since she'd arrived there, the guards had stood close enough that the scent of their after-meal coffee teased her senses. Close enough that she could hear all their trivial exchanges. She'd been privy to complaints about the randomness of checkpoints into the West Bank, how a family member of one of them had a baby on the roadside because they were denied crossing and access to their doctor in time for the delivery. Most heartbreaking of all, how they missed family divided by the wall, family they rarely saw anymore because of the many restrictions imposed on their people. Each of the accounts tightened the knot in her stomach. She'd been taught to ignore the other side of the story, but the more she learned, the harder it became to pretend it didn't exist. As much as those accounts saddened her, she had to steel her heart and hone in on the pieces of the conversations that could help her case.

She was fully aware of the limited number of days left on the deadline, but terrorists, especially radical ones, were unpredictable. When heavy steps sounded in the hall, she rolled to her knees, her eyes fixed on the door. Her breath stalled in her lungs when the sound came to a halt outside her cell. After what seemed like a lifetime, the person moved away and Rachael released a shuddering exhalation.

"Do you have a light?" A hushed voice speaking in Arabic drew her attention to the rudimentary orifice on the wall.

Rachael rolled to her feet and, taking careful steps, stood underneath it, listening for more. The abrasive scrape of a match reached her ears and soon the pungent smell of tobacco smoke wafted into the cell.

"Why are we still waiting?" A second man's voice drifted to her, his impatience evident.

She recognized the voices as two of the guards that escorted her caretakers.

Smoke drifted into the room again on the heels of the first guard's voice. "Don't ask me. Something about the right time."

The second guard scoffed. "I know when the right time is for all these infidels. Now. Now is the time."

"The *Rasūl* is the one who will decide the right time. Not you. Not even *Sahib* does." The man's tone changed. Rachael could recognize respect, fear, when she heard it.

"Sometimes I wonder who is really in charge."

"Are you crazy?"

The sound of spitting reached her ears before the second guard's tone turned darker. "The American traitor needs a lesson in humility. That one needs to feel the butt of my rifle. The way he smirks each time he's taken to Khalil. The other two stupid Americans that share his cell have no clue they have a viper in their house."

No! Rachael covered her mouth and bit her lip to hold back her distress from their ears.

"I also do not understand why Khalil caters to him. But it is not for us to say." The scratching sound of sole against dirt reached her ears. "Let's go. The women are bringing the food." Their steps and voices drifted away.

Rachael's heart slammed against her ribs and her hands shook as she slumped back against the wall. "What the hell," she whispered, shaking her head in denial over what she'd just overheard. "It can't be."

She slid down to a crouch, pressing her hands against her lap to steady them. But there was no mistaking what she had heard. *I can't believe it.* Aside from the two foreign dignitaries, the rest of the members of the convoy had been Americans. She knew the drivers had been killed during the assault and had witnessed Norwood and Thompson meet the same grim fate. At the time she and the others were harvested from the convoy vehicles, Stratton, the DSS agent traveling with her in the car, and her boss had been alive. She recalled Stratton calling for Carter over the radio during the attack. Carter had to be the third American they were talking about.

She couldn't visualize any of the three in that light. Mark Stratton, top in his field. His resume read like a long list of brass commendations from his Special Forces days to the diplomatic service in Israel. She frowned and shook her head. Gerald Blair. He had been entrusted with the mediator position because he was a natural in bridging gaps. She shook her head again. The thought that her boss could be a traitor and the cause of her husband's death pained her. She'd been his secretary for months. She couldn't believe that possibility. Her attention turned to the remaining American. Adam Carter. She was not familiar with the DSS agent. New on rotation, he'd only been there for a short time. All their men were highly recommended and selected for the position with care. A traitor among them would undermine the trust on the Diplomatic Security Services.

Her concern escalated to an even higher level when she realized the implications of that betrayal. They were more than pawns in a simple kidnapping. They were game pieces on a much larger board. Her heart tumbled into her stomach. What if Kahlil showed her necklace to the American? Any one of them would recognize it as hers. What if the card fell out of its hiding place the next time it was opened? She had to get it back. She couldn't risk someone uncovering the precious cargo inside.

She dropped her head against the wall. She needed to act. She couldn't afford to wait any longer. She needed someone willing to help, someone who had access to other parts of the building. Someone whom she could trust with a secret that could cost her life. Her stomach turned when she thought about what she was about to do. It would either gain her an ally or take her head.

Rachael had crossed the younger of the two servants off her list almost immediately; she'd refused to acknowledge Rachael's existence during the few times she had brought her meals. The hatred in the woman's eyes didn't give Rachael any warm, fuzzy feelings, either.

Each time Rachael had drawn near, the woman had averted her eyes and hurried from the room as if disgusted to share the space with her. She knew the young woman wouldn't lift a finger to help her.

The older woman was her best bet. The memory of their faceoff with the guard filled her mouth with the metallic taste of blood. Although she had risked a lot with her impulsive reaction, the gratitude displayed in the woman's eyes had given her a glimmer of hope.

Any minute now, one of the women would be bringing her meal. She crossed her fingers that it would be the one she needed to put her plan into action. As if attuned to her musings, footsteps approached her door.

Rachael pushed to her feet and took small steps toward the middle of the room. Her ankle, still sore, was definitely on the mend under the old woman's care. She pulled up the headscarf over her head and waited for the door to open. A jolt of energy surged through her when the woman who occupied her thoughts stepped into the room carrying the familiar battered tray bearing bowls and a teapot.

Satisfaction settled her nerves as the heady aroma of the sage-infused tea tickled her nose. She'd had her greatest hopes confirmed. By tradition, tea was presented to guests as a display of hospitality and to offer comfort. By bringing it with the meal, the Palestinian woman had just granted Rachael guest status, a sign that she was softening toward her. It was her much-needed olive branch.

She watched the woman set the tray on the chair and pour the tea. When the woman glanced her way and gestured, Rachael moved closer and took a seat on the floor next to the offering. She accepted the bowl of water to wash her hands, followed by the small loaf of bread the woman gave her. When she turned to leave, Rachael clasped the woman's hand and tugged gently.

"Join me," Rachael said in English, cracking a smile and inclining her head toward the floor.

The woman's brow furrowed as if trying to understand what Rachael had said.

"Sit with me." Rachael patted the floor.

Indecision warred across the woman's features as she cast a wary glance over her shoulder. Rachael hid her grin when the woman gathered her long dress and kneeled beside her.

Once settled, Rachael presented her with the cup of tea. The woman accepted it with shaky fingers and a fleeting smile.

Rachael dipped a torn piece of bread in olive oil and watched the woman from the corner of her eye. When her shoulders relaxed, she initiated her plan. It was now or never.

"My name is Rachael." She kept her tone soft, friendly, as she spoke casually in Arabic.

The woman's eyes widened and her mouth slacked open. She set the cup on the floor and stared at her intently. "You speak our language."

Rachael released the breath she hadn't even realized she'd been holding. "Yes." She held the woman's eyes with hers. "Will you keep my secret?"

The woman nodded and lifted her fingers to her lips.

A loud whack sounded against the door before the guard's voice, the same voice she had heard outside her window, thundered outside, "You have ten minutes, old woman." When the guard's footsteps faded in the distance, they both sagged in nervous relief.

"My name is Qismah." Her voice was hushed.

Rachael lowered hers. "Qismah. A beautiful name. I was worried about you. I hope the guard didn't hurt you badly. Are you well?"

Qismah nodded. "I am well. Thank you for your help." She gestured with her hand toward the tray. "*Ta'kuliina.* Eat. He will be back soon."

Qismah pulled out the homemade poultice and a bandage and pointed to her ankle. Rachael dipped her head in a small gesture of thanks and took small bites while the woman tended to her injury. Her heart revved before she took the leap of faith.

"What can you tell me of the others? Are they close?"

The wariness returned to the woman's eyes. "They are not gravely injured, if that is what you are asking."

"Are they in the same building?"

"They are in a room at the other end of the hallway."

Rachael scooped some of the spicy chicken from another bowl with the bread to appease her and to give herself time to search for the right approach, not wanting to spook the woman off. After a few moments, she sensed Qismah's scrutiny and met her eyes.

"What is it?"

"I fear for you."

"Tell me, why?"

"I hear things as I serve the food."

Her words chilled Rachael and a quick and frightening thought assaulted her. "What have you heard?"

"The men are anxious to leave this place."

Rachael's mind raced, searching for the right words before she lost her opportunity. She needed to get her locket back.

She took the woman's hand in hers. "Qismah, I helped you once. Now I am asking for your help." Qismah's eyes widened and she pulled her hand away. Rachael softened her voice, falling back on the lessons of diplomacy her father had taught her. "Please, I only want to know if you have seen where the *Sahib* keeps my necklace." The image of him pocketing it flashed in her mind. "The last time I saw it, he'd placed it in his pocket. Have you seen it? Silver. Round. There is an inscription on it."

The woman's eyes swept over her face and dropped to her own hands, but not before Rachael caught the flash of recognition that flared in them.

"Please. It is very special to me. I would like it back." The woman's shoulders stiffened. Rachael backed off and tried a different approach. "Are you married?"

Qismah lifted her head and Rachael saw sadness buried in the depths of her green eyes. "I was. He is dead. We had many happy years together until he was killed trying to stop the Israeli settlers from tearing down our house."

Rachael's heart lurched. Qismah couldn't know about her background. She needed her.

"I also lost my husband. That is why I must have the necklace back. It was a gift from him. A most cherished gift." The sound of approaching footsteps reached them and Qismah hurried to collect her things. "Please promise me you will see if you can find it. Bring it to me. It has sentimental value."

The woman's gaze bounced from hers to the door and back. "It sits on his desk." She ducked her head and gathered the remains of the meal. "I must be ready. The guard comes."

A shiver crawled up Rachael's spine and settled in her chest as the woman slipped out the door as soon as it opened. Her heart squeezed into her throat. When the guard didn't barge in, she expelled a deep breath. Qismah hadn't mentioned their conversation. A good sign. It was out of her hands now. She just hoped that the leap of faith she'd taken didn't bite her in the ass.

Chapter Twenty-One

A Message

*S*ALMAN STOOD BY THE WINDOW, his gaze lost in the vastness of gray beyond his compound's walls. Hebron had expanded its tentacles into the desert as far as the eye could see, as far as they had been allowed to. It was what he couldn't see that made him yearn for days past. Days before they had become the new Berlin, segregated and confined.

Born a few years before the Armistice, he'd been old enough to remember the destruction and carnage in Falameh that had killed his father. Old enough to witness firsthand his family's eviction from the lands they had nurtured and loved for many generations. Life had never been easy before, but when they had been severed from their roots without the head of the family, their lives had become even more difficult.

Malleability was the word. All of his people shared that trait. They adapted, morphed, made do with what they had to continue their plight. And now they would do so in a new way. The modern way. The Americans wouldn't have a chance against the new threat.

They were always so engrossed in meddling in other countries' businesses that they would miss an Intifada erupting underneath their feet.

He rubbed his chest to soothe the tightness around his heart. He wouldn't be there to see his idea, his plan, flourish. He was too old to last long enough to see it carried out to fruition. What mattered was that many of his people would, and he was satisfied with that. He just needed to remain in the shadows a little while longer to make sure all of the pieces fell into place at the right time.

Once this step was complete, he only had to give it one more nudge before the machine was engaged and nothing would be able to turn it away from its final destination. It was imperative that his identity and whereabouts remained unknown so that nobody could quash the fire he was about to rain down on them all.

The Americans thought they were best at catching others unawares. They would get a taste of their own medicine.

Salman covered his face with the scarf and called for the servant. The young man walked in, keeping his eyes lowered to the ground as he'd been instructed.

"Bring me one of my couriers. I need to send a message."

Rasūl was a fitting nickname. He'd make the Americans understand how it felt like to have their trust, their promises broken. He'd be the messenger of pain.

Chapter Twenty-Two

Ready or Not

GEORGE DIDN'T WAIT FOR CASSANDRA to bring the phone to her ear before he began rattling, his voice full of the usual George-like enthusiasm. "You might be on to something, Cassie."

She drew in a deep breath, excitement threatening to subdue her usual caution. "Georgie, that's music to my ears. I take it you unearthed more on Abboud?"

"Have I told you how much I hate it when you call me that?"

George was a constant presence in her new life and had quickly found a way into her heart. "Did you just pout? Here I thought it was my special nickname for you. Should I change it? How about GG? G-man? I got it, G-string. Yeah, G-string. Trev will love that one. Maybe I should have him add it to your dating profile." A grin tugged at the corner of her mouth. She considered him family and couldn't help but tease him when the opportunity presented itself.

"You are an evil, evil woman."

Cassandra struggled to hold back the laughter that bubbled up her throat and lost. She hadn't laughed like that in days. "How about we start over. I'll be good, George. See? I used George."

"Just so we're clear," humor bled through George's words, "I know you have no plans to stop."

She brought the banter down a few notches. They were wasting precious time. "All kidding aside, I'm itching to hear what you have."

George changed gears to match hers. "Your boy is living the American dream. Freshman at Virginia Commonwealth University, right in the heart of Richmond. Major undeclared."

"That's not unusual for a first-year student." Cassandra pulled up the area around VCU on her screen.

George added, "He's on a full ride. Tuition for the year all paid up. Unemployed, but can still afford a loft near the campus."

Her curiosity was piqued. "So his family is supporting him a hundred percent?"

"That's the thing. His family lives a modest life in Clarksburg, West Virginia. No flash. No credit cards. They're frugal. The tuition was paid directly from an offshore account. I'm still working on unravelling that mess. Tracing accounts as we speak. Gotta dig deeper for that. Also, the parents receive a monthly deposit from the same account. Enough that Abboud doesn't have to work."

"Okay. That is a red flag. Update me when you know. What about friends? Any social life?"

"A few associations from the mosque he frequents. He also has an American girlfriend under wraps."

"What do you mean 'under wraps'?"

"Under wraps as in he doesn't seem to want the fam to know about her."

"That's a nice tidbit. It appears Abboud might have an exploitable vulnerability." The wheels in Cassandra's head started spinning. "Is there more?

"I've included some additional information in the file, along with some video footage. Most are older than a few weeks. With Abboud away from the campus for the holidays, there was nothing to grab from the university's security cameras."

"Only video? No intercepted calls? Come on. You've got the big guns. There's gotta be something hanging out there."

"As a matter of fact, there *is* more. I managed to isolate some interesting communication between him and a government intern. And, before you ask, I'm sending you the audio files, too. I also added an old MI5 report from the investigation into the father's murder. I think you'll find it interesting." Excitement rebounded in George's voice. "It gets better. Remember how we picked up a known signal at ground zero of the kidnapping?"

"Yes?"

"I found old calls between the intern and that phone. Trev was right all along. It's all linked, Cassie. All of it. A big messy cat's cradle."

The additional information painted an intriguing picture of Abboud. She needed eyes on him. Needed to assess his interaction with the girlfriend. Most of all, she needed a face-to-face. Only then could she analyze his expressions correctly.

"Ready or not, George, here I come."

"You're what?"

Cassandra chuckled at the sudden high pitch in his voice. "You heard me. I'm taking the next flight out across the pond. I'll send you my itinerary as soon as it's booked. I'm coming off the bench, George. Time to dust off my Farm training. Let's hope I haven't grown a little too rusty."

"Cassie. You can't be serious. You haven't done any field work in what? Three years? Trevor's not going to like this one bit."

"If there's one thing I know, it's that Trevor trusts me. I want

Trevor home. I'm pretty damn sure you two are doing everything in your power to get him back, too. Besides, this case has been driving you guys up the walls and keeping Trevor up at night. It's in my best interest to help out. It's a substantial lead, George. If it pans out, you guys might be able to close it for good. There is no way I can pass this up."

"What do I tell Trev if he asks?" A thread of panic laced his voice.

"Relax. He won't. Hey, the files just hit. Thanks for coming through on such short notice. I owe you one. Talk to you when I'm stateside."

"Cassie, wait. What did you mean earlier by dating profile?"

"You should ask Trev the next time you talk to him," Cassandra laughed, then disconnected the line. The poor guy would be dwelling on that for a while.

Within minutes and for an outrageous sum, she managed to secure a first-class seat on the first flight to Virginia that afternoon. Trevor would be proud she had suppressed her frugal side that day, and only because, aside from the pressing need to reach Naveed as soon as possible, she needed room to work without someone lying in her lap while she reviewed sensitive material. Thanking the heavens for online booking, she trotted up the stairs to the third floor and made a beeline to the state-of-the-art equipment room embedded in the back of the storage closet's wall.

She tapped the key into the hidden panel and the door opened, revealing the myriad surveillance equipment they kept at hand for all purposes. She never tired of hearing Trevor talk about all the latest gadgets added to the stockpile. A sweet longing made her sigh when she saw the new cameras Trevor had purchased to replace the ones they had abandoned in Russia.

She didn't miss the harrowing days they'd spent there, nor the fact that Trevor had almost gotten himself killed, but she did miss having an active role in a high profile case. She was about to rectify that problem.

Cassandra nabbed one of Trevor's small high-powered cameras and a micro voice recorder she'd need for her little piece of surveillance before locking the room. Next, she made a pit stop in the bedroom to pack her duffel and unearth a heavier coat from the closet. She'd need layers if she was going to be doing surveillance in the middle of the Virginian winter without turning into an icicle. Falling back on ingrained skills she'd acquired during her time with the CIA, Cassandra packed only the bare essentials. She wouldn't need much.

Adrenaline coursed through her veins, and the rush was intoxicating. Her whole body vibrated with energy. It felt good to act on her intuition and be rewarded with operable intel after such a long dry spell.

She didn't expect to stay in Virginia long, just long enough to get what she needed. Long enough to extract what she wanted from Naveed Abboud, whether he voiced the words or she read him like an open book.

Chapter Twenty-Three

Covers

*S*EAGULLS' CRIES MINGLED WITH THE *sound of crashing waves and the dinging of a distant buoy. The Morrígan's bow broke the waves, its white sails pregnant with wind. His parents stood on the vessel's deck, smiling and waving at him. Trevor watched silently from the dock as the gap widened, his throat blocked, his arms heavy as if made of concrete, unable to voice his terror or signal them back.*

The farther they sailed, the harder it became to discern the yacht from the stormy gray background, as if it was becoming one with the growing waves. The insistent dinging of the buoy grew in direct correlation with the sea's anger.

The loud ring of his secure satellite phone scared Trevor awake. "Fuck!" He grabbed the device from the desk, swiping the screen as he recognized the caller's ID. "You better have good news."

"I've been messaging you on chat for a while. I assumed you'd have your phone on you even if you were AFK." George knew he'd want to know if things had taken a turn. Good or bad.

Trevor looked at the computer screen and saw the many messages in the open window. He rubbed his eyes, still groggy from the brief slumber. "I wasn't away from the keyboard. I was asleep on it. First shuteye in days."

"Well...you may be going home soon enough." The smile in George's tone made Trevor's senses perk up.

"We got something?"

"Damn right. Your hunch was spot on, my friend. It took them a little longer than we expected, but we have movement."

"About time. Do you have coordinates?"

"Not yet. Surveillance is in progress. I'll get back to you once we have something. But I'd say it'd be safe to mobilize the men. I'll have all the intel in a neat package for you as soon as we pinpoint the target."

"Brilliant. I'll notify Hanson and Nelson."

"Oh, by the way, Cassandra is working it on this end, too." A long pause silenced the call. "She's made some inquiries, and from what I could get so far, there might be something of real interest in the direction of her investigation."

"That's good. Knowing Cassie, she'll dig up valuable information." A fist formed in his stomach at the mention of his wife. He ached to talk to her, to hear her voice, but knew that calling would make things harder for both of them. Maybe even crack the crystal-thin state of their truce. Just by thinking about how they'd parted made his insides burn. He chose instead to focus a hundred percent of his energy on the case and on getting all of them out of there as quickly as possible. "How is she?"

"Hanging. She sounds as stoic as you do, but she's not one to complain about things. Particularly not one to bitch about the way you dumped her and zipped to Jordan."

"Hey! You're supposed to be my friend. Besides, I was following orders. And she has way more resources in Dublin than she would have if she was here. You said it yourself: she's working on the case and doing what she does best."

A loud sigh sounded on the other side of the line. "Fine. I'll give you that. Don't blow this, Trevor."

Trevor let his head hang. "Do you think I don't worry about that every day?" The consulting job with the NSA that had started as a way for him to support his personal quest had turned into a time drain. The overwhelming pressure of working critical cases that took priority over his own had been unexpected. His need for closure always hung in the back of his mind, interrupting his sleep, making him second-guess himself. But when he was working those cases, helping solve mysteries, collecting evidence to put some nasty individuals away for a long time, he found purpose. He knew there would come a time when he would have to pick one. Or none. Maybe then he could just take over the family business and lead a normal life. Would Cassandra enjoy normalcy in their lives? A nine-to-five job, vacations in sunny places for longer than a couple of days or without putting their lives at risk, Christmas dinners with friends instead of being stuck at home burying their noses in a critical case. He frowned when he couldn't come up with an answer. "Message when you have something solid."

A bleak pause filled the line. "I will."

"Thanks, man." Trevor stared off into space for a few seconds after the call disconnected. George was right. He couldn't blow that. He'd have to choose soon enough. Maybe this unwanted break was the perfect time to find himself. Get his head straight. But not now. He had work to do.

He cracked his knuckles and got to the infiltration he'd been entangled with when he'd fallen asleep at the keyboard. The Israelis sure knew how to secure their systems. Yet it was nothing he couldn't crack with a little more ingenuity and brute force. He smiled as he tackled the challenge with renewed enthusiasm.

It didn't take him long to find the right strategy to establish access to the information he needed. By the time IT security began a lockdown, he already had the files he wanted. With those in hand, he rose to his feet and stretched his arms behind him to loosen sore muscles from his long vigil over the last couple of days. Time to mobilize the troops.

The Crew men had been on edge until they'd received the good news that Acer had survived the transport to Ramstein Air Base in Germany. He'd been stabilized and would be flown stateside for rehab as soon as possible. But that meant they were down one man for any upcoming operation. They would have to worry about that very soon. The good news was bound to lift their spirits a notch or two.

Leaving his makeshift control room, Trevor headed to the quarters he shared with Hanson and Nelson.

Nothing seemed to faze Hanson; but although it didn't show on the surface, Trevor knew that Acer's injury had shaken the man. He sensed an underlying restlessness in him as if he couldn't wait to be done with the mission and get away as fast and far as he could.

He walked in to find Hanson on his bed reading an old copy of Hustler, a cut-off straw hanging from the corner of his mouth. He looked up and smiled at Trevor's raised eyebrows.

"Is this a non-smoking dorm?"

"I quit a long time ago, but from time to time, the urge sneaks up on me." He held the straw between his fingers and took a fake drag from it. "It took some time to realize that if I'm going to die, it better be by someone else's hand and not my own." The crooked smile did nothing to mask the serious look in his eyes.

Trevor avoided going down that dark road. He didn't want to think of death when they were about to go into a powder keg.

"Works for me." Trevor looked around. "Where's Nelson?"

"Gym. He grumbled something about going nuts with the wait. Two days without developments. The man is ready to blow. Told me to make sure he was notified of any changes. He didn't leave the attitude behind when he left."

Trevor laughed. "That I can believe. As much as I would love to prod him and see him turn a nice shade of green, it's not the time for fun and games. We need to get him back here."

Hanson's eyebrows rose an inch. "We've got movement?"

At Trevor's nod, Hanson reached for his radio and requested Nelson be paged back to the room.

A few minutes later, Nelson strode in. Sweat dripped from his temples, soaking the collar of his t-shirt, adding to the damp display of his exertion in the weight room. He glanced from Trevor to Hanson as he used the front of his shirt to wipe the sweat from his face.

"So, what do we have?" His green eyes exuded more loaded questions, unusual for a man who'd often chosen to conceal all semblance of emotion behind a wall of formality or anger.

Trevor felt a prick of recognition. He'd been like that before he'd fallen for Cassandra. He'd hidden his identity and his personal struggles, even from his best friend. What could Nelson be hiding?

"George called. He's monitoring movement."

"Do we have a location?"

Trevor could almost feel waves of nervous energy wafting from Nelson.

"Not yet. I wanted to give you all a heads-up. It won't take long now that the wheels are turning. If my suspicions are proved right once again, we should be close to zooming in on solid coordinates. I'd recommend you handle any prep you need done for a new incursion. The ballistic results on the spent shells at the scene of the kidnapping suggest at least ten distinct weapons were used."

Nelson frowned. "What ballistic report? The CIA hasn't received any report from the Israelis yet."

"Let's just say I have my sources."

"Nice job, Bauer," Hanson smirked. "I'll need to get some more guys down here. We have two other troops coming out of rotation. I'll get that worked out right now." Hanson dropped the magazine he'd been holding onto the bed and left the room.

Trevor wasn't privy to the details of the troops' missions, but he knew the men were in constant movement around the globe. Knowing the high priority of their operation, Hanson would get the resources their mission needed.

The air in the room thickened once Trevor and Nelson were alone. There was a strange unease in the way Nelson moved to his luggage and pulled out his toiletry kit.

Glimpses of the times he'd had direct contact with Nelson since meeting the man flashed in Trevor's mind. The way Nelson had behaved when Cassandra had told him about their engagement; his meddling during the first months of their marriage contrasted with the way he'd come to their rescue in Russia, even when animosity still shone in his eyes; his furtive tumble with Nikol…. And then, nothing. He hadn't been in contact since.

Trevor had to admit that, aside from Nelson's strong disapproval of their marriage, his treatment of Cassandra in Russia and since then had been more fraternal than romantic. The switch had been swift and silent. He knew Nelson was hiding something; what better way to get it out in the open than to bait him?

"Been in touch with Petrovna?"

Nelson went rod-stiff. Bingo.

Nelson slowly turned around to face him. He took a deep breath before asking, "Why exactly do you want to know, Bauer?"

"To be honest," Trevor taunted, "I'm just trying to make sure you don't poach my wife." He wasn't—he knew he could trust Cassandra. Trevor was fairly certain he would have to rescue Nelson's ass from her if he ever crossed the line.

Much to Trevor's surprise, Nelson didn't bite. At least, not as he would have expected. Instead of being angry, Nathan's gaze turned somber.

A pained groan threatened to tear out of Nathan's lips. Bauer couldn't have known about his feelings for another married woman. He couldn't have known of the guilt he'd marinated in for years. He couldn't blame Bauer for thinking that way either, and had to concede that Bauer had been gutsy enough to confront him.

"You don't have to worry about that. Marriage puts any woman off limits for me. There is such a thing as a strict moral code." *Maybe too strict for my own damn good, but I abide by it.*

"In that case, what about Nikol? She's single. Or was when we last had contact. She's also a firecracker. You'll need to move faster than slug speed if you want to have a chance there."

Nikol Petrovna. Russian Secret Service. Beautiful. Hot-headed and deadly. They had a lot in common, more than the secret lives they both led. He'd allowed her to see more of him than any other before. They had both exposed themselves during that platonic one-night-stand, and not in a kinky way. They would never have fallen prey to that weakness had they expected to see each other again. All the shame, all the guilt. He was glad he hadn't crossed paths with her since, and wasn't concerned she'd spill his secrets. After all, he was privy to her share of shame and guilt as well. In a twisted way, they'd come to trust each other.

"I don't plan on making a move at all where Petrovna is concerned."

Bauer's grin grated on him. "Are you still pissed she kicked your ass that day?" The wide grin turned into a frown. "I don't get it. At least, not after the morning you two came out of the room looking like you'd enjoyed your time together."

"Cut it out, Bauer." Nathan kept his cool. If Bauer hoped to reap rewards with the conversation, he'd be very disappointed.

Bauer's smile died and his expression turned serious. "Why are you so bent out of shape with this mission?"

It'd been clear that Bauer suspected something since the day Rachael's video was broadcasted. Nathan had to use every ounce of control he'd possessed to suppress his reaction to seeing Rachael bound to that chair. Fear—no, terror—had almost paralyzed him, and that was a dangerous response for a man in his position. He couldn't allow himself to become vulnerable. Nathan knew Bauer had the skills to search wide and dig deep. In mere minutes, Bauer had managed to acquire information that probably would have taken Nathan weeks via the normal channels. Nathan could deny his interest in the case all he wanted. He could also threaten Bauer with prosecution if he invaded his privacy. He doubted any of that would have any effect on the man. Bauer was a bloodhound locked on a scent. Nathan had to move fast to throw him off course, and the only way he could do that was by telling him the truth. Just not all of it— merely enough to help hide his true feelings in plain sight.

"Phillip Moore. I told you the truth when I said we met a long time ago. I was in England for an internship." Bauer's eyes locked on him, almost the same way Cassandra's did when she was analyzing expressions. Unsettling, to say the least. "He'd become a close friend long before he helped me through a dark period of my life." Nathan held Bauer's eyes. "My younger brother committed suicide while in basic training. Jay couldn't handle the hazing, which became particularly brutal after one of the guys in his unit discovered he was gay." Pain uncoiled in his chest. No matter how much time had passed, remembering Jay's loss always caused pain. Nathan combed his hair with his fingers and forced a deep breath into his lungs.

Bauer's eyes lost their humor. "I had no idea, man. Very sorry."

"Phillip had lost a brother in Iraq, so when I broke down in front of him after finding out about Jay, he took me under his wing. I returned stateside long enough to attend Jay's funeral and then I was back in England, burying myself in work to forget. Phillip was there for me when I needed someone to save me from losing my mind to grief. We grew even closer. He became the older brother I wished I'd had." Nathan relived those days. They still had the power to crush him, yet they felt so far removed from his reality now. "Then Phillip married Rachael." He took a deep breath and continued, the familiar simmering slowly building in his stomach. "I joined the CIA shortly after and both our lines of work demanded time and commitment. We hadn't seen each other for years until he reached out a few weeks before he was killed. He needed information. Information I couldn't disclose to him. It would have broken too many rules. Jeopardized ongoing cases."

Bauer's frown deepened and he cocked his head, narrowing his eyes. "Basically, what you're telling me is that your strict moral code killed your friend." Bauer didn't wait for confirmation. "At least, that's what you believe. Now you're seeking redemption by working your hardest to rescue his wife."

Nathan held his stare, neither confirming nor denying. Bauer had seen a little more than he'd wanted. The controlled release of information wouldn't hold him off for long.

"I want Rachael out of there alive." Truest words he'd spoken in a long time. He witnessed a shift in Bauer's eyes. Nathan hated the faded compassion in them.

"We'll get her out of there." A ring of stubbornness graced the Irishman's tone, and for once he was thankful Bauer was on his side.

"Thank you." Nathan had never expected to ever voice those words to Bauer, but he truly meant them. Bauer didn't question or razz him about the information he'd shared. He didn't press the buttons Nathan had exposed to his perusal. For the second time since Russia, he could see why Cassandra had fallen for the guy. He cleared his throat, pulled his shirt over his head, and tossed it into an improvised laundry bag. Grabbing what he needed, he looked over at Trevor once again. "I'm hitting the shower. I'll meet you all back in the control room in a few."

"Sure. We should have more details as the day progresses."

Shower rooms in military bases were never empty. The place was as clean as one could expect from a service area, but the scent in the air made it clear the facilities were used by men who spent long hours, sometimes days, in the same clothes. The rule was get in, get out—fast.

Nodding curtly at the men standing by the door, he strode to the main shower room. Stripping out of his sweats, he hung them and the towel on the available hook, sparing them from the wet floors before claiming the closest showerhead. He placed soap and shampoo on the metal shelf that ran the length of the wall and turned on the tap.

Stepping under the tepid flow, he closed his eyes and let the water sluice over his body, hoping it would wash away the memories that had cropped up after the conversation. He wasn't so lucky.

His heart churned at the memory of the day he'd learned of Jay's death. He'd received the news from Luke over a brief international phone call. Only Phillip's prompt intervention and leveling presence had dragged Nathan from the edge of the abyss that had gaped in front of him like a monster waiting to swallow him whole.

Hopelessness and guilt had ravaged him, torn him apart. The memory of his father's outbursts flashed in his mind, the disappointment in his words echoing in his ears bringing with it the bitter taste that had flooded his mouth back then. It had driven Nathan to stay as far away from home as he could. He'd often spent holidays on campus, giving flimsy excuses of being swamped with coursework, even though he'd sorely missed his mother and younger brother.

"He died not knowing how much I loved him."

"Bollocks. He knew." Phillip's tone had been steady and calm.

If the words had come from any other, he'd have burst into a rage at the assumption.

"How can you say that with such confidence? You didn't know him."

"I've gotten to know you well. The good parts you've shared with me all involved Jay, so it's safe to assume he had the same good memories from your time together. He knew."

"Yeah…but I hadn't been home in a while. I've avoided going home for years. I should have been there for Christmas this year. What if—"

"You have to stop thinking about guilt and self-punishment. It won't do you any good. Focus on all the things you can do to honor your brother's memory. Make him proud." Phillip had patted his back in camaraderie as they sat at the bar.

Nathan had looked up from his cup to find understanding gleaming in Phillip's eyes.

"Is that how you've handled it?"

"Yes. Or at least I try to."

Phillip's words of comfort had acted as the thread holding him together since then.

The little burn of guilt he was all-too familiar with once again flared up along his breastbone, and he braced himself for the brunt of the pain he knew would come. Not being there for his little brother when he needed him had devastated Nathan. And he'd repeated the mistake with Phillip. Tension balled in his stomach. Nathan definitely wouldn't make the same damn one with Rachael.

As he rinsed the lather from his hair, he realized that sharing what little of himself he could with Bauer had lessened some of the weight he'd shouldered for a long time. The weeks at the Farm had taught him to deceive, sell, exploit, and psychologically access those around him, and most of all, roleplay. Everything in his life since the day he'd completed the program had been stowed away in the shadows. When he'd graduated as a CIA official cover operative, he'd welcomed the challenge with near glee. At the time, all he wanted was to bury himself in work, to the point where the Company would be all he was.

The lying and keeping secrets from those he cared about made him question at times the very purpose of his role within the Company. It had become particularly harder since Phillip's death. A bitter taste filled his mouth and Nathan suppressed a sad laugh at the irony. The man had pretty much lit the beacon pointing him to the CIA, yet he'd had no knowledge of how far he'd climbed.

He braced his hands against the wall, head hung low under the strong flow as the many cases he'd worked during those years washed through his mind. He'd believed he could make a difference, and he had. He hadn't joined the CIA for money, fame, or sex. He didn't expect public recognition for any of his successes; none of those who joined the CIA did. There wasn't any of that to be found in the service—but along the way, having to keep those accomplishments tucked in a dark corner had become a heavy burden. Nobody knew him for the good he'd done; they only saw the mask he'd become. Anger and disappointment churned his insides. Even the extent of how much pull he'd used when he'd intervened on Cassandra and Bauer's behalf in Russia had to remain a secret. By providing the Bauers access to the safe house and a way out of from under the shitstorm they had caused, he'd almost exposed his role and ruined his career. That little slip had placed him in timeout to safeguard his identity and his many other cases.

His cover depended on secrets. With everything else slipping out of his control, the only thing he could direct was his effort into the cases he worked. And for that, he needed his cover to remain intact. Relationships would never be easy. He'd accepted that. It's not like he could call home with a line like, "You can have dinner without me, honey. I'll be late spying on the governor." The only thing he seemed to excel at was his job. Since he could never have Rachael, he'd resigned himself to a life in the Company for as long as he was of use, even if it came with the hefty price of solitude. His muscles quivered, his pulse sped as anger flushed heat through his veins. He punched the wall, using pain to crush the feeling of helplessness that threatened to engulf him.

Opening his eyes, he saw the strange stares the men shot at him. He took a deep breath and shut off the water. They had a job to finish, and not having all their heads in the game could mean the difference between life and death. The deadline was approaching too fast; he couldn't fathom the possibility that they couldn't reach the hostages before time ran out. The thought sobered him, a strange heaviness taking hold of his limbs. He also had an enemy of the state to catch. He'd handle that as proficiently as he'd managed to keep who he really was under a tight cover.

He patted himself dry, wrapped the towel around his waist, and headed back to the room for a quick change into a suit, his cover's disguise. He hoped the time for donning the fatigues he'd brought would come soon enough.

Chapter Twenty-Four

Choose

CASSANDRA SLID THE KEYCARD INTO the slot in the lock. When the indicator light flashed green, she pushed the door open. She walked in, closing the door behind her, and was welcomed by soft jazz and warmth. She thanked whoever had set the thermostat at a comfortable temperature as she stripped off her jacket. The room's warm air caressed her skin, rubbing the numbness from her nose and cheeks. She traced the music to a clock radio sitting on the nightstand. Above it, a wall sconce cast a soft glow into the room. A king size bed lay centered against the wall, its white down comforter turned down for the night, two little chocolate squares nestled on one of the fluffy pillows. Housekeeping's little welcome home.

She dropped her duffel and jacket on the bed, then flipped off the music. The quiet that enveloped the small room brought back memories of other cities, other hotel rooms, other housekeeping welcomes during her time with the CIA. Those little touches no longer held the same appeal as they had back in the day. She'd had a taste of what real homecomings were like. They now involved crazy movie-themed door chimes, cluttered desks, and warm, strong arms wrapping around her the minute she stepped through the door.

Cassandra shoved all thoughts of home from her mind, choosing instead to focus on the lead that she was about to get up-close and friendly with. She crossed over to the wooden desk situated in front of the window and set her backpack on it. The red display on the alarm clock reminded her it was just past midnight. Her mind hadn't stopped during the flight. Making good use of the inflight internet access, she'd spent it reviewing everything George had forwarded, including the audio and video files. She'd studied the area around the complex where Naveed lived, looking for inconspicuous places to set up camp. Luckily, it sat across from a strip mall, its public parking area the perfect base for her surveillance. She'd shot a quick email to George asking him to check what kind of security system was used at Naveed's building, and, if possible, to get her the entry code. She'd also plugged all of Naveed Abboud's known hangouts, including the mosque he frequented, into the GPS on her phone. More important-ly, she'd established a facial expression baseline using the video footage.

She itched to get the surveillance started, but she could feel her reserves draining. She was fairly certain she wouldn't encounter much movement at that time of the night, and made an executive decision to recharge her batteries. She couldn't afford to make mistakes because she was too tired to think straight.

With a deep sigh, she removed her laptop from the backpack. While she waited for the screen to come to life, she retrieved the small box wrapped in manila paper she'd collected from the front-desk clerk at check-in. She sat at the desk and stared at the box with the name *Cass James* written in bold black letters across the top. Her stomach twisted and her chest grew tight. She'd left that name behind only a little over a year ago, but it already tasted foreign on her tongue. Registering under that name—like the contents of the box—was a safety precaution. As Cassandra tore through the packaging, her thoughts reeled back to the reason that box was now in her possession.

"I've boarded and should be airborne shortly," she'd said when George answered the call.

"Cassandra. Since it's obvious I can't stop you, you have to promise me you'll watch your back. I'm kind of attached to my own fine ass, and would hate to have it served to me on a platter by an angry Irishman."

"You worry too much," she'd chuckled.

George hadn't seen the humor in it. *"Did you miss the part about angry Irishman? I mean it. I've actually heard him growl whenever you've taken chances. If you run into any complications, you get your ass to my place. I'm only a three-hour drive from Richmond."*

"Me? Take chances? If it makes you feel better, I promise. I'll even pinky swear."

She had to admit that even before that call she'd already felt naked going in without her weapon or some form of backup. Adding his concern to the unease running thick in her veins, once in flight, she'd reached out to an old friend from her Agency days who owed her a few favors.

Although they hadn't had much contact after she'd left Langley, their camaraderie had picked up as if it had been yesterday since they'd last talked. He'd been responsible for dropping off the box and its contents—a SIG-Sauer P229, extra ammo, and holster—at reception. She opened the box and a trickle of relief flared in her chest as she lifted the two-tone black-and-silver pistol, inserted the magazine, and took aim. Its weight felt just right in her hand. Not that she thought she'd need it, but bearing in mind the events of the past year, it didn't hurt to be prepared for the worst.

Returning her gaze to the laptop, she set the gun aside and sent a message to George, letting him know she'd arrived at her destination and checking to see if he'd received her earlier request. She'd wanted a guaranteed way to enter the building without having to trick some unsuspecting tenant to ring her in. While she waited for a response, she pulled her phone from her pocket and her stomach tumbled when she tapped Trevor's name. No calls. No text messages. It bothered her that he hadn't called or at least sent her a text. She craved the constant contact they'd had prior to their argument. It was as if she was jonesing for her next fix of him.

"You can't avoid me forever, Brennan," Cassandra grumbled. But dwelling on his avoidance only made her the pot calling the kettle black. Their angry words, the hurt in his voice, echoed in her mind and she squeezed her eyes closed, feeling utterly miserable for the things she'd said to him. She could just as easily have sent him a message, bridged the gap, but she worried that if she tried, it would make things worse. They needed to talk about it face-to-face, clear the air, and move on. And it was with that purpose she had crossed the Atlantic. The faster they had a bead on Waldo, the faster he'd be back home.

With a long, exhausted sigh, Cassandra pushed back from the desk and stood. A hot shower and soft bed were calling her name. A shiver raked frigid fingers up her spine as she stripped out of her travel clothes, grabbed what she needed for the shower, and stepped into the marble enclosure. She turned the tap and soon her toes tingled, thawing under the piping-hot water. As she washed the many hours on the plane down the drain, her thoughts returned to Trevor and her years with the CIA. In the past, before she'd met him, a job was a job. You planned, executed, completed it, and moved on to the next. While she missed the excitement of the types of cases she'd worked in the past, the challenge and spontaneity of her work with Trevor had changed everything. It was no longer just a job. She had more skin in the game. It was personal, and she was determined to do her part to shoulder some of the stress her husband had been living under since before she'd met him.

Feeling human again, she stepped out of the shower. Back in the room, toasty and dry, she dressed in layers to fight the chill during the stakeout she planned to take on later that morning. She left the top layer—a pair of black jeans and a black cable sweater—folded neatly on the chair for easy access. It wasn't worth slipping into pajamas when she had to be up in only a few hours.

The sound of an incoming email drew Cassandra back to the desk and the tension stabbing her gut eased a tiny bit. George had come through with the access code. That man was the Grand Mage of the internet right after her husband, that was for damn sure.

She shot off a quick thank you, repacked her bag, and dropped it by the door. Barely able to hold her eyes open, Cassandra slipped under the comforter and snuggled in for a reparative snooze. She closed her eyes and let her mind drift to the last moments she'd shared with Trevor, recalling every inch of his firm body, her whole being aching for his touch.

"Damn you, you treacherous mind," she whispered burrowing deeper into the covers. A few hours were all she needed, then game on.

BASED ON PREVIOUS surveillance, Abboud routinely performed the five daily *Salaah* in congregation during school breaks. She decided to take a chance that he would stick to his routine and drove to the mosque to wait for him after her much-needed shuteye. It didn't take her long to find it. She had the address and surveillance photos showing the building with the white-washed siding and a small deck on the front.

Her position directly across from the two-story house gave her a clear view of the building used as a mosque by the local Islamic community.

Mature trees lined the walkway and obscured the front door and windows. She sat for hours in the cold car, sipping not-so-great coffee from the cup she'd brewed in her hotel room and snapping pictures of anyone who entered the building. She smiled when Abboud arrived on schedule and disappeared into the mosque only to emerge again an hour and a half later as the pinkish-yellow light of dawn broke across the sky.

When he cleared the trees and stepped onto the sidewalk, Cassandra zoomed in on his face and set the camera to record. Abboud's eyes were fixed under a heavy frown, his lower jaw tense, his lips pressed firmly together in a line. It wasn't the serene image of someone who'd just had a conversation with a higher power. Without his knowledge, he broadcasted his emotional duality to her. His guilt shrouded him like a dark cloud as he put distance between himself and the meeting place. It niggled her curiosity. Something or someone had gotten under his skin during his brief time in the mosque.

Cassandra shadowed Abboud all morning, and, as a true shadow, she followed him everywhere, capturing video, taking pictures, and analyzing them while waiting for him to make his next move. For the most part, it was predictable—pretty damn close to what she had pieced together from what George had found on him.

She witnessed the guilt dissipate and a clearer portrait of Naveed Abboud formed in her mind. He enjoyed his ready access to technology yet was allowed minimal access to it to communicate with his brother with whom, based on NSA records, he hadn't had contact in years. Naveed lived the life of a privileged man, which conflicted drastically with the beliefs he was supposed to abide by and the faith he followed. He had a hard-on for big-ticket items, no matter what they were. He spent close to two hours in a local retail store testing gadgets. The way he loved to shop, he could easily give Jessica a run for her money. He enjoyed high-priced coffee, too. Who was she to judge? She had the same affliction. She just about drooled when she was tackled by the delicious bittersweet aroma of fresh brew during the stakeout. That kind of personal gratification could never happen in the world he'd been taken from as a young child. It was considered a sin. Naveed Abboud was Americanized, right down to his accent. He was also afraid, and very much divided about his beliefs.

All day, she observed the emotional markers of that in his expression. He went to the mosque for each prayer at each designated time, and each time, he left the place with the same duality of emotions mirrored on his face. The furrowed brows and tense mouth were telling signs.

Ashlyn, the girlfriend listed in his dossier, was already seated in the restaurant when Cassandra followed him there. The curvy blonde only had eyes for him. Ashlyn's gaze brightened and a sweet blush of color swept across her cheeks when she saw him. Cassandra took a table from where she could observe their interaction and listen in without attracting his or the girlfriend's attention. Not that he was paying much attention to his surroundings. He also only had eyes for the girl.

She found it amusing that he masked it around his girlfriend. He was all smiles and happiness around her, but his fake happy-go-lucky attitude didn't fool Cassandra. While others may not have caught the lie behind the smile, she had. The girlfriend, on the other hand, was transparent. Her love for him shone in her eyes—even a blind man could see it.

At the end of the meal, Naveed begged off spending the evening together. The tone of his voice and shaded look in his eyes as he deflected her questions were indicators that he wasn't happy about not being truthful. Disappointment pinched Ashlyn's face.

From the discussion that followed, his avoidance was becoming a habit of late. He soothed her concerns, promised her it had nothing to do with any other girl, that she was the only one he loved. Soon her lips tilted into a full smile, pulling another one from him.

It was the first real smile Cassandra had witnessed that whole day. The girlfriend was his Achilles heel, and quite possibly the primary reason for the emotional conflict displayed so clearly on his expressions but hidden from the one he cared for most.

When Cassandra spied Abboud waving for the check, she left ahead of them, a tactic used to keep her watch undetected. She walked out of the restaurant and dove into the mom-and-pop copy shop beside it. She leaned her shoulder against the red painted doorway and waited, eyes glued to the restaurant's door. She blew a hot breath into her cupped hands, then shoved them deep into her jacket pockets, trying to stave off the cold biting at her fingertips. For the second time that day, she wished she'd brought a pair of gloves. Abboud and his girlfriend would be leaving the restaurant any minute now.

As if on cue, the couple stepped out, Abboud's arm draped protectively around his girlfriend's shoulders, his head leaning closer to hers, listening to something she said. Ashlyn's laughter broke through Cassandra's rumination. She pushed from the doorway and followed the source of the infectious sound, keeping a discreet distance until the oblivious couple reached a movie theater and purchased tickets. She captured a few more photos of them together before they disappeared inside, then checked to see when the movie they'd selected let out. Luckily for her, it was a longer one.

He'd be alone that night; it was time to make her move. An

acute sense of satisfaction unfurled in her gut and spread up through her chest like wildfire as she strode back to the car, her brain already working all the angles and possible outcomes. She now had a reliable baseline to go by when she interrogated him later. Reaching the car, she slid in behind the wheel and pulled her cell phone from her pocket. Her thumbs flew across the keys.

Wish me luck, Georgie. I'm going in.

The plan was to enter his apartment and engage him when he returned home. It was the safest and most private spot for them to have their little talk.

Cassandra shoved her small lock-pick case into her jacket and discreetly holstered her gun in the shoulder piece that her buddy had included in the package. She glanced at her watch. By her calculations, the movie would let out in another hour. The brisk evening air washed over her as she left the warmth of the rental. The sun had taken a nosedive, and only the light dripping from streetlamps lined the street. Pulling up her hood to ward off the chill brushing against her neck, she shoved her hands into her pockets and walked toward the pedestrians at the corner crosswalk.

Abboud's complex was located in the center of the red brick historic building across the street. At the green light, she mingled and strolled up the street, past sleepy dark retail windows to the main glass entrance. Cassandra resisted the urge to look over her shoulder as she punched in the memorized code and grinned when the deadbolt clicked open. She pushed through the door into the tiled lobby, breathing easier when she didn't find anybody there.

The place was quiet. The winter-break lethargy was in full effect. Only a few students were still around, most having left for the holidays. Only locals or those holding local jobs remained. Tapping into the floorplan in her head, she found the stairwell situated to the left of the elevator and took the stairs to the second floor. Her cheeks burned when the jog up the stairs reminded her of the one in Monaco and how Trevor had welcomed her back to the room. Her pulse raced as she reached the top. She paused, mapping the area in her head, filling in the gaps that the one-dimensional floorplans couldn't reveal. She exited the stairwell onto a wide common area decorated with Cape Cod colors. The light-brown wood-laminate floors, blue-gray walls, white trim, comfortable lighting, and exposed beams with interspaced skylights made the place almost worthy of a magazine spread. To her left, an army of stackable washers and dryers sat in a glass-walled room; to the right, a bank of soda vending machines. Abboud's two-bedroom apartment was located at the end of a hallway branching off the large space. Cassandra padded down the well-lit hall, her shoes making no sound on the plush carpet, to his door.

Other than the front entrance, the building used conventional key locks. A ripple of excitement spread from her chest to her fingertips. It had been a while since she'd used her lock picks and looked forward to practicing her skill. She watched and listened for incoming traffic and, seeing none, pulled out the cloth case and slipped out the two pieces she needed. With one eye on the hall, she jimmied the lock. Within seconds, it clicked open. *Like riding a bike.* Patting herself on the back, she tucked the tools back into her pocket, pulled out a compact flashlight, and stepped inside.

The door opened onto a small sitting area sparsely furnished with a gray overstuffed couch, matching chair, and blond-wood coffee table. Beyond the sitting area was an L-shaped kitchen with black cabinets and matching countertops. The apartment was pristine. Not a magazine or cup littered the area. Cassandra closed the door behind her, taking care to stay away from the large window facing the street. She strode with cat-soft steps down the hallway that led to the two bedrooms.

She spared no time before rummaging through drawers, checking under beds, and searching inside closets. His cabinets were filled with brand-name jeans and t-shirts, another sign of his enjoyment of American commercialism. But other than living the high life on a budget outside his means, nothing indicated he was more than what he appeared to be—a college student.

In the second room, she checked the desk drawers. Under the glow of her Maglite, she flipped through the files in the first drawer. School projects and notes. The other drawer was locked. Cassandra picked the lock, and as she eased it open, a CZ P-07 pistol greeted her. The gun was one favored by Special Forces. *A hobby? Or a tool?* It was the only sign there was more to Naveed than met the eye, a weak one at that, but one that could possibly tie him to something outside of campus life. After a thorough search, she found no other weapon in the apartment.

Cassandra's mind spun that little nugget of information in her head as she checked the safety and tucked the gun into the waistband at her lower back. Better safe than sorry. She flashed the light on her watch. The movie would be ending about now. She added the time it would take for Naveed to drop off Ashlyn and drive home. Not a long wait. Her heart raced in expectation of what would happen shortly.

She retraced her steps back to the living room and paced the floor, impatience twisting her stomach into knots. Fifteen minutes later, footsteps approached the door. She flattened against a spot next to it where the wall tucked back. She could barely breathe when a key turned in the lock and the door opened. From her vantage point, she watched Naveed Abboud close the door behind him, flip the wall switch on, and move further into the room without detecting her presence. Keys still in his hand, he stopped as if he'd forgotten something and turned around, only to lock eyes with Cassandra. She witnessed shock, fear, and on its heels, desperation flutter across them in a wave.

She lifted her palms out, showing she was unarmed. "Navee—"

His arm struck out; the left hook caught her across her cheek-bone. A soft cry escaped her lips as her head snapped back and she staggered to regain balance. The force of the hit surprised her, but she was familiar with that kind of pain. She'd taken worse from deadlier men. She deflected his wild backswing and used his momentum to pull him toward her. His accelerated breathing fanned her face, his hands reached for her shoulders, but she anticipated his move. Grabbing his right wrist, she shoved the palm of her free hand up against his chin, breaking his hold and knocking him away.

Cassandra's cheek throbbed and her lip stung where sweat met the split skin. She could already feel the pain of the bruise and the swelling as blood pulsed in that area. Out of the corner of her eye, she saw him scurrying and before she could stop him, he scrambled down the hall toward the bedrooms. Without missing a beat, Cassandra followed and, just as he had reached the locked drawer, she struck again with a well-placed kick. Another grunt escaped his throat as the force of the double kick threw him flat on his back. In a swift move, Cassandra pulled his gun from its hiding place at her lower back, stomped on his wrist, pinning it to the ground, and dropped her knee in the center of his chest. The sound of their panting mingled in the otherwise silent space. Gun aimed at his forehead, she tilted her head so he could see her eyes.

"Are we done here?" She lifted an eyebrow, waiting for his response. His gaze shifted from her to the barrel staring down at him. Defiance darkened his eyes. Their simple little chat had just gotten more complicated. She realized she'd have to use every possible dirty trick in the book if she was to get anything useful out of him. "Ashlyn is a beautiful woman. Maybe I should call her over to join the party."

Naveed's body stilled, his eyes widened, and fear washed the defiance from them. Cassandra held her breath, hoping he'd realized he had no choice but to listen. He nodded and relief washed over her. She hadn't wanted to hurt the young man any more than she had to. She held her position over him until his body relaxed into the rug. She pushed off him with a long breath.

"Stand." Naveed rolled to his knees, his nervousness palpable. She gestured him up. "Easy now."

He pushed to his feet and faced her, maintaining his silence. His aggressive reaction was on par with finding an intruder in his home; the need to defend himself was understandable, even if the intruder was a woman. But the lack of words surprised her. From the expression in his eyes, he was trying to make sense of her presence and coming up empty.

Cassandra nodded to the chair on the other side of the room, keeping him under the aim of his own gun. "Sit."

Hands raised, Naveed sat in the gray upholstered low-back chair.

"Let's try this again, shall we?" She studied him as she wiped the blood pooling at the corner of her mouth with the back of her hand, assessing the damage. The adrenaline jacking her veins subsided and sweat glistened on her temples. She could hear George in her head. *"Seriously? What were you thinking?"*

"Who are you? What do you want?" His low rasp drew her attention back to him.

"Who I am doesn't matter. What I want is a different story." She sat on the arm of the couch and rubbed the tender spot on her jaw. Cassandra returned the gun to the band of her pants and studied him before continuing, "I have a few questions about your father."

Confusion shadowed his eyes. "Why would you want to ask me about my father?"

Cassandra held his eyes. "I'm referring to your biological father, Ahmed Abboud. Not the one who raised you."

His body tensed and his hands clenched the armrests. Cassandra caught a flicker of surprise in his eyes before anger set in. She'd hit a mark.

"I have no idea what you're talking about. My father is Farooq Abboud; he owns a restaurant in Clarksburg, West Virginia."

"I don't have time to fool around. I *know* your father is Ahmed Abboud, a known extremist responsible for several bombings in London in the late eighties and early nineties. He was detained for questioning after a bombing in 1999. He died while in MI5's custody before he could give the name of his accomplice."

His head rose and his eyes narrowed. "My father did not simply die in custody. He was murdered by MI5."

Cassandra shook her head. "And here I thought your dad lived in Clarksburg."

His eyes widened and his throat moved as if he were trying to swallow back his words.

"What if I told you that I also know that MI5 was cleared of any wrongdoings in that case? That I have seen a document exonerating them and pointing fingers at the same organization responsible for putting him in London that day?"

Anger reared its head again and colored his tone. "You are lying. He would never have killed my father. It was those bastards at MI5."

Cassandra narrowed her eyes, focusing on his expressions to gather from them the words he wasn't saying. "Who would never have? And how can you be sure?"

Naveed tipped his chin defiantly higher and pursed his lips, doubt now taking hold.

She pushed his buttons, hoping to hit the right ones. "You were what? Ten months old when your father passed away? All you have to go on is the rhetoric that your family and your sponsor have fed you. Your education, this,"—she opened her arms and embraced the room—"the things you like to own, the whole life you've created here, hasn't been handed to you for free. It has a price, doesn't it? Compliance. Isn't that why you haven't introduced Ashlyn to your family or friends?"

Within a matter of seconds, myriad emotions crossed Naveed's face. Microexpressions ranging from disbelief to anger, relief, and finally fear completed the full spectrum. Cassandra knew he was on the fence, close to leaping in either direction. It was not just her words that were nudging him. It was his own internal struggle. She'd witnessed it all day.

"The man who set it all up. The one who pays the bills. I need to know everything you know about him. What's his plan for the kidnapped diplomats?"

"I can't tell you that. You don't understand." His hands shook and he gripped them together.

"You'd be surprised." Cassandra could totally understand the concept of misplaced duty. The desire to do what was expected when deep in your soul you knew something was off. It was time to shoot that arrow. To take aim at his Achilles heel.

"What do you think he will do if word gets out about Ashlyn? A well-placed call, a whisper in the right ear? That's what puts that fear in your soul, doesn't it? That harm could come to her like it did to your father. Deep inside, you've always known something was not right. You are an intelligent man, Naveed. Think. You have been misled. Your father was taken from you by one of his own. Why would MI5 kill the only man who could identify him? The question you should be asking yourself is why you are protecting the one responsible for ordering your own father's death when he became a threat." Cassandra bluffed her way through without the need for a good cop to balance out her bad cop act. "Do you want the same to happen to your girlfriend?"

His head snapped up and he stared at her. Naveed hesitated, on the brink of breaking, and yet, she could see that the indecision warring inside him could sway him the wrong way. She knew he was struggling against a strong current of indoctrination.

"Talk to me. This can be your one chance to live the life you want with Ashlyn. A life without looking over your shoulder. Will you sit back and protect someone who is capable of so much hatred when deep in your gut you know it's wrong?"

Naveed dropped his eyes to his hands clenched in his lap. A tense silence enveloped the room. A mélange of nerves and butterflies ricocheted in her stomach, waiting for his decision.

"Choose, Naveed."

Chapter Twenty-Five

A Wolf in Sheep's Clothing

*T*HE CHAIR CREAKED WHEN KHALIL took his seat in the small room. Every one of the hostages had been to that room at least once. All had been interrogated and roughed up. Appearances were paramount to the success of their plan. The door creaked when the guards brought the American traitor to Khalil's presence. The man strode in, hands bound, the indifferent look on his face quickly changing to the calculating expression Khalil had gotten used to seeing in private.

Khalil cocked his head and quipped in Arabic, "I see my men haven't roughed you up enough today."

"That was never part of the deal," the man hissed in the same language, contempt bleeding from each word. "Neither is this." He nodded at his tied hands.

Khalil raised an eyebrow as a warning, unimpressed by the man's tone. "You're a big boy. You can handle it."

"Have you mentioned your personal touch to the *Rasūl?*"

"Americans," Khalil laughed, shaking his head. "When you said you'd do anything to get your share, were you lying?"

"No. Of course not." The American's eyes hardened. "Years devoted to the business and what do I get? Assigned to a thankless job. I believe I deserve a little more than that. I'll help your cause if you help mine."

"Then stop complaining. This is not The Hilton. You get no special treatment. It would defeat the purpose of the deal."

"Fine. Why am I here?" The American leaned back in the chair and rested his bound hands on his lap. "Isn't the deadline in two days? When and how do you plan to release us?"

"The *Rasūl* sent a change in the plans."

"Change? What change?"

"He believes your role will be more secure and you'll be even more well regarded if it appears the liberation was negotiated under bigger pressure."

"Fine. So what do we need to do? Rough us all up a bit more? Christ. Next thing on the menu will be hot pokers."

"Tomorrow, you'll be brought out often so that your cell mates know you've been talking. Make sure you give them the idea you've found a way through to me."

"What about Ms. Moore?"

"She may be key to swaying public opinion. The public is always more touched by the suffering of females." Emotions Khalil couldn't quite identify crossed the man's eyes. He could almost swear he saw…glee? "I won't go too far. I'd hate to see such beautiful skin marred." Her beauty tempted Khalil; her feisty spirit did more than that. "Pity I can't keep her for myself."

The guards prompted the man to stand.

"Don't be fooled," he said before leaving. "She's smarter than you think. Moore would have been proud."

Khalil had a bad feeling about him. He'd mention his concerns to the *Rasūl* when they met again. "You knew her husband?"

The American stopped midstride into the hallway and looked over his shoulder, his eyes full of cold disdain. "You could say that. I met him on the day he died." The icy tone in the man's voice and the smirk curving his lips sent chills down Khalil's spine.

THE MOVEMENT AND the voices outside her door had drawn her to peek through the cracks. Nothing in the world could have prepared her for the crushing blow she received when she recognized the man's voice. The statement made in fluent Arabic made her skin crawl. There was only one person Phillip had met the day he died. His killer.

No! Rachael spun around and leaned against the door to keep herself from collapsing to the floor. She shut her eyes tight and held back the scream that threatened to escape her throat and give her away to the men outside.

Despair gave way to anger. She wanted to break through the door and beat the bastard to a pulp. A traitor and a killer. How could she have missed it? He'd been right under her nose. Her thoughts tumbled into dreadful clarity. Everything made sense now. He had access to the files, freedom to come and go from the embassy at all times—freedom to roam the building without raising suspicion. *I'm a fool.*

The locket became more important than ever. She had to get it back. Without hard evidence, knowing his identity was useless. She needed the other bits of information she'd collected to piece it all together and complete Phillip's dossier. Rachael's stomach churned uncomfortably with mingled disappointment and relief.

The traitor had stolen her chance to say goodbye to Phillip, to part without guilt. He'd also eliminated any chance she might have had with Nathan. She doubted he'd ever forgive her for implying Phillip's death was his fault. Nathan was stoic in his suffering, and she knew she had hurt him more than he allowed her to see that day. Now that the time had arrived to close that door behind her, all she could feel was a deep-seated sadness. Her only way of saying goodbye would be to put that wolf in sheep's clothing away forever and move on with her life.

Chapter Twenty-Six

Minus One

ATHAN'S PHONE CHIMED ON THE floor beside the bed, pulling him out of a semi-sleep. He swiped it from the floor, tapping to answer and bringing it to his ear in one single motion. His eyes caught sight of the clock on the wall. Twenty hundred hours. Only a few hours after the briefing had ended, and he'd had very little sleep. No rest for the weary.

"Have you seen the news?" Franklin's tone put him on high alert.

"No. What's happened?" He sat up, already reaching for clothes.

"It's bad, Nelson." Dread engulfed Nathan and settled in his gut. Gory images all starring Rachael overwhelmed his senses. "We got the green light. Get those boots on the ground."

Nathan released the breath he didn't even know he'd been holding. The team had been in a holding pattern, waiting for the DOD's blessing, ever since they'd received critical pieces of intelligence from Miller and Cassandra. Decisions of that magnitude required a lot of bureaucratic legwork, which explained the long wait. If things were rolling faster, it could only mean the urgency had overridden caution.

"On it."

The second the line went silent, he stormed out toward Bauer's control room, mind reeling with the possible reasons for such swift approval of the raid. He burst through the door in time to observe Bauer's expression change into a painful grimace, his eyes glued to the laptop in front of him.

Nathan closed the distance to Bauer's desk in two strides. "What the fuck is going on?" He looked down to see a popular video-hosting site open on the internet browser.

"They uploaded a new video." Bauer raised his gaze to meet his and Nathan's stomach plummeted.

"Show me." His heartbeat slowed to a crawl when Bauer played the video from the beginning.

A man wearing the typical *mujahideen* clothing, face partially covered by a black headscarf, eyes full of hatred flashing at the camera, held court in a sparse room in front of the Palestinian State flag, the same used in Rachael's video.

"America, you were warned. No action on your part means action on ours."

The video transitioned to an outdoor scene. The camera zoomed in to show one of the hostages, clearly one of the males, hands bound behind him and head covered with a black bag, standing tall in a cage. As the camera zoomed out, it showed the hostage wearing a white *thawb*. His build suggested he was one of the DSS agents captured during the attack.

Nathan could foresee the developments even before they began unfolding before his eyes. A sacrificial lamb. Dressed in white. Whoever that man was, he had been readied to die.

The video panned to the field beside the cage showing a beaten dirt area surrounded by tall walls. The few *mujahideen* in the clip had hidden their faces behind black scarves or balaclavas. Two of them dragged the man from the cage, herding him to the open area where another man waited, holding a long, wide sword. No words were exchanged among any of those on camera.

As they forced the hostage to his knees, it finally dawned on him what was about to take place. He began pleading for his life. *"No. Please. Don't do this."*

Those around him were unmoved by his words. One of them shoved his head down. He struggled against it once, twice. The man punched him on the side of his head, stunning him.

Nathan braced for it, but nothing ever prepares anyone for the gruesomeness of a beheading. The man wielding the sword raised it high in the air and swiftly brought it down. The hostage's black-shrouded head rolled to the side at the same time his body slumped forward. Blood sprayed, seeped, and pooled, forming a red halo around the body.

The video transitioned back to their leader. *"Six minus one makes five. We will continue to act if you continue to support the raping of our state with your inactivity. One hostage for every day of silence."*

A wave of numbness spread from Nathan's legs to his chest and his stomach constricted. Having been privy to grisly scenes before did not make him impervious to the morbid image. He squeezed his eyes shut and took a deep breath, his nostrils filling with the metallic odor from memory. When he opened them, he saw the same shock and disgust mirrored in Bauer's expression. The face that usually sported a smartass grin now furrowed into a deep frown.

"How do they sleep at night?"

Nathan had no answer. He averted his eyes from the screen, set on avoiding the repetition of the macabre act.

"We need to ID him. See what you can pull from the video. And alert the team—we have the green light. Briefing in thirty in the greenroom."

Nathan turned on his heel and left Bauer in charge of gathering the men and getting all communications ready for the raid. In their shared quarters, he wasted no time to suit up into full tactical desert gear. Unbeknownst to the team, he'd received the same intensive physical training as Special Forces operators to fulfill his non-cover role. The suit was a clever disguise of his less-suave facet, the one that made him capable of holding his own against any of the Crew men. Whether the situation required physical strength or mental fortitude, he had to be equipped to handle any adversity.

Ready to jump into the fire with the team, he headed back to the greenroom for the briefing and what promised to be the beginning of a very long night.

Chapter Twenty-Seven

Golden Ticket

EVEN BEFORE CASSANDRA LEFT Naveed Abboud under the care of agents who would take him and Ashlyn under protective custody, there was no doubt in her mind that she was heading to Jordan. If Khalil Abboud was detained for questioning, she wanted to be there for it. Her skills would be crucial in determining the veracity of anything he told them, and having the truth from the get-go would make the capture of their main target much easier. As soon as she returned to her hotel room, she called George to report on the intelligence she'd acquired.

"I'm sending you my notes via email. I've included all of the other intel I had collected on Abboud as well as my observations. I believe that will give them a better understanding of what we're dealing with."

"As Trevor says, brilliant! I would kiss you if I could, Cassie. I'm pinging Trev as we speak. Now for the important part. How was it? Had the rust settled in, or was it a walk in the park?"

"Not a bit of rust in sight. It felt pretty damn good, actually."

Exhilarated and alive, apart from a bit sore, she wanted to add, but knew that would trigger a world of problems.

"Great! What time do you get in? Do you need a pickup?"

"Sorry, George. Change in plans. I cashed in a few favors and was able to hitch a ride on an earlier flight out of Langley later this afternoon."

"Give me a shout when you get back to home sweet home. I want to hear all about how it went. You know I have always considered taking on field work. I live vicariously through your and Trevor's adventures."

If she told George she had no intention of returning to Dublin and that the favors she'd cashed in involved a military transport to Jordan, George would freak and rat her out to Trevor—or even worse, Nathan—in seconds flat. Either one or both would intervene and she would end up on a redeye to Dublin. Swearing George to secrecy was also out of the question; it would put a burden on his shoulders and cause conflict between the two friends. She couldn't put him in that position. So she kept it to herself.

"You got it. I'll be in touch once I've landed."

"All right. Be safe. Oh! Want me to pass any message along?"

She almost chuckled at the oh-so-not-subtle tone in his voice. George and his cupid complex. She had to think long and hard on that one. As badly as she wanted to break the ice, she couldn't risk them discovering her plan and grounding her.

"That's okay, Georgie. I'll send him a message myself." She paused, considering whether she really wanted the answer, but had to ask. "How is he?"

"I'm not going to lie. It's been tough. He's right in the middle of it all and it hasn't all been pretty. Particularly not since Acer's injury."

Cassandra flinched inwardly. She'd read the report on that snafu. Her husband was a complex man and would shoulder anything that went wrong on his watch, even if it hadn't been his fault. She was more determined than ever to help him. Now that she'd exhausted her capabilities away from the heat, it was time to jump straight into the fire.

"Thanks for letting me know. I gotta go. Catch you later."

She took a deep breath after she hung up. She cleared her mind of all thought and let her eyes meander over the delicate details of the wallpaper. She was crashing at a friend's house. The old CIA friend who had arranged for the delivery of the handgun to the hotel, the same friend who'd arranged the transport to Germany.

A soft rap on the door pulled her attention. "Come in."

The door cracked open and her friend's wife's worried expression made her cringe. She came in and put a bottle of pain-relief pills along with a glass of water on the side table.

"I thought you might need this." Her expression didn't display surprise, nor did she question Cassandra about her injuries. She'd probably connected the dots. "Do you need anything else? Something for your eye?"

Cassandra tentatively touched her cheek. The area around it was tender and puffy. "How about a magic wand to make it go away within the next few hours?"

The petite woman, about her age, wrinkled her nose and the hint of a smile quirked at the corner of her mouth. "I wish I had one. Would come in handy. It looks like you will be sporting a shiner for a little while. Sorry."

"I guessed as much. Thanks again for taking me in. I should be out of your hair later today."

"Don't be silly. Now try and get some rest."

"Once my head hits the pillow, I'll be out like a light." Cassandra gave the woman a quick hug.

"I bet." The woman paused at the door. "There're extra blankets in the hall closet and we're just a little further down the hall if you need anything. Good night."

The woman closed the door on her way out, leaving Cassandra alone with her thoughts. If the beginning of the day was a sample of what was yet to come, she'd be facing Armageddon when she landed in Jordan. Sleep was just what she needed to meet it head on.

Chapter Twenty-Eight

Ready, Set

*E*XPECTATION REFLECTED IN EACH OF the soldier's faces. Aside from those who'd been there before the first operation took place, the Crew now stood two more units strong, bringing the new incursion numbers up to seventeen of their own.

Their full contingent crowded the room for the raid's briefing, eyes fixed on the large monitor covering most of one wall and proudly displaying the SOCOM and the 8th Special Warfare Logistics Group's logos. The small talk among them died down when Hanson called all to attention.

"As you are well aware, we've been running against a tight deadline. The seven-day window to comply with their demands was to expire tomorrow. We've always viewed it as seven days to track those bastards down and retrieve our people before more blood was spilled." Hanson lowered his gaze for a moment as if looking for a better way to break the information. There was none. "We are sad to report that the terrorists ignored their own deadline. They have executed one of the hostages. We have reason to believe the deceased is one of ours. Navy SEAL Adam Carter. A Diplomatic Security Service man." Muffled conversation erupted among the men and hushed to silence when Hanson continued, "We've received the green light to proceed. We're officially executing Operation Red Falcon tonight. Bauer will go over the details of the mission and what we can expect to face during the incursion. I'll brief you on the action plan and contingencies once he's done."

All eyes turned to Trevor. With a few keystrokes, he pulled up the surveillance video on the screen.

"Since Operation Argus Strike, we'd had eyes on the target twenty-four seven in hopes it would lead us to the hostages' location. Two days ago, it yielded results. We picked up actionable movement." He played the video George had captured. "The male resident traveled south across the border into Israeli territory. He made no stops along the way, other than the usual checkpoints." Trevor fast-forwarded the video, showing the satellite footage of the man's trajectory. When the video reached a crucial part, he returned it to regular speed and continued his discourse. "His final stop was at a remote compound forty miles south of Tel Aviv. When he arrived, he was greeted and thoroughly frisked by armed men." He zoomed in on the sequence of events, showing the man's car being checked. The image on the screen left no doubt the men were heavily armed. They all watched as one of the men walked around the car waving some sort of box around it. "As you can see, they were careful in screening the visitor. The device they are using to check the car may be familiar to those who've worked with covert surveillance operations. That device detects any tracking signal broadcast from the vehicle."

The video showed that, once checked, the driver proceeded to the open patio area in front of the main structure. A man exited the building and met the newcomer outside. After exchanging the usual *Salaam*, they walked back in together. Trevor paused the video and zoomed out. The image encompassed the whole compound.

"The building is protected by twelve-foot privacy walls." He pulled up the 3D mockup of the house's blueprint and circled a few areas at the back of the building. "The hostages are located in these cells. Points of entry are here, here, and here." He outlined the areas the men would use to enter the place.

John Norton raised his hand, caution in his eyes. "How can you be sure that's the right place?"

Trevor couldn't hold back his sense of humor. "We asked a magic eight ball." He observed the change in their expressions from neutral and focused to heavy frowns all around. They were not used to acting on hunches. Special Forces men dealt in absolutes and they also knew that operations like this could take years to come to fruition. The idea of such quick action backed up by solid data was almost unheard of. Trevor almost laughed at the lack of confidence displayed on their faces. "Just kidding." Hanson shook his head and lowered his gaze to the floor, visibly fighting laughter. Some of the soldiers chuckled at the joke, but the majority remained sober, still not comfortable with the quality of the information presented. "Several pieces of intel led us there, but there was some deduction involved as well. Up until a few days ago, we had no idea where to begin searching. The abduction happened during a short satellite blackout so we had no video of the event itself, nor a way to follow a trail to them. The video upload that led us to the raid in Jaba' was just one of the pieces of the puzzle. Once we tracked the man to that location, we collected and analyzed all satellite video surveillance of the area retroactive in time to the day of the attack. We were able to locate footage showing that truck's—" Trevor circled the truck on the image "—arrival at the compound. It took a lot of man-hours, but we found what we needed to confirm to one-hundred-percent certainty we have the right target."

Trevor played another clip, this time of the truck arriving at the compound. The image was grainy due to its lower resolution, but they could all identify the western clothes of those escorted from the back of the truck by armed men. Six people in total, their heads covered with black bags. The same number of hostages taken that day. He paused the video at the hostage lineup before they disappeared into the compound.

"Alright." Norton flashed his pearly whites in a broad smile, the first Trevor had seen on the man's face since the mishap with Acer.

No matter how many times Nathan had seen the footage since Bauer's team had locked on it earlier that day, he felt it like a punch to the gut all over again. He couldn't take his eyes away from the image, his attention fixed on the captive he'd identified as Rachael. Although they all wore pants and two of the diplomats had smaller frames than the bigger, bulkier Secret Service men, he'd seen Rachael up close, had memorized how she moved. He didn't need someone to identify her for him. His heart had told him it was her.

"Nelson." Bauer's voice snapped him out of his trance.

Nathan took over the briefing, going over the absolutes of the mission. Number of expected hostiles and non-hostiles from estimations based on the ballistic report as well as thermal imaging captured over the span of the last couple of days, the blueprint of the entire cluster of buildings within the walls determined by analysis of the same data, order of ingress of the teams involved in the rescue operation, what intelligence to recover, and last, the directive to capture their leader.

The intelligence Cassandra had gathered from Naveed Abboud had been crucial to determining who they were dealing with.

"We've traced the operation to Khalil Abboud." Nathan waited until Bauer pulled up the few known pictures of Abboud on the big screen. "He's the oldest son of Ahmed Abboud, the man responsible for at least one bombing in London in '95. Ahmed was assassinated in MI5 custody while being questioned about that attack. Khalil was only ten years old then. We are aware of other terrorist acts committed with the same explosive signature in other European cities not long after that. Khalil Abboud was too young to have been the mastermind then. Intelligence collected indicates he's not the top dog in the organization. *But,*" Nathan stressed, "he may be the only person who can de facto guide us to its leader. Naveed Abboud was unable to give us a description, but confirmed his brother had met the man they call the Messenger face to face. He assured us Khalil was with him within the past month finetuning the kidnapping plans. Khalil is key to helping us ascertain his identity." Nathan's eyes roamed the room, broadcasting the seriousness of the directive. "It's imperative that Abboud is detained and brought back for interrogation *alive.* No ifs or buts."

A palpable silence descended upon the room before Hanson broke it. "You heard Nelson. The insurgents are puppets. If we are to stop the global threat this group presents once and for all, we need to find the one pulling the strings. Other than Abboud, we are taking no detainees. Memorize the face and make sure you have the card with his ugly mug with you for identification purposes. We don't want any fuck-ups. You also must be able to discern shooters from non-combatants. Secure and segregate non-hostiles. We don't want this operation nicknamed Red Bloodbath down the road. We want to rescue the hostages as cleanly as possible. Our mission now includes the recovery of Carter's body for DNA matching. We'll bring our man home."

There was no public display of grief, or any other emotion for that matter, but one could almost feel the hardening of their determination to succeed while Hanson listed the entry team's order. "Heinz, Ranger, Reaper, and Mac will join me." Hanson turned to look at Nathan. Disapproval flashed in his eyes when he added, "Nelson will be replacing Acer to complete Bravo One. We'll ride Raptor One."

Nathan had seen the frown on Bauer's face earlier when he'd joined them all decked in fatigues. He'd ignored the question in his eyes then and ignored the new questions now. The beauty of his clearance level was that he didn't have to explain anything to Bauer.

Hanson gave them the lineup for the other two teams and their assigned helicopters, as well as their infiltration order.

Pointing to the digital display, Hanson continued, "Feel free to study the 3D computer model of the building and the breach order. We've trained long and hard to handle situations like this. Follow procedure and we should be in and out as planned. We ride out at zero hundred hours. Be ready." Hanson dismissed them and the men scattered to prepare for the mission.

Nathan could feel the hairs on the back of his neck stand up when Bauer came up behind him. He turned to face him, ready for the criticism and inquisition about to rain down on him. Instead, he found a glimmer of admiration in the man's eyes.

"So…you were serious about that redemption, huh?"

"I'm always serious, Bauer. You should have learned that by now."

"I've learned more about you in the last few days than in more than a year married to your former partner."

Nathan was glad Bauer hadn't formulated that as a question. He couldn't possibly tell him that Cassandra never knew the real him. That would cross a very fine line. He shrugged it off.

"Aren't you lucky."

Bauer narrowed his eyes. "You could say that." He cocked his head and a bitter smile curved his lips. "I won't hide the fact that I would love to be riding out with you, but I think my wife might still want me alive, so I'll stay here and support your asses out there."

Strangely, the weight on Nathan's shoulders dissipated as the moment to act approached. He had no doubt Bauer would pull his weight to get the job done. Had it not been for his ingenuity, they would still be waiting on pinpointing a location.

"You better deliver again."

Bauer's smile faded. "I plan on doing that."

"Well…I have to get ready."

Nathan was unable to identify the emotion that flashed in Bauer's eyes in the long pause before he replied, "Me too."

Nathan frowned as he watched Bauer walk back to his desk where a few of the men stood waiting for him. He could swear he heard a second meaning behind Bauer's words, but there was no time to question him. He still had to pick his weapons from the cache used by the Crew and reassure Hanson about the small change of plans. Nathan drew in a long breath and left him to answer the men's questions about the blueprints. He had much bigger fish to fry.

Chapter Twenty-Nine

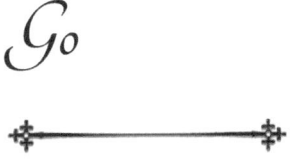

Go

HE THREE STEALTH BLACK HAWK HELICOPTERS whirled dust clouds in the air, creating an eerie fog-like effect over the lit landing pads. The Crew troops lined up in the hangar waited for the time to board. They all wore their full assault gear—black fatigues, helmets equipped with night vision goggles, flashlight, and camera—and packed their weapons. Controlled anxiety was the name of the game. Most of the men, unable to remain quiet for longer periods of time, checked whatever other equipment there was to be checked: Velcro straps for the proper tightness of holsters and chest plates, safety switches on weapons slipped on and off, radios turned to the correct frequencies. Nathan had done all that and then some before he had reached the hangar. He wore the same high-precision uniform as the Crew men and had checked every pocket in his pants, every piece of equipment, with calculated focus—a routine he'd used in the past to get into the right frame of mind. His two radios had been checked: on one ear he'd hear the direct communication from the command net, most precisely Bauer; on the other, he'd hear chatter within the troops on the ground. He'd made sure he was well rested, even though he'd been too amped up to sleep for long stretches since they'd arrived in Jordan. His mind drifted to the checklist for the incursion even in his sleep.

Bauer would be taking over the communication support. With unprecedented access to a much wider array of higher resolution infrared cameras, he would guide them over the command net frequency in the search-and-rescue of the hostages. Strangely, the knowledge that the man that he'd seen in the past as an adversary was in charge of guiding his every step into unknown territory did not worry him.

Hanson was in charge of the operation on the ground and had drilled his team on several scenarios during the remainder of the day. He'd assigned the supporting troops and had gone over the order of ingress and breach with the primary operators. He had not shown one iota of trepidation about the mounting responsibility. The fun-loving Hawaiian-shirt-wearing womanizer was suddenly gone, having given way to the ruthless, fearless soldier he was underneath the bright smile and jokes. Nathan had a hard time connecting the two sides of the real Hanson, but getting to know this new, lethal side of him made Nathan happy to have the soldier on his side for that operation.

Almost as if reading his mind, Hanson walked toward the lines, shouldering his suppressed H&K 416.

"Let's roll!" he yelled over the noise of the rotors, signaling to move to the assigned helicopters. The lines moved fast, and soon Bravo Team hurdled into the first chopper. They were airborne minutes later. Once they cleared the airfield, the birds banked to the left toward the border for the long flight south.

The men, used to the tension before each operation, dozed off right away, conserving their energy and getting as much rest as possible before the final approach. Nathan did the same, and soon the sound of the rotors and the sporadic radio chatter became background noise.

"TEN MINUTES."

The call seemed to be the switch to alertness. Nathan opened his eyes to find all the others coming out of the same sort of trance and beginning their last checks. It was almost a compulsion; call it a military OCD of sorts. The same way carpenters measured twice and cut once, operators checked their equipment several times before jumping in the line of fire.

"Five minutes."

Nathan's heart raced, not with fear, but with the anticipation of seeing Rachael. Within the next hour, he would face her again. He hoped this time would redeem the last. The men pulled their balaclavas into place and tugged on their straps one last time.

"One minute."

The crew chief slid the door open for the final approach and the men began clipping their fast ropes for the descent. The wind and noise inside the cabin increased and they all communicated with signs. Nathan followed the troop's example and lowered the night vision goggles over his eyes. Everything went green and bright. He looked out the door and caught a glimpse of the outline of the compound. Due to the small window of opportunity, they had to deal with some moonlight instead of complete darkness for cover. The building looked eerie; not one light shone through its windows. The strike had been planned for well before the first prayer of the day, hoping to use the element of surprise to their advantage and keep the fire exchange to a minimum.

"Bauer, are you with me?" Nathan called as they made the final approach.

"Did you think I was going to miss being in your ear and out of your reach?" The satisfied tone in the Irishman's voice almost made Nathan laugh. Almost.

"I can still hurt you when I get back."

"Not if you are happy with the outcome—and I plan to do my best from here to reach that happy outcome."

"Good. We're on the same page then." Nathan held his MP7 close to his chest as they got into position.

"Go, go, go!" Hanson's voice blasted through the troop net. Two by two, the men fast-roped onto the front courtyard. The other troops did the same in the back courtyard.

"Bravo Team on target. Report, Charlie. Report, Delta," Hanson whispered over the troop net.

The other teams called back their status.

"Charlie Team on target. Setting charge."

"Delta Team on target."

"Roger. T-minus ten."

They all braced for the cracks of the breaching charges. With the noise, the element of surprise ended. They expected fire once the hostiles were awakened.

"Fire in the hole," Hanson reported immediately before the explosives went off. Nathan's pulse raced. He followed the men in tight formation as they walked through the door into the long series of hallways. Within seconds, they began to hear unsuppressed gunfire coming from the back of the house.

"Charlie under fire."

"Roger." Hanson took the lead through the corridor to the center of the house.

"Two men are running toward the front entrance, toward you,"

Bauer called in.

"On your six!" Norton, at the end of their line and covering their back, called the threat's location. They turned around just in time to return fire. The two combatants fell to the ground, still clutching their AKs.

"Bauer, where do we go now?"

"To your right. About ten feet in, I see a cluster of warm bodies inside the door to your left."

"Roger." Battle sounds reverberated in the distance. The fire exchange, clearly defined between suppressed and unsuppressed automatic weapons, rang in spurts interspersed with the troops' calls over the radio with their status and the distant whimpers and cries of non-combatants.

"Found the prayer room. It's clear," Delta Two called in.

"I got a non-combatant female and two children," Charlie One reported.

"Roger. No vests?" Hanson replied.

"Nope. All clear."

"Take all non-combatants to the prayer room. Keep them away from the fire exchange," Hanson instructed as he advanced into the building toward the cell indicated by Bauer.

Nathan blocked out all noise and forced a deep breath, calming his thoughts for the breach. Using a smaller charge, they splintered the latch. The door almost came off the hinges.

"You call that subtle?" Nathan quipped sarcastically, but knew that the breach had the purpose of stunning any enemy beyond the door as well. Hanson pushed it open and they proceeded with the wall flood.

Disabling the night vision goggles, they lit the room with their helmet flashlights. They found the two foreign diplomats huddling in the corner. They looked roughed up, but not in terrible shape considering they had been imprisoned for over ten days. Unable to see in the darkness, they trembled in fear of their rescuers.

The Korean diplomat spoke in his own language then switched to English, "Please. Don't hurt me. I have family," he begged.

"United States Special Forces. We're here to free you. Can you tell us where the others are?"

"Thank you! Thank you!" Goh Min-Sook grabbed the hand extended to him and stood on unsteady feet.

Jason Wolfe stumbled to his feet. "They split us up last night. I don't know where they took the others."

"What about the woman?" The words grated Nathan's throat. "Do you know of her?"

"She's never been with us. I don't know where they took her."

They had to find her before the insurgents moved her. Now aware of the operation, they could try to use the other hostages as leverage, and if so, the risk of casualties would soar.

"Bauer. Talk to me."

"I'm on it. We have heat signatures all over. I'm trying to locate the right cluster."

"Look for a single one. She may have been segregated."

"Roger."

"Find her for me, Bauer."

"Working on it, Nelson."

★ ★ ★ ★ ★

RACHAEL'S PULSE THUNDERED in her ears as she strained to make out the sound that had just sent her heart racing. She'd been dozing off and on in tandem with the revolving sounds of the compound and had just fallen into a deeper sleep after *Isha*, the evening prayer, when everything had gone quiet for the night. She stared into the dark room, listening. There it was again. A sharp thwack. The sound of fireworks. No. Gunfire.

Adrenaline flooded her veins, catapulting her off the thin pallet. She pushed to her feet and darted across the floor to stand under the opening in the back wall. Shouts and screams erupted, sprays of automatic gunfire hitting concrete and wood. It was like the world had exploded outside. A sick feeling enveloped her. Had another group decided to snatch them from Kahlil? It wasn't unheard of. The lure of such a treasure, American hostages, had to be tempting for those minor groups looking to grab their fifteen minutes of fame. Another hail of automatic rounds erupted, this time closer.

The fist in Rachael's stomach clenched. She ran to the door and tried to catch a glimpse of the outside through the crack. She only caught the blur of movement, the sound of rushing steps, but she couldn't identify any of it. Doors slammed nearby, a woman's voice cried out, a child whimpered. The sound of shots ricocheted in the hall and Rachael hurried to the far corner of the room. She crouched low, eyes focused on the entrance to her cell while rolling the odds of making a run for it in her head.

Heavier footfalls drew closer to her door. In the dark, she tapped the floor around her, searching for something, anything, to protect herself, and, finding nothing of use, she braced for the worst. A simultaneous bright flare and loud bang deafened her for a moment. Icy fear twisted around her heart as the familiar clang of the metal lock falling against the door and the creak of hinges warned her that the door was being forced open.

The thumping of Nathan's heart eclipsed the flashbang of the breaching charge. From that point on, he was numb to anything but the need to break down that door, driven by a deeper need to verify that Rachael was indeed in that cell. Alive. Well.

Bravo Two and Three had stayed behind to cover the two hostages and escort them back to the landing zone while Hanson and

Nathan proceeded to find Rachael.

He kicked the splintered lock and tugged on the handle, only to find the fragmented lock still held. Hanson pulled out his bolt cutters and stuck them between the door and the jamb.

"On three, pull it out. One, two—"

Nathan grabbed the handle and pried the door open. The helmet Maglites flooded the room with bright white light. A chamber pot sat in the far corner beside the rug-covered pallet. Rachael wasn't laying on it. His pulse galloped when Hanson's flashlight illuminated the other side of the room and he saw her. Everything went out of focus but the image of Rachael, in the same dirty clothes she'd been wearing in the video, looking pale and a bit thinner than the last time he'd seen her this close. Weary, but alive. She sheltered her narrowed eyes from the lights and pushed her back against the wall.

"Is that her?" Hanson asked.

"Affirmative."

"Grab her. We need to get out of here."

Nathan's legs felt heavier with each step he took toward her.

"Who are you? I'm not going anywhere until I know who you are."

Nathan smiled at the feisty tone in her voice. Yes, that was Rachael. His Rachael.

"US Special Forces, ma'am. We are here to take you home," Hanson said.

A shuddering breath escaped her and her lips opened in a bright smile. Nathan had to force a deep breath into his lungs once he realized he'd been holding it for too long.

Her smile faded and lines formed on her forehead. "Did you already find the others?"

"Two are under custody. My men are looking for the others."

Nathan kept his silence, unsure if it was the right time to identify himself to her. As much as he wanted to scream from the rooftops, they were not out of danger just yet.

He reached for her and relief almost knocked him to his knees when he finally got to wrap his fingers around her arm. She was solid. Not a dream or figment of his imagination anymore. She was there, and he was going to take her home. *Like I promised you I would, Phillip.*

The troop net frequency crackled to life. *"Bravo Leader, this is Charlie Leader. We found the body."*

"Do you have an ID?"

"Affirmative, Bravo Leader."

"Copy. Charlie Two can take him to the LZ. The rest remain on the targets."

"Roger."

"Delta Leader, do you have a status on the target?"

"Negative, Bravo Leader."

"We'll tackle this quadrant once we deliver the hostage to the chopper."

"Roger. Rover said he might have seen the target heading your way but couldn't be sure."

"Copy."

Rachael's pulse raced in her ears as a niggling sensation took over. The fire exchange ringing in sporadic bursts outside no longer scared or surprised her. Instead, recognition teased her senses as the taller soldier wrapped his hand around her arm. His height, the way he moved, the way he stood, all brought Nathan front and center in her mind. She shook her head.

It couldn't be him. Her mind had played tricks with her before. Even Stratton had reminded her of him. She frowned, trying to make sense of it. Stratton had reminded her of Nathan because of the suit, the stance. Not because he actually had the same height as Nathan or because he made her think of him every time he moved. Not the way the soldier holding her arm in a protective yet firm way did. He prompted her to move without a word and his silence intrigued her even more.

The other man who had identified them took the lead at the door. "How many?" he said as if to himself, and she understood he was talking to someone over the radio. As he peeked outside, gunfire erupted. He ducked back inside.

"Fuck!" He used the doorjamb as cover against the enemy fire. "Charlie, we need backup."

"Roger, Bravo Leader."

"Cut the lights and cover her," he whispered to the tall man and pulled his handgun out of the holster. Hanson didn't have to command him to do what his instincts already screamed.

"Charlie, take a left on the next hallway. Follow it to the end. I see three heat signatures. All armed and not any of our guys," Bauer's voice came through the command net, guiding them.

The room went dark for a moment before Nathan's eyes adjusted again. Hanson lowered his night vision goggles and crawled toward the door. From that low vantage point, he peeked first then opened fire. The thudding noise outside told her he'd hit at least one mark.

Flashlights went on as he stood, blinding Rachael once again.

"Charlie, where are you?"

"Heading your way, Bravo."

Seconds that felt like hours went by before fire erupted outside again. Hanson stood again and peeked into the hallway, advancing and signaling Nathan to follow him. They stepped into the hallway just as more gunfire burst. Scrambling to shield Rachael with his body, Nathan caught a glimpse of the shooter as he ducked into another hallway to avoid Hanson's return fire.

"Hanson, it's Abboud," Nathan called in.

"Are you sure?"

"Positive. Bauer, can you see a heat signature?"

"Clear as day. He's not alone. I can't define who is who from my end but I see at least five warm bodies."

"We need Abboud," Nathan reminded them all. They were in a bind. Shooting their way out of there was a lot more difficult when they needed one of the hostiles alive.

Chaos consumed Rachael's heart and mind. She wasn't going crazy. She'd recognize that voice anywhere, even muffled by the balaclavas both men wore. She froze, eyes glued to his back. After all those years wondering what it would be like to be that close to him and what she would say, her mind drew a blank. Even if a tendril of anger left her wanting to hit him hard, as hard as the blow of knowing he'd been in contact with Phillip before his death, she still wanted him.

"Charlie, circle back to the big room. I'll herd them your way," the man Nathan had called Hanson said.

"What are you thinking?" Rachael could feel the tension in Nathan's words.

"When I head their way, you take her out of here. We'll kill two birds. I'll push them back toward Charlie and we can catch the elusive Mr. Abboud while you get her safely to the exfil zone."

"It's not SOP and you know it." Rachael couldn't see their faces, but there was no question that they were not seeing eye-to-eye. "You said it yourself. We follow procedure. I don't want to be the next one flown to Ramstein, do you?"

Having been around Intelligence for years, Rachael understood the gist of the conversation. As usual, Nathan was sticking to the rules, abiding by them.

"I don't plan to. It's the only way."

Even she could see Hanson was right. She expected Nathan to waste time analyzing things to death trying to figure out another way, but after a brief pause, Nathan took a deep breath.

"Fine."

Hanson nodded. "Charlie, what's your position?"

Hanson took a stance by the door while Nathan reached for her arm again, positioning her immediately behind him. He clutched his weapon expertly, with confidence. She could barely reconcile the charming, suave, and torn younger Nathan with the hard, clinical man standing in front of her holding an automatic weapon as if it was an everyday thing for him. But then again, ten years had gone by since she'd fallen in love with him. Ten years that she'd spent battling that same love, unable to extinguish it even when his actions had caused her pain. Not even her anger had prevented him from invading her mind since Phillip's death.

The thought brought her self-imposed mission back to the surface. Stunned by Nathan's presence, she'd forgotten the reason she was there in the first place.

"Roger. We're in position," Hanson spoke again. "On three. One, Two, Three." Hanson burst through the door, shooting in the direction the hostile shots had come from.

Nathan reached behind him and pulled her closer. "Hold on tight, Rae." The gentleness of his voice almost undid her, but she couldn't let her heart misdirect her now.

She shook his arm off and stood her ground. "We can't leave just yet, Nathan."

Nathan's heart sank to his knees. When she called him by his name, he realized she'd recognized his voice when he'd talked to Hanson. Letting her name slip from his lips hadn't been the smartest move, either. Whatever grudge she had against him had to be put on the backburner. They had to reach the landing zone to make it on the first helicopter out of that hellhole. Nathan had to get her moving. He turned to look at her. Her features, illuminated by the Maglite on his helmet, only showed determination laced with the same anger he'd seen in her eyes the last time they'd talked. *I don't ever want to see you again.* Her eyes hardened and his heart tumbled.

"Rae—"

"No. Don't. I need to recover something from one of the rooms. I'm not leaving without it." Her tone was decisive.

"What can be that important that you are willing to risk your own life for it?"

"A locket. It was a gift from Phillip. Khalil, the man in charge of the compound, took it from me and I need it back."

A vivid picture of Rachael on the day he'd visited her in California flashed in his mind. The image had been branded there; he could recall every inch of her. Nathan remembered seeing the silver chain gracing her neck, its pendant hidden beneath her shirt's neckline. Her insistence in recovering it could only mean she was hanging on to Phillip's memory, honoring him in death. He admired her actions, but the thought tore a gash into his heart. He'd never be enough for her. He'd known that when he'd taken the mission. He hadn't expected anything different, but reality struck him harder than he'd expected.

"You owe me this, Nathan. You owe us both this."

The gash bled freely. He'd been indebted to Phillip from the day he'd met Rachael and couldn't suppress how she made him feel. The more his attraction grew and matured into what he now recognized as love, the more he'd concealed it and prayed it wasn't clear as day to everyone. He'd made the mistake of disclosing he'd wanted her once. He wouldn't make the mistake of telling her how much he still loved her. Instead, he'd show his respect and honor through his actions.

Turning the troop net off, he nodded. "Take the lead."

Chapter Thirty

No One Left Behind

❖———————❖

"*B*AUER, DO NOT, I REPEAT, do not broadcast."

"*Do I want to know?*"

"No."

"*It's just you and me. For the record, I'm shaking my head. But strangely proud, like a Jedi Master after his Padawan learns a new mind trick.*"

Nathan ignored Bauer's movie references and turned to Rachael. "Where are we going?" Sweat poured from his temples. He hadn't worn full tactical gear in a while and was feeling the effects of the extra weight.

"Just follow me."

Nathan frowned, but, compelled by the urgency in her voice, complied. Before she walked out, he cleared the hallway and stepped out ahead of her, whispering back, "We need to hurry. We're cutting close to the exfil window."

"This shouldn't take long. Give me your handgun."

A flush of adrenaline tingled through his body. He knew she'd been married to a British Navy officer, but didn't expect her to be into guns, particularly not with such confidence. It was the confidence that assured him she knew how to handle one.

He pulled his H&K 45C from the holster and handed it to her. The compact issue of the gun used by many men in the Special Forces was a bit too big for her hand size, but she managed it just fine.

Upon taking it from him, Rachael retracted the slide and checked the magazine load. The ease with which she completed the weapons check came from muscle memory. Curiosity niggled at Nathan once again, but this wasn't the time to question her about it. He'd have that little talk with her when they weren't literally dodging bullets.

She drew in a deep breath and closed her eyes. "Don't freak out. I'll have to do it with my eyes closed," she whispered.

Stepping into the hallway, she turned to the right and, with her eyes still shut, continued down the hall as if in a trance. Nathan realized she was counting her steps. She'd mapped out the way to wherever she had to go in her mind and was now recalling it from memory. His frown deepened. Every agent who was worth his salt knew to observe the environment, count steps, memorize everything.

She continued down the hallway in confident steps while Nathan, eye to his weapon's sight, covered her progress.

"Nelson, what the fuck are you doing? You're heading in the wrong direction."

"Not now, Bauer."

Rachael stopped some fifty feet from her cell and, opening her eyes, turned to face a door.

"This is it."

"This is not the time to play games, Nelson."

"I'm not good at playing games either, Bauer. Just cover our six, will you? And no word to Hanson."

"*Fuck, fuck, fuck,*" Bauer muttered.

"Cass needs to invest in soap to wash that dirty mouth of yours."

"*Just wait until you're back. You'll hear a lot more from me.*"

Nathan signaled for her to take cover to one side while he did the same on the other. Room clearing in these circumstances was always a dangerous deal. The images from the first incursion flashed in front of his eyes and he shook his head to get rid of them. He reached for the handle, verified it wasn't locked, then pushed it open from his cover.

"*No heat signature in the room,*" Bauer interjected.

"Better safe than sorry."

Moving slowly, Nathan performed the corner check, then flooded the room, Rachael close on his tail. He flipped the light switch once he confirmed no one was there. A low-wattage yellow glow enveloped the room. He studied the place more carefully. It was furnished modestly. A rug on the floor and a sleeping pallet to the left. A few file cabinets sat against the far wall, a wooden desk and chair arranged in front of them. No electronic devices other than a video camera, which sat on a tripod pointed at a flag draped on the wall to the right. The same flag he'd seen in the videos. The carved armchair Rachael had been tied to sat immediately in front of it. The makeshift studio. Anger simmered in his stomach. That's how she knew where to go. She'd been in that room at least once before.

She closed in on the desk, tucking the gun in her waistband. "Help me find it."

Nathan followed her, but decided to tackle the cabinets instead. "How do we know it's really here?"

"I heard him refer to it as his office when they brought me here. One of the servants told me she'd seen it in here before."

"Did she say exactly where?"

"No. But it shouldn't be hard to find. There's not much to search."

An orchestra of suppressed and unsuppressed gunfire played in the background while they sifted through the drawers, scrambling against the clock. In one of the cabinet drawers, Nathan located paperwork in Arabic. To be on the safe side, he pulled a folded bag from one of his pockets and began stuffing the papers in for later analysis. He also discovered several tapes hidden in the back of the drawer. He assumed they were the original recordings made in that room. The tapes followed the documents into the bag. He exhaled a deep breath. He anticipated he'd be carrying months of work with him once they were finished.

"Nelson, Hanson's men apprehended Khalil Abboud. They're headed to the LZ. Get your ass out there. They just called for exfil."

"What's the ETA?"

"You've got less than ten minutes. By the way, thought you should know the gig is up. Hanson figured out you're not where you're supposed to be. Needless to say, he's not happy."

Nathan shot a look at Rachael. Her attention completely focused on finding the locket, she'd missed his question to Bauer.

"It has to be here. Why would he move it?" Rachael asked herself, only to realize she'd spoken out loud. She'd managed to keep her anxiety under control up to that point, but as the proof she needed remained unaccounted for, her control slipped. She sifted through the last drawer, her pulse beating faster as she rummaged through its contents only to come up empty. "It *has* to be here."

She let her eyes roam the room; it lacked hiding places, storage, or a safe. Rachael put herself in Khalil's shoes. Sitting at the desk he'd sat at countless times, she closed her eyes to hone in on what she had learned to dive into the psyche of the man.

"Rae. We need to go. Our ride will be here in—"

"Give me a minute."

She'd seen something in the way Kahlil looked at her, in the way he talked to her when he'd first visited her in the cell. She opened her eyes and turned her attention to the pallet. She pushed from the chair and dropped to her knees beside it. Her pulse beat in her ears, her stomach twisted in knots as she tossed the blankets aside and lifted the squalid mattress. Relief washed over her when she saw the silver necklace and the locket underneath.

She snatched it and squeezed it against her heart. She had everything required to give Phillip and herself the peace they needed.

Nathan watched the range of emotions careen over her face. Relief merged with the determination that had already been stamped there. One had to have been exceptional in his public and private life to draw that kind of response even after death. He added envy to his list of sins.

"Are we done here?"

His question seemed to wake her from a daze.

"Yes." She stood and slipped the delicate silver chain over her head.

He turned the troop net back on and reported in, "Bravo Leader, do you copy?"

"Nelson, where the fuck have you been?" Nathan scrunched his face at the loudness of Hanson's reply. Shots fired in the background again.

"Heading your way. We should be there in a few."

"Move your ass."

"Roger." He wasn't going to justify his decision over the radio. He'd have a private chat with Hanson once they were back on base.

They made their way through the hallway tracing back to the entry. Rachael gasped when they came across the bloodied bodies of the dead hostiles. That was her only response. She puzzled him with every step they took. Her reactions didn't jive with those of a typical civilian on seeing such a gruesome scene.

As they reached the doorway, another report came through. *"Bravo Team, this is Eagle one. ETA is two minutes."*

When they reached the doorway, Nathan could already hear the sound of the helicopter blades chopping the air in the distance. In the barely lit night, he could define the contours of bodies scattering the courtyard. They painted a sad portrait of the consequences of hatred and ignorance.

"I see you. Do not cross the courtyard. Do you copy?" Hanson ordered as soon as Nathan stepped from the shadows.

"Copy." Nathan shoved Rachael back behind the wall and shielded her with his body.

"There's a sniper hiding somewhere and several other combatants on standby. They're like cats on a laser beam. Any light source gets shot at. We had to take cover in the barn-like structure by the LZ directly in front of you." Nathan took aim with his MP7's night scope and caught a glimpse of movement in the building that fit the description. *"They have more ammo than we do. Some are standing strong. We need to conserve our ammo for when the bird gets here."*

"Got it." Nathan slipped his goggles back on for a wider view of the surrounding area.

"What's happening?" Rachael asked from behind him.

"We'll make a run for it when the helicopter gets here. Be ready, but hold your fire until we make a break for it."

She nodded and retrieved his gun from her waistband, taking a more casual but still tense stance. The wind gusts picked up as the helicopters approached for the exfiltration and the rotor wash reached them. The three black fuselages camouflaged against the dark sky, only seen clearly under the green hue of the night vision goggles. They kept a safety perimeter and, due to the limited space for landing in the courtyard, were following the landing order established during the planning stages. Delta Team would be the first to evacuate and would cover the exfiltration of the other teams from above.

The first Black Hawk descended smoothly and was hovering a couple of feet off the ground when sparks shot out from the electric pole by the front gate in tandem with the blast of an ear-shattering grinding noise. The tail of the helicopter broke apart and spun out of control, raising a dust cloud as the rotors sliced into the dirt ground. Within seconds, the aircraft came to rest at an awkward angle. The radios exploded with action.

"Cover them!" Hanson yelled as two of his men ran from their shelter under pot shots from the enemy to the helicopter to extract the pilots from the crumpled shell. *"Command, we have a situation."*

"Roger, Bravo Leader. We have you under bird's eye view. We are deploying a Chinook from the closest possible base. ETA is two hours and thirty-five minutes."

"Negative, Command. We need exfil stat."

"Stand by, Bravo Leader."

"Are you fucking kidding me? They put me on hold?" Nathan could almost have laughed at Hanson's outburst if their situation wasn't so troubling. *"Eagle Two, do you copy?"*

"Loud and clear, Bravo Leader."

"How many can we squeeze into each of the remaining helos?"

"Eleven all decked out. Thirteen max. That's cutting it too close."

"Fuck." A silent moment stretched before Hanson's voice came through again. *"We'll load the hostages and as many we can put on the two birds. Ranger and I will stay behind and wait for the supporting team. Eagle Two, do you copy? Watch for wires or you'll end up like Eagle One. Land as close to us as possible. Sending our exact coordinates now."*

"Roger, Bravo Leader."

"Hanson, this is suicide." Although Hanson was most likely not inclined to hear him out, Nathan had to be the voice of reason. "We stand a better chance if we stay together and take them out one by one. We can retrieve weapons and ammo from the dead. No one left behind, remember?"

"The mission is to get the hostages to safety. By keeping them here for longer than absolutely necessary, we'll be jeopardizing the entire mission. There's nothing saying we can't leave two of ours behind for a later retrieval." Hanson's tone left no space for argument.

"You two won't be able to hold out for that long."

"You haven't been through the missions we have, Nelson."

Nathan thought about replying to that with the list of high-risk operations he'd manned on his own, but he couldn't. They were all top secret, not for bragging rights. As the top CIA operative in charge, he had the power to give approval to the op changes on the spot, but to give his approval would be self-serving. Hanson's plan would take Nathan from the line of fire while leaving the two soldiers behind to face certain death. He couldn't let that happen.

"Delta Team can escort Abboud and the male hostages on Eagle Two. Once they take off we'll support your and Mrs. Moore's egress to Eagle Three."

"Negative, Bravo Leader. I'll stay. I'll cover Mrs. Moore to the bird. But once I deliver her to you, she's under your care. Just make sure she gets back to the base safe and sound. I'll stay and wait for the Chinook."

Rachael gasped beside him. In the flurry of activity, he'd forgotten she was beside him, listening in on his side of the conversation. From the worry clouding her eyes, she had drawn her own conclusions from what he'd said.

"No offense, Nelson, but this is fucking crazy. Who's talking about

suicide now? What happened to the no-man-left-behind motto you just spewed to them?" Bauer interjected from command central.

"Shut up, Bauer. You're no Jiminy Cricket. Besides, as you all pointed out, I'm not one of them. That doesn't apply to me. I work alone. Always have and always will. Bravo Leader, do you copy?"

"Nelson—"

"This is not a request, soldier. As your immediate superior, you will do as I've ordered."

Almost as if to prove his point, another barrage of fire sounded outside. They took cover behind the wall.

"Bravo Leader, we can't wait here. We're sitting ducks."

The radio went quiet only to crackle again, *"Roger, Eagle Two. Prepare for exfil."*

Rachael wouldn't have believed hearts could break, but the intensity of the pain in her chest while they waited for her turn to board the Black Hawk could only mean hers had. Aside from the brief visit three years earlier, she'd avoided any contact with Nathan, so she'd missed the metamorphosis he'd undergone over the years. Gone was the soft-spoken young man who'd stolen her heart. He had almost fooled her for a minute. It was obvious to her now that he'd never been a follower. There was a leader behind that mask. A leader who would never let the men under his command place themselves at risk if he could do it himself. And by doing so, he was signing his own death sentence.

"You can't do this." The words escaped her lips before she could contain them.

He took a deep breath and looked at her. She couldn't see his expression hidden under the balaclava, but she could see the conflict in his eyes.

"I don't have a choice."

"What about the first idea of keeping everybody barricaded until the Chinook gets here?"

"Hanson is right. Staying could put you and the others in un-necessary danger. The earlier we get you out, the better."

"So, this is it then?"

"I trust they will make sure you get to the base."

She wanted to scream, shake him, go back in time to change eve-rything that had happened that day. From the moment she realized he was there to rescue her to the moment she had used their past to gain his cooperation. What if she wouldn't have delayed their arrival to the LZ? Would that have changed the chain of events that led to that moment? Would she have still been forced to say goodbye again, this time possibly forever?

A part of her wanted to stay behind with Nathan, forgo any semblance of safety. She had lived her life on the safe side and it had only gained her heartbreak. Nathan's appearance when she needed him most was a sign to take chances, maybe also to give chances. The other part of her knew she had to finish what she'd started, close Phillip's case. The more she dwelled on what she had learned about that bastard traitor, the more she understood she couldn't ignore it. It was a matter of national security. There was more at stake than one woman's broken heart and lost love.

She tightened her grip on the gun and followed Nathan's direc-tions, conserving her ammo for when it was their time to race across the open field. When the helicopter made its approach, Rachael's gut turned once again. Soon she would be forced to leave Nathan behind.

"Cover the bird!" Hanson commanded.

The insurgents who still held positions within the compound had lurked in the shadows, quietly waiting until the helicopter landed to open fire again. It was widely known that any American soldier or hostage caught dead or alive was worth their weight in gold. Their sporadic gunfire was rebutted with rounds of suppressed fire from the soldiers providing cover support for those boarding the first bird.

"Tell everyone, helmet lights off. They can't find us in the dark. The helo is a sitting duck. The cockpit dashboard is a big X-marks-the-spot. They need to get in and out ASAP or they'll be lit up at the hands of some lucky fucker with a rocket launcher," Hanson's voice crackled over the troop net, and Nathan observed through his night vision goggles the lights disappear one by one as they prepared for the dash.

The thirteen people scurrying for the first helicopter consisted of Delta team, the two pilots of the downed helicopter, the four male hostages, and the target, Kahlil Abboud. Within seconds, they were all jammed into the cabin and the bird climbed into the dark sky.

"Ready?" Nathan turned to Rachael, taking the time to let his gaze wash over her features one last time before he switched off his flashlight. He knew that there was a possibility he could make it out of there alive if he could find a good hiding spot and wait it out. But, if this was his day to die, he would die knowing he'd accomplished the most important mission of his life. Rachael would be safe, and that was all that mattered to him at that moment.

She nodded and they took positions behind the wall by the door, waiting for the right time to cross the courtyard to her ride out.

"Hanson, do you copy?"

Hanson took his sweet time to respond. *"Affirmative, Nelson."*

Nathan took a deep breath. "I have a bag full of intelligence material. You'll need to deliver it to Director Franklin at Langley."

Hanson replied in a curt tone, *"Roger."*

"And Hanson," Nathan paused, hesitant to say the words he needed to say.

"I'm listening."

"For what it's worth, sorry I pulled rank."

Hanson didn't reply. By keeping his quiet, Nathan recognized Hanson understood where he was coming from. His whole life had been a huge unsaid sorry. He didn't want to part ways with more things left unsaid than strictly necessary.

The helicopter landed, idling rotors whipping the air around them. From their perch, Nathan kept watch through his night vision goggles while Bravo and Charlie Teams, carrying Carter's body bag, boarded the helicopter under hostile fire. The glare of the helicopter instruments once again provided the insurgents with one hell of a bullseye.

"Your turn," Hanson called in. *"We have your back covered. Be quick."*

"Roger." Nathan turned to Rachael and found tears glistening in her eyes. They almost had him convinced that she felt something other than the hatred she'd voiced so clearly to him. It would be too ironic to find that out when they were about to be separated, quite possibly forever. "I should be back at the base in a few hours," he managed to lie. Just another added to a long list of them.

"We both know this is a suicide mission."

"Why does it matter? You once said you never wanted to see me again."

"I...," her voice faltered. "It would have made things easier."

"Nelson, we can't wait any longer. Move it."

Nathan pocketed away those words for when he could dissect them and exploded into action. Rachael followed on his heels as they made a break for the helicopter. The men kept the incoming fire under control. Hanson pulled Rachael onboard and caught the bag Nathan tossed him.

The rotor wash and whomp of the blades made it almost impossible to have any conversation without the use of the radio. "Take care of that. It may be critical to National Security."

"I'll make sure it gets to the right hands, stat. Just get your ugly ass back to base. The Chinook is inbound."

"Copy."

Hanson saluted him. Nathan hadn't expected that gesture of respect from the operator. He returned the salute as the dark aircraft began to climb. Nathan ducked under the assault of the vortex of dust the helicopter kicked in the air and was just about to retrace his steps to the hiding spot when a shot rang in the distance. Nathan was thrown forward, the air sucked from his lungs, as he landed face first in the dirt. A fiery bolt of pain seared his back where the bullet had struck. He struggled to catch his breath while a loud ring muffled his ears.

"Nathan!" He heard Rachael's yell in the distance as he fought through the pain blurring his vision. His MP7 had slipped from his grasp and lay inches away from his fingers. He sucked in a painful gulp of air and hissed between his teeth, concentrating on moving his hand forward to retrieve possession of the rifle.

"What the fuck!" He heard Hanson's cascade of curse words through the troop net at the same time something hit the ground not far from him with a thud.

"Where were you hit?" Rachael's urgent voice sounded right above him and he thought he'd died for good. But the gentle hands frantically patting over his shoulders, arms and legs were real. "Can you feel them?"

"Yes," he groaned, as a new barrage of fire landed around them.

"Nelson, do you copy?"

He forced air into his lungs. "Copy."

Another round of gunfire rang out and impacted metal. The helicopter still hovering close to the ground had taken a hit.

"Nelson, tell her to get her ass back on board."

"Rae…you need to go. No time."

"I'm not leaving. Tell them to go without me. Now." She turned and waved them off.

"No. Get on that helo, Rachael."

"Who's going to force me? You?" She rolled him to his back and helped him sit. "Tell them to go." She draped his arm over her shoulder and forced him to his feet.

"Why are you doing this?"

"Move it, soldier, before you get us both killed."

His gut churned, deep desolation consuming him until there was no hope.

"Rae—"

She leaned closer and yelled into his mic, "Get the hell out of here!"

Having been privy to her stubbornness earlier that night, he knew they would be arguing it forever and a day, placing her in even more danger. Shaking his head, he commanded the team, "Bravo Leader, proceed with exfil without Mrs. Moore. Notify the inbound bird of the change."

"Roger. For the record, you two deserve each other."

The Crew men returned enemy fire and covered their hobbling retreat to the temporary safety of the compound's entryway. Nathan glanced up just in time to see the Black Hawk's nose dip as it picked up speed and disappeared into the night, leaving them behind.

Chapter Thirty-One

Peeling Layers

✦————————✦

ATHAN SWALLOWED PAST THE LUMP in his throat and drew in a deep breath. The weight of the gear and the contact of the back plate against the area of the impact made him extremely uncomfortable. He sucked in another deep breath and grimaced as pain radiated across his back.

The fact that Rachael was still in that hellhole and had willingly placed herself in that situation for him had left him speechless. He wanted to be angry with her, wanted to make her understand how rash her decision had been, but he couldn't. He sat with his shoulder propped against the wall while she watched for incoming threats, her outline visible against the gaping door.

He unsnapped the chin strap and let his helmet roll to the floor before pulling off the balaclava covering his face. He dropped his head, appreciating the cold air against his exposed skin.

Rachael moved closer and, without a word of warning, slipped a hand between his vest's back plate and his shirt, palpating his back clinically.

"No need to fret. It hit the plate. Knocked the wind out of me. There will be one hell of an ugly bruise in a day or two," he reported it to her matter-of-factly. It wasn't anything new to him. He'd been there, done that.

Rachael withdrew her hand as if she'd touched an open flame. Another shot rang out and she stood, gun in hand. "Do you think they will find us here?"

In the distance, Nathan heard the cries of a young child. It reminded him that the compound was also home to non-combatants and that the Crew men had escorted some to the prayer room during the assault. Civilians who were not on their side. One more thing to worry about.

Nathan shifted, searching for a more comfortable position, and cringed when pain shot from his back to his neck. "To answer your question, most likely. We can't assume nobody saw us hide here. We gotta move."

"What do you think they'll do?"

"If they find us? You don't want to know." He recalled the images in the last video broadcast and took a deep breath, trying to think it through. Although Khalil Abboud had been captured, Nathan knew he wasn't the one pulling the strings. Those still out there were loyal to a greater cause, to someone at the top of the totem pole, and they would continue to hunt them as a prize. In fact, they'd just become even more valuable now that the others had been rescued. Using them to set an example of what happened when you pissed off their leader would garner them major points with their organization. "Our only hope of living through this is to find a way out long before the Chinook gets here."

"Did you have that in mind when you decided to stay behind?" Her tone was slightly flippant, like a mother chastising a child for not wearing his coat on a cold day.

He managed a smile. "You give me more credit than I'm due."

"I don't remember you being this impulsive." The waning moon's light was barely enough to allow him to see movement, but he could detect the humor making its way into her voice. While he wished he could see her better, turning on any light would be like waving a red cape in front of not one, but many angry bulls.

The metallic click of the gun's magazine being released and then the retraction of the slide releasing the bullet in the chamber echoed in the room. A repetitive scrape of metal followed when she removed all the bullets from the magazine and then proceeded to reload them. It was the second time that she'd completed a weapons check that night.

Nathan's humor evaporated. "I don't remember you being able to handle guns so well."

He heard the hitch of her breath before she spoke. "Ten years, Nathan. There're a lot of things you don't know about me."

"You could say that." *But I want to know you, everything about you.* He didn't voice that thought. There was no point.

"So, what's the plan? Or do we even have one?"

"I'm counting on Bauer."

"Bauer?"

"The Irish pain in my ass who pipes in when he's not needed, says nothing when he is." It suddenly dawned on Nathan that the radio had gone silent. No snarky comeback from the other end shot through the connection. "Bauer? Do you copy?" The signal remained as silent as before.

Shots rang out in sporadic bursts. Rachael shuffled closer to the doorframe and peeked out.

"Don't return fire. They're baiting us. If we fire back, we announce our position and they'll swarm down on us."

He pulled out the radios and realized their digital displays were black. He played with the buttons. One of the units, the one used for the troop net frequency, was completely dead. The other had a weak glow, indicating a possible low-power issue. He traded the units' batteries and, after playing with the buttons, was rewarded with a crackle as the thing came back to life. Relief washed over him.

"Bauer, do you copy?"

"What the hell happened? One minute you were there, the next you were gone. I was starting to believe bullets didn't ricochet off your fluorescent green skin after all." The tone of Bauer's voice contradicted his humorous remark.

Nathan kept his voice to a whisper. In the dead of the night, any noise carried far. "Funny boy. Listen, we have no time for jokes. Not sure how much longer the battery will last." On cue, the radio crackled again and Bauer's voice cut a little.

"—Mrs. Moore—you? Franklin req—status update."

"She's alive and yes, she's here with me."

A short pause hung before Bauer continued, *"Glad to hear it. I checked—Chinook—on route. Same ETA."*

"That's not soon enough. We have to get out of here now. If we wait, we're sitting ducks. And I'm very fond of my feathers."

"Do you—any preference?"

"Anything that takes us out from under their crosshairs."

"Got it. Give me—minutes to think this through."

"Clock's ticking."

Rachael dropped to a knee next to him and leaned closer. "What did he say?" Her sweet breath laced with a hint of mint tea caressed his cheek, shortcircuiting his brain for a moment.

"He's looking into it."

Precious minutes went by before the radio hiccupped to life again, static cutting into Bauer's every other word.

"There—several heat signatur—active in the compound—if we

managed to establish—with the Israeli—support from them after deploy—non-authorized infiltration in their territ—it would still take hours—team of operators down there. Same—that it will take—Chinook to get there."

"Is there a breach in the wall, gate, something we can use to just walk out of here under the cover of darkness?"

"Not—I could see. You'd—scale the walls."

"No equipment at hand." Frustration bubbled in his stomach. This couldn't be the end. He wouldn't accept it. Not when Rachael's life hung in the balance.

The radio crackled once more and Nathan's blood turn to ice. That radio was their last lifeline.

"—truck. Si—ard." With that last broken message, the radio's digital display went dark.

"Fuck!" Nathan wanted to punch something to disperse the feeling of helplessness threatening to engulf him. He eased his back against the wall and stared into the dark, looking for answers to their problem. In his head, he reviewed the briefing on the compound and Bauer's presentation on how he'd gotten the bead on the hostages.

"This truck." Bauer had circled the vehicle in the bird's-eye-view photograph of the compound. The truck. It was parked on the north-side yard, by the main house. If they avoided alerting anybody to their presence, they could stay within the cover of the house for most of the way. He'd seen the blueprint showing the doors used as ingress points by the incursion teams. One of them had been the door that opened to that same courtyard. It would have been breached earlier, making an easy exit point to the area where the truck had been parked in the briefing pictures. If they were lucky, that truck was still in the same location with enough fuel to take them as far from the compound as possible.

"How far have you gone within this building?"

"Only as far as the office where we recovered the locket." Curiosity rang in Rachael's tone.

"That's north. Can you guide us back there in the dark?"

"Yes."

He retrieved his helmet and reached for his gun. "Let's move out." Bracing himself against the wall, Nathan slowly rose to his feet. Before he could take a step, Rachael was beside him, wrapping an arm around his waist to support him. His heart did a cartwheel at the innocuous touch.

"How's your back?"

"All good."

It was then that he realized she was limping. "What happened to your leg?"

"I twisted my ankle during the attack. It was healing pretty well—"

"Until you jumped off a helicopter to cover me." His self-worth took another hit. "Next time, you better leave when I tell you to."

"Good thing there won't be a next time."

The knot in his stomach tightened. The I-don't-ever-want-to-see-you-again rule was still in full effect. Once they were out of there, he'd never see her again. He'd warmed up to the idea that he could regain her friendship, earn her respect. While he was a quick learner when it came to anything related to his work, his love for Rachael had pushed him to make stupid decisions, second-guess himself, and question his every move. That was never good for a man in his position.

In silence, they made their way through the darkened hallways, alert for any incoming threat. Luck was on their side as they hobbled past Rachael's old cell and by Khalil's office. As they hit the last stretch, muted conversation in Arabic and the weak glow of a candle spilled into the hallway from the last room before the outside door.

Rachael left Nathan leaning against the wall and, going down on her hands and knees, approached the door.

"Hush, hush. They are gone now. You can go to sleep," a woman murmured to a whimpering child.

Warmth replaced the cold running in her veins at the recognition of Qismah's voice.

"The bad men are gone, now," the old woman said.

Rachael, once so sure of Qismah's cooperation, couldn't quite count on an alliance. From the woman's point of view, the rescue operation hadn't been any different from the Israeli occupation that had caused her husband's death. Could she risk reaching for help, risk having her warn the remaining *mujahideen* of their location?

She weighed the pros and cons of pushing through. In the end, it came down to having no other choice. She could either trust her instincts and reveal their presence, hoping Qismah would facilitate their escape, or sit there and wait under the risk of being captured before their chariot arrived.

She pushed to her feet and limped through the open doorway before Nathan could stop her. Startled, the woman's eyes widened. Rachael gestured for Qismah to stay quiet.

The room was scantily furnished with the usual sleeping pallets and mats. A dresser and very few pieces composed what looked to be Qismah's living quarters.

The child whimpered and Rachael soothed the little one in Arabic. "It's okay. Nothing is wrong. I'm a friend."

"How—?"

"I had to stay behind. A friend needed my help."

"A friend?"

"Yes. He won't hurt you, I promise. We just need to reach the truck, the one they used to drive me and the other hostages here, and we'll be gone. We don't want to put you and your child in danger."

"If they know I helped...."

"I know. You don't need to help us. Just don't alert them. We're only passing by."

She nodded, accepting the agreement in silence. "I have never forgotten your kindness." Qismah walked to the end of the room, grabbed a couple of blankets, and handed them to Rachael. "It's cold out."

"Thank you."

As she turned to leave, Qismah held her by the elbow. "You are limping again." She reached for a jar sitting on the dresser. "Take this." Qismah placed it on top of the pile. Rachael inclined her head a second time, this time in gratitude.

"Allah yusallmak." With Qismah's blessing, Rachael turned and, limping toward the hallway, exited the room.

Nathan waited for her just outside, where the glow of the candle illuminated the hall just enough for her to see his face for the first time since he'd opened the door to her cell. She felt a shock run through her and her breath caught in her throat. He'd worn the knit face mask for the entire time they were searching the office. Now that she could see him without that barrier, it made the whole thing more real. He was really there. Her fingers itched to reach out, to touch his face. To make sure he was flesh and blood, not a figment of her wildest dreams, but she kept it to herself. That was definitely not the right time to disclose her fragile emotions to his perusal.

Nathan noticed Rachael's shift, her pause when she came out of the room carrying blankets. She spoke fluent Arabic. Another unexpected facet of hers. He knew she spoke her father's language, Hebrew, fluently, but had not expected her to know Arabic.

"She can't help us. That would put her and the children in danger, but she's promised not to alert the men."

"That's more than enough." As they walked past the door, he

saw a petite woman sitting on a pallet on the floor, a child on her lap. She didn't disguise her surprised look at seeing him, but as promised, she didn't call the guards. He nodded in respectful acknowledgment and moved from her line of sight as fast as his body allowed him to.

When they reached the side of the house, they encountered the signs of the earlier breaching. The metal door hung by one hinge, leaving the side wide open for easy egress, but also a perfect funnel for target practice. If any of the armed hostiles had access to a night vision scope like his, they were toast. Making use of his MP7's scope, he scoured the surrounding area and, finding no sign of activity, prompted Rachael to follow him outside. The truck was parked some twenty feet from the side of the building. They crept to the vehicle without disturbing the silence. Nathan tried the door, praying they'd left it unlocked within the security of the compound walls. It wasn't as if anybody could steal it out from under their noses and their AKs like Nathan was planning on doing.

With a click, the door eased open and he signaled for Rachael to climb in ahead before following her in and closing the door behind him.

Sitting in the driver's seat, Nathan pulled his Gerber tool, a standard item in any operator's kit, from one of his pockets and cracked the steering column's cover. He yanked on the ignition wires and, with quick strokes, stripped them like a pro car thief.

"Get down on the floor and cover yourself with the blankets. I don't know how many tries it will take to hotwire this sucker, but once they hear the engine turning, all hell will break loose."

She took cover as instructed and he took a deep breath before taking the chance. The truck's engine coughed and spurted once; voices rang out in the distance around the house. His pulse kicked into full throttle. He was breathing hard as he tried a second time, with the same results.

"Come on, come on!" he yelled at the truck, willing it to come to life, to no avail. As he tried for the third time, he heard the first spray of bullets hit the frame. He ducked and continued to attempt the ignition. Sparks flew as he rubbed the wires together while the voices outside became louder as the men closed in on them. "Come on, piece of shit. Move it!" Almost as if disgruntled at the curse, the truck sputtered a couple of times and the engine growled to life. "Yes!" Putting the truck in gear, he floored the gas. The truck's headlights illuminated a group of armed men as he turned the corner to the front of the building. Caught by surprise, the men began shooting at the truck as he drove by.

Nathan pressed the pedal to the floor, picking up the necessary speed to break through the metal panel gates fronting the compound's entrance. "Hold on tight!" he cried out to Rachael, the dings of the bullets against the back of the truck punctuating his words as he crashed into the gates, breaking them apart and giving way to their escape.

His attention was immediately drawn back to Rachael. "Rae. Are you okay?" She nodded back and he released the breath he didn't realize he'd been holding. He checked his mirrors. No headlights followed them yet and hopefully never would. "We're clear. You can come out now."

Rachael climbed onto the seat and scooted closer to him. "Where are we headed?"

"Based on what I can remember from the maps shared during the briefing for the rescue, this road runs through the Devira Forest. It's only a few miles away." He continued to monitor their six carefully, hoping to avoid a high-speed chase in the rattling truck.

They drove in uneasy silence until they reached the forest. A few hundred feet from the entrance, Nathan located the perfect hiding spot for the truck. Working together to conceal it, they stripped it of any useful items. Nathan found more blankets in the bed of the truck, and Rachael retrieved a couple of bottles of water from under one of the seats, most likely those items intended for use during the hostages' abduction.

Bundling everything into two of the blankets, they each shouldered one and followed a nearby trail into the thick tree line. They walked for half an hour, their progress hampered by the ache in his back and the condition of Rachael's tender ankle, when Nathan's shin connected with a solid wall and he lost his balance.

Rachael grabbed the back of his vest and stopped him from tumbling into a hole in the ground. "Easy, I got you."

The sudden movement shot pain through his back again. "Damn it." Nathan took a deep breath, and with a quick burst of light from his Maglite, inspected the area. Satisfaction warmed his chest and the knot in his stomach loosened as he studied the sturdiness of the ancient stone structure. It was half-buried in the ground, with a small entrance only visible if someone stood right above it. Perfect for a temporary hiding place.

"We wait for rescue here."

With only a couple of water bottles to last them until they were found, they'd have to conserve energy and heat for as long as possible. Without rebuttal, Rachael stepped down into the ancient cave-like structure, balancing on the stone steps as he illuminated the way. The entrance opened up into a wider space with limestone-lined walls and a dome-like ceiling. Temperatures in the Negev desert during the winter could reach well below freezing, and that included their shelter. Placing the flashlight on a ledge on the stone wall, Nathan grabbed two of the blankets and covered the floor to provide the necessary insulation from the frigid ground. The single thermal blanket from the survival kit sandwiched between the remaining two blankets they brought from the compound would provide excellent heat retention.

"Lie down," he coaxed her and she complied, exhaustion etched on her face. It was as if she was going into shock or nosediving into an adrenaline crash. Once she lay on the makeshift bed, he turned the lights off and joined her, pulling the other two blankets over them.

His pulse thundered in his ears when he wrapped his arm around her waist and pulled her back against his chest. The move was a practical one, their shared heat a needed survival measure to ensure neither of them suffered from exposure. But Nathan's mind, his heart reacted with joy. He'd never expected that they would ever be in this situation, particularly not in this position, but if that was what fate had to offer him, he'd take it gladly and silently—even if his mind reeled with the events of the night, with the new fascinating dimension of the woman he cradled in his arms. The same, and yet so different from the woman who'd stolen his heart all those years ago. As much as his mind wanted answers, his body screamed with exhaustion.

Burying his face in her hair, he filled his lungs with her scent and welcomed some much-needed sleep. He'd have time to peel all those layers soon enough.

Chapter Thirty-Two

Instinct

CHIRPING STARTLED NATHAN FROM A DEEP sleep. He could barely remember the last time he'd slept that well, particularly considering the circumstances. He opened his eyes to the reality of their rudimentary shelter. The reddish haze of dawn bounced off the stone walls, illuminating their rough-hewn hiding place. The pain in his back had been replaced by a dull, generalized soreness. Broken bones or bruises were easy to handle. It was the emotional wounds that took longer to heal. His bruised back wouldn't stop him from finding their way out of there when the time came. He'd most likely need it looked at when he returned home, but he wasn't worried. Home. The apartment minutes from Langley where he housed his suits wasn't home. Had never been one. He thought of his family's home. It hadn't felt like home long before he'd left it.

He lowered his gaze to the woman pressed against his chest. She had turned toward him during the night, and now her face brushed against the front of his chest plate when she breathed in and out. She should be uncomfortable laying against the rough material. Instead, she looked rested, peaceful. And at that moment he realized where home was.

His mind went blank of everything but Rachael. No wonder he'd slept so well. For the first time since meeting her, he was truly at peace. Didn't matter that they were hiding from hostiles in the middle of a foreign country. Didn't matter that they still had to find a way out of there. All that mattered was the quiet in his soul.

He soaked in the sight of her. Her golden skin, the reddish highlights of her dark hair under the morning haze, the shape of her lips. God. What he wouldn't do to be allowed to kiss those lips, cover them with his, breach them with his tongue, taste her. His body reacted to the image painted in his head, his blood pumped faster, his breath followed right behind it. He closed his eyes and stilled his mind to keep his desire under control, but it was of no use. His cock hardened, his pulse raced wildly.

He had her exactly where he'd always wanted her. In his arms. She took a deeper breath and snuggled closer, completely unaware of his inner struggle, and a sliver of fear went down his spine. He didn't want that moment to end. He didn't want to see anger in her eyes when she opened them and realized whose arms encircled her. He didn't want to hear words of repulsion from her lips. He wanted that moment to last forever.

Loving her had become ingrained, a part of him, an instinct. He couldn't think of any stage of his adult life that he had been able to completely erase her from his memory. Having her beside him, no matter how rough the ground was, no matter how tough it got in the hours to come, made it all worth it.

Unable to keep himself from enjoying the rare moment, he lowered his eyes, only to meet hers staring at him. His heart halted with a thud. He froze like a deer in the headlights, unable to find the right words to justify his body's reaction to her.

"I'm—"

She pressed her fingers against his lips, stopping the measly excuse he was about to give. His heart played a full military tattoo in his ears when she brushed her fingers from his lips to his cheek. All he could see was the troubled expression in her eyes, the war she fought mirrored his. The hand cupping his cheek slipped behind his neck. Gently, as if she was afraid he would turn away from her, she brought his face closer to hers until their lips were barely touching. His breath mingled with hers, collided. Seconds of pure bliss and hell hung between them.

He fought that war within himself, a war he'd mastered over many years. The drive to have her, possess her, and be possessed by her on one side, the need to keep his distance on the other. It was a hard war to wage. In the end, when she closed the gap and pressed her lips against his, he knew he'd lost.

From the moment Rachael woke in Nathan's strong arms, his face hovering scant inches above hers, she knew she'd lost her restraint on the attraction that had simmered under the surface since she'd met him. She'd needed to be close to him, experience that kind of proximity to accept that, like the very air she'd breathed, she had needed him for as long as she could remember. She still needed him. Now more than ever. She brushed her lips across his, once, twice. His ragged breath stroked her cheek and turned choppy, telling her he was just as affected by that first gentle kiss as she was. She slanted her lips over his again, savoring their heat, the soft brush against hers, capturing that perfect moment in her heart before he had a chance to reject her.

An ache grew in her throat and moisture slipped into her eyes. To finally be that close to him was everything she'd imagined. No. It was pure heaven. Her entire body ignited with a yearning that she'd never experienced before. She was still reeling from the way he'd stormed back into her life. This older Nathan was sexier, more virile, and way more dangerous—to others as much as to her own heart— yet he still carried that vulnerability she'd seen in his eyes ten years ago, and that strict sense of honor of his. That thought acted as a wakeup call. She had carried her love for him tucked away for so long that it had felt natural to kiss him. Her bold move came crashing down when she recalled his words. *No matter how much I've wanted you, I could never—. You're Phillip's wife. You'll always be.*

Reluctantly, she stopped the lingering kiss, took a shaky breath, and rested her forehead on his chest plate. "I'm sorry. I had no right to do that."

At that moment, she wished she could forget the past, turn back the clock, and redo her life except for him. Pretend for even a little while that he was hers and had been all those years. She couldn't chastise Nathan for his principles when she had taken that same road herself. She'd gone ahead with a marriage she knew was not based on mutual love only because she had given her word. Somehow, looking back, she realized Phillip would have possibly understood her love for Nathan if she had come clean right away. The realization made her sorry for both of them, sorry she had stolen the opportunity to have given them both a chance.

Almost as if responding to the thoughts in her head and not her words, Nathan lifted her chin until his striking green eyes caught and held hers. "Don't ever be sorry, Rae." His eyes brimmed with heart-rending tenderness as he threaded his fingers through her hair, brushing the loose strands away from her face.

Beams of sunlight washed down into their sanctuary and cut across his face. Almost of their own accord, her fingers reached out to trace the arch of his brow, the bridge of his nose, brush across the sharp angle of his cheek. She wanted that moment to last forever, even though she knew it would be gone the second they were found. Nathan would most likely rebuild his walls, uphold his code. Her heart thrummed in her head. Eyes drawn to his mouth, she struggled to keep her distance. Now that she'd had a taste of it, it was more tempting than ever. Her pulse grew louder in her ears as her thumb caressed his lower lip.

"What are you doing?" His voice broke with huskiness.

A million butterflies scrambled in her stomach as her eyes met his again. "I…I'm committing you to memory just in case—"

His lips curved into a sad smile. Nathan's hand came over hers, lifted her fingers to his lips, and he kissed them. "I'm not going anywhere. We're leaving here together." He leaned over her again, placing a chaste kiss on her brow. He pulled back just enough to hold her gaze once again. Time stood still, eyes locked until, gradually, the air was charged with sexual tension. She felt the change in the way he held her, the way his eyes followed the movement of her tongue when she moistened her dry lips. And then, paradise.

Cautiously, he lowered his face to hers and trailed kisses along the bridge of her nose, across her cheek, and finally to her mouth. Her heart swelled, her pulse jumped as he ran the tip of his tongue across the seam of her lips. Rachael's breath hitched and her lips parted, inviting him to take his fill. He dipped his tongue past her lips and swirled it against hers. She'd always wondered what it would be like to have Nathan's tongue plundering her mouth. It was all and more than she'd imagined. He made her feel alive, whole. Rachael moaned softly under his sensual assault. She ran her fingers through his short crop of hair to the nape of his neck and held him to her, afraid that if she let go she'd find it was all just another dream.

Nathan grasped at the edges of the fantasy he seemed to be living, worried the hit he'd taken had been worse than he'd initially thought. Hallucination was the only logical explanation for her kissing him back. He considered the consequences of going down that path, taking what she was offering, and realized he was willing to risk an eternity in hell for that stolen moment of bliss.

Her lips were as soft and plump as he'd imagined, her touch warm and firm as she shifted closer, wrapping her arms around his neck and pressing the length of her body against his. He deepened the kiss, alternating the dipping of his tongue with the nibbling of her lips, and burned hotter when she sucked his lower lip into her mouth, grazing it with her teeth.

"God." He couldn't hold back the moan from escaping his throat.

She stilled and he opened his eyes, about to kick himself for ruining the magic of the moment. Instead of guilt and admonition, he saw only a reflection of his desire in her eyes.

Holding his gaze, without a word, Rachael straddled his hips. With slow, deliberate motions, she released the Velcro straps on his vest one by one. Once it was loose, he sat and helped her lift it over his head. She dropped the heavy piece to the ground beside them and sank back to rest on his thighs. Her eyes clung to his, an air of expectation radiating from her as if waiting for him to make the next move.

His mind went fuzzy, but his reaction to her unspoken invitation was of a primal nature. With trembling fingers, he unbuttoned her shirt, dimly aware of the ache in his back, but unwilling to give it notice. When the last button came undone, the sides fell apart, revealing her no-nonsense bra, the silver locket nestled between her breasts. The plain cotton garment was a big turn-on. Fancy lace would have been wasted on her. She was already the most beautiful woman he'd ever seen or would ever see. As she shrugged the shirt off her shoulders and tossed it on top of his vest, he knew he was a goner. His heart chugged even faster when she reached for the silver chain, pulled it over her head, and set it on her shirt. This moment was proving to be much more than his wildest dreams.

She caught the hem of his long-sleeve tactical shirt and with a tug, pushed it up over his head. He jerked it off and tossed it aside. The cold air caressing his bare chest was no match for the feverish heat that rippled under his skin when she set her hand above his heart. It thundered in there so loudly, he knew she had to feel its vibration under her touch.

Disappointment rushed him when her hand fell away, but it was soon replaced by awe when she turned her back to him and lifted her hair. With another unspoken invitation, the bra was now his to remove. A ragged breath squeezed from his lungs as she faced him, letting the straps slide down her arms. Her nipples puckered in the brisk morning air. He had to swallow past the lump in his throat.

Rachael's skin tingled where his fingers and eyes touched her. Her heart jumped to her throat as she reached for him, gathering him in her arms until their bodies met, skin to skin. Their moans mingled in the small enclosed room on contact. He buried his face in her neck and tightened his hold around her waist, pressing her tighter against him. Time seemed to stand still. She could feel his heart thudding against her own.

"God. I've wanted to hold you like this for so long." His words brushed her neck, sending a spray of goosebumps across her exposed skin.

She wanted to tell him she'd dreamed about it, too. Afraid he'd pull back, she remained silent, hoping her actions would speak for her. She cradled the back of his head and cupped his jaw. Looking deep into his eyes, she lowered her mouth to his. A groan rolled up his chest. He gripped the hair at the nape of her neck, holding her as he took control of the kiss, plunging his tongue into her mouth, exploring, teasing. His lips slid across her cheek, trailing kisses along her neck to the swell of her breasts.

Rachael melted under his touch. This is what had been missing in her life. The complete and intense awareness of every pore in her body under his touch. She dug her fingers into the corded muscles of his arms and leaned back, giving him full access to anything he desired. She gasped when he tightened his arms around her and swept her to her back beneath him. His ragged breath, moist and warm, mingled with hers as he reclaimed her mouth in a soul-wrenching kiss.

Her heart faltered when he pressed his hard erection against her thigh. Wanting to feel every inch of him against her, she shifted her hips to accommodate his weight, ever so conscious of his touch as he ran his fingertips along her waist to the underside of her breast. Nathan softened the kiss and raised his head, eyes now focused on his thumb as it caressed the gentle swell.

"So beautiful."

She sucked in a shallow breath when he leaned forward and drew the tight bud into his mouth. A shiver of need raked up her back. He rolled it in his mouth gently, laving it with tantalizing possessiveness.

Her body was in flames, the feel of him tight against her was overwhelming. She closed her eyes, entranced by the intense need awakened inside her. She arched her back and gasped when he accepted her offer, sucking, flickering, and nibbling on her sensitive skin. She moaned when he broke that contact and pulled back from her. She opened her eyes and found him hovering above her, eyes darkened, an unspoken question buried in them as his hand slid down her stomach to the swell of her hip, his finger tracing the edge of her waistband to its button. She understood his request. Rachael held his gaze, grazing her hand down his arm until her hand met his and nodded.

Relief, caution, and expectation all collided in his chest when she gave him consent to proceed. He fought to retain some semblance of the mature individual he considered himself to be rather than some bumbling teenager at his first sexual experience. She made him feel like those ten years had not existed, as if this really was his first time.

He kneeled between her parted legs, and when he'd undone the button and zipper, she lifted her hips, helping him slip her slacks and panties down. For a long moment, he couldn't move. There she lay, bared to him, and all he could do was pray this was real, she was real, afraid that touching her would end the dream.

Sensing his hesitation, she sat up and kissed him before reaching for his belt. His breath hitched in his lungs when she tugged on it with hands that trembled as much as his. Mind-blown, he helped her undo the many fastenings. His heart slammed in his chest when she eased the combat cargo pants and boxers down to his knees, springing his erection free. He discarded the pants on the growing pile of clothing, oblivious to anything but the vision in front of him.

Holding his gaze, Rachael leaned back onto the blankets and extended her hands to him. Heat whooshed over his body. Fighting to remain in control, he kneeled between her parted thighs and moved his body over hers. The brush of skin on skin as he covered her almost drove him out of his mind.

She moaned and he froze. "Am I too heavy? I can—" He began to roll off of her.

She wrapped her arms around him, stopping him. "Shh. You are just perfect where you are."

Relief washed over him. He would stop if she asked him, but he knew doing so would probably kill him. He moved his hand down between them, his fingers caressing the skin of her inner thigh, seeking her heat. Fierce want engulfed his body when he found her already wet. This was not a dream or a hallucination. This was very real. Nathan groaned and leaned down once again, covering her mouth with his. *God help him. She would be his today and he'd be hers forever.*

A wave of pleasure coursed through her body when he poised the crown of his hard erection against her heat. He shifted his weight off her. Bracing himself on his forearms, he gazed down at her, almost as if giving her one more chance to say no. She curled her hand around the nape of his neck and brought his mouth closer to hers.

"Please, don't stop."

His eyes darkened and he captured her mouth in a searing kiss. Her skin tingled on contact when he hooked her leg high on his hip. With gentle pressure, he buried himself inch by inch, their moans mingling in the silence surrounding them. A hot ache grew in her throat when he released a low moan and tipped his head back, his expression tight with desire. He dropped his gaze to hers again and pulled back until he was almost free of her before he thrust forward again.

She was lost in a world of sensations she'd never experienced. Instinctively, she wrapped both legs around his hips, pressing him to move. Awe, joy, pleasure mingled in his expression and it made her heart sing. Their groans blended as their bodies found their tempo, a harmony that bound them together.

Flames licked across her skin and her inner walls tightened around him. He moved faster. Harder. Demanding all of her. Her head pressed back against the blankets, her body grew taut, and her heart slammed against her ribs. Nathan held her tight, urging her to let go, and she did, shattering into a thousand pieces.

"Nathan!" He caught her shout in his mouth, his tongue thrusting deep, exploring.

Nathan loved watching her passion spill over her face and her body shuddering around him in climax. His own climax was riding upon him, licking flames up his spine. Rachael's body pulsed in such a deliriously perfect grip around his, he couldn't hold his need, his desire any longer. At the sound of his name on her lips, he released all his restraints. He drove again and again until he was thoroughly spent. Spasms racked his body with each involuntary squeeze of hers while he lay atop her, her legs still locked around his hips.

Minutes went by before she released her hold on him. He took the opportunity to reverse their positions, pressing the length of her against his side, her leg hooked over his thigh. With a deep sigh, she tucked her face into the crook of his neck and placed a gentle kiss on it.

Rachael's breath slowed and leveled as she fell asleep in his arms. He was unwilling to follow her example. Instead, he watched over her, studied every curve, every swell of her golden skin while replaying every single second over and over in his mind. He'd wanted her for too long before that shared moment, and had been forced to keep his distance. Now that the line into intimacy had been crossed, that the bounds he'd demarcated himself had been erased, he was sure he couldn't let her go.

Knowing she couldn't hear him, he whispered the words he hoped he'd one day be able to say out loud. "Will you be mine?"

Somehow, the idea of being rescued wasn't so exciting anymore.

Chapter Thirty-Three

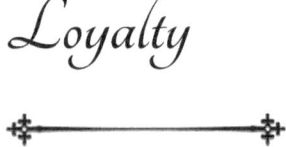

Loyalty

HE SOUND OF APPROACHING STEPS reverberated through the hallways outside the cell. Khalil didn't move, didn't turn to look at the door when the clanging of keys signaled someone was about to join him. Not that he could anyway. He'd been handcuffed to the bed, both hands secured to the metal frame.

The door opened and then closed behind his visitor. Khalil kept his eyes fixed on the ceiling. He heard the grinding scrape of a metal chair against the concrete floor, then the shuffle of someone sitting on it.

"How much fun when the tables turn, huh?" the traitor whispered in Arabic close to his ear, making him jump inside his skin.

"You shouldn't be laughing. You are walking a dangerous line. Possibly thinner than mine," Khalil responded with the same tone, same language, turning his head to face the man. A cynical smile curved his mouth just like it always had before. He'd showered and changed into sweats and a shirt that appeared a bit too loose on him.

He looked different from the suit-wearing man he'd plucked out of the convoy less than two weeks earlier. The icy cold sheen in his eyes hadn't changed, though.

"I think you are wrong. No. I know you are wrong. Without you, he gains security. Without me, the *Rasūl* will have lost every possible chance to influence the government from within. I can still find a way to garner the support I need to reach a position of power, and when I do, I'll be faithful."

Khalil scoffed. "You, faithful? Do you even know the meaning of the word? I admire the *Rasūl's* ability to create powerful means to reach a needed end and believe he was sent to free us from the oppression we've lived under all these years, but he made a big mistake trusting someone who would betray his country for power and not for a higher motive."

"So eloquent." A low chuckle punctuated his words. "Who are you to say anything? You betrayed your mentor."

"I didn't—" Khalil frowned, unsure what the man was referring to. He'd never betrayed the *Rasūl*. Ever.

"Yes, you did. You alerted the CIA of the hostages' location, and that's how they found us."

"But I didn't."

The thought sent frigid tentacles slithering down his spine. Khalil had been in a position of privilege until now. The *Rasūl* had trusted him to execute the plan, and now that he'd failed, Khalil doubted that he'd ever be in the same circle of trust again. The *Rasūl* would trust the American over him.

"No, you didn't, but that's what the *Rasūl* will hear. From me. And you'll be a dead man either way."

He was right. If the *Rasūl* believed he had something to do with it, Khalil wouldn't be given a chance to explain. One thing Khalil had learned through the many years he'd known his mentor was that he hadn't reached the heights he had through forgiveness. Would he believe he had nothing to do with the whole thing? That he hadn't betrayed his confidence? The *Rasūl* would coax the answers from him in his own way. It didn't matter that there were no answers to be had.

Khalil's blood froze in his veins. "You can't do this." If he did, he would sign his death warrant. No matter where he hid, he'd eventually be found and killed.

"I can. I will, if you don't do the right thing and take care of a little problem. Yourself."

"I don't understand."

"The US military is skilled in all torture techniques. They will use them to take every drop of intelligence they can from you. There's no question in my mind you will cave. And that is a problem."

Chills racked his body at the memory of the many times he'd witnessed the *Rasūl's* own methods for carving the truth from those he suspected to have betrayed him. The many times those subjected to his methods had succumbed to the extreme torture. Kahlil had enjoyed the learning experience of watching the *Rasūl* deliver painful blows and excruciating burns, never once questioning what it would feel like to be the one on the receiving end. Now that he did, a cold film of sweat covered his skin. If the Americans were even close to what he could do, he'd be happy if he died quickly.

The American continued his train of thought. "If you cave and reveal how far and wide the *Rasūl's* organization reaches, if you reveal my participation in it, you will effectively destroy any possible chance it will ever come to realization." His smile faded. "You will destroy my chance of reaching the senate, and eventually the presidency. The plan was always to be a long-term one. It would have gotten a fast track if I'd returned a hero who managed to negotiate the hostages' release without intervention. But the plans have changed, and just like the *Rasūl* always says, we need to adapt. Move on. That means you are a threat to the Palestinian State simply by breathing."

Khalil let his words sink in as far as they could. And it finally made sense. He was right. He couldn't allow himself to be the boulder in the middle of the road.

"Did you come to terminate the threat?"

"I can't do that. They signed me in. If you turned up dead after I left, they would know it was me."

"Won't they be suspicious you are talking to me?"

"They think I'm trying to get information from you. I said we had a good rapport while in captivity. The others confirmed my story."

"So how do you plan on handling this?"

"They have arranged to bring a specialist to interrogate you here. You'll have what you need under the chair in the interrogation room. I'll make sure you have time. Do what you need to do and I will tell the *Rasūl* of your loyalty."

Upon receiving Khalil's nod, the man stood and walked to the windowless metal door. He knocked twice and the clanging of keys sounded outside before the door opened and he exited without a glance back at Khalil.

Chapter Thirty-Four

Seeing Ghosts

ASSANDRA STOOD ON THE TARMAC at Ramstein AB, watching as the large cargo plane—her ride to Amman— taxied on the tarmac until it came to a stop. Its gunmetal-gray fuselage, brightly lit under the strip's lights, squatted on the snow-dusted tarmac in stark contrast with the dark background. Its engines whirled with power and the smell of burnt jet fuel assaulted her nose. She scanned the area. Only the relief flight crew and support crew were out on the tarmac. Ramstein was only a short hop before the cargo shipment left for its final destination, Jordan.

She waited at the edge of the hangar while the ground crew went through the aircraft's checklist. A blend of anxiety and anticipation warred in her chest when a man holding a clipboard started toward her.

Only five more hours or so and she would see Trevor again. A wave of apprehension swept over her. She wasn't sure what her reception was going to be like when she landed at the Forward Operating Base. She'd ignored orders. She'd ignored Trevor's wishes for her to stay home where he thought her safe. Twice. She hadn't done that to be contrary or stubborn. Trevor had always told her to trust her instincts, follow her gut. She had and got the results they needed. Now they told her to get her ass to Jordan, and she would. Her instincts had never let her down, and she wasn't going to turn deaf ears to them now. She sighed heavily at the thought of what waited for her in Jordan. She knew that no matter how positive the outcome had been this far, Trevor was going to be rip-roaring pissed.

Come on. Just open already. Let's get this over with.

As if reading her thoughts, the ramp separated from the tail. She shouldered her backpack, and clutching her duffel's handles, approached the man.

"Bauer?" the flight crewmember called out.

She barely heard him over the constant whine of the plane's idle engine.

"That's me."

He escorted her to the ramp and motioned her forward, a grin stamped on his face. "Your chariot awaits. Apparently, you scored a golden ticket. Sit anywhere. You can play musical chairs if you want. The entire plane is yours today."

Cassandra followed him up the ramp and selected a seat in the middle, against the side of the cargo plane. The plane's cargo load sat on pallets in the center. Securing her bags, she harnessed herself in. The crewman checked her and gave her the thumbs up.

"We lift off as soon as the tower clears us. I'll check on you later."

As he turned away, Cassandra caught his arm. "What's our ETA?"

"Ten hundred hours local time."

She gave him a thumbs-up and sat back against the seat. The area around her was pretty bare. Cargo anchored with wide, white canvas straps lay near the tail. The silver-and-gray interior was impersonal, no fluff, no frill, which was fine with her. Fewer distractions. Her stomach balled when her thoughts turned to the uncertainty of her flight out of Germany. Minutes stretched before the engine finally screamed louder and they started moving slowly toward the strip. Deafened by the sound of the powerful turbines, she leaned her head back and closed her eyes as she felt the push of takeoff. The engines growled as the plane fought to break away from the earth's gravitational pull. Once they leveled off at cruising speed, she pulled her earbuds from her pocket, shoved them in her ears, and hit play. Soon, her playlist helped block out the grueling engine noise and break through the helter-skelter in her brain. She dropped her head back against the seat and closed her eyes, this time meticulously organizing her thoughts and losing the battle to stay awake.

"Ms. Bauer?"

Cassandra snapped open her eyes and glanced up at the crewman hovering over her.

"ETA fifteen minutes."

She straightened in her seat, alertness finally making its way through. "Got it."

The man disappeared through the cabin door, leaving her alone with her thoughts once again.

She had been so out of it she hadn't even noticed the time. As she felt the gradual descent, anxiety and excitement flowed like dual currents under her skin. She would be joining the action soon. The plane dipped and squared for the approach and she braced for the touchdown. Cassandra held on to the straps of her harness. The plane jerked and she bounced in her seat. It sped down the runway and slowed to a stop before taxiing to the unloading area.

Minutes after the aircraft came to a complete stop, the crewman was back, motioning her to follow him to the tail. He pressed a button and the ramp lowered, allowing blinding sunshine into the belly of the plane. Stepping out onto the sunlit ramp, he pointed her in the direction of the hangar. Cassandra nodded. Her stomach twisted in knots and her heart thumped uncomfortably as she made her way to the exit. *Time to pay the piper.*

Squinting against the bright sunlight, Cassandra took her dark wire-rimmed sunglasses from her backpack and slipped them over her eyes. She leaned against the metal siding of the maintenance hangar entrance, staring out at the tarmac.

A low growl diverted her attention to the road. She shaded the top of her glasses and saw a military Humvee on a trajectory straight for her. Her heart jerked in her chest and her stomach tightened as it pulled to a stop a short distance from where she stood. Trevor stepped out from behind the steering wheel. Leaning back against the door of the truck, he folded his arms across his chest, eyes narrowed and indecipherable.

It had only been one week since Cassandra had last set eyes on Trevor, yet it seemed like a lifetime. Her eyes drank him in. His long muscular legs were clad in wrinkled khaki cargo pants, a tan t-shirt peeked from under the unbuttoned white shirt, his sleeves rolled back to the elbow displaying his lean, corded forearms. The man could turn her into a puddle just by standing there. She'd love nothing more than to run into his arms. His stormy blue eyes and lips pressed into a tight line held her desire to throw her arms around him in check.

Oh, yeah, he was pissed. All the certainty that she'd done the right thing by heading semi-unannounced to Jordan fled under his relentless stare. She shouldered her backpack and grabbed her duffel. Cassandra didn't know how she'd managed to walk on rubbery legs, but she had. She approached him with steady steps and a hesitant smile. She came to a stop a few feet away from him.

"Hey, you."

Unsaid words stood between them like the elephant in the room. The fact that she had ignored their superior's orders to stay out of Jordan was probably simmering deep inside him. His expression was a blank canvas; the only hint she had on his state of mind was the muscle tightening in his jaw.

She had to swallow around the lump lodged in her throat. She wanted to reach for him but clenched her hand instead until her nails cut into her palm. He had to hear her out.

"You're pissed, aren't you?"

Trevor exhaled a deep breath. She could have sworn he'd been counting to ten. "Why shouldn't I be?"

"About the things I said before you left—"

"They're in the past. I was already over them by the time I arrived here. In fact, you may have been right about me not being fit for the whole Special Forces thing." Even though his words gave her a little bit of hope, his eyes still held a hard edge. He broke his stiff stance and his eyes flashed with frustration as he shoved a hand through his unruly dark hair. "I'm mad because I just realized that my peace of mind, my anchor, was all in my head, because you'd become an international traveler, tackling something dangerous without even backup. Something that could have turned very ugly, very deadly, very fast."

Cassandra's fingers itched to smooth the tight lines framing his eyes. She squirmed inside and kept her hands to herself. She'd hurt him deeply. She set her bags on the ground, mind racing, searching for the right words to make it right. Deep down, she knew there weren't any. *One baby step at a time.*

She cleared her throat. "I'll explain about that, but first you have to hear me out." She took a deep breath. "I never meant to hurt you. You're one of the most capable, resourceful men I have ever had the pleasure of encountering in my life. You're a risk-taker. Hell, you have nine lives. You have proved that time and again. Not many could have pulled off what you did in Russia. The world would be a better place if there were more men like you. It's one of the many facets I love about you and one that scares the hell out of me."

A surge of hope flared in her chest when she saw the stern line of his lips soften. She drew in a deep breath. "I let old insecurities get the best of me. It was never about you. It was all about me, a terrified me. Terrified of losing you. Knowing that you were being placed in a dangerous situation again, that I couldn't do anything to help, turned me into someone even I couldn't recognize. You said that you wanted me safe at home. Well, I wanted you safe at home, too."

Worry that she was fighting a losing battle gripped her chest. Tears pooled in the back of her eyes, blurring her vision, and she was grateful her gaze was shielded by her sunglasses.

"I…I know that I can never take those words back. They've been said. But I hope you understand that they never came from my heart and that not once did I ever believe them. I hope you can forgive me." She took a few more steps toward him.

The tightness in his jaw eased, but the surge of relief that loosened the knot in her stomach was short-lived. He cocked his head, narrowed eyes scanning her face carefully before he closed in on her and gently removed her sunglasses. His sharp blue eyes swept her face, widened as they caught the bruising around her eye, and then narrowed again as they locked on the cut on her lip.

"What the hell? What the fuck were you thinking, going off on your own?"

She resisted the urge to touch her face and blurted in a rush, "I had a lead that I couldn't pass up. I knew in my gut that it was something hot and if I waited for you guys to debate it to death, we'd have lost the window of opportunity. It was essential to the case and it yielded very useful intel. Another piece of this puzzle. As for coming over, you know damn well you'll need me to confirm that anything Kahlil Abboud divulges is true. If I'd told you earlier I planned on heading over, you and Nathan would have pulled strings to have me escorted on a plane home."

Her voice trailed off when, without a word, Trevor stepped closer. Her pulse jumped as he put his hand under her chin, tipping her face up. His thumb gently rubbed across her lip. When it reached the corner of her mouth, he pushed her hair back from her cheek and his eyes darkened. He brushed his fingertips in a feather-light stroke along the black and purple bruise shadowing her eye.

"I'd have killed him."

"He was just a kid. I pretty much scared the shit out of him." She covered his hand with hers. "This was my fault. Can you believe I forgot to duck?"

He looked down at her. His eyes held a world of emotions. The one that shocked her the most was the relief she saw in them. She tightened her hold on his hand and cupped his cheek.

"I'm so sorry, Trevor. God, you don't know how sorry I am."

His gaze turned hot, possessive. Heat ignited in her belly at that one single look. The baby steps had just turned into a giant leap.

Trevor couldn't hold back the need to take Cassandra in his arms and hold her close, as close as he could, and never let her go. The knowledge that she'd been hurt when he was nowhere near to help her sickened him. Suddenly, it dawned on him what she might have gone through, sitting at home waiting for him to come back to her.

"Come here, you infuriating woman." He pulled her close, encircling her with his arms. He held her tightly for several heartbeats before tipping her face again and gently covering her mouth with his. All of his repressed anxiety dissolved under the touch of her lips and relief surged inside him. She cupped the side of his jaw, sinking into the kiss. With a sigh, Trevor broke the kiss and leaned his forehead against hers. "God, I missed you, Cassie girl." He trembled with the effort to hold his composure in check.

"I've missed you too, Mr. Brennan. Let's not do this again. I missed your texts."

She cracked a mischievous smile and his heart fluttered in his chest. "Agreed." He caressed her cheek, thankful to have her there after all. "I'm sorry I missed your birthday. I had plans—"

"I know. And that's all that matters."

"We'll have to make it up to each other later." He pressed a kiss to her lips and turned toward the vehicle. "We need to get back. Work awaits." He grabbed her duffel bag, tossed it in the Humvee, and held the door for her. Once inside, he handed her backpack to her. "Abboud is waiting for you, Cassie."

The name appeared to sober her. "Where is he?"

"In a holding cell at the base. They were having him moved to the room we will be using for the interrogation"—he glanced at his watch—"just about right now."

Cassandra squared her shoulders. Trevor admired her ability to snap back into agent mode, ready to tackle business.

"Has he been stewing long?"

"Yeah."

"Good. I'll need to set up the camera before we start. I want to capture as many of his microexpressions as possible. They'll happen so quickly, within a fraction of a second, that I might miss some of them while we talk. I can review them as we go; they may yield something valuable."

Trevor turned the engine and put the vehicle into gear.

"This is what you do. I trust your instincts, but I don't like that you'll be in the cell alone with him. Hanson granted me permission to join you in case you need someone to throw a laptop at him or something."

Her mouth curved with humor. "Gotta love teamwork."

STERILE WALLS AND bright white lights. Why did Westerners think that would put fear in anyone's heart? It was nothing compared to the fear that crawled in his gut, placed there by his own failure. The guards sat him down on the chair and checked his handcuffs to make sure they were tight. Then they left him alone in the room, locking the heavy metal door behind them.

A verse of the Qu'ran made its way into his consciousness. *Nor take life—which God has made sacred—except for just cause.* Making sure the Americans didn't gain access to any of the compromising information he had on the *Rasūl* was his just cause. As much as Khalil feared the man, he also admired the lengths to which he would go to fulfill their purpose. Khalil would rather die than put the *Rasūl* in the crosshairs of the American government. Khalil would do what he had to do, handle it the way an honorable man would.

He knew they were waiting on the arrival of the person who would take over his interrogation. He was running out of time. Thankful they had no means to handcuff him to the table, he flipped the chair upside down. It was as the American traitor had said it would be. He dug his fingers under the tape, holding the blade to the bottom of the chair to avoid making noise. He had to be careful not to attract the attention of the guards. He jerked it free and moved to a corner of the room, out of sight from the door.

Sitting with his back against the wall, he studied his cuffed hands, visualizing the path the knife would take, the blood that would weep like tears from his wrists. His pulse beat erratically, the muscles in his forearm tensing as he pressed the edge of the tip against the tender skin of his inner wrist. His eyes focused on the dot of crimson that bloomed on contact. Entranced by it, he sucked in a deep breath and sank the blade deep into his flesh. He hissed against the sting as he slid the razor-sharp edge along his veins. Immediately, blood welled and flowed down his palm, trailing down each finger, staining his pants and the floor.

He drew in a tattered breath and switched the blade to his bloodied hand, chanting verses of the holy book to give him the strength to go through with it. The second cut was not as clean, the action made harder by the blood-soaked handle slipping in his grip. He tossed the blade to the side and dropped his head back, focusing on the beat of his heart. The heart that had held true to their cause.

THE RIDE TO the base was quick. The mountains and the ground as far as the eye could see had a golden hue. Everything looked so magical, ageless. The only thing that felt real was the warmth of Trevor's fingers entwined with hers, his thumb rubbing the skin of her wrist. The vehicle halted in front of a two-story stucco building that spanned the length of a football field. On the front steps, Hanson, dressed in fatigues instead of the civilian clothes she'd seen him in last, waited for them. The surfer dude had been replaced by the far more lethal Special Forces operator she recognized him to be when he'd shown up on their doorstep. His eyes were sharp, assessing.

"Ready?" He didn't waste time with pleasantries.

At her nod, he turned on his heel and led the way inside. They walked down several corridors for what felt like forever. Trevor held on to her hand, squeezing it from time to time in what she'd thought was reassurance to her, but as she studied his expression, she realized he'd been reassuring himself.

Hanson slowed down and stopped next to a door flanked by two guards. He turned to face her. "What do you need?"

"I just need to set up the camera."

"How long do you think it will take?"

"Depends. We might have to break so I can study some of the footage or exchange memory cards. Other than that, I intend to stay in there for as long as it takes to get what we need."

Hanson nodded. On his signal, the guards opened the door and she took a step toward it, Trevor right behind her.

Upon entering the room, her heart jumped to her throat as the metallic smell of blood assaulted her nose. Her eyes anxiously searched for the source and quickly located the man sitting on the floor to the left of the door, his back against the wall, head slumped forward, the pool of blood around him slowly spreading.

"Call the medics!" She dropped to the man's side, slapping her palms against one of his severely carved wrists, frantically attempting to staunch the blood oozing between her fingers as all hell broke loose outside the cell. The man's breath was shallow, rapid. He was slipping into shock. "Trevor! Put pressure on that other wrist. We need to stop it before he bleeds out." For the second time since he'd met Cassandra, Trevor had his hands covered in blood. He'd tried to save Allison in Paris, and things hadn't turned out so well then. He didn't see it turning out any differently now. He continued to apply pressure. Pain must have stirred Abboud back to consciousness. He grunted and lifted his head; the blood loss had made him so weak he didn't seem able to hold it up and it fell back to rest against the wall. His lids opened, revealing dazed, disoriented eyes. As his gaze locked with Trevor's, his pupils dilated, eyes grew wider, and mouth slacked open as a puzzled frown furrowed his forehead. A glimmer of what appeared to be recognition crossed his eyes.

"His pulse just spiked. We're losing him." Cassandra's voice seemed to come from a long way off.

The man's mouth formed words and Trevor leaned closer, placing his ear near the man's lips, straining to hear what Khalil Abboud was struggling to say.

"I...I...thought you were dead—" Abboud's breath caught and he hissed, trying to breathe in. Trevor frowned. He was certain they'd never crossed paths before. The man had to be seeing ghosts, hallucinating as a result of the blood loss. "—Doctor Brennan."

Trevor's mind splintered. A whoosh of blood went straight to his head, the meaning of his words flooding his mind with crazy hope and fear. His heart raced as he shrugged off his shirt and pressed it firmly against the wound, desperate to stop the flow. He glanced at Cassandra as she too struggled to hold back the blood pooling under her hands.

"Fuck! Help! We need him alive!"

"I know. Where's the damn medic? Hanson!" Her voice rang with command.

Even with their best efforts to control it, blood continued to seep between Cassandra's fingers and soak his shirt like a sponge. Footfalls pounded through the door and medics shouldered them aside as they took over the frantic fight for the man's life. Trevor stepped back from the chaos ensuing around them, but couldn't step back from the chaos consuming his insides.

"How the hell was he able to do that?" Hanson asked, joining him.

"I don't know. Those cuts were deep." Trevor scanned the area around the corner where they'd found Abboud and located a spray of blood streaking the floor. His eyes traced the path to a short, bloodied blade. "Fuck. Over there. Where the hell did that come from? Didn't anyone search him?"

The others followed his line of sight and more cursing burst from Hanson's lips. "He was clean. We need this documented. All of it."

Trevor's eyes drifted back to the man still under the hands of the medics. Moments dragged like hours until their focused expressions turned to grim defeat. Abboud lay on the floor, lifeless. The medics called his time of death while Trevor's brain worked under a tornado of thoughts. Hanson punched the door, pacing the room. Cassandra still sat on her knees a distance from the body, frustration etched on her face and a gleam of tears in her eyes. Trevor's own frustration grew over the fact Abboud had died without providing vital information on the mastermind of the kidnapping. His body went numb, his mind muddled with questions. Questions he knew nobody there could answer. He was oblivious to the activity in the room until Cassandra tugged on his arm.

"Let's get out of here so they can do their job. Everything will need to be gone over with a fine-tooth comb."

They stepped out and stood in the hallway for a long time as the buzz of activity continued. Radios screeched and the sound of boots pounding the floor obliterated any possibility of silence. The bedlam in his head reflected the one surrounding them. The noise in his ears ceased when Cassandra wrapped her arms around him, anchoring him to the present.

She leaned back to look into his eyes. "Talk to me. I saw your face. What happened in there?"

Trevor shook his head and held her inquisitive gaze. He searched for the words to explain it all but came up empty. He wiped his hands on his t-shirt as his eyes touched on the ruined shirt on the floor.

"To be honest, I'm not sure. He said something before he died."

Cassandra's eyes sharpened. He could almost see the wheels in her head jumpstarting. She took a deep breath before asking, "Could you make it out? Was it a name?"

"To some extent."

"Then what was it?"

"He said he thought I was dead." Cassandra's confusion mirrored his own. "Cassie, he called me Doctor Brennan."

Her eyes widened and mouth fell open as a gasp escaped her lips. "I don't understand. How would he know that name?"

"I don't know. It seems we'll never know." His eyes traced back to the room where they were preparing the body for transport. Desolation hit him square in his chest, his limbs felt heavy while he grew lightheaded. Not once during the many months he'd been tracking Waldo had he found any indication of a link to his parents in all of the data he'd collected. Not once had he been led to believe that the events of the last few weeks had an alternate connection to his own quest.

"What are we going to do with that information?" Concern spilled from her eyes.

There was nothing he could do now. He didn't have the luxury of time to dwell on the meaning of the connection at that moment. There was still a job to be completed. Nelson and Rachael Moore were still out there and hadn't contacted the base. He needed to get his head straight and back in the game.

"Once George and I find Nelson and Mrs. Moore, I'll deal with that."

"What do you mean, find Nathan? What happened?"

"He joined the Eighth on the raid. Got separated. Long story. I'll fill you in after we get cleaned up." He took her hand in his and led the way to the control room, leaving the gigantic mess of Abboud's suicide behind.

Chapter Thirty-Five

Bare It All

THEY HAD RUN OUT of water by mid-afternoon, but fate, having been on their side all along, sent a heavy rainfall and with it the relief they needed. With their makeshift bed, they moved to an elevated ledge further into the ancient structure.

Safe from the sudden downpour, they focused on collecting water. Nathan made use of one of the water bottles, cutting off the top to serve as a funnel to feed the compact bladder in his survival kit. He sat it under a naturally formed spout off the stone roof, and by the time the rain eased off, they had enough purified drinking water to quench their thirst with some saved for later. He'd then messed with the radio for a while, trying to get it to work, but with no luck.

Leaning against the carved limestone wall, he inventoried their supplies. Although his survival kit was the gift that kept giving, it could only be stretched so far. Not only were they sharing contents meant for one person, they were unable to make use of some critical items like the fire-starting kit, forcing them to resort to good-old body contact to keep warm. His eyes strayed once again to Rachael. Lying naked under the covers since their last lovemaking, she looked like the perfect model for a painting. The simple act of looking at her brought back the same feeling of completeness he felt when buried inside her. His breath quickened, his heart hitched with renewed arousal, and, thanking the heavens his high-compression boxers helped conceal the physical evidence of that, he focused on their options, mulling out loud for distraction.

"We can't go too long without food, and we only have enough water for another day if it doesn't rain again."

Attracted by the sound of his voice, Rachael rolled to her side to look at him. "We can't venture out of the forest on foot. They could be scouring the area. And we can't risk taking the truck out, either. It's riddled with bullet holes."

Unaware of the direction of his thoughts, she untucked the blanket from her side and beckoned him to the ledge. He'd been hungry for her for a long time, and he'd be insane to reject any crumb she threw his way. Silently thankful for her offer, he joined her under the covers. She scooted closer and rested her face on his chest. After a second of hesitation, he draped his arm around her shoulders and pulled her closer. The act felt so natural, so right, as if they had been lovers all along.

He cleared his throat to banish the lump there. "Exactly. Our only hope is to trust Bauer will use one of his clever tricks to trace us. The problem lies in how long it will take for him to do that."

She tipped her face up and looked at him, a pensive expression on her face. "You seem to admire this Bauer."

Nathan paused and thought about her comment. When he'd met Trevor Bauer, he was the last person in the world he'd consider admiring. But with the developments of the last two weeks, he'd come to realize that not only was Bauer worthy of admiration for his skills, but that Nathan was now indebted to him because of them. Through his stubbornness and less-than-kosher approach to intelligence collection, Bauer had located Rachael and gifted Nathan with the moment he'd waited for all his adult life.

"Actually, I do. He and his team tracked you down."

"Ah." If she'd understood how much that meant to him, she didn't let it show. "So, what's the plan?"

"We wait one more day. That's how far we can stretch the water we have. If we haven't been located by nightfall tomorrow, we'll head northeast. We'll save the MRE for tomorrow and have that to pack some nourishment before we head out."

"It sounds like you've got all the bases covered."

Rachael's nonchalant strategy discussion and the fact that she didn't question him about the meaning of MRE—Meals Ready to Eat, the term used to refer to military ration packets—made him itch with curiosity. Eventually, he'd have to voice those questions out loud.

Rachael tightened her hold around his waist, pressing her ear against his chest. She soaked in the heat emanating from his skin, her mind turning to the few times he'd loved her thoroughly since dawn. For every moment she spent in his arms, the higher the conflict inside her grew.

She wanted them to be found, to be rescued, but she also wanted to keep their connection intact. It had taken them years to get to that stage, and now that they'd reached it, she feared it would disappear into thin air when they returned to the real world. Could their newfound intimacy grow into a long-term relationship? She didn't know. Nathan hadn't brought up the subject, and she didn't want to scare him away just yet. Once they made their way out of Israel, she'd find a way to bring it up. They had one more day of pure bliss, and she planned on enjoying every single moment.

His breathing accelerated in tandem with the heart beating under her ear when she hooked a hand behind his neck and gently brought his face down to hers.

"Rae—" he whispered against her lips. His low groan sent shivers across her skin.

Rachael didn't heed the warning in his tone. Grabbing the hem of his shirt, she pulled it over his head, baring his chest to her touch. She ran her fingertips over his skin, exploring and watching as the goosebumps bloomed along their path.

His fingers stroked her cheek softly, almost reverently. Covering his hand with hers, she guided it to her sex. Her lungs seized for a second when he buried one finger inside her and sent her heartbeat careening out of control.

Pushing the blanket aside, he gripped her waist and pulled her into a straddle across his lap. She took a deep breath to steady herself before undoing the fastenings on his pants under his watchful gaze. He lifted his hips from the blanket, helping her to pull his fatigues and boxers down past them. She then rose to her knees just enough to position him. Locking her gaze with his, she slowly lowered her body, taking each long inch of him inside her and eliciting a loud rumble from his chest.

He fit perfectly; she wished they could stay like that forever, joined in the most primal way a man and a woman could be joined. Eyes locked with his, she moved, slowly at first, gradually increasing speed. When he reached for the sensitive flesh of her clit, her body splintered into a million pieces. Nathan careened into his own climax right after her.

She remained on top of him, boneless, spent, hoping that it would never end. Knowing that it could.

WHEN NIGHT FELL upon them, they ventured out of their hiding place to forage the area for any edible plants they could find. Unfamiliar with the local flora, Nathan used his flashlight to carefully examine a few shrubs for characteristics indicating they were safe for consumption.

"Nathan," Rachael whispered behind him. "Here."

He walked toward her and illuminated the area she indicated.

"Malva. That's a lucky find." The enthusiasm in her voice told him they had what they needed.

She grabbed the leaves, still damp from the earlier showers, and they headed back to their temporary shelter. Under the glare of his helmet flashlight, she showed him what to cut out of the leaf, and explained how it was a central staple in the local gastronomy. He felt her eyes on him while he took a tentative bite, and it surprised him. The flavor and texture fell somewhere between lettuce and cilantro, without the dominant herby taste. Her lips tilted into a full smile and he smiled back, enjoying the somewhat domestic moment.

Rachael had become a riddle from the moment they'd left her cell. From challenging him to get her locket back to jumping out of an in-flight helicopter to stay with him to wielding a gun, she was a puzzle with more pieces than he'd ever imagined existed. Some of the things she did were familiar to him simply because he'd learned them from either the Farm or his special training. But he couldn't connect the dots between the Rachael he knew and those things. Curiosity got the better of him.

"How do you know so much about handling guns and all this survival stuff?"

She continued to chew on the leaves, eyes diverted to the ground, but he knew she had heard him. Somehow, her silence spoke louder. Rachael had changed a lot in the years they were apart, but it had been a shift for the better. While he'd fallen for a girl, he was floored by the woman she'd become. Determined and strong, yet soft and caring. There was a lot about Rachael he needed to know, needed to fill the gaps so he could see the whole picture, the how and why she ended up as a hostage in the Middle East.

"It doesn't matter to me how you got involved in whatever put you here, Rae. All I want is the chance to help put it to rest. I don't want to see you hurt ever again."

A whirlwind of activity revolved in Rachael's head. Her loyalties to her former employer were no longer a barrier. Her focus until now had been to uncover Phillip's murderer. Now that she knew who had killed him, everything made sense. The when, where, and how were now combined with the why to paint the picture of the man who had taken Phillip's life. By knowing whom, she'd accomplished her personal mission. All she had left to do was to use the tools she had at hand to put that man—no, animal—behind bars.

Nathan asked her to trust him with secrets she had carried for a long while. Her parents had no idea she had asked for their help to secure the job with that in mind. They just believed she was starting her life again from a clean slate, away from the job neither of them approved of. She had masked her intentions from all.

She wasn't alone. Rachael had once assumed Nathan held a government desk job, something related to politics, since that was the focus of his studies ten years ago. Now, she was sure that wasn't all there was to him.

He didn't have the appearance of a desk jockey or someone who held a morose job of any kind. His muscles were defined, she assumed, by constant workouts necessary for his job, and of course, the fact he could handle weapons and was included in the rescue as one of the operators told her she'd been way off her mark. Putting all the pieces together, she understood she and Nathan had something in common. They both hid behind a façade.

Whatever role he played in her rescue, she needed to trust him with the information she'd gathered. Deep inside, she knew she could. Forcing a deep breath into her lungs, she raised her gaze to meet his.

"I was hunting Phillip's murderer."

Nathan didn't understand what she meant. His frown deepened as he searched for answers. "What do you mean by hunting?"

"A couple of years after our wedding, Phillip was transferred to Israel." Nathan kept his eyes trained on her. She swallowed before she continued, "In the course of liaising with the Israeli government, he came across a joint investigation into an old MI5 case that led him to a possible infiltration in the US Embassy."

Rachael's account fit Phillip's request for a list of government employees working abroad with links to Washington, information so critical Nathan couldn't hand it out, not even to an old friend.

"After Phillip's murder, I came across several notes of his." She paused, a sad smile curving her lips. "He was methodical in his thought process, he liked to draw mind maps to figure things out. I followed the trail he left behind and it led me here."

A pang stroked his chest at seeing the expression in her eyes. She still missed Phillip. He shook his head at the feelings their conversation brought to the surface.

"That was bold," he said. "Still doesn't explain the guns."

"That comes from my training within the Shin Bet."

His muscles tensed in surprise. The Shin Bet was Israel's Intelligence branch in charge of internal affairs. Her work there would have given her keen insight into terrorism and many of the insurgent organizations in the region. Shock and awe converged in his brain. They had been apart for ten years, and yet they'd followed the same footsteps into Intelligence and counterterrorism. He couldn't hold back the laughter. It started out as a small chuckle and turned into a belly laugh. Rachael stared at him, a confused expression on her face. He settled back against the wall, wiping the tears from his eyes.

"Are you going to share, or do I have to force it out of you?"

She looked so beautiful, all flustered and puzzled, he wanted to reach out and kiss her. He raised his hands in defeat.

"If what I know about the Shin Bet's methods is true, you'd have it out of me in seconds."

"Something like that."

"How long have you worked with them? And are they aware of your personal crusade?"

"I resigned after Phillip's death. I had to leave Israel." Her gaze sobered. "Too many memories."

He could relate. He hadn't been able to return to his family's home after Jay's funeral. Too many memories of his brother bombarded him when he did.

"I've shown you mine," her eyes lightened up with curiosity. "Now it's time for you to show me yours. What have you been doing all these years? I'm willing to bet it isn't administrative work." Her eyes scanned the weapons and chest plate arranged neatly against the wall.

He'd missed her wit. He really had. He'd even missed how she could throw him off balance with one sentence. He pondered over the choice he had to make. Share only the bare minimum, or bare it all. Operatives were instructed to only share their roles with their spouses and after marriage. If he shared that with Rachael right now, it would be in violation of those regulations. But he was tired of lying, sick of concealing. If they ever had a chance to be together, they had to build upon the truth, and that had to start now.

"After I graduated the Academy, I applied to join the CIA." Her eyebrows rose and she finally got the humor in it. "Yeah...Intelligence. Meeting Phillip fired up my interest, and I wanted more field work." *I wanted to keep my mind off you.* "I guess it was a good fit."

He watched the humorous glimmer in her eyes morph into questions.

"I'd met other American and British Intelligence operatives before. Most have the basics like I do. Weapons handling, evasive maneuvers, and all that jazz. None of them gets involved in high-risk operations. Not like you did. I saw you in action. You were like one of them."

He sucked in a sharp breath. *Bare it all.*

"You're right. I have some extra skills up my sleeve other official cover operatives don't. I work under direct orders on select assignments, and I'm non-cover when the case calls for it, Rae."

Her eyes darkened with understanding; being in Intelligence herself, she would know what being a non-cover operative entailed. All of his missions had been kept in classified Top Secret files to which only a few very select people had access. Not even his coworkers had knowledge of his activities. He'd become an expert at improvising, modifying, adapting, and overcoming. So much so that his boss had offered him the even bigger challenge of taking non-official cover jobs, delving deeper into the bowels of his own government.

"Like the one here. Cases involving US citizens infiltrated in the government and supporting terror organizations from within." He rejoiced in the feeling of accomplishment when his work led to exposing traitors and those bent on causing harm to their own people. The mere contemplation of the consequences of those actions had he not intercepted their wrong-doings made him grind his teeth.

Her frown deepened. "You're here chasing a traitor?"

He nodded. A job he had yet to complete. "That, and overseeing the rescue operation, since the two cases are tied."

"And the traitor you seek is an American. Working in Israel. At the embassy."

He nodded again. "Yes."

"Have you found him? Do you know who he is?" A strange urgency rang in her tone.

"I was given a list of possible suspects. I haven't been able to uncover any concrete evidence pointing to any of those on my radar." Frustration boiled in his blood.

"I may have what you need." Rachael reached the locket she'd not worn since the moment she'd taken it off before they'd made love the first time. Opening it, she plucked something small from it and handed it to him.

A micro SD card. He looked at her, confused. "What's on this?"

"Pictures I took of documents showing the embassy's list of personnel working there during the days the leaks were reported. Useful, if you are going to use a process of elimination to obtain concrete evidence."

The meaning of her words slammed into his head. "I'll get to it as soon as we are back on the base. Might not take me long to narrow it down to one name." *I'll have fulfilled my mission, and then we can talk about where this is going,* he wanted to add.

"You'll need that only to corroborate what I already know." A flash of pure hatred, unadulterated anger, crossed her eyes.

"Rae?"

"My cell was the closest to Khalil's office. I overheard them talking in fluent Arabic. He never expected me to know the language, was never worried I could understand when he—" her voice broke, her eyes, still clouded by anger, glistened with tears. "I know who the traitor is."

Chapter Thirty-Six

Hansel and Gretel

THE CONTROL ROOM WAS SILENT. No big support crew, no sounds of radio static. It was barely light out, and Trevor sat at the makeshift desk he'd been using since he'd arrived, staring at the screen, focused on pinpointing their location. Cassandra, sitting at the desk next to Trevor's and writing a full report on the events after her arrival the day before, was the only other person in the room. Trevor had been sitting in the same uncomfortable chair for hours. The tension of the hunt tugged at his neck and shoulders, making the time in there feel much longer.

Stopping to stretch, he caught Cassandra looking at him with the same preoccupied expression of the last hours.

"He'll be fine," he said soothingly.

"I hope so." Cassandra left her chair and closed the distance, leaning against his desk to face him.

"We'll find him and Moore. The base hasn't been the same without him. I almost miss his green hue around."

"Trevor." Her chastising tone made him chuckle.

Strangely, Trevor understood that Nelson mattered to her on a completely different level than he meant to her. He realized it didn't bother him anymore.

"I've made my priority to get him back so we can get home. Besides, the accommodations on base were not created with couples in mind. Particularly not us."

She gave him a slap on the shoulder. "Seriously."

"I'm very serious." He pulled her onto his lap and kissed her. It was meant to be just a peck, but he couldn't keep from deepening it, breaching her lips with his tongue. Footsteps in the hallway disrupted the moment. He broke the kiss and leaned his forehead against hers. "I want you again." She'd been the only thing stopping him from going crazy, from going over the words Khalil Abboud had whispered in his ear. He saw his need mirrored in her eyes.

"So, what do you have?" Hanson asked the instant he crossed the threshold into the control room and nodded at Cassandra. She stood beside Trevor, keeping a hand on his shoulder, almost as if understanding that he needed that link, that connection.

Hanson exuded a controlled kind of nervous energy, as if ready to explode into action at any moment. Trevor had gotten used to seeing him in his combat fatigues instead of the signature Hawaiian shirts and cargo pants he'd worn in Dublin. In Jordan, he'd been all business, no play, from the get-go. Still, from the little he knew about the man, he recognized that Khalil Abboud's suicide had affected him. Trevor just hadn't been around him in private long enough to figure out why or how. Since Cassandra had arrived, they'd been moved into separate quarters, leaving Hanson the room to himself. The wait to locate Nelson had left Hanson a lot of alone time to ruminate on things.

Trevor looked up from his computer screen. "We're still working on pinning down their position."

Doubt flashed in Hanson's eyes. "How do you know this is not a total waste of time? They could be dead by now."

Trevor held his stare and spoke with confidence. "I can say with almost one-hundred-percent certainty they escaped." What he couldn't say was that knowing what he knew about Nathan Nelson now, he was confident of the man's capabilities to handle those circumstances.

"How? The Chinook pilots reported no sign of friendlies while they set the charge on the downed Black Hawk. They had to bug out under hostile fire before it detonated. If Nelson and Moore were caught before they got there—"

Trevor was confident on his findings. He'd combed the Chinook's forward-looking infrared imaging system videos for hours. "The onboard recording. It wasn't what the FLIR footage showed that told me they are alive. It was what it didn't."

"I hate when you talk in riddles."

Cassandra chuckled. "Welcome to my life."

Hanson turned to her, a bit of his humorous self peeking through. "I don't know how you do it."

"Me neither, most days. But I love him anyway."

Trevor shot them both his best offended look. "I'm right here, you know. I can hear you."

"Right. Where were we?" Hanson returned his attention to Trevor, a lighter gleam in his eyes.

Trevor shook his head at their banter and continued with the explanation. "The Chinook flew around the whole compound, searching for them. Here are some stills I took from the video footage." He pulled up the green-hued infrared images of the side courtyard. "Here are the pictures of the same courtyard immediately before we lost communications."

"Okay…what am I looking at? I see things have changed,

moved, the truck is missing. But how does that prove any connection to Nelson and Moore?"

"I was right in the middle of telling him about the truck when the radio signal went down."

"And?"

"Add that to this"—he pulled up more stills showing the wrecked gate—"and you get a better picture of what happened there after you left."

"Son of a bitch."

"Yep. They made it out of there alive. He was gung ho to leave the place when I talked to him. He found a way."

"Can't you just get some satellite footage of the area and track them down like you did before?"

"We're on it. The truck was easier because it was daytime footage. We have cameras rolling on sensitive areas at all daylight hours. We could rewind and fast-forward for hours to track the truck's trajectory. We don't normally have nighttime footage of locations without prior knowledge an operation is taking place, but luckily, because there was an operation, we did have cameras rolling that night. George is sifting through the whole thing trying to figure out the path of the truck after the exfil."

"Do you have an ETA on when I should have the men ready for retrieval?"

"Can't tell, but it shouldn't take us much longer. Hansel and Gretel must have left crumbs behind we can trace." Trevor withheld his knowledge of Nelson's deeper connection to Phillip Moore; it was not for him to disclose what Nelson had shared in confidence.

Hanson took a deep breath and stood straighter, a new purpose in his eyes. "I'll get my men briefed and basics taken care of. We'll just need a go." With a nod, the special operator left them alone again.

Cassandra squeezed Trevor's arm and leaned in for a quick peck before returning to her desk.

"Let's get back to business." No-nonsense Cassandra was back.

He watched her as she sat at the desk, tackling the grueling report-writing. He studied her focused expression, thinking how lucky he was for having her in his life. Shaking the image of what he would have become without her, he opened a secure chat window with George to gather the latest information on Nelson and Moore.

Cassandra stared at the screen, blind to the words she typed. Trevor had assumed she was worried about Nathan. She was. But she also worried about him. Since they'd moved to Dublin, he'd learned to hide his emotions fairly well, the bugger; what he didn't realize was that he let a lot slip when he was unaware she was observing him or when he was under a lot of stress.

She turned her eyes to Trevor, probing him again. When Abboud was declared dead, Trevor's hopelessness had been written in capital letters on his face. They hadn't had time to look into what Abboud could have meant by calling him by his father's name, but she knew it would come, and with it, the search for the truth about the Brennans would be on the forefront of his mind. She could only hope it didn't consume him more than it already did.

Ignoring the heaviness in her chest, she returned to writing up her report. She planned to have it done before they were on a plane back to Dublin, hopefully sooner than later.

TREVOR HAD JUST returned from having lunch at the mess hall when the ping on his screen alerted him of the incoming message.

We got them.

"Yes!" Trevor said out loud, attracting Cassandra's attention.

She walked over to his desk. "What's up?"

"George has something."

Trevor typed in a reply. *Coordinates?*

Sending you the footage as well as the exact location of the truck. Couldn't pick up any heat signature in the surrounding area, but they have to be there. Lots of ancient structures in the forest. If they are hiding in one, with the area's frozen ground, I wouldn't be able to pick them up easily.

I'll pass the information to Hanson right away.

I have full satellite cover on the area. If things change or I get more details, I'll pass it over.

Thanks, G.

Trevor wasted no time in notifying Hanson. Within the hour, Bravo Team was loaded on the chopper, heading back to the northern edge of the Negev desert, still unsure if what they were about to attempt would be a rescue or a recovery operation.

Chapter Thirty-Seven

Farewell

S TEEL GRAY CLOUDS GREETED THEM at dawn, the gloomy weather a perfect reflection of Nathan's mood. Neither subsided as the hours went by. The weather could be easily explained and justified; after all, it was winter in that part of the world. His personal gray clouds, on the other hand, were caused by the tempest in his head.

From the moment Rachael had disclosed what she knew about the man he'd been hunting, there was a gradual but noticeable shift in her. When she talked about Phillip's murderer, he recognized the glare in her eyes. Anger, hurt, pain. There was also a shadow in them he couldn't quite identify. One thing was very clear to him. All those years she'd been driven by grief, by loss. It was also clear she wasn't quite ready to let go.

Phillip had been an exceptional man. He'd offered guidance when Nathan had needed it and been the model Nathan had looked up to mold his own life. Unfortunately, he knew that mimicking Phillip wasn't enough to make Rachael love him with the same depth she dedicated to her late husband. The thought made his chest so tight he thought it would split open. He could never measure up to the man.

His eyes centered on Rachael, sitting by the entrance, gaze lost in the forest. She'd withdrawn into her own world after their conversation, making Nathan realize his fantasy was coming to an end. Deep inside, he'd known their stolen moment was too good to be true, too fragile to withstand exposure to the outside world. His whole body ached, and not from the impact on his back, but from knowing he may never feel whole again. A part of him would always be missing once they parted ways.

They'd had no sign of rescue overnight, and with their limited water supply, they couldn't afford to stay there another night. Their only hope was to set out at dusk, traveling at night to avoid crossing paths with insurgents.

Keeping his feelings locked in his chest, he returned to the makeshift bed. He needed to get his head in the game, prepare for the inevitable and the unforeseeable, save energy for their hike into the night and for the disappointment he knew would come.

Rachael heard shuffling behind her and turned around just as Nathan stretched on the blankets and draped an arm over his eyes. He'd been strangely deflated since their talk the night before, and his silence prompted her own.

She found herself questioning the time spent chasing answers for the sake of soothing her conscience. She'd loved Phillip, just never how he'd deserved to be loved. Once his murderer was brought to justice, she could finally be free of the guilt that ate at her all these years. She'd be free to love Nathan. She didn't regret the hastened way things had happened between them. God no. He made her shiver with a simple look of those green eyes of his, as if he could see into her deepest dreams and wishes. His simple presence made her feel right. Most of all, he made her feel alive, complete, when he was buried deep inside her. For a single day, she had believed they could finally put everything in the right place. Right all the wrongs, turn back the clock to the day they had first seen each other. But things were not as simple as they seemed.

Nathan had wanted her. There was no question in her mind he'd wanted her. Even if he hadn't confessed to it three years ago, it had been evident the day before. But he never inferred anything deeper than the physical fulfillment they both had taken from it. As much as she'd reveled in every second, she wanted more than sex from him, more than companionship this time around. She wanted the whole shebang, she wanted his love. And that was the only thing she wasn't sure of right now.

Questions rolled wildly in her head like tumbleweeds in the desert. Rachael had been so quick to take chances she didn't realize she could be making the reverse mistake she'd made in the past. She'd married a man she didn't love and fallen for a man who didn't love her. The irony. She imagined fate having a very good laugh at her expense.

He'd been quiet, back to the collected and distant Nathan she remembered from ten years ago. Maybe having her there had sated his hunger for a woman he couldn't have all those years. And if that were true, she should prepare herself for the upcoming fall from heaven. A sharp pang engulfed her. Once again, someone she cared for was being ripped from her, but this time he'd be alive, breathing, while she would be grieving for the one thing that seemed to evade her grasp.

AFTER AN HOUR of unrest, Nathan gave up on the idea of sleeping. Instead, to keep his mind busy with something other than Rachael, he'd methodically checked the weapons, gathered the scattered equipment they'd be taking with them, and repackaged all unused items in his survival kit. When the sun began to lower in the distance, he had everything ready and waiting for them to set out. He'd tried to ignore the fist in his stomach, but it grew tighter with every passing minute.

Fear had never been a part of his life on the job. At least, it hadn't been until now. He'd avoided certain death while on a few missions without too much concern for his own safety. He had nothing to lose then. Now, after what they'd shared, more than anything in the world he feared the words of rejection he expected to spill from her mouth at any moment.

Although the temperature was falling, he felt himself burning inside, the control he'd held in check since he'd taken her slowly falling apart. Not that he'd had any control over anything since she'd touched him, since she'd kissed him. His stomach rolled. The impending loss of the dream cocooned in that hole in the ground made him want to punch the wall, destroy something in return. Not the most mature or controlled thought he'd ever had in his life.

Outside, the last vestiges of the day were being slowly swallowed by the night. A flashlight went on behind him. Movement caught his eye and he turned to see Rachael kneeling beside the nest they had created with blankets. She was pulling one off the pile, about to fold the blankets they'd used as a bed, destroy the last proof that what they'd had wasn't just a figment of his imagination, that it had been real. He felt like he'd been kicked in the balls. And he snapped. He rushed to her as she was about to pull another blanket from the pile.

"Nath—"

He covered her mouth with his, silencing her words. He didn't want to hear them. He wanted her to know she'd always be his, to leave an imprint in her mind, on her body, the bone-melting satisfaction that would ruin her for any other man she came across in the future. The thought of other men having her burned his insides and pushed him harder. He parted from her and held her gaze as he undid the buttons of her shirt once again, only this time there was no gentleness or hesitation.

He kissed her again, nipping at her lips as he pushed her shirt from her shoulders. He needed her to know he wasn't going to be gentle. She moaned but didn't push him away. Instead, her hands sought his pants with similar urgency. Their fevered search for each other's skin paid off when they finally came to lie once again on the blankets.

She parted her thighs to accommodate him when he kneeled in front of her, his hand seeking the heat between her legs. Holding her gaze, he spread her folds and rejoiced at what he found. She was so wet. Half of him needed the rush, needed to be fully seated in her, needed the knowledge they were one; but knowing this could be their final farewell, he'd take the last of their time together to savor the moment. She reached for him and cupped his face with her hands. Their warmth soothed his frenzy. He brought his fingers to his mouth and the moment he tasted her on them, he knew he had to have more.

He bent down and covered one breast with his lips, suckling on it until the nipple pebbled in his mouth. She threw her head back, her dark hair cascading over her back like a satin curtain. He placed a gentle kiss on her exposed neck where her pulse jumped under her golden skin, then another between her breasts, another on her stomach. He heard the distinct hitch of her breath when he continued to slide down until he could place a kiss on the sensitive skin on the inside of her thigh. She leaned on her elbows, small moans of approval escaping her lips as he inched closer to his target.

With as gentle a touch as he could muster, he spread her folds and covered her clit with his mouth. God, he tasted heaven in her. He stroked her clit with his tongue in a slow, deliberate swirl. Her breathing picked up speed, racing along with his. Her low moans became louder with each flick, each roll, until she splintered. She cupped his neck and jerked when he sucked it into his mouth as she trembled, still under the effects of her orgasm.

He traced the path back atop her, enjoying the little shakes for every kiss he deposited on her skin. When they were face to face, he held her gaze in awe. She was so beautiful. Her hair formed a dark halo around her head, her eyes still displaying the relaxing effects of her orgasm. For that moment, for those stolen minutes, she was truly his.

His heart stuttered and her breath hitched when he positioned his cock, gently rubbing its crown in her juices for lubrication. In a single long movement, he pushed deep inside.

"Oh God." His whole body burned with sensation. Her heat enveloped him, drew him deeper. Leveraging his weight on his elbows, he hovered inches above her, eyes lost in the pleasure emblazoned on her face. Her lips parted, a long moan escaping them when he withdrew his full length and then buried himself again to the hilt. In silent reverence, with each pull, each push, he gave more of his heart to her.

Rachael's heart thrummed against her ribcage when Nathan swept her into his arms. It was as if he'd read her mind. She was incapable of rejecting the precious gift of having one more time to remember him by. Instead, she delighted in how completely he filled her. She sensed a different intensity to his need, so different from the previous times. Before, Nathan had been the considerate lover, giving before taking satisfaction, but almost afraid to push limits, as if he'd expected her to run. That vulnerability had vanished.

She locked her gaze with his and found a hint of desperation there. His face was taut, his jaw rigid, his eyes burning with lust. She reached out to soothe him, but he captured her hand before she could touch him. She lost her breath when he secured one hand then the other above her head. His eyes gleamed with desire. An army of butterflies fluttered in her stomach as he lowered his head closer. The rest of the world disappeared when his mouth claimed hers, tongue thrusting deep, exploring, demanding, laying claim. She could taste herself in his mouth, and somehow that was the sexiest thing she could have experienced.

If he wanted to brand her, he'd achieved his goal. Everything dimmed except for him, what he was doing to her, how he was making her feel. Those were amplified, enhanced with each move he made. She wanted this. Craved this. She melted into the kiss, sucking on his tongue, swirling hers around his in a frenzied dance.

"I want you, Nathan," she breathed into his mouth.

"You have me."

He nipped at her lower lip and ground his hips against hers. Her muscles tightened instinctively around him and she rocked her hips in tandem, moaning at the feel of his shaft pressing deeper inside her with every thrust. She was going up in flames. Every inch of her body was attuned to every inch of his. The sensation of his pelvic bone brushing against her sensitive flesh engulfed her and her eyes fluttered closed. Head pressed back against the blankets, she met his grind.

"Open your eyes, Rae. I need you to look at me." Nathan's voice was a rough whisper.

Rachael complied and, meeting his gaze, drowned in the passion that mirrored her own. At that moment, she wanted to share everything with him, wanted him to know she was free to follow her heart.

"Nathan, I…."

He kissed her, swallowing those precious words before they formed on her tongue. She took it as fate forcing her to keep them to herself. Instead, she showed him.

She entwined her fingers with his and wound her leg over his hip, pressing her heel into his ass, bringing him closer, wanting to please him as much as he pleased her. Satisfaction swirled in her chest when he exhaled sharply and a deep groan rumbled in his chest. Lines of concentration formed on his brow and sweat beaded on his temple. He pumped faster, surged harder, deeper, with each thrust. Waves of ecstasy washed over them with each push of his body into hers, each rise of her body seeking his.

"Yes." The low hiss sounded strange to her own ears, but she couldn't help it. The tide of another orgasm was rising quickly, overriding her senses. She was all feeling, all over.

Nathan shook along with his voice. "Jesus, Rae." Leveraging his weight on their entwined hands, he thrust faster, deeper, angling just right to tap her sensitive bud with his groin. Her hips found and matched his rhythm, lifting, tightening, taking all of him.

He fought his release. He wasn't ready to let go of the feeling, let go of their union just yet, but as the sounds from her throat grew higher in pitch, his restraint became weaker. He went still for a moment, hoping to subdue the flames licking at his spine and extend their experience, but she had a different opinion on it. She clamped her legs around his hips and, detangling her hands from his, set them firmly on his ass, guiding him to move.

An electrifying sensation took him over when she ground against him in a sensual circular motion. "Nathan, please."

Engulfed by an overwhelming sense of urgency, he yielded to the natural compulsion to sway his hips. The gentle rocking grew rapidly into a crescendo until she clenched around him in a delicious ripple, bringing his orgasm forward. His scream of release mingled with hers and filled the air with the sounds of their shared crest. The thrill of release rolled through him in waves, emptying him.

Rachael wrapped her arms around him and squeezed tight. Her hot breath fanned over his neck and he could feel the rapid beat of her heart against his chest. He slipped into a haze, not asleep but not really awake, each stolen second with her a fantasy of its own.

In that moment of complete peace, a thought speared his mind. What if that was really all of it? Could he go a lifetime keeping his love to himself? He'd made a vow for honesty, a vow to bare all of himself, and he was not being true to that vow if he kept the most important thing to himself.

He raised his head to look at her, the weight of the words crushing his chest.

"Rae...."

"Hmm...." She kept her eyes closed, a smile curving the tip of her mouth and making him lose his train of thought.

He'd been lost in wonder when a repetitive sound breached the edge of his conscience. He cocked his head and listened carefully, seeking to identify what it was, and jumping into action when he did.

Rachael's expression changed to surprise, eyes narrowed and inquisitive when he broke their contact and reached for their clothes.

In a swift motion, he gathered the items scattered around them from the ground.

"Get dressed." He handed hers over and quickly slipped into his before grabbing the intermittent signal device from his survival kit. "Stay here until I know it's safe." Without waiting for her agreement, he ran toward the clearing a few hundred meters from their hiding place and looked up, searching for the source of the noise.

The sound of the helicopter blades chopping the air became increasingly louder. Since the insurgents had no access to aircrafts of any kind, he felt safe to assume that whoever was flying in the area was a friendly. He just hoped it was their own team, and not some Israeli pilot bent on blowing any possible signal off the face of the earth. He caught the outline of the chopper in the distance, no bigger than a coin, above the tree line, against the last traces of daylight. As the sound became louder and the helicopter drew closer, he was able to identify the familiar shape of a Black Hawk.

His chest tightened. He was happy they were leaving that hell-hole, but disappointed to see their newfound intimacy come to an abrupt halt.

Setting the signaling device down, he turned around, planning on going back for Rachael, and found her already behind him. She'd made one of the blankets into a pouch and had the few items they brought with them in it, the MP7 hanging on her shoulder.

An involuntary smile curved his lips. He should have expected that. Taking the weapon and the improvised sack from her hands, they stood side by side, eyes locked on the aircraft. *See us, see us, see us* played on repeat in his head together with *Go away, go away.*

His heart thundered in his ears when the helicopter veered to the side and straightened its course toward them. Within minutes, it was hovering above them.

Nathan saw a head stick out the side and then disappear inside before the Black Hawk reduced altitude and landed in the clearing in front of them.

The downwind from the blades whirled a cloud of dust from the ground. A man wearing the same tactical uniform as his climbed out when the bird touched down. As he got closer, Nathan recognized him as Hanson.

The operator slapped his back and yelled over the rotor noise, "Let's get you two home."

He ushered them to the helicopter and was the last to board before the Black Hawk climbed into the air, its nose dipping as it picked up speed for the long flight to the base.

Chapter Thirty-Eight

Pop Goes the Weasel

✤————————✤

SQUEEZED BETWEEN NATHAN AND SPECIAL Operator
Hanson, Rachael wondered how those men could endure
such flights over and over again. The cabin of the Black
Hawk was dark and crowded. The whirring of machine noise
battering her ears made it impossible to have a conversation, and the
vibration of the aircraft seemed to be transmitted directly to her seat
and the barely-there cushion she sat on.

Rachael leaned her head against the seat, her hands clasped in her
lap, mostly to stop her from reaching for Nathan's. Each time his
thigh pressed against hers when he shuffled in the tight space, an
electric current hit her system and she wasn't sure if the vibrations
resonating through her body were from the helicopter or that touch.

She wished there was light in the cabin so that she could see his
face, could reassure herself that what had transpired only hours ago
hadn't slipped away into the night before they'd approached the
hazy, barely visible silhouette of the Black Hawk. Once they'd
climbed in, Nathan had said very little to her, leaving her to make

wild assumptions from his silence.

An intangible sense of dread grew in the pit of her stomach the closer they got to the base. Once all was said and done, she wouldn't have the what-ifs she'd had in the past to comfort her, to make her dream about him. Now she knew his taste on her tongue, the feel of his body sliding over hers, his heady scent. While in the past she could only have imagined what it would be like to be with him, from now on she could draw from memories of the real thing. She was certain those new memories would be more a curse than a blessing down the road.

"We're almost there. ETA ten minutes," Nathan yelled over the rotor noise.

She placed her hand on his thigh in acknowledgment and the muscles in his legs bunched under her touch. When she pulled it back, a surge of satisfaction swelled in her chest. Not so indifferent after all. But then the possibility that he was embarrassed of being seen with her crossed her mind and deflated her smugness. She avoided touching him for the remainder of the flight.

Activity bloomed in the cabin as they approached the base. A vibrant sense of accomplishment emanated from the men. Some held their silence, others were loud enough that she heard a joke or two as they secured their weapons and gathered their gear when the bright landing pad appeared in the distance through the front window.

After spending so many days uncertain of what the future would bring, uncertain if she would make it back alive, being on that flight surrounded by some of the best-trained soldiers in the world felt surreal. Even more overwhelming was the certainty that soon she'd be able to bring down the bastard who killed Phillip.

With the SD card entrusted to Nathan, it was now a matter of securing the hard evidence to support an indictment. Blood pounded in her head. She wanted it to be over. Her jaw tightened, her fingers curled into fists. Would the monster still be at the base? Would she be able to keep her cool? The bird shook during the final approach and she sucked in a quick breath. She'd soon find out.

Hanson leaned near her ear. "We're just getting ready to land."

She nodded and held onto the straps of her harness as the aircraft leveled and descended. The second the landing gear touched the tarmac, the operators efficiently exited. Nathan and Hanson were last, and both extended a hand to help her to the hard surface of the runway, almost as if they knew she was walking on rubbery legs.

Warm engine exhaust clung to the air while the rotary blades' downdraft kicked her hair across her face. Nathan gripped her by the elbow, guiding her toward the massive building sitting alongside the flight line. She pushed the hair from her face and saw a group of people standing in a halo of lights outside the entry to the building.

As the three of them closed the distance to them, she could discern more of their faces against the bright light, but none of them were familiar to her. A woman with shoulder-length auburn hair, her features holding startling similarity to her own, broke from the group. Rachael's heart froze when she ran up to Nathan, threw her arms around his neck, and kissed his cheek.

"I've never been so happy to see you." The woman's smile brightened with affection.

When his arm circled the woman's waist in a familiar hug, Rachael's steps faltered. She suddenly felt self-conscious of the filth of her long confinement clinging to her and an inkling of jealousy pricked under her skin.

"What the hell are you doing here?" His tone held a degree of warmth, chastisement, and confusion all in one.

"Imagine my surprise when I got the call." Rachael's attention was drawn to the owner of the Irish lilt. A dark-haired man, almost as tall as Nathan, his intense blue eyes flashing with exasperation, joined them.

The woman shrugged. "Turns out you needed my help here after all. Well...you would have if...." She stopped her sentence halfway. "Long story better left for later."

The Irishman draped his arm around the woman's waist in a more possessive manner and shook Nathan's hand. "Good to see your green skin is all in one piece, Nelson."

Rachael caught Nathan's narrowed eyes and the back-off look he'd shot at the clearly unfazed couple before he reached for Rachael's arm and drew her into the circle.

"Rachael Moore, let me introduce you to Trevor Bauer, the man I spoke to you about, and his wife Cassandra."

Unexpected relief washed over Rachael at hearing their connection and she smiled. "So, you're Bauer."

He took her hand and a warm smile curved his lips. "You can call me Trevor."

Cassandra shook her hand next, but her hold lasted longer. Her eyes swept Rachael's face, studying her as if searching for any and all of her hidden secrets. Uncomfortable with her probing stare, Rachael flicked her gaze to Nathan, seeking reassurance. Nathan nodded at her and Rachael returned her gaze to Cassandra.

Soon a mix of speculation and approval edged Cassandra's eyes. The corners of her mouth tipped into a smile. "It's nice to finally meet you, Rachael."

Hanson interrupted their friendly acquaintance. "Nelson, Bauer and I need to update you on some critical developments ASAP. We'll also need to debrief you and Mrs. Moore. How about we regroup at zero seven hundred for that? It should give you both time to clean up and get some rest. I'm sure the last two days haven't been easy."

Rachael almost let the sad laughter that bubbled in her throat escape. She avoided Nathan's eyes and simply nodded in acknowledgement.

"I'll show you your accommodations." Hanson turned and the whole the group started toward the door.

Anxiety pressed down on her with each step. She couldn't wait any longer to know the status of the others.

"Did everyone make it back safely?"

Trevor nodded as they stepped into the building and started down a long hallway.

"Yes. They were cleared by medical and have been given a clean bill of health. In fact, Wolfe and Goh Min-Sook were transported to their own embassies in Amman. Blair is still here. He refused to leave until you were found." Reservation saturated Bauer's tone. "I regret to inform you that DSS Agent Carter was killed in the line of duty."

Rachael's heart bled for the youngest member of their diplomatic escort. The anger that had been swirling in the back of her mind pushed forward. Carter had been another one steamrolled simply because he was in the wrong place at the wrong time. Her stomach turned at the callousness of it all.

"What about Mr. Blair's security detai—"

"Rachael! You're safe." Gerald Blair walked out of a room in front of them and pulled her into a hug. "We were so worried about you."

Rachael smiled at him as she stepped back from his embrace. "Thank you."

"Mrs. Moore. Welcome back." She hadn't noticed Stratton walk in behind Blair.

Rachael froze. The overly sweet tone coating his voice skated up her spine.

"Thank you." She had no idea how she managed to speak with the lump in her throat. She studied Stratton. A little bruising was the only indication that he'd been held hostage. Gone was his well-cut black suit. In its place were a pair of fatigues and boots, the standard shoulder holster already strapped in place, ready to perform his duty, to show the world how heroic and selfless he was. The weasel. Instinctively, she narrowed her eyes, her hands balled into fists.

"Rachael?" Nathan's concerned voice sounded far in the distance.

She wanted to hurt Stratton as much as he'd hurt them all, particularly for what he'd done to Phillip. Instead, she banked her anger and pasted on her best diplomatic smile, one her mother would have been proud of. She held to her resolve to let justice play out and for that, she'd need hard evidence. Lashing out at that moment would have been pleasurable, but it would have compromised the case.

"I'm okay. Just happy to see everyone safe."

Nathan paused, looking at her, a deep frown creasing his brow. She cracked a small smile to reassure him, and that seemed to be enough.

"If you'll excuse us." Hanson's tone denoted his rush. "My team is heading stateside this afternoon and I want to get on that plane with them. Mr. Blair, can you take Mrs. Moore to her room? It's the one to the left of yours."

"Of course."

She could almost feel a physical touch when Nathan's gaze brushed over her face once again. After a brief pause, he nodded and followed Hanson, Trevor, and Cassandra down the hall, giving her time with her boss and Stratton. She followed Nathan with her eyes until they disappeared through a door.

When they stood face to face, Stratton extended his hand. "I'm sorry we didn't make it out of there the way I would have hoped."

"I'm sure you tried your hardest." She struggled to keep her sarcasm locked in her chest. "My deepest condolences regarding your fallen colleagues. Norwood, Thompson, and Carter were good men."

She looked into his clear blue eyes and was finally able to see the coldness in them.

Other than a clenched jaw, there was no display of emotion. "Yes, they were."

A wave of lightheadedness hit her and she extended her arm, seeking to steady herself on the wall.

Blair's eyes widened. "You need some rest. Believe me. I had never slept so well in my life than on the day we arrived at the base. I'll show you the way to your room." He swept his hand out, indicating they should walk, and she fell into step with him.

He continued to fire nervous commentary at her and she tried to keep up the best she could.

"—No one would tell us where you were. We had no idea you were even in the same place. I was afraid those savages would do something—" He stopped himself, leaving the meaning of the sentence hanging in the air.

"They didn't. I was concerned about your well-being, too. Luckily, I was just a few feet from the interrogation room. I heard when you were brought over, so I knew you were alive but was afraid to call out." She sensed Stratton's stare and realized her mistake. "I wasn't sure about Stratton, though." She looked at him, feigning a concern she didn't feel. "I'm glad you didn't suffer the same fate as Carter," she added, hoping to throw him off her scent.

"If you were that close, could you hear anything of value from their conversations and interrogations?" Stratton's tone was cool, indifferent, but his eyes showed a glimmer of caution.

Rachael glanced at him, hoping to dismiss his guard. "Not really. None of them spoke any English."

Rachael's heart raced. She could feel the weight of his eyes dissecting her, determining her threat level just as they walked by the room Nathan and the others had walked into earlier.

She paused by the door and sought out Nathan. He stood by the desk, talking with Trevor, looking to whatever was displayed on the screen of Trevor's computer. He turned his gaze to her and held hers briefly before reaching into his pocket and pulling something out, then handed it to Trevor before giving her a quick nod. He was still in agent mode, from what she could tell. His dedication to the job at that moment was reassuring considering that, in her gut, she knew Blair's innocent blabber and her slip may have given Stratton food for thought. The faster he could get the evidence put together, the faster they could get Stratton out of circulation.

Blair continued down the hall, stopping at one of the doors in the corridor. "Here you are. Get some sleep. I'm hoping to arrange a flight out of here some time tomorrow."

"They want to debrief me at seven."

"I'll see if I can get something figured out." Blair patted her back and slipped into the room beside hers, leaving her with Stratton.

His eyes almost burned holes in her. She avoided his gaze. "Well, I guess I should get that sleep." She turned to the door, hoping to put as much distance between them as possible.

"I should have known," Stratton said in Arabic. The venomous words caught her by surprise and gave him the answer he was fishing for.

Out of the corner of her eye, she caught the faintest blur of motion before one of his hands wrapped around her neck and the other covered her mouth. The chokehold was a vice cutting off her oxygen supply. She struggled against his grasp, pulled at his arms, kicked back at his knee.

She felt his quick intake of air, music to her ears. Satisfaction that she'd inflicted some measure of pain on him unfurled in her chest. Rachael swung her foot back to deliver a second blow, but Stratton pulled her against his chest and applied tighter pressure on her neck. He caught her neck again in the v-hold of his arm, pressing on her windpipe and immobilizing her.

He reached for the door and she fought him. She knew that if he could get her in there, she'd be dead. She had to avoid being locked in a room with this man at all costs. She leveraged her weight on the arm choking her and lifted her feet from the ground, pushing with all her might against the door.

They tumbled back against the opposite wall, knocking a bulletin board on the ground. The noise reverberated through the long hallway, but she was deaf to anything but the beat of her heart.

She heard the heavy sound of boots running toward them, Nathan's voice yelling her name and Hanson shouting orders.

Stratton scrambled from the ground, his arm once again wrapped on her neck, but this time he used her as a shield. Her breath hitched with the click of a gun being cocked and the kiss of cold metal into the side of her temple. The men stopped dead in their tracks.

"Stratton. Let her go," Hanson commanded in a calm voice.

Threads of fear wrapped around her heart. She'd come so close. All that time wasted chasing answers. It couldn't end like this. The emptiness she'd felt since leaving the forest expanded in her chest and she squeezed back the moisture tearing in her eyes.

All that wasted time waiting to be free to go after her heart's desire. She sought Nathan's eyes and tried to tell him all the things she should have told him before they left.

"Rae, it will be okay." Nathan's voice trembled, his eyes locked on her face. She saw anger overtake fear in his expression.

"Don't listen to him. It won't," Stratton whispered in her ear, sending an icy trickle running down her spine. Her neck burned and her pulse raced out of control as Stratton half-carried half-dragged her toward the end of the hall to an exit door.

The air had cooled when they stumbled out. In the distance, she saw the glare of the landing pads where the helicopters sat in wait. Still careful to keep her in front of him, he looked around as if unsure where to go. She heard him chuckle before she saw what he had seen. A Humvee parked next to the building.

They had almost reached the vehicle when Nathan burst through the door at the same time as light flooded the area, blinding them. Stratton faced the men, holding her tighter against him.

"Give up, Stratton. You know you can't go far. What are you going to do? Hightail it all the way to Israel to join whatever organization has covered your ass all this time?" Nathan's tone was deadly as he moved closer, hands up and no weapon in sight.

"I don't have to go far. The night is my friend." Stratton's voice was cold, exact, as he pointed the gun at Nathan and then at her again.

Nathan's green eyes locked with hers and Rachael's heart tumbled to her knees. They'd flashed with tenderness, a small comfort, before morphing into a dangerous gleam. The lamps illuminating the perimeter cast harsh shadows across the taut skin of his cheeks.

As Stratton lugged her closer to the vehicle, regret knotted her stomach. Regret for the things she had said to Nathan years ago. Regret for the ones she didn't today. She should have told him that she loved him when she had the opportunity. The closer they got to the armored vehicle, the slimmer the chances she would ever be able to say those words to him.

Eyes locked on her, Nathan took another step closer as Stratton stopped, his back to the side of the Humvee.

"Open the door," Stratton said.

Rachael froze. Once inside the Humvee, the only way to get to him was with brute force and heavy artillery. If she got in it with Stratton, she'd be dead—either by his hand or by friendly fire. She hesitated to comply.

"Open the damn door." Stratton pushed the gun harder into her temple. She saw Nathan flinch, his hands clench into fists. Stratton gave her a shove and her ankle gave out. She slipped from his grasp and he scrambled to move behind his living shield.

Nathan's expression changed into a cross between pain and anger. "Hanson?" His lips barely moved, but she heard begging in his tone. As soon as the name left his lips, a shot rang out.

Stratton was thrown against the truck and down on the ground, taking her with him. She struggled against his arm, pushing it off her. The gun slipped from his limp fingers to the ground. Her ears rang; her entire body was numb with shock as she stood on wobbly legs only to be taken into strong arms as chaos reigned around her. Soldiers rushed out from the building and secured the area, quickly making sure Stratton was disarmed and the threat had been eliminated.

"Clear!" one of them called out.

From the safety of Nathan's arms, she looked at the lifeless body at her feet. *It's finally over.*

Chapter Thirty-Nine

Home

*F*EAR WASHED OVER HIM WITH the force of a tsunami. The scene played in slow motion and held still—that terrifying moment he thought Hanson could have missed his mark—until Rachael pushed Stratton's body to free herself from his crush.

It took him that split second to realize the mistake he'd made by not telling her straight up how he felt. Telling her how much she meant to him. The huge mistake of not fighting for what he wanted. And he wanted her. Would always want her. He was a fool for not seeing it until that moment. Nothing would change it. Losing her would be like losing himself.

He didn't know how his legs had carried him, but he'd closed the distance in a few strides, and the moment he had her in his arms, he was whole again.

"Rae." Nathan buried his face in her hair and murmured in her ear. "I thought I'd lost you again."

She clung to him just as tightly. "You'll never lose me."

Nathan turned her face up to him and he caught a hint of desperation in her eyes, a mirror image of the emotions swirling in his chest. He kissed her, an intense, penetrating kiss that burned deep. She wrapped her arms around his neck and melted into the kiss, bringing the magic they had created in isolation to life among the many people surrounding them. He'd thought he'd never have the opportunity to voice his feelings to her. He'd have to be insane to let it slip through his fingers again. He held on to her, putting the words in the right order in his head. Hoping she'd see they were meant to be.

He pulled back from her, but before he could spill his guts, she blurted out, "I love you, Nathan."

As the words slipped from her lips, relief flooded her eyes. Rachael pressed her cheek against his chest again, hiding her face from him.

Nathan froze. He closed his eyes and shook his head, uncertain he'd heard her say it. Considering the terrifying moments he'd just lived through, he couldn't quite trust his ears. He pulled away from her again, tipped her head back, and searched her eyes. He couldn't identify all of the emotions swirling in them, but it was the vulnerability hinted there that tugged at his heartstrings. He couldn't have heard it right, could he? Nathan kept his calm, hoping to conceal that his heart had just jumped into his throat. He didn't want to be mistaken.

Rachael caught his face between her hands and stared into his eyes. "Do I need to say it again? I will. I've loved you since the day we met."

Something squeezed his heart so tight his chest hurt. He let his breath out in a whoosh when he realized he'd been holding it for too long. It wasn't a dream. It wasn't just a figment of his imagination. It was real after all. *I've loved you since the day we met.* He replayed the sentence in his head over and over until it erased all of the uncertainty of the past.

He cupped her face in his hands and placed a kiss on her forehead, then another on her lips. He stared into her eyes and saw so much emotion in them it made his stomach clench. Love. He realized that's what he had seen in her eyes earlier while Stratton held her captive. His mind juggled the fears of not measuring up and tossed them out.

Having her in his arms at that moment, having her give him those most cherished words made him realize he'd wandered through life with no direction except for the compass leading straight to her. She was and had always been his true North. He knew they would have to sit down and talk about Phillip, lay it all out so it could never come between them, but at that very moment, he was ready to bare his soul once and for all.

"God. I love you, too, Rae."

The most beautiful smile curved her lips. Tears glistened in her eyes as she rose to her tiptoes and claimed his mouth. The chaos around them disappeared into the haze. His pulse thumped in his ears and he savored her taste, the feel of having her pressed against him, this time with the promise that it would happen many times in the future. He had found his home.

Rachael wrapped her arms around his neck and deepened the kiss. His breathing kicked up a notch. Oblivious to his surroundings, he threaded his hands through her hair and met her heat with his.

The sound of a throat clearing invaded his consciousness. He broke from the kiss and sought the source of the noise. He found Bauer standing a couple of feet from them, his arm around Cassandra's waist. A knowing smile played in their eyes.

"Sorry to interrupt. Hanson wants to get the debriefing done earlier than he'd planned. With the new developments, there's no real reason to remain here. We can continue the search for their leader from the comfort of our homes."

Nathan nodded. Indeed, there was nothing keeping them there. But then, he wasn't quite sure where they would go from there, either.

Rachael, almost as if tuned in to his disquiet, stepped forward.

"That sounds good. I'm assuming you know how to contact Nathan?" At Bauer's nod, she continued. "If you need me to clarify any detail of my statement, you can find me there."

Bauer raised his eyebrows and Nathan noticed when Cassandra squeezed his hand in a gentle warning.

Nathan shook his head, letting a smile crack through, and took Rachael's hand.

"You heard her." He then turned to Rachael once again. His pulse raced when he locked eyes with her. "I have a condition for that relocation, though." A confused look clouded her expression. "Marry me. I don't have much to offer but my loyalty, my honesty, and my love. That's all of me."

Her eyes brimmed with tears, her lips trembled when she cupped his cheek, and with a shaky breath, gave him his dream.

"You're all I ever wanted."

Rachael brought his face to hers, and what began as a quick kiss slowly deepened until they were interrupted once again, this time by a loud groan.

"Do we have to stand here and watch them? Jaysus, get a room. Freakin' rabbits." Bauer's voice was lost in the racket of laughter that followed as they started toward the door.

Chapter Forty

Closing Doors

One week later

CASSANDRA SAT CROSS-LEGGED ON THE soft brown rug in baby Connellan's nursery, a laundry basket filled with freshly laundered baby blankets next to her.

She watched Jessica flutter around like a butterfly from one drawer to the next, adding the final touches to the room. The pink floral long-sleeve tunic Jessica wore brought out the rosy hue in her cheeks and enhanced the blue of her eyes. There was a certain beauty in her movements. As heavy as she was with child, and as much as Cassandra liked to tease her, Jessica didn't waddle. There was more of an elegant glide to her steps. As with everything Jessica did, she'd totally owned her pregnancy.

Cassandra pulled another baby blanket onto her lap and folded it. Jessica had assigned that task to her as a penalty for having taken off for the US without a word of warning. Instead of the intended punishment, the task and the tranquility of the space soothed her.

She and Trevor had been back in Dublin for a few days already, but Jessica was still pissed off at her for not letting her know she was leaving the country. Stephan hadn't been too pleased with her and Trevor for jumping into the fire again, either. Cassandra could swear that he'd blamed her for the little false alarm that had sent them speeding to the hospital the night Jessica found out about their little adventure in Jordan. Trevor had teased that the baby already knew its honorary uncle and auntie were headed home and was anxious to meet them. Cassandra had just been glad that she hadn't missed the second most important event in Jessica's life.

Jessica was the little sister she'd never had. She couldn't miss being there for the little one's arrival. A flood of affection coursed through her. Cassandra would move mountains for her, and was certain that Jessica and Stephan's child would have her wrapped around his or her little finger in seconds flat. Cassandra brushed the corners of her eyes with her fingers and wiped them on her jeans. Hell. That baby already had a good solid grip on her.

To make it up to her best friend for the scare and to give Trevor some breathing room, Cassandra had placed herself at Jessica's beck and call. After a couple of days, she was beginning to have some serious regrets. Jessica took full advantage of the at-your-service offer, and Trevor, not having her around to nag him into talking, still wasn't sharing what was niggling at him. And she knew something was bothering him, something he didn't want to share or talk about just yet. She took a deep breath and placed the folded blanket on the pile.

Jessica's touch on her shoulder startled her. "How are you feeling? Still sore?"

She nodded. "I've felt like crap for a couple of days now."

"Who wouldn't? If I had gone through what you did, I'd be in a fetal position in my room for a month."

It had taken a little while for reality to set in once they had returned to the safety of their home. The fight with Naveed Abboud had taken a physical toll, while witnessing Khalil Abboud's death had taken a deeper psychological one. Both she and Trevor reeled over it in different ways.

"I'm okay."

"I'll take your word for it. At least your color is back, so that's a good sign. It means I get to put you back to work. Are you sure the crib is alright where it is?"

Cassandra took in the beautiful nursery. It was magazine-cover worthy, ready to welcome the little tyke. It didn't need a speck of change.

"Ah…no. I refuse to move that crib one more time. Each time we do, you move it right back."

"I just want to be sure." Jessica walked over to stand in the spot where she wanted it. "Right here. It's closer to the window."

Cassandra loved that the arched dark-wood crib had been placed in the middle of the room. She glanced out the window at the light rain bouncing against it. She shook head.

"Stop the madness. It's perfect right where it is. Besides, the baby will get a chill by the window." She could easily imagine Stephan and Jessica standing in silent watch over their sleeping baby, able to see him or her from every angle. Had that nursery been in her house, she would have placed the crib in the same spot.

As soon as that unexpected thought crossed her mind, an image of Trevor sneaking out of their bed in the middle of the night to watch their baby sleep sent a surge of warmth spreading through her. She immediately squelched the thought. *Geez. Between Jessica and Tatiana, all the baby talk must be getting to me.*

She set the folded blanket on the rocker and caught Jessica's too-astute-for-her-own-good gaze.

"This whole nesting thing is out of control. And it's kind of freaking me out. You're supposed to be resting, not running around like a crazy woman."

"I know, right? You should have seen Stephan's face when I wanted to move the furniture in his den around. I could swear he turned pale and broke out in a sweat. I had to vow to stay away until the baby arrives," Jessica chuckled, smoothing a hand over her belly.

Cassandra grinned. "Have you tried the door? I bet he's locked it."

Jessica snorted. "Much good it'll do him. I could always have you pick it."

Cassandra smiled and tried her best to pay attention to Jessica's chatter, but the mention of picking locks sent her mind rolling back to the events of the last two weeks and their impact on their lives. Her heart ached for her husband. Although he'd tried to hide it, she'd seen the shadows haunting Trevor's eyes. The unanswered questions Khalil Abboud had left behind were the direct cause of those shadows, of the silence.

He'd done that before. When they had returned from Prague emptyhanded, Trevor's demeanor had changed. She'd noticed he'd become less passionate about the hunt, less confident he'd get the closure he needed. Once he'd been dragged into more NSA cases, it had seemed to lighten the load, and she'd forgotten how difficult it must still be for him to not know.

The hidden looks he'd been giving her of late reminded her of those days and were what worried her the most. A small part of her was afraid to open the door to that discussion, afraid it would invite a massive vortex into their lives, one that would suck them in whole. But she knew it was barreling toward them, whether she wanted to acknowledge it or not. She drew a deep breath, grabbed the last blanket, and focused her attention back on Jessica, catching her discourse on Stephan's latest baby antics.

"Speaking of your hubby, please tell me he's not really upset with me." Stephan had become a good friend and it would sting if he was really mad.

A sparkle entered Jessica's eyes. "Stop being so silly. He was just worried. Your gangrenous eye reminded him of the mess in Monaco. You know he cares for you and Trevor and would hate to see you two hurt. Add the good scare he had when we thought the baby was coming and poof, there went my calm, collected, and very logical husband. The worrywart took his place. He was happy you were coming over today to keep a watch over me while he popped into the office. Oh!"—a serene smile curved Jessica's lips—"I think the baby just woke."

She crossed the room and placed Cassandra's splayed hands on either side of her round tummy. The floral print on Jessica's top seemed to come alive with each baby kick and roll. Cassandra gazed up at her and couldn't hold back her own smile.

"She's a feisty bugger."

"Well, it could be a little boy."

The baby kicked again and Jessica's belly jerked to the side like it had a mind of its own.

"Holy shit. Are you sure there's only one in there? It feels like a whole soccer team."

Jessica smacked her hand playfully. "Bite your tongue, woman. One at a time, please." She raised her blonde eyebrow mischievously. "If I'm having a whole soccer team, I want the whole baby-making-tryouts experience to last for many years."

The baby flipped against her hand and a sudden yearning exploded across Cassandra's mind. It wasn't the first time she'd wondered what it would be like to carry Trevor's child. To have their own baby kicking inside her.

They hadn't really spoken about it, but Cassandra knew Trevor wanted children. From his conversations about his family, she felt his deep-seated desire to share the things his parents had shared with him with their own son or daughter. A tingling started in the pit of her stomach and spread to her limbs. The idea of becoming a parent simultaneously scared and fascinated her. She worried about the type of mother she would be when she'd had so little feminine influence in her early life. And yet, in that moment, soaking in all things baby, she realized that just as she had with Trevor, she would be willing to take that chance, to share that special gift with him.

Cassandra handed Jessica the baby blankets she'd folded when she crossed near and followed her progress at the changing table.

Just like they had never discussed having children, they had never openly put it on hold until he was through with seeking answers. It had been an unspoken agreement from day one. Cassandra had understood why he craved closure. He was haunted by dreams, by theories of what had really happened. They took all of his energy, his enjoyment of simply being alive. Closing that door behind him would allow them to move on with their lives, allow them to reach for all those unspoken things they wanted but couldn't allow themselves to have.

She couldn't deny the possibility that they might be chasing their own tails; wasting their time with a case that seemed pretty clear-cut to the agencies involved in it from the beginning concerned her. It also worried her that with each brick wall they hit in the search, Trevor withdrew further into his own head, but she knew that was a door he had to close himself.

She had no doubt in her mind that it would happen. It didn't matter to her whether it was tomorrow, one year, or ten years from now. She would follow him wherever he may go and, regardless of what lay at the end, they would have each other, they would have their share of the happiness they deserved.

"Okay. I think we're done for now." Jessica brushed her hands together, a satisfied smile curling her lips. "Since you're not going to humor me by moving the crib, I'll just have to recruit Stephan when he gets home."

Her friend's humorous tone carried her back from her brooding. Cassandra chuckled and pushed to her feet.

"Good lord, I've got to warn him." Whipping her phone from her pocket, she swiped the screen.

"Hey, give me that." Jessica made a grab for the cell and Cassandra held it out of her reach.

She grinned. "I dare you to waddle for it."

"Shut up," Jessica grinned back, trying to grab it again.

Cassandra took a couple of steps back while frantically typing and reading aloud as Jessica advanced, "Stephan! RUN. She's at it again. Save your Irish ass!"

Jessica's undiluted laughter filled the room and she threw a pillow at her. "I'm not that bad."

"Did you seriously just say that?" Cassandra raised an eyebrow, tossing the pillow back on the rocker. She let her eyes take one last look at the nursery. "The room is lovely and doesn't need any changes. Having the baby in it will make it perfect. Promise me to take it easy. No more shopping. The room is a ticking time bomb. One more piece of clothing and the dresser drawers will explode. Think pastel onesies everywhere."

Jessica grinned and herded her toward the door. "Fine. I promise. Now move it. Hungry monster on board. I need food."

The thought of food was unappealing. "If it's okay with you, I'll pass. I don't think my appetite is back yet." She hadn't been able to stomach much since witnessing Khalil's suicide. She shook her head to shake the image and checked the time. "I'm going to head out. As much as I love spending time with you, there's this really tempting

Irishman waiting for me back home." As she approached, the front door opened, allowing the earthy smell of peat to flow into the hallway as Stephan strode in. "Look, perfect timing. I'll leave you to do her bidding, my lord."

"So early? Would you like to stay for dinner?" Stephan prompted.

"Still a lot to tidy up with regards to the last case. Thanks for the invite. I should get moving."

She hugged them both and headed out, promising to call the next day to check on Jessica. She pulled her phone out of her pocket as she slipped behind the wheel of their sedan.

Done here. I'm heading home.

His reply was almost instantaneous. *I'll be waiting, a ghrá.*

Her pulse kicked up a beat and a warm heat flooded her chest. The prospect of another night in his arms catching up for the time they had spent apart brought a smile to her face. She was suddenly feeling much better.

Chapter Forty-One

Truce

 HE FAMILIAR TUNE OF THE Imperial March reached
 Trevor in the office. Not expecting any visitors or
 deliveries from work, he frowned, but welcomed the
interruption. He'd had enough dark thoughts to last a lifetime.

He padded downstairs, conscious of the quiet in their home. It
still freaked him out after the constant buzz of activity he'd been
surrounded with in Jordan. The silence was even more blatant when
Cassandra wasn't around. She'd been visiting Jessica often since their
return, strategizing and plotting each minute until baby Connellan's
arrival. For all he knew, she might have created a detailed plan
Stephan was to follow when Jessica went into labor.

Although under normal circumstances he would have preferred
to spend every waking moment in her company a million times over
solitude, he appreciated the space she'd given him. He needed time
to deal with what he'd learned in Jordan, or, more accurately, with
the things he hadn't. Time to deal with a dying man's last words.

For a week, those words had been weighing him down like an

anchor, keeping him drowning in confusion, in heartache. Khalil Abboud had tied that anchor to his foot and hadn't stuck around to help free him from it. Not that Trevor thought anybody could. He had to pry it off himself. And he would, even if he had to chew his leg off to reach the surface.

With the patience of Job, Cassandra waited quietly in the wings for when he was ready to talk about it. She'd left him to his own devices, given him berth to get his head around that mess. But he knew couldn't keep her waiting much longer. He'd seen the determined gleam in her eye. If he knew his wife, she was already plotting to handcuff him to a chair until he'd exposed all his demons to her perusal.

Trevor took a deep breath before opening the door, ready to dismiss whoever had come knocking, and stopped dead in his tracks on seeing who stood on the doorstep. He raised an eyebrow.

"You?"

Nelson faced him, hands in his pockets. He squinted and shuffled his feet.

"Maybe this was a bad idea."

"Cassie is at the Connellans'. If I know my wife, she won't be back until she drills them on safe driving procedures while under pressure." Nelson frowned, confusion clouding his eyes. "They're having a baby soon." It was clear Nelson didn't get his humor. "Never mind. She's not here. Come back another time if you want to talk to her."

Nelson shifted his weight, his expression changing as he appeared to carefully weigh his next words.

"Actually. I'm here to talk to you."

Trevor's surprise grew tenfold, now enhanced by curiosity. "Really? Why would you want to talk to me?"

A horn blared down the street. The mid-morning traffic around

St. Stephen's Green, while not bad, was constant, and people busied the sidewalk to and from workplaces in the area at all times.

Nelson looked behind him at the passersby and nodded at the door. "Can we do this inside?"

Trevor ran through every possible scenario that could result from a private conversation with Nelson, and he wasn't comfortable with the majority of them.

"I don't have any tranquilizer darts on hand. Do you promise to count to ten if things I say piss you off? Maybe I should have said when." He knew he shouldn't run his mouth, but it was an unavoidable compulsion.

"Very funny. I'm here in peace. Need me to pull out the white flag before you invite me in?"

Trevor threw him a matter-of-fact stare. "Do you have one handy?"

Nelson shook his head while giving him a droll look, this time laced with humor. "Come on."

Jordan had changed everything. He'd not have considered agreeing had Nelson shown up a few months ago, but now he found himself wanting to know what he had to say.

"Fine." He stepped back, allowing Nelson in, then closed the door behind him before leading the way up the stairs. Upon reaching the vast open-concept first floor, he headed straight to the fridge. "Can I get you a glass of water? Beer?"

Nelson dismissed him with a wave of his hand and Trevor grabbed an energy drink for himself. He settled on the couch while Nelson took the chair to his left. Trevor set the can on the coffee table and leaned back; his stomach fluttered and pulse quickened waiting for Nelson to begin talking. Nelson's discomfort was visible in the way he sat, stiff and formal.

"Where's Rachael?"

"She's with her parents in California until I get back. After everything, they wanted to spend time with her." Nelson's eyes told him he was happy she was being watched while he was away. Trevor knew that feeling. After Cassandra was released from the hospital, he could barely keep his eyes off her. "I can't blame them."

Silence came over them once again and Nelson's forehead pulled into a deeper frown. He lowered his gaze to his hands then back to Trevor, but still didn't say a word.

"So?"

Nathan realized it was a really bad idea the minute he'd rung the doorbell. The knot in his stomach had grown with each step he'd taken toward the couch he'd slept on when he and Hanson had been there.

He recalled the verbal confrontation that had happened then. And he knew he'd deserved the classic mouthiness that followed. Bauer surprised him, though, and in a good way. His impulsive streak had accomplished what straight-laced diplomacy couldn't. And, in an incongruous kind of way, Trevor had brought Rachael back into his life. Nathan owed him that. He forced a deep, easy breath into his lungs.

"The day we flew to Jordan, you schooled me on the many types of sexual satisfaction—"

Trevor leaned back into the chair, eyes narrowed, hands waving at him. "Whoa! Dude. Let's stop right there. I don't like where this is going."

Nathan shook his head. "Just hear me out, okay?" he continued when Bauer settled down again. "I had no frame of reference. I won't say I was a monk, but I wasn't"—he searched for the word—"versed in the difference you were talking about." He forced a deep breath into his lungs in preparation for what he had to say next. "When Rachael and I...I realized I never knew the difference. Even after

Cass—"

"Stop right there. I don't want to know. I don't *need* to know."

"Yeah, you do. You need to understand I regret crossing that line, but I can't take it back. I can only hope you and Cass will give me a chance to prove I'm not the guy you thought I was, or even the guy I truly was. Rachael changed everything."

"What do you want from me, Nelson?"

"Nothing. I want to give something back. You helped me get Rachael back. You went above and beyond to locate her, and I want to pay you back for your help with my own. I want you to let me help you with your parents' case."

Trevor's heart slammed against his ribs. Once the surprise of the offer subsided, he considered it carefully. He'd dug a bit more than he'd expected and shed some light in the shadows surrounding Nelson. He knew how far Nelson's clearance went and that he'd have access to a lot of resources far beyond the digital world he lived in, resources he himself couldn't reach. His chest tightened with the need for closure. Nelson dangled a juicy carrot in front of him. It was tempting, but also fickle.

Nothing could guarantee that he would find the answers he needed if he accepted his help, neither that he would like them. The farther he walked that path, the harder it would be to stop; he had considered quitting while he was ahead. While his wife still had love in her eyes when she looked at him.

He'd have to think long and hard about whether or not he could go on. Whether he could afford to lose what he had if he kept at it. The sobering thought guided his decision. He inhaled deeply and nodded.

"I appreciate the offer. It's nice to know you'd be willing to do that for me, but I'll have to pass on it. At least for now."

Nelson leaned forward, eyebrows raised in wide arches before his eyes narrowed into questions Trevor couldn't answer.

"I never expected you to give up."

"I didn't say I'm giving up. The decision to continue needs to be made with Cassie's help. After all, it affects both our lives."

Nelson gave him a curt nod. "Understood." He pushed to his feet and Trevor did the same. "Well, if things change, give me a shout. You know how to find me." Humor streaked his tone. He approached Trevor and extended his hand.

Trevor lowered his eyes to the outstretched hand before raising them to meet Nelson's. He saw no sign of the anger that used to live in their depths. After digging up a lot more than he cared to know about the man, Trevor realized that Nelson could actually turn out to be someone he could call a friend one day. Slowly, he took Nelson's hand in a tight handshake. For now, all he hoped for was a long-standing truce.

Chapter Forty-Two

*J*ESSICA MOANED SOFTLY AS PAIN flared once again, plucking her from sleep. *Lovely. What else was new? More aches and pains, as if there weren't enough already.* She rolled to her right side, hoping the change in position would ease it.

"What is it?" She felt the brush of Stephan's fingers on her arm as he spooned her.

Almost as if soothed by the sound of his voice, the uncomfortable, annoying cramp subsided. She rolled back to face him.

"It's nothing. It feels just like it did the other night." Jessica dismissed it in her mind. "The last time, the doctor said if it was labor I'd also feel my belly tighten." She paused, focusing on her body. "Nope, no tightening." She snuggled into him as best she could. "Don't worry so much. Everything is fine."

She felt him move away and when he drew close again, a light glowed between them. He was checking his watch. She placed her hand on his chest, curious as to what he was up to.

He rested his chin on her head, his low voice rumbling through her. "I'm not taking any chances. I'm going to time you."

"You're wasting your time. I'll be snoring soon."

"Humor me."

A short time later, when she was just falling asleep, the same twinge woke her up. She let a soft moan escape her lips and shifted, searching for a more comfortable position. They came and went, and by the third time, Stephan murmured, "Jessica, these cramps are coming ten minutes apart."

She snuggled into his chest, seeking comfort once again. "Seriously. It's the same thing as before. No point in leaving the comfort of our bed to be poked and prodded and then sent home for another month. I'll be fine in the morning." The little humph he made in his throat was a clear indicator he was still not sure of it.

A couple of hours later, she wasn't as sure of it either. The cramps hadn't subsided; in fact, they had become not only more frequent but also more painful—so much so, she'd been unable to even take the little naps in between them. Thoughts scattered across her mind. *Could it be?* She didn't want to go through the craziness of another false alarm. But this cramping was different, it was steady, and there was now also a dull ache in her back.

She opened her eyes and saw Stephan standing next to the dresser. The lamp's yellow glow illuminated the worry on his face like a billboard. He was as restless as she was. An uncomfortable swell of uncertainty poured into her. She rose to her elbow and pushed the hair from her face.

"I think we should call the doctor."

Her words were like an electric prod. Stephan sprang into action. Snatching his cell off the dresser, he circled the bed to her side and crouched beside her. He punched in the numbers and set the phone on the side table as she laid her head back and breathed through another cramp.

The call rang once, twice…the sound amplified by the speaker-phone grated her nerves. She heard the click of the connection and Stephan blurted without waiting for an answer, "We're in labor. The Connellans. I…I mean, we think Jessica is going into labor." The brogue in his tone was thicker than usual, his voice a little unsteady.

"Bloody hell, old man. Why are you calling me? Shouldn't you be taking her to a hospital or something?"

"Shite. Trevor? How the hell did you get on the line?"

"You tell me. You're the one who called me." Trevor's chuckle flowed over the connection and Cassandra's voice sounded indistinct in the background. "Stephan. Apparently he thinks I can deliver babies now, too."

Jessica giggled. The annoyed look on Stephan's face was classic. "Bye, Trevor." She reached for the phone, disconnected the call, and dialed the correct number, opting to talk to the doctor herself. "Doctor O'Malley? I think we have the real alarm, now."

The doctor's calm voice immediately soothed Jessica's nerves. She was one of the most highly praised doctors at Coombe and in great demand. They'd been lucky to have her. When she was overcome with pain again in the middle of the discussion, she handed Stephan the phone.

He set it on speakerphone on the side table and sat on the bed beside her, reaching for and squeezing her hand. "Hi, Doctor O'Malley. This is Stephan Connellan. Jessica is most likely in labor this time. Contractions have been spaced about ten minutes or so apart for the last couple of hours, but appear to be coming more frequently now. When should I bring her in?"

"Can I speak to her?"

"I'm here. We have you on speaker," Jessica said when she could talk again. The last one had been more intense than the previous ones.

"Is he always so direct?" Laughter laced the doctor's voice when she spoke.

Jessica laughed. "You just got a taste of his boardroom voice."

The doctor asked a few questions, and after hearing her answers on the type of pain she was feeling, told her to head to the hospital for a checkup.

"It could be another false alarm, but I'd like to be certain."

Jessica caught Stephan's gaze and held it. A twinge of excitement mixed with worry danced in her chest and she saw the same mirrored in his eyes.

"Okay. We should be there in twenty," she replied, and disconnected the phone.

The bed dipped when Stephan pulled her into his arms. "This could be it, *a stór*."

Her stomach fluttered and she forced herself to settle down. "I hope everything is okay, though. I'm kind of nervous all of a sudden." She brushed a hand over the baby.

He helped her from the bed and she sucked in a deep breath as another cramp stuck its claws in her. After a moment, Stephan tipped her face up to his. "I'm sure everything will be fine."

She searched his eyes. He tried to hide it, but she knew he was just as worried. Maybe more. She pressed a tight kiss on his lips. "Let's get going."

Jessica's heart was beating a mile a minute. She had been waiting for that day and it was hard for her to believe that it was finally there, albeit a few weeks sooner than she'd expected. A part of her wanted it to be another false alarm; the other itched to hold their little baby in her arms.

When they reached the bottom floor, Stephan handed over her coat. She shrugged it on and picked up her cell phone from the entry hall table where she'd left it. If she knew Cassandra, after that little misdial she was probably lying in bed with the phone in her hand, waiting to hear something. Jessica pulled her up on the screen and tapped on the keys.

We're off to the hospital. We'll keep you posted. Oh, and tell Irish I'm sorry for hanging up on him.

Her response was immediate. *Okay. We'll be waiting to hear. *fingers crossed* Love you.*

Stephan helped her to the car, opening the door for her and making sure she was comfortable before taking his place behind the wheel.

He leaned over and placed a soft kiss to her lips. "Ready?"

"As ever," she smiled back.

STEPHAN FROZE BY the door. His heart stuttered, his stomach sank to his knees, the same knees he didn't think would hold his weight for long. His eyes traced the most beautiful picture before him. Jessica sitting by the window, framed by blue sky and sunlight. She had on a plain white hospital gown that screamed purity and made her look like a Madonna painted by one of the masters. Her hair formed a wavy blonde halo around her face, pure adoration glittering in her eyes. As if that image wasn't striking enough, a smile curved her lips as she admired the newborn child cradled in her arms, her fingertips gently brushing over a tiny hand, the baby's fuzzy dark hair a stark contrast to the creamy pale skin of her breast.

He'd thought he had felt every single overwhelming emotion since meeting Jessica. He was wrong. Nothing else compared to seeing them like that for the first time. He could almost feel his heart grow bigger with love.

Jessica turned her gaze to him, the love they radiated when directed at their son extended now to him. His chest warmed up with the recognition.

"How long have you been there?"

He cleared his throat before he spoke, afraid he'd choke up if he didn't. "Long enough. You two look peaceful. I didn't want to disturb." He padded closer, his eyes locked on hers.

As she adjusted herself on the chair, the baby slipped off her nipple. He whimpered, squirming and nuzzling her skin, seeking to latch onto it again.

She chuckled and helped him find his source of comfort once again before turning her gaze back to Stephan. "Hungry little guy."

"You look so natural doing that."

A smirk graced her features. "After you left, I tried to feed him. I was about to cry when this amazing nurse came in and helped me. Once she showed me what to do and how to do it, it was a matter of trial and error until we found the right way for us."

"Didn't take the two of you long to do that." Stephan reached for the baby and caressed his soft dark fuzz, then the curve of his cheek.

"You wouldn't say that if you had been here an hour ago." Her self-deprecation was countered by the broad smile she flashed him.

"I'm sorry it took me so long to get back. I swear I lost all sense of time and space after last night. My mind was going a mile a minute. I ended up having to take a cold shower so I could think straight enough to know what to bring back."

Jessica muffled her laughter with her hand when the baby squirmed again. "I should have hired a cameraman to record last night for posterity's sake. Your expression when you realized I was in labor was priceless."

"I may have lost a few lives during his delivery, too."

"Yes. He's as stubborn as his dad. Which brings another subject to the table. Now that we know he is a boy, we'll need to settle on the name. I'm sure our parents are probably already halfway here; they'll want to know what to call him." Jessica gently switched the baby to her other breast. He watched as lines formed above her eyes as she concentrated on getting the baby latched once again. After a few tries, she relaxed, a tender smile curving her lips as she adjusted her hold of their little treasure.

"Are you okay with what we had discussed? I mean, we can always—"

"No. I agreed with it." Stephan lowered his gaze to his son once again. "Padraig Conor Connellan." The words caught in his throat.

"Such a big name for a small baby."

"He'll grow into it nicely." Paternal pride swarmed him. Flashes of conversations he'd had with Conor in the past now made absolute sense. He'd do anything to protect Padraig from harm.

"Yes, he will." Jessica slipped her hand in his and drew him closer for a kiss. Jessica had completed him in a way he could never have imagined before. His heart swelled to life once again, this time to make room for the promise of more to come.

Chapter Forty-Three

Priorities

*T*HE SOUND OF THE DOOR CLOSING in the distance alerted Trevor of Cassandra's return. His mood instantly brightened. She had left earlier to visit the Connellans again, already hopelessly in love with Padraig. He followed her progress through the house by the sounds she made. The clinking of the keys in the porcelain key holder by the door, the footsteps crossing the hardwood floors on the first level and stalking up the stairs. She burst through the doorway, all smiles.

"I gather you got your baby fix for the day?" He welcomed her quick peck on the lips as he typed the closing arguments for a report on the digital surveillance processes that resulted in the recovery of the hostages. There had been a sudden interest in Operation Countermeasure's activities since their return, not all of it positive, and Trevor hoped the report would clarify the importance of their team to national security. He paused to follow her around the room with his eyes.

"He's so damn cute. I feel like squishing him." Her delight was nearly palpable.

"Please don't. His parents wouldn't appreciate it." Cassandra laughed, dismissing his feigned concern. "How's Jessie doing? All well on the motherhood front?"

"Jessie is a natural."

Cassandra reached for a hairband and carelessly tied her hair into a ponytail, missing a few wisps at her nape. He was sure she did that on purpose to drive him crazy. He smiled.

"Has Stephan bubblewrapped mother and child yet?"

"Surprisingly, no. He's pretty mellow, actually. You can clearly see he's a goner, though." Humor permeated her tone as she approached the file cabinets and selected a couple of folders from it.

"I'm sure I would be too if he were my kid." Cassandra slowed in her tracks and her smile dimmed. He rushed to explain. "I mean, when the time comes for us, I'll be as gone as he is."

"Got it." Cassandra continued across the room and sat at her desk. Pulling the keyboard closer, she began typing away.

Trevor wanted to kick himself for the slip. Although they had never really had the talk about children, from her reactions to the subject in the past, he'd assumed her feelings about it weren't the most positive.

He could recall her face last year before his birthday when he suspected she was hiding something from him. At the mention of a possible pregnancy, she'd laughed it off, thinking him crazy. He also recalled his reaction to it, the turmoil in his head at that possibility, the taste of the longing it had left in his mouth. Yet he could wholeheartedly understand her reaction. Her mother's death affected more than her relationship with Robert; it had changed how she looked at relationships as a whole. Almost the opposite effect his parents' disappearance had had on him, making him pursue things with more passion, without giving too much thought to the consequences. He took a deep breath and returned his eyes to his monitors, avoiding her scrutiny.

He'd thought about children in the past. Many times. But then his crusade had been a priority. The same crusade he'd questioned when Khalil Abboud had died, leaving him with a bigger enigma on his hands. Could he lead a normal life without answers? Could he let go? He'd never considered it possible. That was true until Cassandra.

The Connellan's baby only added one more variable to the already-complicated equation. As far as he knew, Cassandra was more than okay with holding off on children until they had tied up all the loose ends. What if that wasn't the case? From her reaction to baby Padraig, he saw a change in that, a small twinkle in her eye that told him he was missing something. What if he'd been so focused on the case he'd become blind to the things happening around him? He studied his wife's focused expression, her eyes locked on her computer screen.

Was closure worth jeopardizing his future with her? His stomach contracted. He stood at a crossroads. To one side, he saw a blurry path covered in rocks, some sharp, some the size of boulders, a route impossible to tread without incurring some damage. That path was also darkened by thick, angry clouds, and it had become a lot more dangerous and deadly with the newly emerged link to the terrorist organization. To the other side lay a smooth, paved path edged with colorful flowers, topped with a blue sun-drenched sky and peppered with butterflies.

For anyone else, choosing one would be a no-brainer. For him, not so much. He was drawn to the treacherous path, even if the smooth one called his name—more like yelled, *"You! Yeah! The dumb one."* He could almost hear it.

In his mind's eye, he also saw the opposite pictures they painted of their future. One showed Cassandra holding a child—dark curls framing chubby cheeks, blue eyes mirroring his own. Laughter rang in his head as the image played out. The other churned his gut. It depicted Cassandra walking away from him, fed up with waiting for him to find his definition of closure.

His hands trembled and he grew lightheaded all of a sudden. Seeing the aftereffects of his actions so clearly, Trevor knew exactly which one to choose. He knew he had to let his parents go.

The thought hit him like a stab to the solar plexus. His breath caught in his throat as he explored how he could find purpose in his new life. It didn't take him long to figure it out. His chest tightened as relief and grief weaved into an overwhelming cascade of emotions. He'd put his energy and drive into becoming the best husband and father he could be. He'd honor his own father's memory by following in his footsteps. By becoming the man his father had always trusted he would be. By making Cassandra smile every day of her life, the way his father had made his ma smile. By being an integral part of his children's lives the way his father had been of his. His eyes burned with tears he'd needed to shed for a while.

"Trev?" He raised his eyes to find Cassandra's worried ones staring at him. "Are you okay?"

He blinked away the tears and cleared his throat, releasing the breath he'd held. "Yeah. I am."

A deep frown marred her beautiful features. She left her chair and closed the distance. Leaning against his desk, she placed a hand on his forehead. "You look like you're coming down with something."

Trevor brought her hand to his lips. He pressed a kiss on her palm and raised his gaze to meet hers. "I'm all right."

"What's on your mind then? And don't say it's nothing. I'll kick your ass. I'm done waiting."

He chuckled at the threat. He knew she would follow through

on it, too.

"Feisty." Leaning back against his seat he took a deep breath, bracing himself for sharing his thoughts with the woman with whom he hoped to spend the rest of his days. "I've been thinking."

"Oh, boy," she piped.

A half-smile, half-cringe curved his lips. "Hear me out."

Cassandra's expression sobered. "I'm listening."

"If my parents' case had crossed your desk before we met, what would you have written in your report?"

"Trev—"

"No. Just give me a straight answer."

Cassandra diverted her eyes to the wall behind him, as if choosing her words carefully. After a few moments of silence, she returned her gaze to his. The desolation he saw in their depths spoke louder than anything she was about to say.

"I'd have recommended the case be closed. There's no evidence of foul play. I'd note that the authorities handled the case appropriately and had followed the correct procedure when they labeled it an accidental death."

Silence descended between them. Trevor's heart raced along with his pulse. He knew she was right. He'd been chasing ghosts all along. "I agree."

Cassandra's disbelief was almost laughable if it wasn't a sad display that she hadn't expected that response from him. "What do you mean, you agree?"

"I'm ready." Her eyes widened with understanding. "It's time to let go."

Cassandra reached out and cupped his cheek, her soft touch soothing the inferno raging in his stomach. "Are you sure?"

He held her gaze and nodded. "There's just one last thing I need to do before I can truly let go." His voice broke and for a second he thought he'd go adrift, but the familiar warmth of her touch kept him anchored. "The Sligo house. I need to go there."

"You've needed that for a while." A hesitant smile curved her lips.

"Yes. You're right." She would have read that easily from his disquiet when they had last been in Sligo. "Will you come with me?"

Cassandra's smile grew wider and brighter. "Need you ask? You know I've been dying to see the house you grew up in."

If he was doing that, he was going all the way. "Maybe we could air the place out. Use it every now and then."

"That's a wonderful idea."

"Even better, I could set up a satellite uplink at the house and we could work from there for a part of the year."

"Definitely, oh mighty Geek," she laughed, but muffled it when he raised his eyebrows.

"Gotta have a decent connection."

"Check. Without it, we—I really mean you—would be curled into a fetal position within seconds."

He laughed, shaking his head, his heart released from the fist that had squeezed it for such a long time.

"Do you think we could leave for Sligo in the morning?"

Cassandra's dream was coming true. She'd thought she might need to pinch herself to be sure she wasn't really sound asleep. But before she could truly believe it, she had to make sure they weren't moving too fast.

"So soon? Are you sure you don't want to think about it a little more? You know, come to terms with the idea first?"

"The sooner, the better. It's taken this long to get to this point. I don't want to lose momentum."

"I get it." And she did. Trevor had always worn his emotions on his sleeve. It was easy to discern the tumult in his head when he looked like he'd been trampled by wild horses. Cassandra ached for him. She knew it had taken a monumental effort on his part to reach the acceptance stage, but it signaled a new beginning, a brand new life for both of them.

She had no idea what had brought that conversation about, nor the emotional upheaval that had prompted his new resolution. Whatever it was, it had come at the perfect time.

From studying his expression, she knew he'd had more than he could take in for a day. She couldn't—wouldn't—add to the heavy burden he already carried. Her chest warmed at the thought of sharing the news with him. *Soon.*

"Do we need to book a room at that dreamy bed-and-breakfast again?"

He shook his head. "We can stay at the house. It will probably need a good airing out and dusting after being closed all these years. Come to think of it, heating might be a problem. Are you up for roughing it?"

Heat flooded her cheeks. She could think of many ways the problem could be remedied. "There's nothing that a little body heat can't fix."

"I like how you think, Mrs. Brennan." A wisp of sadness flitted across his features. It lasted only seconds, but she'd caught it none-theless.

She leaned forward and brushed her lips over his. "How about you show me how it's done, Mr. Brennan?"

The devious glimmer chased the shadows from his eyes.

"Happy to oblige." His dark blue eyes crinkled at the corners with his broad smile. He skimmed his palms over her legs as he pushed to his feet. Turning her around, he guided her to their room for what she hoped was a full demonstration of his body-heating skills.

Epilogue

None the Wiser

THE M4 MOTORWAY WAS CLEAR by the time they got on their way to Sligo. Cassandra studied Trevor as he drove, his eyes fixed on the road. Lines of tension tightened his mouth and creased his brows on and off. It was as if he had an ongoing inner battle taking place in his head.

Would he hold true to it? That was yet to be seen. Could he let go of the unwavering persistence that made him the stubborn man he was? That had made him push limits when she'd pushed him away, that had driven him to reach her while injured and fighting the unexpected in Russia? Could he truly give up seeking the truth about his parents? An uncomfortable thought popped up in the back of her mind. Maybe the real question should be, should she want him to?

Her overly cautious side wanted to settle into a normal life with him, grow gray with the passing of time—and not because she was worried sick that he would run out of luck during one of his stunts. A sharp pain sliced through her at the thought of losing him. She wanted to make decades of memories with him. She wanted to cradle their baby in her arms. To have him at her side to share the joy, the overwhelming love for someone who would share the same love they had for each other. To help shoulder her fear of having another special someone in her life she could lose.

But deep inside, she had an inkling that if he didn't follow that quest to the finish, regardless of how it ended, it would slowly kill the Trevor she loved, the spontaneous and crazy one, the curious and daring one. She didn't want to see him become a shell of what he was.

Her eyes moistened and she turned her gaze to the scenery, needing a different focus for her thoughts. Soon the beauty of the land overtook her. There was a good reason Ireland was called the Emerald Island: regardless of the time of the year, the landscape never shed its green mantle. She feasted her eyes on the checkered green pastures dotted with sheep and whitewashed stone cottages. Soon her eyelids grew heavy and she let the peaceful scenery and soothing music flowing from the speakers flush away her convoluted thoughts.

★ ★ ★ ★ ★

"WE'RE HERE."

Trevor's voice sounded strangely choked to her ears. Opening her eyes, she saw the rawness of his emotions swirling in the dark blue pools of his eyes.

She turned in the seat and scrutinized the home where he had spent the first years of his life. The house his family had considered home, even after their move to Dublin, and where they had flocked for family gatherings and special occasions. It was where the heart lay for them all.

The house had cream walls throughout the façade. The main section had matching gables topping massive windows on both floors. The same pattern was repeated in the adjacent sections of each side of the main entrance. Although the house had been uninhabited for six years, the landscape was in pristine condition, its gardens trimmed, the small trees and bushes carefully wrapped with tarps to avoid winter's deadly kiss. As if waiting for them to return any day.

Trevor stood beside the car, eyes lost on the top window above the main entrance. Cassandra walked around the car and joined him, burrowing into his arms, hoping to comfort him during the emotional havoc that day was already delivering. She eased back, giving him the space he needed to voice his thoughts.

"I can almost see her standing there. She enjoyed the view of the lake from that window. That's where she used to read to me when I was little." His voice broke when he turned to look at the view he was describing.

She rubbed his arms in support, encouraging him to continue with his reminiscence. He dropped his gaze, a frown pinching his eyebrows together.

"God...I sound pathetic. No wonder you had no trust in me going into the operation. I must sound like a lost puppy or some shit," he huffed and pressed his palms over his eyes before combing his messy hair with unsteady fingers.

"No. You sound like a devoted son who misses his parents a lot. You love them. And you never do anything on a small scale. When you love someone, you love them with all your heart. I know that. I feel it myself." She intertwined her fingers with his. "Do you want to come back another time? It doesn't need to be done today."

"No. It does. Let's get this over with." He squeezed her hand and removed the ring with the house keys from his pocket as they approached the door.

Trevor's heart beat a mile a minute. His pulse raced in his ears and the scenes seemed to play in slow motion as he unlocked the door and pushed it open. The inside of the house looked as if time had never passed. It was obvious that it had been uninhabited for all those years. There was no delicious scent of cooking coming from the kitchen, no sound of laughter coming from the family room; but the memories echoing through its halls and rooms screamed at him louder, sharper.

"Remind me to thank Stephan for this," he said, gesturing at the house. Stephan had ensured the upkeep of the place.

"I will." She looked around the room, curiosity flooding her face.

He knew he had to walk her through each room, remember all of the good moments, and then maybe he'd be able to pry away the fist clamped around his heart.

"Come," he said.

Tugging her by the hand, he moved through the foyer toward the family room. The big fireplace dominated the room. Stone masonry framed the open pit where peat once burned, filling the house with the comforting scent he associated with family, with constancy. Memories of Christmases past and many other occasions they had sat around the fire charged his brain.

Strangely, although his pulse still raced and his heart still beat like a bass drum, the pain of walking into the home that meant so much to him had receded from a sharp stab to a dull ache. Maybe, just maybe, confronting the echoes of the past had been the best idea he'd had in a long time.

"We had great laughs here."

"I can almost feel it," she replied. A gentle smile brightened her expression.

"Do you like it?"

"What's not to like? The place is gorgeous, the view is breathtaking, and it's all part of you."

"There's a lot more to see." He tugged her hand again and took her around, telling about his mischiefs growing up there. He showed her the kitchen and where he used to sit doing his homework or reading while his mother cooked. His mouth salivated as he recalled the tantalizing taste of her signature stew. He went from room to room, stopping to brush his fingers on old pictures, to hold knick-knacks his mother had cherished, to peruse the books in his father's study and scribbled notebooks in his drawers. With each step taken, each room unveiled, the freer he felt. A smile crept on his lips as he remembered the many rainy days spent playing hide-and-seek indoors. The house was big and harbored many nooks and crannies.

"Remember when I told you about the games my mother used to play with me?"

"You mean the games that turned you into the sleuth you are now?" Cassandra raised her eyebrows, a matching smile playing on her lips.

"Yes. Those."

"It was here, right?"

"Yes. I remember her making me look all day for one puzzle piece she had hidden. I had spent weeks on a large puzzle, and when I got to the last piece, it was nowhere to be found. She said she had hidden it in the house and that its hiding place was obvious." He shook his head.

"And it wasn't?"

"Not to an eight-year-old kid. I can see her logic now, but it frustrated the hell out of me back then."

"Where did you end up finding it?"

"In the attic, of all places. I believe I mentioned it before, but when Da bought the house, the attic was converted into a playroom. For some reason, the previous owners had built little hiding spots throughout the house. Maybe to hide money or something, but the fact is that it gave my mother hours of entertainment and me lots of hunts."

"Yes, you mentioned you found all her hiding places." Cassandra's smile widened.

"I did. But her little games continued. She used the hiding spots, in particular the one in the attic, to hide things from Da." Trevor chuckled when he recalled one of the times they'd hidden his father's birthday gift there. "Want to check it out?"

"Show me."

Excitement burned through him. The good memories had the desired effect. He no longer feared facing the emotions being there brought to his chest. The slow burn was now comforting, like downing a shot of good whiskey. They climbed the first set of stairs and he pulled her by the hand past the bedrooms. He caught her peering inside as they walked past.

"We'll look at them later," he said excitedly. "This is way more fun." He led her to the attic door and climbed ahead of her in a quick jog to the top.

Sunlight filtered through the semicircle window immediately under the gable. Trevor turned the light on so they could reach the farthest end of the attic where the roof met the floor. They crouched there and he pressed and pushed a piece of wood to the side.

"Wow. You need to tell me how the heck you discovered this spot."

"Elementary, dear Watson," he chuckled. "The puzzle I was putting together was of a cross section of a house. It showed all the rooms, with furniture and all. The missing piece was from the attic. I could eliminate the rest of the house and focus my efforts here." He popped it wider and stuck his hand inside, the same way he had done many years before. "It took me a while to search the room for hiding spots, but I found it in an envelope in he—" He froze as his hand touched something in there.

He felt the object and his pulse accelerated when he realized what that was. His ears rang and the bongo drums went wild in his chest. Cassandra must have noticed his tension because her eyes widened when she saw his face.

"Trev? What is it?"

TO BE CONTINUED

NOTE FROM THE AUTHORS

Thank you for reading **Alternate Connection**, the third novel in the Countermeasure series! We hope you enjoyed Nathan and Rachael's story. Stay tuned for more of the Countermeasure Series soon and its spin-off series The A.W.E. Crew!

If you enjoyed **Alternate Connection**, we would appreciate if you'd help others enjoy this story too.

Recommend it. Recommendations from friends are the number one decision-maker for many readers. Please help other readers find this book by recommending it to friends, readers' groups, and on social media sites.

Review it. Please tell other readers what you liked or didn't like about this book by reviewing it at one of the major retailers, review sites, or your blog.

Sláinte!
Chris & Cecilia

Find more of Countermeasure at your retailer.

Visit your retailer today for the complete list of books in the series.

SPECIAL SHOUT-OUT

To the Facebook C&C Hub group members for their continuous support and help with all things C&C and for being part of our little family.

To the members of the Countermeasure Discussion Group on Facebook, your enthusiasm for our characters is a constant source of joy. If you are reading this and would like to join the group, we'd love to have you.

To the members of the Codename: HEAT group on Facebook, your great discussions make our gears turn and inspire more and more of our stories. Keep them coming! Codename: HEAT is a discussion group focused on all things Romantic Suspense. If you are a RomSus fan, you need to be there!

ABOUT THE AUTHORS

CHRIS ALMEIDA & CECILIA AUBREY

Writing had touched Chris Almeida and Cecilia Aubrey's lives in different ways throughout the years, but never took flight until 2010, when Chris and Cecilia met and began roleplaying online as a hobby. It was through playing fictional characters in a sort of improv written theater that writing took a central position in their lives. The transition from roleplaying to novel writing was smooth, and they attribute the ease of writing realistic characters to their ability to live the scenes through roleplay.

Chris and Cecilia have since chosen to release all their titles independently. They have several short stories and two novels published under their own label, Éire Publishing, and are vocal supporters of independent publishing done right. They are currently working on the next novel in their series. Through all the chaos and laughter, they still hold true to their roots, bringing their favorite roleplay characters and stories to life.

Be sure to connect with them online!

To receive updates about new releases and a free copy of "Uncharted," subscribe to their newsletter:
chrisalmeida-ceciliaaubrey.com/newsletter

You can find updated information about the authors and the upcoming books at:
chrisalmeida-ceciliaaubrey.com
countermeasureseries.com
facebook.com/Authors.ChrisAlmeida.CeciliaAubrey
twitter.com/CAlmeidaCAubrey